Tripp

In the Company of Snipers

Book 23

Irish Winters

COPYRIGHT

Tripp; In the Company of Snipers, Book 23

Cover design: Kelli Ann Morgan, Inspire Creative Services
Cover image: Paul Henry Serres Photography, www.paulhenryserres.com
Interior book design: Bob Houston, eBook Formatting
Editor: Linda Clarkson, Black Opal Editing and Proofreading

ISBN Paperback: 978-1-942895-01-5
ISBN eBook: 978-1-942895-02-2
Library of Congress Control Number: 2021906846

In the Company of Snipers

You can find Irish Winters

On Facebook:
https://www.facebook.com/author.irishwinters

On Twitter:
https://twitter.com/irishwinters1

If you're an e-reader:
For news on upcoming releases, sign up for
Irish Winters' Newsletter at IrishWinters.com.

For more information about all my books, visit
IrishWinters.com.

IN THE COMPANY OF SNIPERS

This series revolves around former Marine scout sniper, Alex Stewart, and his covert surveillance company, The TEAM, home-based out of Alexandria, Virginia. An obsessive patriot and workaholic, he created the company to give former military snipers like him, a chance at returning to civilian life with a decent job, security, and a future.

This is not a serial with each book ending at a cliffhanger. *In the Company of Snipers* is a collection of passionate love stories involving strong women and men who are tough enough to take on the world alone. Each is a stand-alone read, complete in itself.

Spoiler alert: Every story contains adult scenes including sexual situations (some explicit), language, and violence. I don't write sweet romance, so be forewarned.

Book 1, *ALEX*, reveals how The TEAM came to be, as well as how Alex met Kelsey, how they fell in love and fought all odds to stay together. Each of the following books is a complete romance in itself, where, in the course of an active TEAM operation, one agent comes face to face with his or her demons. The men and women I write about are all patriots and warriors, dealing with what they've lived through or mistakes they've made.

It's my hope that you will come to realize along with my heroes...

Love changes everything.

Prologue

US Army Corporal Tripp McClane jerked his cell phone out of one of his many tactical vest pockets and glared at the caller ID displayed on the cracked-to-shit screen. Trish again. Damn her. What now? That girl had more problems than anyone he'd ever known. Which was saying something, since he'd joined the Army, and now knew more people than just the locals back in Letha, Idaho. His hometown was a goodbye, good-riddance, speck of dust stuck between Caldwell, Idaho, and Ontario, Oregon. On the border to No-Damned-Where. The scenery might've been gorgeous, but the mess that had been his home life? Trish had made that as ugly as shit.

Which was why his mother had moved her to the East Coast after he'd deployed. It was Andrea McClane's last-ditch effort to get her daughter away from the small-town mentality, where entertainment had everything to do with booze and drugs. She'd moved to show Trish a different, smarter way to live. To submerse her in a town filled with the diversity of military families, hard-charging professionals, and winners. But mostly, to get her away from her trashy, drinking, drug-addict friends.

"I'm working," he clipped, instead of asking, "What now?" He didn't want to know.

"Yeah, well, I'm working, too, you fuckin' jerk!" she screeched. "You seen Mom today? I mean, you heard from

Mom? God, it's not like you ever Facetime or keep in touch, you ass." With every word, the pitch of her voice turned more shrill and demanding. Which meant Trish was using again. *My poor mother.* "She's not here. I don't know where she is, and I need a ride to the effin' bus stop, and I'm tired of—"

"I don't have time for this," he replied tersely. "Call me back later."

"Listen to me, damn you!" Her voice vibrated as if she were stomping her feet or banging her head. A brother could only wish she'd knock some sense into the empty space between her ears. "For once! Can't you focus on me instead of your fuckin' job for once? Damn you! I'm important, too, and I need—"

Click.

I... I... I... Trish's all-time favorite word in Webster's dictionary. Make that her go-to *letter.*

Tripp hung up without listening to the rest of what would've been a drawn-out, tiresome rant mingled with more ugly words, dramatic tears, and vicious threats. Fraternal twins should've had more in common, but not him and Trish. The cell went into his pocket. His attention went back to Army business.

If Mom wasn't home, she was probably next-door babysitting Benson's three little girls, her usual schedule since Mr. Benson died of a heart attack during last fall's Virginia deer hunt. Mom was compassionate. She actually thought of others, unlike Trish, who only ever thought of herself. Tripp flat didn't have time for his sister's tantrum this morning, not in the middle of the sensitive Afghan prisoner transfer he was handling.

Abdul Ikram, an Afghan youngster of fifteen years, had killed eleven civilians in yesterday's bombing at a mosque in downtown Kabul. Out of sheer dumb luck, Tripp and his six-man squad had been patrolling a block away when the explosion rocked the city. They'd intercepted Ikram within minutes of the attack, thankfully, before he'd detonated the suicide vest intended to kill any first responders who would've gotten to him first.

First on-site, Tripp had simply manhandled the kid to the ground and defused the vest. It turned out to be an oddly sophisticated item for a poor kid dressed in rags. From there, the US Army took the scrawny teenager into custody. Ikram spent the night inside Camp Eggers detention facility. There, he was allowed to shower and eat, then dress in clean clothes, an orange jumpsuit with EGGERS stenciled on its back.

After Tripp watched the kid snarf the simple meal of canned turkey hash over brown rice, with a side of green beans, he knew damned well the kid had been starving. That detail and the vest told Tripp plenty. Ikram wasn't the mastermind behind the attack, but hungry kids did the damnedest things to survive. Tripp had no authority to question or interrogate the boy, so he kept his interaction friendly, hoping to get him to talk, to tell him who'd set him up. No go. For the entire night, Ikram was wide-eyed, frightened, but mute. After Tripp's efforts failed, the kid curled onto the narrow cot in his solitary cell, faced the wall, pulled the OD green blanket over his head, and effectively shut the US Army out.

But USA rules of engagement prevailed. Any and all Afghan prisoners had to be turned over to Afghan National Security Forces (ANSF) as quickly as possible after apprehension. Since Tripp and his guys did the catching, their CO, Staff Sergeant Wolsey, assigned them the 'privilege' of escorting Ikram to the rendezvous point. And since Major General Jalandar Ali of the Afghan National Army Commando Corps wanted to meet the man who'd taken Ikram down—without getting himself blown up—the meeting should've taken place at the Morehead Commando Training Center, six miles south of Kabul, at zero-five-thirty this morning.

Should have. Didn't. Still might if Major General Ali ever showed. He was two hours late, and Tripp was tired of waiting. He rolled his shoulder as the first orange-pink fingers of a beautiful sunrise stretched across the eastern horizon and promised another hot-as-hell day.

By now, Tripp was antsy as hell, glancing over his shoulder, and tired of the delay. His squad was just as wired. Ikram stood in the middle of them, still wearing orange, with his hands cuffed in front of him, and still not talking. Tripp didn't blame him. He didn't want the attention this meeting with one of Afghanistan's top dogs would garner, either. Nothing good ever came from the dubious distinction of tackling an armed but skinny-as-hell teenager, who had no sense in his empty head, to the ground. It was luck that Tripp hadn't killed the kid. Tripp almost had. Might've been a righteous hit, considering the body count in that mosque, but hurting children was out of Tripp's comfort zone.

The tackle itself was automatic, a jock skill left over from high school. As the middle linebacker for the Letha Leopards, he knew damned well how to intercept, tackle, and hang on tight to a pigskin. That ability alone was the reason he and his team were alive today. That and the fact that Ikram was small for his age. Tackling the dumbass had felt more like tackling a bag of sticks than an offensive lineman. But that was Afghanistan. Nothing and no one was what or who they seemed.

At last! Major General Ali's military jet touched down on Morehead's private runway. It was now zero-seven-thirty. Guess he thought he was more important than the US Army, which he'd kept waiting. The ass.

Tripp's cell phone rang again. Without checking caller ID, he reached into his vest pocket and thumbed the power off. *Not now, Trish.*

Major General Ali's military entourage cleared the jet's stairway. To look at the pomp and fuss over this guy's arrival, you'd think the medal-bedecked, tan-uniformed, asshat strutting toward Tripp was divine instead of mortal. There had to be twenty armed ANSF commandos accompanying him, not to mention the stone-faced civilians in light tan suits who'd met him on the tarmac, or the soldiers in the convoy of camouflaged military vehicles driving alongside his royal highness. For hell's sake, US presidents didn't travel with this much security.

Was that the Afghan equivalent of Secret Service? Tripp didn't know and didn't care. He wasn't anyone special and had just done what any other American soldier would've done—his job. This shitshow needed to be over. He had work to do.

Because it was a shitshow. Every last one of those commandos marching with Ali could've passed for an American GI. They wore damned near the same style of US Army uniforms, from their camouflage patrol caps down to their tan combat boots. Hell, even their weapons were probably paid for by the red, white, and blue, only via the black market. These guys looked like USA wannabes, trying to look tough. Tripp was damned sick and tired of being Big Brother. The USA needed to wrap this country up in a shitty brown bow, give it back to the warlords, and bring America's men and women home.

As the sun cleared the wall of mountains to the east, the morning turned into another scorcher. The tall, slender Afghan soldier walking alongside Major General Ali tipped his head into Ali's brimmed field officer cap and pointed at Tripp. Ali nodded. His index finger traced the thin mustache over his top lip. His dark black eyes went cold and flat, as he aimed for Tripp.

Tripp never blinked, just stared the man down like he would any other belligerent. Generals put their pants on the same way grunts did. Ali wanted a power struggle? He'd get it. Signed, sealed, and delivered, courtesy of US Army Corporal McClane. Tripp didn't back down from anyone which was why he'd never aspired to OTS, Officer Training School. What did it matter if he pissed off this jerk?

General Ali marched right up to him, the bright sun glinting off all the shiny crap pinned to his chest. Not much glinted off Tripp's chest. Tactical vests didn't shine.

"You," Ali bit out. He'd taken one step too many and was now inside Tripp's personal space. "You are the American soldier responsible for apprehending this pig?"

So much for courteous introductions.

As if to make a point, the general turned and spat at the already cringing teenage terrorist. "Kneel! You will kneel to me, or I will have you caged and burned alive. Here! Now!"

Cowering, Ikram fell to his knees and hid his face behind his cuffed hands. The poor damned kid. He didn't stand a chance against this bully. Something dark and feral inside Tripp lifted its head and bared its fangs. He hadn't yet officially transferred his prisoner over to this pompous ANSF prick. Didn't know if he would now. Despite the agreed-upon ROEs between the USA and Afghanistan, Ikram was technically still in Tripp's care. True, terrorists didn't deserve much respect. They didn't get it in America; they got less in this country. But Ikram was just a stupid kid, and nobody deserved the treatment Ali was dishing out.

"Yes, sir, I'm Corporal McClane," Tripp answered respectfully, keeping his tone neutral, even as his blood began a slow boil. "My team and I intercepted Abdul Ikram one block east of—"

"But you," Ali snapped, one side of his upper lip lifted in a snarl. He stabbed a finger into Tripp's chest, pissing him off. "It was you. You are the one. It was you who stopped him from completing his assignment."

Calling what Ikram did an assignment made it sound as if he had a boss, which he probably did. How else would the kid have acquired that many explosives, a suicide vest, and a push-button detonator? But Ali also made it sound like an accusation, instead of something Tripp should've been proud of. Nothing he'd done yesterday, except preventing more deaths and taking Ikram under his wing, felt right.

"*We* did, yes, sir," Tripp replied. "My team and—"

"Not *we*. There was no we. Your men did not bring this… this…" Ali muttered some curse Tripp couldn't interpret quickly enough. "You alone took this piece of camel shit down. You alone took the detonator from him and ended his fatwa. You!"

Tripp couldn't decide if the man wanted agreement or confession. He refused to give either. There was no I in his team, damn it. Again, he quietly replied, "*My team and I* ended this young man's attack before more civilians were killed, sir. We were lucky. We were in the right place at the right time. It happens." *Get over your effin' self.*

Ali's head bobbed once. He grunted, but not as if he'd conceded the power struggle. More like he'd accepted a challenge. Without another word, he jerked the Russian-made pistol out of the holster on his belt and fired. The poor, unsuspecting kid folded back onto his skinny legs like a deflated, punctured accordion. The top of his head was gone, splattered against the pants of the American soldiers standing behind him.

Automatically, Tripp's pistol sprang to his gloved hand. His six-man squad followed suit, and it was showdown in Dodge City, with really bad odds.

"You son of a bitch!" he hissed at the glowering bastard standing so close that Tripp could've strangled him with his bare hands. "He was just a kid!"

General Ali turned magnanimous. Holstering his pistol with a swaggering head bob, he put one palm forward, as if placating a stupid American. As if he hadn't just murdered a child. A sinister smile curled the corners of his thin lips. "My country and I thank you for your service, Corporal McClane," he announced loud enough for all to hear. "That is your name, is it not? You are United States Army Corporal Tripp McClane, right? Or is my intelligence incorrect?"

Tripp was done being nice. He didn't answer this pompous dickwad, and he didn't lower his weapon. Couldn't. Could barely think straight. Willed his nostrils not to inhale the sickening scent of Ikram's blood and brains cooking on the sizzling tarmac. Focused solely on the wrinkles lining the forehead of the asshat who had cold-bloodedly murdered a fifteen-year-old boy.

"Come on, Tripp. Don't make waves," Spike, his best buddy, muttered as he hip-checked Tripp. "Sergeant Wolsey just drove up. We gotta go."

"Yeah," Tripp growled out of the side of his mouth, his mind numb at the awful turn of events. "Yeah. We do."

But red-hot rage still burned low in his gut, the same kind of rage that had propelled him out of Idaho and into the Army two years ago. The kind that would get him and his men killed if he acted on it today. It might've gotten him out of the mess his sister made of his family life, but here, in this godforsaken part of the world, it could get him court-martialed. Or dead.

Like a USA robot with a script programmed into its perfectly manicured data banks, he repeated the official words he'd been instructed to say during the prisoner hand-off. Legal words he had to say. Thinning his lips, he bit out, "By the authority of the US Army, I relinquish care and responsibility for prisoner one-zero-one-two, Abdul Ikram, a fifteen-year-old child…" *You son of a bitch!* "…over to you…" *You pig!* "Major General Jalandar Ali of the Afghan National Army Commando Corps." *You worthless piece of shit!*

Would've meant more if Tripp had lowered his weapon before he'd said it. Close to fifty weapons now stared down at him and his squad. Dozens of the darkest black eyes promised retribution.

Well, bring it on.

Trickles of sweat rolled down Tripp's temples, off his forehead and into his eyes, at what could very well happen next. His pulse hammered for his own brand of retribution. His finger, still on the trigger, begged to squeeze off a round, to empty his double-stack magazine into Ali's smug face. All those yes-men might win this fight, but by hell, Ali wouldn't.

The big, brave man with brass on his chest, not in his pants, sneered. "You tell me that nonsense now? Are you a fool?"

Yes, actually... I can be.

Tripp's lower lip curled over his bottom teeth. He breathed through his mouth, fighting for composure and that damned elusive thing called discretion. Nothing about this transfer had gone right. US Army Rangers had trained every last ANSF commando. *Those* commandos excelled at fighting the Taliban and ISIL, had in fact, never been beaten. There was no way *these* jerks were those same trained men.

Spike hip-checked him again. "Take a step back, buddy. Sarge'll have your ass if you screw this up."

Tripp stared Ali down, not going to blink, gawddamnit. "For what? For letting this shithead kill a kid in cold blood?"

"Don't forget, Ikram was a terrorist, and you know it, and... Atten-shun!" Spike snapped to.

The rest of Tripp's squad did as well. Not Tripp. Wolsey could wait his turn.

Damned if his CO didn't step directly into Tripp's line of sight with an amicable, shit-eating, "Major General Ali. Staff Sergeant Wolsey here, pleased to make your acquaintance, sir." With one hand now firmly braced over the top of Tripp's pistol, Wolsey forced his aim to the tarmac instead of the asshole. "I trust everything is in order. That the transfer went well."

Was Wolsey blind? Had he missed the murdered kid at his feet?

"It did," Ali replied smoothly, his chin lifted while he petted his scrawny excuse for a mustache again. "It is too bad you arrived late. The prisoner tried to escape. I was forced to execute him. Tsk, tsk."

Tripp blew. "Escape, my ass! You son of a—!"

Wolsey twisted Tripp's wrist, a sure signal to shut up. "Well, sir, it's war," he told Ali without emotion. "Unfortunately, things like this happen. Thank you for taking the time to meet with us today, General. You've been a great help. We appreciate all you do for us."

All you do for us? Like murdering children?!

"It is my pleasure," the liar replied with the grace of every politician on the whole damned planet.

Tripp wanted to throw up. The world turned red and hazy, but not because of the pretty sunrise pouring over the horizon. His head worked like that when he was about to lose his temper. When he'd been forced to witness atrocities and murder—and do nothing!

"About face," Wolsey barked, his hand still an iron manacle on Tripp's wrist as he forced compliance Tripp didn't want to give. But he was smart enough to follow orders. He kept his big mouth shut until he and his squad were almost to the OD green wall of US Army deuce-and-a-half trucks now parked at the edge of the runway. When had they arrived?

Tripp glanced over his shoulder. General Ali was staring at him. Still preening. Gloating. "That bastard just killed a kid in cold blood, Sergeant Wolsey. I hadn't even transferred military authority when he—"

"What part of about face do you not understand, soldier?" Wolsey growled while speed-walking to the rear of those trucks. "I'm trying to save your dumb ass, McClane. Move it."

"Why? What's going on?"

"It's war, damn it. Forget Ikram. Kids play with bombs, they end up dead. End of fuckin' story."

"But someone else forced him to bomb that mosque. I damned well know it, and so do you. Wanna bet that someone was Ali?"

There was no sense arguing. Wolsey's pearly whites were set and his square jaw was clenched like the bulldog he was. All Tripp could do was follow orders. His was not to question why. His was just to do and die. And… "Bullshit! These ROEs suck! They're wrong! He was just a skinny kid. We're better than that. I could've gotten him to talk. I know I could've!"

"Get your ass in the truck. We need to be gone."

Tripp's guys had already boarded. Spike was waving for him to climb in. Tripp had one foot on the tailgate, ready to jump up when he noticed all the tailgates on these trucks were down. A couple dozen fully-armed, geared-up, badassed soldiers were waiting inside each deuce-and-a-half. Wolsey knew something Tripp didn't.

"Ali?" Tripp asked, even as he hung suspended by one arm from the canvas soft top.

"That bastard's not Ali, damn it," Wolsey declared vehemently, "and those men with him are not ANSF commandos. That's Ali's son of a bitchin' brother, Anwar Khan, the Crimson Sword of Allah. He's a terrorist, and he's here to kill his brother, then takeover this facility. We need to be gone before hell breaks loose."

Right on cue, the lethal rumble of America's finest guardian angel of the skies eased its silver wings over the far end of the tarmac. An A-10, aka the famed Warthog, every US service member's best friend, was headed straight for Khan's little army. Now there was a sight a man could believe in.

Tripp's jaw dropped. "But he looks just like Ali."

"Well, he's not. Ali's the one who notified us that Khan and his men were headed here. It's Ali who asked for air support."

"Khan's got inside help if he's made it this far with this many armed men."

"You think?" Wolsey groused as the first A-10's magnificent barrage shook the Earth.

"That's why he killed Ikram. Khan sent him into that mosque, didn't he?"

The ground vibrated and bucked beneath Tripp's boots, as the A-10's thirty-millimeter GAU Avenger cannons began hitting their marks. Man, he loved the blistering sound of payback. He dropped back to the ground to watch.

The A-10 was commonly called *'a gun with an airplane attached,'* and for good reason. That Gatling-style Avenger delivered powerful, precise destruction that was, right then, raining hell on the ass who'd killed Abdul Ikram. It took Tripp's breath watching the killer bedecked with phony medals, run for his life, only to disappear in a gray plume of pulverized concrete.

After one pass, the coup was over. Nothing remained of Khan's attempted take-over, nothing except smoking carcasses, ash, and a runway that needed repair. For the most part, Morehead Commando Training Center was safe. The A-10's pilot dipped his wings in a brotherly salute as he flew over the rumbling line of deuce-and-a-halfs. Talk about righteous kills. This take-down was the perfect revenge for the death of a frightened, hungry, Afghan boy.

"I fuckin' love America!" Tripp declared as he hoisted himself aboard. "Let's go home, guys."

Chapter One

Three Years Later

Junior Agent Tripp McClane stood in the shadows near the entry gate to the Winkler Botanical Preserve in western Alexandria, Virginia. Dusk came early in autumn. This was his second night back on the streets since he'd returned to the East Coast. He was anxious, ready to continue the late-night masquerade he'd begun in Seattle. Here, within spitting distance of the nation's capital.

Like last night and those before, he'd camo-painted his face and purposefully darkened the skin around his eyes for his graveyard shift. Dressed in midnight black, from his leather jacket to his steel-toed work boots, he was one with the shadows. No one who knew him during the day would recognize him now. He intended to keep it that way.

This was his mission, his purpose in life. Protect the weak. Destroy those who would harm or do them wrong. It had begun at the stroke of one damp, chilly midnight in Seattle, the emerald gem of the great Pacific Northwest, and the site of Tripp's last job. All he'd wanted was a cup of Seattle's famous coffee. Instead, he'd come across two stout morons assaulting a five-foot-nothing blonde who shouldn't have been on Pike Street so late nor so alone. They'd cornered her in an alley, between a delivery truck and a red-brick building.

They'd already slapped and pushed her around. Her winter coat was on the ground at her feet and her hair was undone. She'd been crying, pleading with them to take her briefcase. To just let her live.

And Tripp had seen red. Gawddamnit. No woman should have to plead for anything, least of all to be allowed to live. The breeze off Elliot Bay was brisk and bitter that night. As was Tripp's response. Without thought or strategy, he'd tossed his coffee and roared to her rescue. Knocked both men down and out before they knew what they were up against. He'd saved that woman's life, possibly her virtue. Maybe her mind. All those things he hadn't been able to do for a skinny Afghan teenager on the other side of the world.

When all was said and done, Tripp had called the police, then begged off into the shadows once their blues and reds flashed onto the scene. With her safely in good hands, Tripp stepped away from what could have been notoriety and applause. Instead, he opted for anonymity and the reward of knowing that a man could still do good in the world, more if he kept his identity hidden.

A vigilante was born that night. Well, not born. Make that revived. Tripp had always had an overprotective, zealous streak. After saving that one woman, he became more of the same. A man in the shadows. A punisher and a savior. A warrior.

Did that make him a lawbreaker? Absolutely. Did he care what his new boss would say if he found out? Nope. Tripp might work for Mr. OCD, aka Alex Stewart, during the day. But he worked for the blind Lady Justice after dark. The scales of truth in her right hand had proven faulty for too long. Too many bleeding hearts over the years had set enough scumbags, perverts, and murderers free, and, in the process, allowed more innocent deaths. Tripp meant to change those dynamics. He was the sword of vengeance in Lady Justice's left hand, the swift, final end of the road for all who got in his way.

He paid—visits—to local miscreants and bastards. He dealt brutal, if not healthy, doses of comeuppance, but only to those who had it coming. Back in Seattle, he'd prevented two assaults of women in dark parking lots. He'd thwarted a bank job in progress, the looting of a street side ATM, and a bloody home burglary. Tonight's work was cut out for a guy like him. He pulled a pair of black gloves over his already tender knuckles. It was time to get down and dirty.

The two college-aged young men he'd been following, had just skirted the CLOSED sign to the Preserve. They should've known better than to enter the shadow-filled park after dark. Yet Tripp understood. Young people were full of angst and raging hormones, and that combination made them stupid.

That anyone believed these two should *hide* their feelings, *pretend* to be like everyone else, or spend their lives *lying* to themselves just to get along, annoyed the shit out of Tripp. Which was why he'd been following them since they'd left their adjoining apartments on Seminary Road, just north of the Preserve. All because of a convo he'd overheard in a local biker bar last night. A plan to torture and kill this specific couple. To make an example of 'those people'. To remind the world what the Bible said about 'them' and the self-righteous 'us.' As if the bastards hunting these two tonight had ever read the Bible.

But when the leather-clad, gin-guzzling, big-mouthed biker named names to go with his despicable plan, well, that cinched Tripp's plans for the evening. He'd located these two young men and found out they were just nineteen-year-old freshmen at the nearby community college.

Tonight wasn't about trespassing. Tripp wasn't here to prevent misdemeanors. But he did care that tonight, these quiet trails and shadowy hideaways were haunted by dangerous bigots. That these two gullible kids only had eyes for each other. That they had no concept of situational awareness or self-defense.

His nostrils flared with disdain for bullies who thought themselves above the law, and for terrorists who used the good books for their evil machinations the whole world over. Even in America.

Slapping one gloved hand to the top bar of the gate, he vaulted his six-foot, five-inch frame over the weak excuse of a barrier and landed quietly on the other side. His job was clear. Protect the innocent. Engage the aggressors. End their reign of terror before another innocent died. Do it all over again tomorrow night. Wash. Rinse. Repeat.

Established back in the 1980s, the Preserve had once been a pig farm. Although located in the middle of a busy metropolitan area now, it still boasted thickly forested trails, a good-sized pond full of ducks, a quaint wooden bridge, and man-made waterfalls that fed the pond. But tonight, it boasted trouble.

The boys had just crossed the bridge when a sinister voice rumbled from the shadows, "Hey, hey, hey. Look what we got here. A couple of light-footed fairies."

Five hefty, leather-jacketed adult males stepped out of the dark, boxing the two college kids in. The taller kid spread his feet as if prepared to fight back—or run. The shorter, stockier kid, turned to the bridge, his palms forward, ready to placate the aggressors blocking his way. Which was the worst possible tactic when faced with bullies. Placation never commanded respect, not unless it was delivered with force. At which point, it ceased being passive.

Strike hard. Strike fast. Never give a fuckin' inch. That was how you placated a bully. Not with chit-chat or good manners. Never with compromise.

Kids these days. They had no idea how ugly the world really was. It would've been smart if these two had brought something to defend themselves. But Tripp doubted it. When the back-and-forth convo deteriorated into pleading, more name-calling, and five baseball-bat, tire-iron, chain-wielding asshats against two unarmed college kids, he stepped into the weak glow of the lamp, still on the wrong side of the bridge.

"Shut the fuck up!" he ordered.

That worked on the college boys. By then, they were back-to-back, and knew they were in serious shit. But the bullies threatening them took Tripp's command as if he were the grand marshal at the Daytona 500, and had declared, "Drivers, start your engines!"

One stomped back over the bridge like a troll, power-posing and swinging a Louisville slugger. The idiot behind him looked like a fool straight out of Rhinestone Cowboy, Inc. His shiny leather jacket bedazzled, all right. Those big boy pants had more glittery zippers up the sides than a zipper factory. He looked like a sparkling fool, whirling that heavy tow chain over his head like a lasso. Tripp had seen children in other parts of the world with less clothes who were ten times scarier.

He charged before Mr. Baseball crossed the bridge. With a quick, hard chop to the jerk's windpipe, the game was over. Mr. B collapsed in the middle of the bridge, bug-eyed and gasping on all fours. His bully club rolled into the stream.

Rushing Rhinestone Cowboy next, Tripp grabbed both railings, drew his knees in, and delivered a swift, well-aimed kick to the center of the guy's glittering chest. Gasping, Cowboy stumbled back. Tripp followed through with a solid right cross to Cowboy's chin. A solid left jab left the tough guy on his knees, drooling, and cross-eyed. He hadn't taken a single swing, but he was down.

Chaos took over. The tall kid took a punch to his face, his assailant the beefy boss who'd called this ambush. The shorter kid was already on his side on the ground, crying, and getting his ass whipped by the other two thugs.

Tripp went after the boss of this shit show. With a flying leap over the two morons thrashing the shorter kid, he caught Mr. Boss-man with both boots, square in the center of his thick, barrel chest. Knocked the bastard off the skinny kid and off his feet. Down Tripp rolled into a carpet of Virginia creeper with the guy, groping after the knife that had flashed at him as they'd gone down.

Not willing to play hide-and-seek with a blade he didn't need and possibly couldn't retrieve, Tripp bounced to his feet, ready to end this pathetic battle. Eager to keep the kids safe. The adrenaline in his blood surged like pure fire, its flames licking at him to do more. It all came back to that other young man who'd died on the other side of the planet. Ikram. That was why Tripp was here tonight and would serve America as one of its few vigilantes. To take down men like these jerks.

To somehow, make amends for letting that other mother's son die.

Tripp didn't hold back, and he never offered quarter. It wasn't in him. Not during these late night come-to-Jesus meetings. Just attacked with all of his pent-up fury, threw straight punches and inside hooks until the big guy dropped to his knees. Did Tripp care when the lead jerk whined like a pussy? Did he stop administering justice or punishment? Hell, no. Cupping his fists, he clubbed the bastard senseless. Then, with sweat stinging his eyes, he turned to the last two asshats standing.

Side-by-side, they'd stopped beating the kid crying at their feet. Too little, too late. Tripp stalked forward like the badass he was, gawddamnit. His fists curled into iron. Snorting a plume of frosty vapor through his flared nostrils, he told the fools who still thought they were mean enough to take him, "You should run."

"Who are you?" the wimpier, skinnier of the two asked.

"I'm your fuckin' nightmare." He stomped a boot forward. "Now, run!"

"This ain't none of your business, dickwad!" the other bully snarled, wiping the back of his hand over a bloody lip. Which meant one of the college kids must've gotten in a lucky punch.

Tripp raised his right arm and fluttered his fingers, taunting the two fools to come, try him. "It's you who's got no business being here. Run. Tell your friends. I'm coming for every last one of you."

The weaker of the two stepped back and grabbed the other's sleeve. "Come on, Monkey. Let's go."

"I ain't goin' nowhere, Chum." The ballsy bastard stomped a menacing boot back at Tripp. "Why don't *you* run, shithead? Go home to mommy. These streets are ours. Tell her I said so!"

Big mistake. Tripp hadn't come here to argue, and no one badmouthed the woman who'd raised him—ever. He didn't growl. Didn't waste another breath on this loser. Just attacked. Head down. Head on. Right shoulder tucked. Left fist first. Threw a punch straight into Monkey's ugly face. Then followed with a blistering barrage of left, right hooks to the guy's soggy middle.

Monkey wheezed, but never raised a hand to block the shots.

Tripp ended the one-sided fight with an over-handed punch to the guy's head, then an upper-cut to his big chin. His face was hamburger by then, and he was out cold. As stiff as a corpse, he planked face first. His forehead bounced on the hard-packed ground.

TKO. If he lived. Tripp was long past caring whether murderers like these five survived the brutal beatings he dished out. Just like Anwar Khan, the Crimson Sword of Allah, these guys thought they were untouchable. He fuckin' thought otherwise.

With evil intent, he turned to the last bully standing, but by then, Chumley was gone, and the two college kids were shakily helping each other to their feet. "Hey, m-mister," the taller one sputtered. He was holding his gut with both hands and blood from his nose ran down his chin and neck. "You saved our lives. Th-thanks."

"Yeah," the shorter kid wheezed. "My mom and dad'll want to meet you."

"You've got parents who care?" Tripp asked in disbelief. It wasn't that long ago that people disowned kids who were 'different.' "Then why the fuck are you out here tonight? Why aren't you somewhere safe? In a coffee shop or… or home?" He'd almost said, "in bed," but figured these guys didn't need any encouragement.

"Yeah, sure," the short guy huffed. He was on his feet by then, unsteady and leaning into his friend. Hell, they were both leaning. "We've got parents. Good parents. But moms and dads get a little overprotective sometimes, you know what I mean?"

"And now you know why," Tripp snarled. "You know where the free clinic is over on King Street? Go there. Get yourselves checked, then call an Uber or a cab and go straight home. Talk to your parents. Tell them what happened here tonight. Just leave me out of it."

"You're really a good guy," the taller kid breathed. "You're like one of the Avengers. You're a hero."

"Like hell I am."

"You're my hero," Shorty murmured.

Tripp cut the hero-worship, star-struck, bullshit off. "No, I'm not. Get the hell out of here, and forget you ever saw me!"

"Yeah. Sure," the shorter kid said again, his voice so damned gentle and patient, Tripp worried he'd met an actual canonized saint.

Stabbing a gloved finger in the general direction of the clinic, he bellowed, "Go!"

"We're going. But if you ever need any—"

"I said get the hell out of here! Run!"

Finally. That vehement blast propelled the two back across the bridge, over the gate, and out of the Preserve. Tripp followed in the shadows, needing to be sure they made it to the clinic without more trouble. Which they did. Once they were inside, he intended to call it a night and head home. Morning came early. So, did his real job.

Chapter Two

Darn. The sun had set hours ago, and Ashley Cox was late leaving her office. Really late. She'd been promoted today. She was now an outreach coordinator for Alexandria, Virginia's Health Department. As a newly appointed, trained public health educator, it was her job to locate and teach—if possible—individuals in need of a certain type of preventative medical care. Unfortunately, the real teaching these guys needed had more to do with keeping their pants zipped, than how to eat nutritionally or perform emergency CPR. And therein lay Ashley's problem. She didn't like most men. The belligerent sperm-donor in her life was the worst role model a daughter could get. Then, there was that other guy… *No. Not going there.*

Stalled at the building's front entrance glass doors, she debated the benefits of staying the night inside, as opposed to walking outside to get to the metro station. She could sleep here. Why not? Her office was small and tidy, not as large as her boss, Terry Chandler's, but it was clean. She could sleep on the floor. Her light jacket would make a decent blanket. She could freshen up in the women's restroom before anyone arrived tomorrow morning. Who would know?

Sure, the couch in her boss's office would make a more comfortable bed. But his office also had floor-to-ceiling windows, and windows weren't all they were cracked up to be. Ha, ha. She rolled her eyes at that unintentional pun.

The Department shared their one-level brick building with the twenty-four-seven free clinic on its west end. As dark as it already was outside, anyone standing on the street could see inside when the lights were on. Like those in the lobby.

But if that person wanted to break in, all they had to do was step past the tidy beds of trimmed wintergreen boxwood shrubs, and those huge windows in Terry's office wouldn't stand a chance. Not like there were drugs or cash or other valuables inside the Health Department, because there weren't. But because the world had grown a lot meaner lately. Some people just wanted to destroy public property. They wanted to make statements.

Lifting both arms over her head, Ashley gathered her long, black hair and secured it with one of several elastics she kept on her wrist. She should've tracked her time better. But she'd been so focused on her first, on-the-job assignment, that she'd stayed way past quitting time, and now everyone else was gone. Truthfully, she was a nervous wreck. This promotion meant she'd be contacting those who'd been tagged as possible carriers of STDs. Talk about having to face her worst demon. This assignment would do it. Notifying women would be hard enough. But men? She cringed at the thought. But it was either get over her male-induced phobia or turn down the promotion. Which wasn't going to happen.

She drummed her fingers on the free-moving bar that would either propel her into the night with all its unknowns, or that she could lock to keep those same unknowns, well, unknown. It would only take one little turn of the hex key at the end of that bar to lock herself in for the night.

Opening the door, the brisk autumn night poured into the lobby with her. She peered out at the busy, lighted street. Darn. If she left now, and if she speed-walked, it'd still be a good fifteen-minutes to the King Street metro station. It sounded doable. A brisk evening walk might even be good for her. There were streetlights on the way, for heaven's sake. This was America. Land of the free. Home of the brave. For once, she could be brave, too.

Couldn't she? *Yeah, sure.*

Well, maybe. With resolute bravado she didn't quite feel, Ashley flipped the lobby light switch off, opened the right half of the glass entry door, stuck the hex key into the locking mechanism, and locked the door that would now prevent her re-entry. With her light jacket on and her over-the-shoulder messenger bag firmly in place, she burst into the night. Determined, darn it. Well-lighted King Station lay directly to the East. One metro stop and a short walk to her apartment-complex past that, and she'd be home. She could do this.

If she hurried.

Facing the wind, she lifted one hand to tighten the collar of her jacket, while sticking her other hand deep into her bag. Once her fingers curled around her secret weapon, the cool, slender cylinder of mace she always carried, she breathed easier. She'd never had to use it before. Truthfully, she didn't venture outside more than she had to, mostly just for work. Nothing else. She had her groceries delivered to her apartment. Anything else she needed, she picked up on her way to or from work. In the daylight. When there were more people. When it was safer. She didn't go out at night, and she didn't take unnecessary chances. Not anymore.

Glancing back at the free clinic adjacent to her now darkened office building, she wondered if it might not have been smarter to call a cab or Uber. She would, but only if she could be sure she'd get a female driver.

She'd no more than cast that notion aside when an arm snaked out of nowhere and circled her throat. "Make one move and I'll gut you like a frog," a man growled against the side of her head. Jerking the strap of her messenger bag over her head, he nearly took her ear off with it. Her secret weapon catapulted out of her hand, end-over-end through the air. The guy cocked his elbow, tightening his hold around her neck and dragged her onto the strip of grass between the sidewalk and parking lot.

Ashley's back hit a wall of solid muscle. A blast of rank, hot breath feathered over her neck. He had a knife under her chin, its blade as cold as ice. A desperate cry climbed up her throat. Tears. Damned worthless tears that hadn't helped last time, blurred her way forward. Off balance, she stumbled. He was going to kill her. It was happening again!

"Why are you doing this?"

"Shut up!" the creep ordered, punching the side of her head so hard with his knife handle, that her teeth chattered, and she saw stars. He let go, and she fell to her knees in the grass, her ponytail swirling over her face.

Thinking this was the end, Ashley rolled to her side, fighting the humiliation that was sure to come. But if she was going down, she needed to see her attacker. Swiping her hair out of her eyes and mouth, she looked up at him. He was taller, definitely heavier, and he'd spoken with a southern accent. But he was younger than she'd thought. He couldn't have been more than eighteen. He was just a young man in ragged jeans with a light-gray hoody pulled over his head. Scraggly whiskers shadowed his chin. Frosty plumes exhaled over straight white teeth. This was someone's child. He had parents, a mom and dad who loved him enough to pay for his braces. Ashley knew it to her soul. He couldn't be a murderer. Until he dropped to his knees beside her and landed a vicious hit to her solar plexus.

Her heart fluttered to a dead stop. She struggled to breathe. The 'poor child' punched her again. Worried what he'd do next, she turned her face toward King Street, and looked at all those cars humming eastward and westward. Surely someone could see that she needed help, that she was under attack. It wouldn't take much for someone—anyone— to stop and ask this young man what he was doing. To make sure he knew he'd been seen, caught assaulting a woman. That ought to frighten him away. Streetlights, darn it. King Street was lined with plenty of streetlights! She wasn't invisible, people!

With a mean hand, he flipped her onto her stomach and straddled her butt. How humiliating! To be attacked, possibly on her way to being raped, where everyone could see but wouldn't interfere.

"Help!" she screamed, her brain overloaded with images of that other day and that other man. That other knife.

Twisting her ponytail into his fist, this jerk pulled her head so far back that she couldn't swallow or scream. "Shut your pie-hole, slut!" he hissed into the side of her face.

"I'm not a… a…" *A that.*

"You're all sluts. Every gawddamned one of you!" He was so close that his saliva speckled her cheek when he yelled. With a hard yank, he pulled her hair nearly out of her scalp.

"Where's the keys, bitch? You got 'em, I know you do. I seen you lock the place up. You the boss or something?"

"Keys?" she managed to gasp.

"Yeah, keys!" Bang, bang, bang! He kept slamming her face into the spongy, icy-cold grass. "Where are they?"

Oh, my God, He's going to kill me! Ashley closed her eyes, ready to die. There was nothing she could say to make this guy understand that he'd never get inside that building. Once the front door locked, the only way in was to break the glass, and that would set off the alarm. The police station was only a block or two away. They'd be here in seconds.

"You heard me! The keys to the drugs. Oxy! That's all I want!" His voice ramped higher with every desperate word and every slam her face took into the grass. Her poor nose was bleeding! "I'll tell you what's gonna happen next. You and me are gonna march back in there, and you're gonna unlock your safe or your cabinet or wherever you keep the shit, and you're gonna give me everything I need! All of it! Understand?"

"Ah huh, sure," was all she could manage to wheeze. By then she was deafened by the abuse, and too frightened at what he'd do next if she said anything else. Or when he found out she had no keys, that there were no drugs where she worked. Only at the clinic. Her entire body ached, and her poor scalp burned like fire. She was sure he'd already cut her neck, though she couldn't feel any sting. If she were bleeding there, she didn't know it. As thin as he was, he was still heavy and agitated and… and mean.

She lay there, out of breath and out of time, ready to die, when the ground vibrated under her chin. A fierce roar split the night. A growling string of vile curses followed. Oh, no.

There were two! Another creep had just joined the first. She buried her face in the grass and cried.

But suddenly, the hefty weight straddling her was gone. Just poof! Gone! One second, he'd been mashing his putrid body into hers, rubbing his… his thing… against her butt. The next, he'd flown backward, as if some giant puppeteer had jerked his strings and sent him flying. His knife skittered across the sidewalk and landed in the gutter.

Gasping, Ashley climbed to her knees and braced one foot to the grass, ready to run for her life at this double threat. Until she caught sight of the magnificent predator now kneeling over her original attacker, exacting brutal vengeance. He wasn't anything like the other guy. Not at all. He was huge, a monster in black from the cap covering his head to his size twenty boots. A growling, cursing monster that made her attacker look like a sniveling little boy. He'd pinned the guy to the sidewalk and was pummeling the kid with wicked, hard blows, from fists as big as sledgehammers. Blood and spit flew, but not his. Still his arm pistoned up and down, delivering bone-crunching, nose-breaking retribution for a woman he didn't even know. *Who does that?!*

Ashley sucked in a long, deep breath that turned to frosted vapor when she blew out her fright. She was too weak to run. She could only stare. Half of her wanted to scream, "Hit him again!" But her other half cried out for mercy, "Stop! You're killing him!"

This man was no savior, no Jesus Christ. No turn-the-other-cheek kind of hero. There was madness in the quick, efficient way he exacted punishment. He was bigger. Meaner. Heavier. He knew how to hurt her aggressor, now turned into a whimpering victim she couldn't help feeling sorry for.

"Don't!" *Punch. Punch. Punch.* "Ever!" *Bam. Bam. Bam.* "Touch this woman again!" the newly arrived, but much angrier man bellowed. "The next time I see you…" *Punch. Bam. Punch.* "…I will…" *Punch. Punch. Punch.* "…fuckin' kill you!" He landed one last fist into the stupid, younger man's bloodied, mashed-beyond-description, face. Those pretty, expensive teeth weren't so straight nor so white now.

But promises like that were hard to unhear. Harder yet to unsee. Or believe. This man, this savior, this fierce stranger, meant to kill her aggressor? For her? Someone he didn't know and would never see again? What was he going to do, camp on her doorstep and follow her around for the rest of her life to keep that promise?

"S-s-stop," she begged, before he voided his promise to kill this kid by murdering him on her behalf.

The man in black lifted to his feet and turned to glare at her. He snapped, pointing a long, condemning finger at her. "You shouldn't be out this late at night! Not alone!"

His words stung. His voice was more heated hiss than speech, full of invective so hot, it sounded like hate, not care or concern. Like a prize bull facing a matador, billows of white, frosty vapor snorted from his nostrils. He stood there flexing his fingers. She was sure blood dripped off the tips of his black gloves and sizzled when it hit the ground.

"I-I-I know, b-b-ut…" Ashley lost her voice in the wild, thrumming beat of her heart. She scurried backward, like a witless crab toward the busy street, with all its worthless illumination and cowardly passersby. Who was the aggressor now? Was she next? Would this guy hurt her, too?

His gloved palm came up and, "Stop!" he commanded, like he had the right to order her around. Like she should listen just because he said so.

"W-w-why should I? Because you're bigger and meaner than me?" she cried, more scared now than she'd been before. "No! I just want to g-g-go home. Don't hurt me, too!"

And he was on her. Like an inky shadow, he captured her and blocked her view of the streetlights, the entire street, and most of the sky. Ashley squeezed her eyes shut. She didn't dare breathe. Couldn't think, her heart was pounding so hard. The power of the gods radiated off this man in black, in hair-raising, frightening mega-gigawatts. He was one with the night, a true jungle predator out for a kill, one who could rip her apart, lap at her entrails, and kick dirt over her carcass when he'd finished making a meal of her.

What a horrible, awful night. Tucking her chin to her chest, Ashley instinctively made herself smaller. She curled into a ball, her arms over her head, and her knees tucked up tightly into her belly, shielding her more tender body parts. Like prey, she was caught with no way to escape. All she could do was try to survive. She flinched at what might happen next. She was a stupid, stupid gazelle and he was a predator.

All the men in her life had been loud-mouthed, belligerent users of women, mean and cruel when it served their purposes. This guy was no different. He'd just proven that in spades. Had he saved her for something worse than death? Was this a power struggle or a rescue? Her poor heart couldn't tell.

Until a band of steel curled under her knees and lifted her carefully off the cold ground. Until the monster who'd come to her aid, cradled her ever so gently against his fiercely beating heart. It, err, he whispered into the top of her shivering, sweaty head, "Hey, there. I'm sorry I scared you, but I've got you now, and he can't hurt you anymore. You're safe now, ma'am. Please don't cry."

"I'm not! B-b-but…" She was. Ashley blubbered, not sure of anything other than she was on the verge of wetting her pants and screaming hysterically for him to put her down. At least he'd removed his bloody gloves and tossed them aside. That was thoughtful. But his big hands still had a firm hold on her. She was still caught.

"Shush," he murmured softly, unzipping his leather jacket and tucking her inside like a little girl. Not that she wasn't already wearing her own jacket, but hers was lightweight, and his was so warm and big. And man, the scent pouring out of his jacket smelled decadently of wind, leather, and testosterone, precisely the scents she seemed to need in her nose right then. They calmed her. Helped her to think and process logical, sensible thoughts. Her nostrils flared, and she was surprised her nose still worked while gushing blood. That inhaling could still feel semi-pleasurable. The unique fragrance wafting off this guy would forevermore remind her of what true masculine strength was. Even as hot tears rolled over her cheeks.

"I promise, ma'am. That guy won't bother you again," her monster guardian angel said as a big, rough hand curved around her head and cupped her jaw.

Like a hapless idiot, Ashley leaned into that palm, her heart still pounding out of control even as she considered the fact that this guy had saved her life. That he was so much larger, thicker, and heavier than she was. He was made of steel and coiled bands of titanium muscle. And she was bleeding all over him.

"Is he… is he still alive?" she whimpered, desperate for a tissue—or ten.

"Do you care?" Incredulity colored that terse question. "After what he did to you?"

"Well, err…" *Kind of.* "Yes, I mean…" How could she not care about an obviously drug-addicted young man? And how could anyone survive the beating this guy had dished out? The kid hadn't hit back. Not once. He hadn't had the chance. He wasn't big enough to take on this man, and he surely hadn't the skills. Yet he'd certainly had no trouble slapping her around, punching her, and—

"Yes, he's alive, but he can't hurt you now. Focus on that. Breathe in. Breathe out. You're safe, and I'm going to take care of you." His voice was a seductive rumble, a masculine purr she wanted to snuggle into. Whoever this man was, he was a safe place. A big, warm safe place that seemed able to read her mind.

Trying desperately to regain a professional sense of decorum, Ashley swiped the back of her hand under her bloody, snotty nose and again wished for a tissue.

Instantly, a travel-sized package of them appeared, courtesy of this man's deep pockets. He punched his thumbnail into the top perforation and tugged several tissues out. "Here," he said quietly, her less important wish granted and perched at the end of his fingertips. "Use all you need. I've got more."

"Th-thank you," she whispered. Taking the offering, Ashley blew her poor, tender nose like a lady, then tucked the disgusting, crumpled tissues into her pocket.

"No problem. I'm here for you. Promise."

Risking a covert glance through her spikey, wet eyelashes, she prepared to be brave and look her rescuer in the eye. D-d-darn. That was a long way up. But so worth the effort.

This was no boy come to her rescue. Uh-uh. This guy was all male. Thick-boned and heavily muscled, like a workhorse. Camouflage tones painted a square jaw. The black and green stripes on his cheeks made his nose appear as sharp as a blade. Thick brows shadowed his blackened eyes. She'd never recognize him without the greasepaint. He was hiding, too.

But nothing could conceal the sparkle hidden deep in those eyes. There was no regret in them for what he'd done; no worry or fear of reprisal or of being caught, either. Only brash, in-your-face confidence. It oozed out of him, scenting the air around her with overwhelming, deep, dark, male pheromones. How would that feel, to be so free of worry? So unafraid of one's shadow? He worried his bottom lip, scraping his top teeth over it while he tended to her. It was such a boyish thing to do. He couldn't hide the dimple in his left cheek, either. His lips were so, so close.

"You're like a guardian angel," she breathed in wonder.

He grunted. "I'm no damned angel."

But he was. The sheer size of him, the width of his shoulders and the breadth of his chest stole her breath. She couldn't decide what color his eyes were, but she knew enough about tragedy to translate the fury she saw banked there. He was a cross between a terrifying devil and an avenging angel, a heady combination of dark and light, of sin and grace. There was more of cinder and ash to his furled wings—if he indeed had any—than flowers, sunshine, and holy water. Besides, wings made perfect if not surreal sense to this crazy, scary night. Surely, he couldn't have shown up as quickly as he had without them, could he? Else why was he here precisely when and where she'd needed him? He was a sight to behold, so much larger than life, and she was so much smaller. So not worth his attention nor his time. And younger. He had to be ten years older.

"Where's your car?"

"I usually take the train home," *With everyone else.* "But…" Ashley swallowed hard, her voice trailing off to no-darned-where. The creep who'd assaulted her, still lay panting frosty breaths up into the chilly night sky. He was just like her deadbeat father, a user and a deadbeat, nothing like the mysterious dark angel holding her tightly. Keeping her safe. A stifled sob choked out of her at the stinging pain all over her scalp. "He pulled my hair!" she cried.

"I know. I saw. He's paid for what he did to you. Trust me, he's paid." Folding her into his arms, the man in black sat down on the grass with her on his lap. His much thicker thighs were warm and solid. His longer, muscled arms and shoulders wrapped around her like castle walls. Strong, high, impenetrable, warm walls.

Somehow, Ashley was surprisingly calm and able to breathe through her fear. In and out. It really worked, just like he'd said.

He tucked a thick chunk of her hair out of her face and shifted it over her shoulder, then smoothed his other hand over her forehead, brushing more tangled strands out of her eyes. "How else did he hurt you?"

She glanced over her shoulder at the silent man bleeding on the ground. "M-m-mostly, he just pulled my hair and p-p-punched me." She still couldn't believe people could be so cruel. "He kept banging my face into the grass, and h-h-he had a knife, and—" Ashley's hand flew to her neck. Her fingers came away sticky and dark. That jerk! "He cut me!"

With two gentle fingers, her angel tilted her chin. His dark eyes turned into shards of black obsidian. His nostrils flared, and she was pretty sure steam snorted out of his nose. "Fuckin' moron!" he hissed. Reaching into the other side of his jacket, her foul-mouthed angel pulled out a small bag of…

Oh, wow. He carried a personal first-aid kit with him? That was different.

"Lean back. Relax," he ordered, opening a small, sealed pack of antiseptic wipes. "It's not very deep, but let's get you taken care of."

Ashley hesitated. She looked like something an alley cat had dragged in or yakked up. Her nose was still running, possibly bleeding, and her cheeks were no doubt bright red. With her fair complexion, a simple blush looked like a fatal case of hives. Tears still dripped off her chin.

When he cleared his throat and nodded his chin at her, oh yeah. Ashley swiped another tissue under her nose, gathered her hair out of his way and leaned into his arm. Somehow, she'd lost her elastic. Wayward strands drifted in the breeze off the Potomac. Some teased over his nose and brows. Some got caught in the scruffy shadow on his chin. He didn't seem to mind. She tipped farther back to allow him to better see what he was doing.

"It's not a deep cut, thank fuck." Her potty-mouthed angel peered closely at her neck.

She found it odd that his continual f-bombs didn't distress her. Despite the sharp scent of antiseptic alcohol drifting between them, his breath was deliciously warm in her face. He smoothed a wipe—that stung!—up the quivering column of her throat. His fingers were spread wide, and his gentle touch was so disconcerting, that Ashley couldn't catch her breath for an entirely different reason now.

With the dark night's breeze swirling her black hair around them like a mysterious, translucent fog…

With this guy's hand so gentle on her throat…

With her rescue so recently, so fearlessly acquired…

Ashley froze, afraid to look at the brash man who held her now. She was caught again, this time in a vortex where time seemed to stand still. The warm scents coming from inside his leather jacket whirled in the same spiral her hair was caught up in. A piece of her battered, frightened heart felt determined to go with it.

Silently, the same way he'd come to her rescue, her fierce savior cradled her jaw in one of his big, rugged palms. Very gently, he tipped her chin up with his thumb. Stark savagery stared down at her. His eyes were so dark, so full of pent-up passion, that her heart stuttered to a whimper. He could kill her. He was that kind of John Cena large and John Wick lethal.

Ashley swallowed hard, her throat incapable of the normally involuntary action. Something was happening. Something good and right and…magical?

Whatever happened next, she wasn't afraid. He was looking down at her, as if he'd just felt that same hint of something rare and wonderful. She refused to extrapolate what that might be. If it was even real. Dreams didn't come true, not for her.

Until his head tilted the barest degree.

She matched the angle of his chin, slanting with her own head and licking her bottom lip. Wishing magic did exist and dreams did come true. For a moment, one brief, star-struck, crazy, meteoric moment, she left herself open to the possibility of a kiss. Her first real kiss.

The purest silence swelled around them. It was happening. Heaven had opened. They were in an invisible cathedral. The rarest celestial blessing *was* pouring down on them and—

HONK! Darn. Someone had finally spotted her. Why now?

With a jolt, her mysterious hero blinked. He dropped his hands. The magic—*Pffft!*—vanished. Straight back up to heaven, where it belonged. Ashley exhaled a frosty breath. Love wasn't real anyway. Why waste time wishing it were?

As if nothing happened—because nothing had—the monster-turned-angel fastened some kind of sticky gauze around the front of her neck. He maintained a professional, indifferent hold this time, pressing the gauze until he was sure it held.

"This will keep for now," he said a little too briskly. "Does it still hurt?"

In more ways than I'll ever tell. "Umm, no," she replied with her steadiest, most unemotional voice. "I'll be okay." *Because single women who live alone have no choice but to be okay.* "Thanks."

The temptation to melt under this fierce man's chin, to breathe deeply of his breath, and imprint his scent into her olfactory receptors for the rest of her life, was hard to resist. But Ashley offered tit-for-tat, nothing more. If he refused to acknowledge what she'd felt between them, so would she. He needed to back off and let her get on with her orderly, predictably boring life.

"Do you have a cell phone?"

She nodded, the top of her head bumping his chin. "Sorry. I didn't know you were still that close, I mean…" She could smell the mint on his breath. "Y-y-yes. It's over there." She pointed at the gutter, where her messenger bag leaned against the curb, as if she'd simply set it there while she'd been busy being assaulted.

"Call the police. Tell them what happened. They'll send an ambulance."

"He wanted drugs, oxy. He… he thought we kept opioids in our building, and that I had a key."

"You work at the free clinic?"

She shook her head. "Just the Health Department."

"I'm glad I was here."

Ashley froze at the quiet declaration of that unexpected *something else*. He didn't expound further, and that was good. This was not a night for mutual admiration, certainly not for whatever that momentary lapse in judgment between them had been. Like that other disastrous time, this was just another night to forget.

He cleared his throat. "Call 9-1-1, ma'am. Do it now. Tell them what happened. Tell them some guy showed up and interrupted that rat bastard before he could seriously hurt you. Tell them I beat the fuck out of him, then ran off like a chicken shit. Can you do that for me?"

"Probably not quite like that," she admitted meekly. Her harshest expletive was *fudge*.

He had the grace to smile. "Sorry ma'am. I tend to forget my manners when I'm at war."

"Why can't I just tell them the truth? That you saved me?"

"Because I'd rather no one knows who I am. I work better this way. Keep my secret, okay?"

"What's your name?" she asked like a dolt. Why would he tell her? It was a secret. Duh.

He did something a little bit magical then. He leaned into her face and pressed those warm, luscious lips of his to the middle of her sweaty forehead. "I'm just some guy," he whispered against her skin, his masculine voice devastatingly deep and sexy. "Call the police, kiddo. Stay off dark streets from now on. Forget you ever saw me. Promise?"

Who could resist? "You'll always be a hero to me," she promised with all of her banged up heart. "My name's Ashley, by the way. Ashley Cox. Please stay safe."

"Do yourself a favor and don't worry about me, Ashley Cox," he murmured before he moved her off his lap, walked to the gutter, and retrieved her bag. Handing it to her, he asked, "Is this your can of mace? It was beside your purse."

"Oh, my, umm, yes," she replied, embarrassed that even with her secret weapon, she'd still been a helpless damsel in distress.

He crouched down beside her, his hands loose between his knees, his alpha male presence overpowering the last of her resolve. "Go ahead," he said, fluttering his fingers to hurry her along. "Call the police. I'll stay until they show."

"Okay." Taking her bag with trembling fingers, she stuffed the mace back where it belonged, then pulled her phone out of an interior pocket. But when she lifted her head to tell him goodbye, that she hoped she'd run into him again someday, her handsome shadow was gone. Just like that. Of course. What had she expected? He was just a man. He'd said he'd stay, but he hadn't. He'd disappeared. Only her attacker remained, and he wasn't breathing too well.

Shaking like the last leaf of autumn about to fall off its lonely branch, Ashley called 9-1-1 and gave the dispatcher her location. In minutes, the Alexandria police arrived, along with a fire engine, an ambulance, and two other squad cars. The officer out of the first cruiser was a woman, thank God. Her partner was male, but both were kind and professional. So were the paramedics who assessed her minor injuries, removed her from the scene of the attack, and stowed her inside the ambulance.

While they double-checked the bandages on her neck, Ashley couldn't keep her eyes from searching the shadows beyond the emergency vehicles. Was he still out there? Was he watching? Did he have any idea how much his being here tonight would mean to her for the rest of her life? Did he even care? Probably not.

But she'd promised. She'd never tell.

Chapter Three

From between the strip mall and Alexandria's Health Department, behind the Dumpsters and recycle bins, deep within the shadows, Tripp waited. He'd told Ashley he'd stay, and he'd meant what he'd said. But not in plain sight. He watched while the first two police officers on the scene questioned her. The female officer hadn't left her side, not until the EMTs arrived and took over. Which was good. Women often needed another woman's touch at times like this. Even the EMTs were extra-gentle with Ashley. One said something that made her smile. They covered her with a blanket and checked her vitals.

They'd better be gentle, because Tripp knew this woman. She was his neighbor. Until tonight, he hadn't known her name, only that she lived next door to him in Olde Town Alexandria. What a coincidence.

He'd noticed her eyeing him the few occasions they'd crossed paths in the hall, coming or going. Who could miss the light in her bright, intelligent, deep-blue eyes, or the long, silky black hair that shimmered down her back like an ebony waterfall when she'd walked by? She was his idea of the quintessential girl-next-door, a delightful vision in rich blue-blacks, with a bright strawberry-pink smile most days.

Ashley was petite, but well-endowed. Yet the few times he'd seen her, she'd disguised her feminine assets behind a dowdy uniform of plain gray pants and too-large, matching gray shirts. Men's shirts that she didn't tuck in, but let hang loose, like heavier women did. Her hair had been pulled back in a stifling bun or ponytail. But tonight, it glistened on her shoulders, like a living adornment he wanted to sink his nose into and run his fingers through. Tripp fought the zing that still rippled between Ashley and him. At the end of the day, he was no one's angel. If anything, he was just another devil she needed to stay clear of.

Because of his late-night activities, he faced most Mondays and getting up at the butt-crack of dawn, like a half-dead zombie. But Ashley had always been bright-eyed and full of energy when he'd seen her. Which, until now, had been damned seldom.

Silently, Tripp watched the other officers attend to the asshat who'd hurt her. They worked just as efficiently with him as they had with Ashley. Just as kind. Tripp tracked them as they searched the scene for evidence. He stayed clear of their flashlights' beams, then waited until the EMTs loaded the *alleged* woman-beater into the second ambulance that had arrived.

God, he hated that word. *Alleged,* nothing. These cops had solid evidence, damn it. They had solid proof that this guy had assaulted Ashley. They'd located and bagged the bastard's knife, for God's sake. It had her blood on it. He'd hurt Ashley, could've killed her. She had cuts and bruises from his hands on her arm and neck to prove it. What more did they need?

Alleged, my ass. In the end, Tripp knew it might still come down to her word against that bastard's. And if he came from money, his crime could be dismissed; he might get a slap on the wrist or have to perform a few hours of community service—or less. How much leniency did men like him deserve? None, as far as Tripp was concerned. Who the fuck else sliced her neck?

It was the same story since the beginning of time. When money talked, assholes walked. Tripp's tenderized knuckles stung, but he'd like another go at the guy. Someone needed to teach him a lesson.

Tripp didn't fade to black until she was safely out of the public's view and inside the ambulance. Until those two EMTs climbed in with her and closed the gate.

It was sheer dumb luck he'd even been there tonight. If not for his decision to intervene in what could've been the beating deaths of two college kids, he wouldn't have come this far west. He usually stuck close to the pubs and boutique restaurants farther east on King Street, along the Potomac River.

Halloween and autumn decorations were everywhere, soon to be replaced by Thanksgiving and Christmas, then New Year's Eve, décor. Tourists were easy marks, especially at this festive time of year. They were plentiful at the other end of this street. So were grifters and pickpockets. Tripp was glad he'd followed his heart and rescued those two young men tonight. If he hadn't tracked them to the clinic...

A full-body cringe roared over him and shivered up the back of his neck at what would've happened. Ashley would've been a statistic come morning, a blip on the news channel. Which made him more certain of his calling. He was the sword of vengeance, by hell. His boss might send him overseas or across the country on company business, but wherever he went, Tripp would never stop protecting innocents like Ashley.

Pretty name for the tiny thing she was. He'd been plenty pissed with her at first. What had she been doing alone on the street after dark? Women, more than men, needed to learn how to protect themselves. The world had changed. It wasn't safe, not that it ever had been. She should've been at home with some big, brooding hulk who would've protected her and held onto her…

Like me.

He shook his head at the stupidest notion he'd had in a long, damned time. Big and brooding, yeah, that was him all right. The Army had made sure he'd bulked up, and his sister had sure as hell given him enough to brood over.

But Tripp McClane was not the settling-down type, no sir. He didn't do easy pick-ups, dates, or long-term relationships, either. Hell, no. He was focused, and he had one mission in life. It, not some woman, would always come first. He was like a priest. A monk. He'd pledged his life, his blood, and everything he owned, to Lady Justice. He was that last thin line between right and wrong on these streets, between evildoers and the righteous silent majority. He *would* dispense punishment, by God, in Seattle, Washington, DC., or wherever. Time and location didn't matter. Wherever he went, he'd never slack off, not when good people needed him. Someone who'd stand in the shadows, unseen but deadly and ready to put psychotic killers, rapists, and power mongers down. Just as ready and able to rescue those who needed rescuing. Like Abdul.

Like Ashley…

Damn. When he'd lifted her off the ground, she'd been trembling, crying, and scared to death. That was when he'd realized she was more child than woman. As light as a fawn, with big, expressive, innocent eyes, she'd been close to falling apart.

He knew he'd frightened her. It was too bad she'd seen what he'd done to the idiot who'd body-slammed her. Tripp felt sorry about her witnessing that. But he didn't give a flying fuck about that guy. Saving her virtue, possibly her life, was all that mattered. Ashley Cox was alive because of him, and she'd get over seeing the punishment her would-be killer/rapist had received. He'd only gotten a small portion of what he deserved, but Tripp would be watching from now on. The next time that scurvy little bastard assaulted anyone, he'd wake up in a shallow, unmarked grave. Tripp would make sure of that.

But Ashley... *Damn*. He couldn't get her out of his head. A sigh breathed out of him remembering the feel of her delicate, quivering body in his arms and on his lap. Of how she'd melted into him, trusted him. Of how she smelled. Wind and cherries were now a sensual lure lingering over the surface of his mind, like a fisherman's fly teasing the rivers and streams. He was the trout, hunting and waiting below. Watching. Hoping.

Yeah, no. Hope had nothing to do with why Tripp hunted these streets and alleys. That frightened woman with tears in her eyes and blood on her neck, she was why he did what he did. Ashley was soft and feminine. Unsure and timid. She needed to stay that way.

Okay, so yeah, maybe it was because she'd leaned into him... Maybe it was the scent of her hair... Or the way her heart pulsed at the hollow of her slender neck... Aw, hell, maybe it was just that she'd been so much in need of a man like him tonight. Tripp didn't know. Yet all those feminine nuances called to something he'd shoved down so deep in his soul, he thought he'd never have to deal with it again.

For sure she'd never recognize him the next time their paths crossed. He wasn't that kind of lucky. Or smart. Smart would be to quit this one-man crusade against evil and to search out the better half of himself. To believe in love again. To settle down and stop fighting the whole damned world. Hell, he was surrounded by a team of happily married guys at work. Every one of them had something he didn't. While he knew there were better things to do with the rest of his life, he also knew his crusade was worth doing. If not him, who would save the defenseless? The naïve and silly-hearted? The normal people who had no clue how ugly life was?

The ambulance flashed its red lights, but no siren screamed as it pulled away, which was damned decent of those EMTs. They'd make sure Ashley got the care she deserved. She was safe with them now. She'd be okay. It was time to call it a night.

Dragging a hand over his head, Tripp smoothed his black beanie off and ruffled his hair. Into his rear pocket the beanie went. The streets were safe again. For now.

Chapter Four

In the darkest shadows, from across busy King Street, he watched, drooling at the luscious scene that had just unfolded. He'd just finished with his latest treasure. Left her where the local police would surely find her. After all, they were still looking, weren't they? Stupidity ran deep within the ranks of Alexandria's so-called finest. If the police were any good, they would've caught him last time. Or the time before that. But they hadn't, had they? No, and they were no closer to catching him this time, either. He knew the game. They, obviously, didn't.

My, but she'd grown more beautiful these last two years. Her hair was longer, silkier. Her voice, more tender. Almost melodic in its terror. Such a delightful morsel and, coincidentally, a woman he remembered. The one that got away…

Destiny, that was the name for coincidental meetings like this. A man could rely on destiny. She pointed out patterns most people didn't see. She supplied signs and prognostications. Promises…

He hadn't known the name of this playmate when they'd met before. But he did now. Ashley Cox. It had a lovely ring to it.

Perhaps the behemoth who'd saved her tonight might check on her later? He seemed like the type, as carefully as he'd handled her… As softly as he'd spoken to her. Wasn't that what heroes did? Wasn't that their pattern? Their style? Their destiny? To keep track of the poor, sweet victims they rescued? To take advantage of their two minutes of fame before they overcame their prey with lies and innuendo that would ultimately end with them in the same bed?

But for now, Ashley Cox—Oh, he loved that name!—was safely hidden out of sight and on her way to some nearby hospital instead of home. He had no choice. If he wanted her, he'd have to follow the fellow who'd saved her. Surely, he'd lead the gallant way to Ashley's hidey-hole. What'd she call him, her guardian angel? Her hero? Not likely. That big guy was only a means to an end. The end of Ashley Cox.

Chapter Five

Ashley drew in another deep breath, then blew it out, sending her black bangs flying out of her eyes and off her face. The rest of her long locks stayed put in the ponytail she'd curled into a good, tight knot at the back of her neck. It was early Monday morning, and she'd just survived one heck of a long weekend. The people in her office would never believe what happened Friday night. Not that she'd tell them. Well, she might tell Terry, her boss. But then again, she might not. Not about the attack outside the Health Department. Certainly not about the dark angel who'd rescued her. Heavens no. One lesson she'd learned early, the less people knew about her personal life, the better off she was. No sharing ensured no office gossip.

Man, she was never staying late again. From now on, her cell phone was programmed to chirp every half-hour all afternoon on work days, reminding her to leave on time with the rest of her co-workers. Talk about scary.

She hadn't wanted to stay overnight for observation at the hospital, either, but the ER doctor had insisted after he found out she lived alone. He'd been worried. She had a small concussion, which explained why her head still throbbed more than the shallow slice on her throat stung. Actually, once her avenging angel had bandaged her, she hadn't thought of her neck again. Only how warm and sure his hands had felt on her skin. How adeptly he'd cleaned the shallow slice, then applied that sticky gauze. How he'd smelled of spearmint and musky male. How he might have kissed her if only...

Her lungs expanded at those delicious memories. Of all the men in the world, she'd met someone who resembled an archangel. Wasn't that just her style? Hide from every other guy, never date, never even think of dating or going out for coffee or... anything. Then find a man worth taking the risk, on the worst, well, second worst, day of her life. Only to realize he wasn't from the same planet or dimension or... whatever.

Ashley shook her head, dismissing those crazy thoughts. Not going there. The adventure was behind her. The cut was already healing. She smoothed her hand over her neck to prove it. Because of her buttoned-up collar, no one would ever know she'd been attacked Friday night. It was Monday morning, and she had a job to do. She was Alexandria, Virginia's one-of-a-kind, outreach coordinator, and she could do this. *Deep breath.*

Autumn weather was humid, not yet unbearable. It'd be the perfect day if not for the nasty task at hand. But she'd get it done, by heck. She'd already called Terry. He knew she'd be in late, that she was handling her assignment. She was prepared to face down any belligerents who might not appreciate the invitation she was about to extend to them. There were three men on her list of bad boys who'd thought they could defy Health Department orders. Not anymore.

She was strong. She was determined. What happened Friday night would not get her down, not like that other time. That encounter had nearly ruined her. To say she'd come a long way from the traumatized woman she'd been back then, was like saying the hurricane currently stretching up the Florida coast was a spring shower. There was a day not long ago she never would've stepped outside her apartment, not even to go to work. But a woman couldn't let past mistakes define her. She knew that now. Not that she'd made a mistake *that day*. She hadn't. But after two years of extreme caution, mixed with months of confidential counseling that her employer offered, she was ready to take her old life back.

Okay then. Another deep breath. If one of these three men thought they could push her around once they heard what she had to say… Well, her trusty can of mace was back in her over-the-shoulder messenger bag, and this time, she'd use it. It was unfortunate the men on her list hadn't yet responded to her phone calls or written notification to come in for check-ups and blood tests. They should have, or she wouldn't have to pay them personal visits today, would she?

Deep, deep breath. Then another and… *Oh, fudge.* Inhaling that deeply was only making her dizzy. Hyperventilating wouldn't satisfy her nervous body's need for O_2. It wouldn't get the dirty job ahead of her done any quicker, either. The only way was through.

Yeah, yeah, yeah…

Ashley glanced down the empty hallway of her safe, secure apartment complex, contemplating a round of good old procrastination. But that wasn't her style, either, and…

Oh-kay then. You got this.

No, I don't.

But you'll still do it. You always do what you're told. You're a good girl. Why change now?

There is that…

Despite her upbringing, or maybe because of it, Ashley girded up her invisible loins of courage, swallowed hard, and knock, knock, knocked on the sturdy apartment door next to hers. Unfortunately, it belonged to her neighbor, the to-die-for handsome, sandy-blond haired man, with shoulders so wide he had to let them pass through doorways one at a time. Mr. Tripp McClane. She was sure he was former military, and that he'd been created with muscles to spare. But the absolute last way she'd wanted to meet him was by handing over the incriminating, accusatory invitation in her now sweaty hand.

This was all his fault. His failure to comply was the only reason she was here today. If he'd answered any of the numerous calls, emails, and letters she'd sent him, he could've saved himself, and her, a ton of embarrassing trouble. But since he hadn't, she was here to make sure he knew he had to be tested. The sooner, the better. Privately, by a doctor of his choice, or by one of the doctors at the clinic. It'd be free, and it would only take a couple minutes. No one else would know unless he told them. He just had to be a man and man up and… Do. It.

A rowdy gang of street urchins, Ashley's gentle term for ladies of the night, which was another fairly obtuse misnomer for prostitutes, had recently invaded the lovely, tourist-friendly streets of quaint Alexandria. Because those enterprising women had taken their kind of stalking to a fine art, a veritable epidemic of STDs now walked the streets in stilettos and glitter bombs, another euphemism for those silly, sequined push-up bras they all wore. What a stupid fad.

While APD had corralled, arrested, and pretty much cleared the streets of those troublemakers, it was now up to the conscientious PMC notification officer—Ashley—to track down and notify their, ahem, johns. And she had to do it today, before the men on her list contaminated others with their disgusting body parts.

Ashley cocked her head, sure she'd heard grumbling inside her neighbor's apartment. "If you don't talk to me now," she told his door sternly, "I'll just come back tomorrow, and the next day, and the day after that. It's my job, but it's not my fault. It's yours. So, open up and take it like a man."

Wow, that almost made her sound tough. She knocked again, louder this time. Determined, darn it. Wielding that official piece of paper like the sword of truth it was.

Another, louder noise came from inside. Pressing her ear against the polished wooden door, she listened intently. Wait. Was he cursing? "For the love of God, what now?"

My heck, he *was* swearing. Well, too bad.

The door jerked open. Inward. And there he was, the same vision she'd glimpsed before, when he'd marched down the hall in all his tanned, golden glory, probably on his way to work. Her neighbor. Mr. McClane. The guy she'd only seen coming and going. From behind. His broad shoulders and straighter erect back were worth noticing. So was his butt. His long legs—

"Oh, it's you," he said more politely than the intense scrutiny in his green eyes declared. "What can I do for you, ma'am?"

Ma'am? Me? He almost sounded respectful.

"I, ahh…" The official notice crunched in Ashley's palm. She had no more words. Her eyes were too wide. The mouth-watering scene standing in front of her was too… too. He'd been working out or something. She must've interrupted him. That was why he'd cussed when she'd knocked. Sweat still glistened on his forehead. His short hair was spiked and wet with it. A single, flesh-toned butterfly bandage peeked above his left eyebrow.

The silly desire to lick the tiny droplets trickling down the steel cords of his neck, before they disappeared beneath the round collar of his short-sleeved t-shirt, made Ashley shift her feet. The shirt couldn't begin to cover the mounded pectorals beneath it. It was white, well, semi-white, since it was darkened with perspiration, between those pecs, and under his arms. He had mounds and mounds of biceps. The hems of that shirt's armholes showed off those tremendous curves quite nicely. Quite nicely indeed.

Knee-length workout shorts drew her attention down over the roped thickness of his muscular thighs to his bronzed kneecaps. This guy was gloriously tanned in all the best places. My gosh, his calves were as thick as her thighs. She blinked, trying hard not to stare.

This man is nothing but fool's gold, her inner, prudish-self reminded her.

Yeah, but… Ashley took a step back, her tongue bone-dry, and her crazy heart hop-scotching up her throat like a three-year-old on a sugar high. "I, ahh…" *Don't remember what I was going to say. When in doubt…* "Hi, there."

"Hey," he replied quickly. A titch of impatience resonated in that one word. He lifted one massive arm and stabbed four straight, bronzed fingers over his head, raking his damp hair back from the most beautiful, angular male face she'd ever seen. Wide, clear, but sweaty forehead. Straight, slender nose. Arched light-brown brows Ashley wanted to trace with her fingertips. A firm chin masked by golden stubble, darker than his hair. More brownish-red than sandy-blond. What a delightful combination. It looked soft and touchable. Was it?

Wherever he'd lived before, the sun had kissed the heck out of this guy. His hair. His lips. His arms. Even his green eyes. Bottle green. Bright, as if they stored sunshine. They shone like that pretty bottle of sparkling water she'd ordered at her favorite restaurant for lunch the other day. Tiny, darker, emerald spokes radiated from huge, black pupils.

When he blinked, she fell in love with the lashes that fanned like smoky paint brushes against the sheen of his perspiration-dampened cheeks. The contrast between the green of his eyes and his sweat-slick, sandy-blond hair, made Mr. McClane a little overwhelming to behold. Yet there she stood, like a star-struck teenager—beholding.

Ashley hadn't expected her first notification of the day to be so, so good. She ran the tip of her tongue over her bottom lip and a steamy heat flickered to life in those beautiful, crystal-clear greens. Something crackled in the air between Mr. McClane and her. Felt like electricity—or lightning.

She slipped her free hand into her messenger bag and clutched her secret weapon, in case he wasn't as nice as he acted and looked. But if he were...

"I'm... ah... I'm... I'm..." —*Here to notify you that you might have an STD*— "Ashley. Ashley Cox. Your n-n-next door n-n-neighbor."

Way to go, girl. Should've led with your job title, not your home address.

The sunshine inside those gorgeous eyeballs brightened, and she was entranced all over again. This job wasn't so bad at all.

He stabbed his thumb in the direction of her place. "You're the lady with the birds."

She nodded. "Yes, well, just one. Peewee. He's not disturbing you, is he?"

Peewee was her Moluccan cockatoo, a pretty boy who loved to greet the mornings, evenings, and sometimes, afternoons, with enthusiasm, that, unfortunately, sounded like shrieking to everyone but her. She used to keep him covered until the dangerous times of day passed, but he'd shriek the moment he spied her anyway. Right now, he had the run of the place. He was her favorite silly boy.

Her handsome neighbor crooked one elbow into the corner of the door jamb over his head, framing the opening with a magnificent bicep, the underside of it embellished with thick ropes of purplish veins and more muscle. His forearm draped casually over his head. All by himself, he filled the space like a beautiful, golden door.

"He always that noisy at the butt-crack of dawn?"

That description of sunrise made Ashley laugh. She nodded, fully aware she hadn't stopped by just to chat. She wasn't one of those gregarious, exuberant women, who had to know everything about their neighbors. Introverts were a closed nation unto themselves, convinced they didn't need most other people. Ashley certainly didn't. For the last two years, she'd been extremely introverted. She could count the number of friends she had on one hand and still have fingers left. And one of those friends was a bird. But this guy was something else.

"His noisy times are usually sunrise and sunset," she explained, in awe of the drool-worthy male watching her intently from beneath thick, sooty lashes. "Otherwise he's quiet. You just moved in?" The oddest question popped into her head. Why did this green-eyed Greek god have black eyelashes when his hair was kissed-by-the-sun blond? How'd that work?

A lazy, crooked smile curled one corner of his mouth. While his top lip was thin, the lower was lush and slippery looking. Wet, as if he'd run his tongue over it before he'd opened his door. She wanted to run her tongue over it.

Say what? Heat slithered up her neck at that salacious thought. Where it came from, she had no idea. It'd been years since she'd had anything positive to say about the opposite sex. Her savior from Friday night didn't count. She'd decided he hadn't been that great after he'd deserted her like he had. Besides, she'd been overdosed with adrenaline then, and everyone knew adrenaline made you see and think things that weren't real. Her sexy, avenging angel was now just *some guy*, like he'd said he was. He wasn't a superhero, and he hadn't even been that good looking. But this man was surely worth looking at. Possibly, even thinking about. Later...

"Nah. Moved in a while ago, but I've been back and forth between here and Seattle the last couple weeks," he replied, licking that lush bottom lip again. "Sorry. Where are my manners? Name's Tripp McClane." He stuck a well-muscled arm and hand in her face. "Sure nice to meet you, Ashley Cox. I've seen you around. We should grab a cup of coffee sometime."

One look at those callused fingers and that work-roughened palm, and Ashley's reason for being there came back to her. There was no way she'd touch this guy. Who knew where that hand and those fingers had been.

He kept talking, waiting for her to accept his friendly gesture. "Yeah, I've got a year's lease here, but I moved to Seattle for my job, then had to move right back. Family problems." He shrugged. "Guess you're stuck with me a while longer."

How horribly nice was that? But, oh, darn. Coincidentally, those rowdy street urchins were also from Seattle, the hotbed of the year's civil unrest and, well, apparently a lot of other things. That had to be where he'd caught his—disease.

Mr. McClane's much larger head canted onto his shoulder. His hand fell back to his thigh. Those mischievous eyes made him look like an adorable, but very naughty, little boy. "What's wrong? You don't like coffee? Hell, hot chocolate then. Or wine. Name your poison. I'm not choosey."

Which brings us back to the reason I'm here today...

Ashley closed her eyes, fighting the fierce attraction for her neighbor strumming through her body. Lifting her right hand to her forehead, she scratched a tense fingernail over her brow, praying for strength to do what had now become an enormously distasteful job. Wishing this man didn't look as breathtakingly fantastic as he did. But he did, and that was probably why he was now carrying around a nasty STD in his pants, that she—*God, why me?*—was here to tell him about. *Please don't let him ask me for a lesson on where STDs come from and how they work.*

He leaned into her. Closer. "Hey, neighbor. How'd you get that bruise on your cheek? Is there something you want to tell me? Is some guy—? Is your boyfriend—?"

"No. I mean, no, I don't have a boyfriend, but yes, there's something I need to tell you, only..." *Darn. Darn. Darn!* A gasp of exasperation sent a loose strand of her hair flying, and Ashley clenched the mace in her bag, again, just in case. There was no way she'd tell this guy what happened Friday. That was her business. Her mistake.

"Read this," she ordered in her most professional voice, slapping the incriminating, folded-in-thirds, official notification into that hard, made-for-sex-that-was-never-going-to-happen, chest. "I'm an outreach coordinator for the Health Department. That makes me just the messenger here, so don't blame me. There's a phone number on the bottom line if you have questions. Whoever answers will explain. Not me. B-b-bye."

That was as much as she could squeak out. Like a chicken, once he slapped his hand over his chest to keep the notice from falling, she turned tail and ran for home, the apartment next door to this Adonis with a sexually transmitted disease. What a shame!

"What the fuck? Hey! Wait up!" he called after her. "Wait! Ashley!"

"Forget we ever met," she tossed over her shoulder. "I'm not your type!"

Obviously. Because I'm no man's type. Not anymore. What kind of guy would want to face her after this debacle of a first meeting? Yeah. That kind. The kind who had unprotected sex with strangers and shared STDs like twitchy addicts shared needles.

Slamming her door behind her, Ashley locked it, then stood with her back against it, out of breath and shaking like a ninny. How unprofessional was that, to dump this mess on him, then run away like a chicken with her head cut off? So unprofessional. Hardly even couth. She still had two more men to face with this awful news. Could she do it? Probably not.

Ashley squeezed her eyes shut, embarrassed for herself and for Mr. McClane and... and... for Peewee! Why not? His lovely Indian-style headdress was now standing on end from her startling, door-slamming entry.

The wood behind her vibrated with the powerful energy of an angry male's knock. "Ashley?" Mr. McClane asked politely, his voice rough and rumbly. He didn't sound as perturbed as she'd expected, and he hadn't really knocked that loudly. Fear magnified everything, that was all. "This is what you wanted to tell me? That I need to get a blood test? Is this all? I can explain."

Ashley didn't reply, just turned to face her locked door.

Did she dare open it?

Chapter Six

Tripp stared at the paper Ashley had thrown at him—for all of ten seconds. *Shit, damn, and son of a bitch!* Another official Health Department notice, like he hadn't seen this exact kind of bullshit before. Trish had done it to him again. Damn her. This lying piece of trash was her work, her stab at him for being the good twin. The nerve of her to name him—her one and only flesh-and-blood brother!—as one of the many lowlife sleazebags she had sex with. He didn't have STDs, gawddamn it! And he'd never paid for sex, but now his pretty neighbor thought he did? Jesus H Christ.

Slamming his door shut, he raced down the hall to intercept Ashley before she got away. What an unreal coincidence, that the woman he'd rescued Friday night was his neighbor. He'd known that then, but deliberately hadn't let on. Thank fuck she hadn't recognized him. That much was good. He'd meant his asking about her bruise as a segue into what he'd hoped would have been a real convo. Guess not.

Too late. Her door slammed in his face. Of course. What'd he expect? She thought he was a douchebag, like any smart, upstanding woman who thought he'd engaged in risky sex with hookers, would. He knocked anyway, convinced she hadn't recognized him. Which gave him a second chance to make a better first impression than the ones he'd made Friday night and two seconds ago.

"Ashley?" He pleaded through the sturdy wooden barrier between them, one fist still against the door. "This is what you wanted to tell me? That I need to get a blood test? Is this all? I can explain." *Please answer.*

Tripp bowed his forehead to the door, embarrassed for her more than for himself. He'd been down this road before. She, obviously, had not.

Because the last two nights on the street had been tough, he'd called in late to work this morning. Saturday night, two punks harassing a homeless veteran, found out how hard asphalt could be. The vet found himself warmed and fed in a local shelter; the kids found themselves in the river, alive, but well-warned not to try that shit again. Sunday night, he'd patrolled the riverbank in case the kids came back, looking for another target.

Which was why'd he'd been giving his home gym a good workout this morning when Ashley knocked. He'd turned his two-bedroom apartment into one bedroom and a modestly equipped weight room with Parkour bars up the walls and over the ceiling. He was lucky. His employer demanded his team maintain above-average physical fitness. To that end, Alex Stewart maintained an on-site gym that provided plenty of strength, core, and cardio, including a more rigorous Parkour workout track than Tripp's. Vigilantes couldn't afford to go soft. They had identities—and women, like Ashley—to protect. The world needed men like him to be all they could be, all the time.

She was a helluva lot tougher than he'd expected. Yes, she was banged up. He'd known which hospital she'd been taken to. He also knew she'd come home early Saturday, but he hadn't expected she'd be back to work today. Or that after what she'd gone through Friday night, she'd still be smiling. Ashley Cox was definitely one of those indomitable morning people. Usually, chipper people annoyed the living shit out of Tripp until he'd had at least two cups of coffee. But not Ashley. She was different. He'd known it the second he'd laid eyes on her. Just seeing her made him smile.

Until now, there'd never been time for anything but quick, hurried greetings. His move to Seattle, then back again to Alexandria, hadn't helped. Seattle was the primary location he'd signed up for when he'd hired onto The TEAM, a locally-owned security business. Working out of the Seattle office would've given him the distance he craved from his troublemaking twin. He'd trained hard, and he'd deserved a break from his family drama.

But he'd no more than settled into that spacious loft overlooking Elliot Bay, when Trish pulled her latest disappearing act. He'd moved back a week ago to help his mom locate his sister. Now this official piece of crap notice. Once again, Trish had screwed his chance to be free of her sorry ass. When hadn't she been a pain in his butt? In everybody's butts? Including his mom's? Short answer, not in this lifetime.

Tripp stared at the crumpled letter in his hand. Mom always said things happened for a reason. Could Ashley please be the reason he was back on the East Coast this time? Not Trish?

Because as much as Tripp didn't want a relationship, he still meant to keep Ashley safe. She didn't have to like him for him to watch her back, uh-uh. She just needed to keep on breathing. He was her shadow, and that would be enough. It had to be. Because he was the night, not a hero. If she knew half the things he'd done… Yeah, not going there.

"Ashley?" he asked again, keeping his tone sincere and pleading. More than anything, he wanted a chance to explain. What better way than by taking her out to coffee or drinks or hamburgers or… man, anything? Maybe just a walk in a public place where everyone could see them. Where she'd feel safe. That was important to her and now, to him.

Dead silence was his only answer, but his gut told him that Ashley was standing on the other side of her door. He knew it. She hadn't struck him as being one of those flighty women who wallowed in drama. Delivering the poisonous notice had been hard for her. He'd seen the trepidation in her eyes. She'd been worried how he'd react. He didn't blame her. What a shitty job for a petite, pretty woman, to have to confront full grown men with devastatingly intimate news. But for a moment before she'd handed over that deceitful notice, he had felt a connection. Hadn't he?

Guess not. She wasn't opening her door.

This debacle was his fault. He'd been crazy-busy moving in and getting back to duty at TEAM HQ. Not to mention his nightly activities. Now that Trish was officially missing, his mom was worried out of her mind. Worse, some kind of hooker convention had recently flooded Alexandria's streets, and that kind of action was right up Trish's ally. Damn her. The girl never knew when to leave drugs and hooking alone.

This carefully worded letter was his only clue. Ashley might be the key to his sister's whereabouts. Oddly, as much as he disliked his twin for her destructive behavior and foolish decisions, Tripp worried about Trish. She was, after all, just a woman, and the streets were hard enough on men.

Tripp tried one last time. Putting it all on the line, he ran back to his apartment and snagged the copy of the results from his last physical, off the unopened stack of mail on his kitchen counter. His new boss, Alex Stewart, was a stickler for order and transparency, crap like that. Since Tripp had spent a couple weeks in Seattle, the notorious hotspot in the nation for STDs, Alex had insisted on proof of a clean bill of health. Not that he thought Tripp was stupid or desperate enough to pay for sex, but because that was The TEAM's number one rule: *Don't ask. Don't tell. Just do what you're told.*

Out of breath and with his apartment door left open, Tripp slipped the results of his physical and the bloodwork that went with it, under Ashley's door. Either she'd believe him or she wouldn't. The next move was hers.

He stepped back and waited, wondering about that phrase, *bated breath*. Now he knew what it meant. One minute passed. Two. Then three, four, five, six. He gave her enough time to read over the damned thing before he called it quits. But then, because this was Ashley, and he really wanted to get to know her, he took a deep breath and waited another five minutes. It'd taken him a while to read through all the medical mumbo-jumbo. Might take her a few minutes, too.

At fifteen minutes, he jogged back down the hall, shut his door, and ran back to Ashley's apartment. At twenty, he leaned against the wall opposite her door, folded his legs, and sat his butt on the floor. He could be patient. She was worth it.

Each floor in this five-level building, the sixth of the apartment complex, offered four separate bachelor-size apartments. He lived on the fourth floor. Ashley's place was closest to the elevator; his was next to hers, beside the fire doors and the stairs that led to ground level. Across from him, a sweet elderly woman, Mrs. Harrison, lived with her dog. Tripp didn't have a clue who lived across from Ashley. He hadn't met that tenant yet.

Mrs. Harrison exited her place, closed her door with a firm click, then double-checked the knob, rattling it to make sure it was locked. This morning, she was dressed in black slacks with a black-and-orange-flowered print blouse, and her usual low-heeled dress shoes. Her silver hair was always curled, trimmed, and proper. She was a widow, close to eighty, one of only two people Tripp knew in the entire apartment complex—if he counted Ashley.

Mrs. Harrison had knocked on his door one night before he'd left for Seattle. She'd needed help opening a jar of green olives. Poor thing. That meeting led Tripp to giving her his numbers in case she needed another jar opened, and inviting her over for dinner a couple times before he'd left town. She was lonely, and he'd had zip for a social life. Three moves in a couple months guaranteed that. But he didn't mind. She and her little dog were two of his favorite people.

"Tripp. What are you doing on the floor? Did you lose something?"

"No, ma'am, just waiting."

"For who? Ashley Cox?" Why did Mrs. Harrison sound surprised?

"Yes, ma'am. How's Chipper?" Chipper was her smelly little dachshund that loved his tummy scratched.

Sighing, she shook her head. "I'm afraid his time has come. He ate one of my new slippers. He's at the vet now, but the prognosis isn't good. Doctor Myers said his gut's twisted, and he's got gastric dilatation-volvulus. Have you ever heard of such a thing?"

"I'm sorry, yes. When did you take him in?"

Gastric dilatation-volvulus, or GDV, was seriously life-threatening. While the condition generally afflicted large dogs, Dachshunds were one of the few small breeds it targeted. The medical condition occurred when a dog's stomach bloated, which it surely would've done after chowing down an entire slipper. Mortality rates increased quickly, because owners with gassy dogs thought the condition would go away like it had before. By the time they realized their pet was in critical distress, it was oftentimes too late.

"Early this morning," she replied, a tremor in her voice. "I was there when the vet's office opened. He took Chipper right in. He's had him all day."

Tripp shoved to his feet. "Is that where you were going now?"

The poor woman nodded, then pressed her fingers to her lips and whispered, "He's all I have. I can't let him suffer, and I won't let him die alone."

"How about I drive?" he asked gently, his feet already aimed to his place and his truck keys.

"That would be sweet of you. The metro's crowded this time of day."

"Can I come with you?" a timid, but sweet, voice asked. Ashley was peeking around the wooden door that had kept him out.

"Sure. Yes, you bet," he replied as evenly as his thumping heart would allow. Man, she looked good. "We'd love the company, but we're just going to the vet, and—"

Ashley's door shut with a resolute snick behind her. She went straight to Mrs. Harrison's side and took hold of the older woman's hand. "I couldn't help overhearing what you said, and I'm so sorry Chipper's sick. Let's get you to your fur baby right now."

Tripp eyed his pretty neighbor. He was right. She'd been standing on the other side of her door. Better yet, she honestly cared about Mrs. Harrison. Good on her.

Chapter Seven

If there was a more excruciating torture than sitting alongside this beautiful woman with her tantalizing hip and sexy thigh pressed tight against his, Tripp didn't know it. But there he was, in his truck with Mrs. Harrison riding shotgun, and Ashley seated between them, her arms wrapped protectively around the clunky messenger bag in her lap. Now Tripp knew why. She carried one of those tiny cans of mace in that bag. Despite her stodgy, man-style uniform, nothing could stop the heat building between them.

Man, he ached to tell her who he was, that he was the guy who'd saved her. But vigilantes lived two very separate lives for a reason. Bringing her into his confidence could get her hurt, might even make her an accomplice or get her killed.

Sitting this close made her nervous. She tried not to touch him more than she had to. But in the confines of his Chevy pick-up, with the rear floor and seat still stuffed with boxes he needed to unpack from his move, there wasn't room to spare. Not that Tripp didn't appreciate every bump and turn that brought Ashley closer. He truly did. He just wished he'd changed into jeans when he'd grabbed a clean shirt before this road trip. Because now, every turn, corner, and stop his truck made, brought the warmth and softness of her against his bare leg. At this rate, he wouldn't be able to accompany Mrs. Fields into the vet's office. There'd be no way to hide what was happening between his legs.

Worse, the ends of Ashley's long ponytail brushing over his arm when she moved, were as soft as angel kisses. That comparison alone should've been the buzzkill he needed to calm the hell down. She *was* an angel, but he was as fallen a devil as a man could get. He'd been to war, had done what soldiers the world over did. He'd served his country, and in the course of that service, he'd ended his share of high-value targets. Didn't regret one of them.

A soldier didn't earn his Ranger tab without facing the two-mile buddy-run in full ACU, Army combat uniform, while carrying a full Camelback, a loaded M4, and a shitload of ammo. He'd destroyed the Malvesti Obstacle Course of the Benning Phase at Camp Rogers, Fort Benning, Georgia. Including the infamous worm pit, a shallow, mucky obstacle course covered with knee-high barbed-wire. The only way through the pit was to crawl over the wire or worm under it, either on his belly or back. He'd survived the plunge into Victory Pond, too, damn it. As well as parachute jumps and extractions where he'd been hooked, along with other Ranger wannabes, dangling from the belly of a low-flying helo.

Not to mention he was outright breaking the law every night as Alexandria's one and only vigilante. But he wasn't so sure he'd survive one more minute of not kissing Ashley Cox's mouth. He was a pig, but she was a luscious breath of sweet, fresh air sitting beside him. The epitome of the girl next door, against his thigh and nearly under the arm that wanted to curl around her and keep her safe.

There went his hero complex, but so what? She *was* a tiny, fragile thing, and he had a gut feeling she might just need someone like him in her corner. He hoped so. It'd be just as nice to have her in his corner. In his apartment. In his bed...

His head sure was working against him today. To keep his mind from planning down to the last detail how great the tender body beside him would feel beneath him, Tripp focused on being the safest, most anal driver on the road. It would've worked if his nostrils weren't striving to inhale every last atom of the cherry-scented shampoo she'd used, or the powdery fragrance of her deodorant. All those unique, womanly pheromones drove a man crazy. Damn, he should've traded his workout shorts for jeans. He could've hidden the spike in his pants then. Now? Not so much.

Mrs. Harrison leaned forward and pointed across Ashley's chest to the red-brick building tucked under two stately magnolia trees on the other side of the street. "There. The vet's office is over there."

Thank God in heaven for small miracles. Dutifully, Tripp flipped his turn signal, then patiently drummed his fingertips on the wheel, waiting for opposing traffic to clear. Once he'd crossed the two lanes of traffic into the vet's parking lot, he pulled into the stall closest to the office door.

"You can't park here," Ashley murmured. "It's for handicapped people only, Mr. McClane."

"Right. Got that. Not parking. Just dropping Mrs. Harrison close enough, so she won't have far to walk. And it's Tripp, not mister anything. Just Tripp."

"Oh, yeah, sure." She bit her bottom lip. "That was thoughtful. I'm Ashley. Just Ashley."

Putting the truck in park, he cast a sideways glance at Ashley. Did she think he was a total jerk just because some piece of paper said so? Never mind. He didn't have time to care about that nonsense right now. In two seconds, he was out of the truck and opening Mrs. Harrison's door. The step down from his front seat was too high for a delicate, older woman like her, and he had yet to install running boards. Most guys didn't need them, and he hadn't been around town long enough to date someone who did. Without asking, he took careful hold of her waist and set her gently on the ground. "There you go, ma'am. I've got you. Watch your step."

"Thank you, Tripp. You're always so good to me."

The moment she looked up at him with those sad eyes, his out-of-control lust for Ashley's body faded. Mrs. Harrison was trying to hide her tears, like most women of her generation did. Acting brave when her world was falling apart.

"You are never a problem," he murmured. He couldn't let her face whatever lay inside the vet's office alone.

Ashley was perched on the edge of the truck seat by then with her bag hanging off her shoulder, looking down at the distance to ground level. Which for a woman her size, probably seemed like jumping off a cliff. She'd sucked her bottom lip in, biting it as she studied the drop.

"I've gotcha," he told her as he carefully transferred Ashley to Mrs. Harrison's side, without inadvertently groping her at all. "Why don't you ladies go inside? I'll park and join you in a minute."

He would've done just that, but Ashley grabbed his wrist before he turned away. "Thanks for letting me come along."

Man, he could've stood there all day, staring into her sapphire-blue eyes and at her peaches-and-cream complexion. "My pleasure," he replied, his voice softer than he cared to admit.

The slender fingers touching him were light as feathers—until she jerked her hand away, as if touching him burned. He had a feeling he could thank Trish for that.

"You have to understand something, Ashley. Your report's one-hundred percent wrong about me. I'm not that kind of guy," he told her firmly.

She tossed her head and sent that ponytail ruffling down her back, like a shiny, ebony wave, body language for, *'Yeah, right. That's what guys like you say.'*

Tripp let further explanations go for now. Chipper needed his mistress and, God willing, there'd be time to set things straight with Ashley later. Once inside the small lobby, he stood at Mrs. Harrison's side while she spoke with the receptionist.

"Oh, I'm sorry," the young man with thick, horn-rimmed glasses behind the counter said as he rushed into the hall that led to the backroom. "Wait here. Umm, don't go anywhere, okay? I'll go get Doctor Myers. He really needs to be the one to tell, err, umm, talk with you."

That didn't sound good.

A quiet sob broke free from Mrs. Harrison. She closed her eyes and whispered, "He's gone. I just know it. He's already gone, Tripp. I'm too late. What am I going to do?"

He did what he would've done if she were his mom, just pulled Mrs. Harrison into his side and held her, his heart breaking for this lonely woman. "You're stronger than you realize," he told her quietly, "and I'm just across the hall whenever you need me. I'm in Alexandria for good now. You're always welcome at my place. But let's wait and see what Doctor Myers says before we panic, okay?"

She nodded, but she was falling apart, and he was falling apart with her. Dogs should live longer, damn it. The world needed them more than it needed the crowds of selfish, entitled people currently overpopulating every damned open green space on the planet. Humans were the current plague. Not dogs.

"And I'm right next door to Tripp, Mrs. Harrison," Ashley added timidly. "You can call me any time. I'll give you all my numbers on the ride back home."

He looked at Ashley then, but she was blurry as hell. Damn it. His eyes were leaking.

Doctor Myers appeared out of nowhere and took Mrs. Harrison by the hand. He pulled her into the hall, then into an empty exam room and shut the door. Tripp took position just inside the door and crossed his arms, prepared for the worst. Ashley went to sit alongside Mrs. Harrison on the padded bench beside the shiny, stainless steel, but empty, exam table. She tucked her bag next to her.

"I'm so sorry, ma'am." Doctor Myers grabbed a box of tissues from the counter, then took a knee at Mrs. Harrison's feet and put the box at her side. "We tried everything to save your little Chipper. I did emergency surgery to insert a trocar, but he went into shock. He was badly dehydrated, and I believe the stress was too much for his heart. Remind me, when did he last eat?"

"When he ate my slipper, l-l-last week. Friday, I think." She buried her face in her hands, her shoulders trembling.

Tripp pursed his lips. Four days ago. Wow. Poor Chipper. That was a long time for the little guy to suffer. "What's a trocar?" he asked the vet.

Kindness gleamed in the gentleman's eyes when Doctor Myers lifted his chin to address Tripp. "It's an obturator, essentially a cannula with one sharpened end. Once it's inserted into distended abdomens, like Chipper's, it allows built-up gases, if there are any, to escape. Unfortunately, his little stomach had twisted by then. I couldn't save him."

"But you tried," Mrs. Harrison cried, patting the vet's shoulder. "Th-thank you for trying to help my little boy, Doctor."

He clasped her wrist. "Chipper didn't suffer, Barbara. Honest. We gave him whatever he needed to stop the pain. I wish I could've done more."

She dabbed tissues under her eyes as tears flowed freely. "I know you do. You've always been real good to me and my baby."

Ashley was dabbing the corners of her eyes by then, and Tripp was eyeballing the box of tissues. "He must've really enjoyed that slipper," he offered evenly, trying like hell to lessen the tragedy by focusing on the joy that smelly fur baby had brought into his mistress's life.

Mrs. Harrison's head bobbed. "Oh, he did, that little rascal. But now he's gone, and… and that's that, isn't it?"

"I can take you to see him if you'd like," Doctor Myers offered softly. "We've kept him warm. I'm sure his spirit's still hovering nearby, waiting to say goodbye to his mom before he crosses over the Rainbow Bridge."

She choked back a sob. "Yes. I'd like that. Thank you."

While the vet assisted Mrs. Harrison to her feet and out the door, Tripp bowed his chin to his chest and stared at the floor. Didn't matter how it came, Death was always a hard motherfucker.

"You're very kind to her." Ashley said that as if it surprised her.

He kept his eyes down. Gray flecked linoleum tile shouldn't look so interesting, but he couldn't risk getting teary-eyed in front of this neighbor. "Yeah, well, I try. She reminds me of my mom, alone in the world, dealing with crap all by herself. Didn't know her name was Barbara until today, though. Been calling her Mrs. Harrison ever since I met her. Out of respect, you know. She's a class act."

"How did you meet her?"

Tripp lifted his head and looked straight into Ashley's eyes. "I need you to understand why my name's on that notification list first."

She crossed both arms over her chest, the compassion on her face turned to stone. "Do tell."

"Did you even look at the results of my last physical that I slipped under your door?"

"Results can be invented or fixed."

Tripp inhaled a long, slow breath, letting his belly expand. He had to give her that. "Well then, how about I give you the phone number of the doctor who gave me that physical, and let her confirm what I'm trying to tell you?"

"Anyone can pretend to be a doctor over the phone."

Exasperated, he ran a hand over his head, then folded his arms across his chest again. "Okay, then, come with me after I take Barbara home. I'll gladly introduce you to Doc Fitz. You saw the date on my report. You had to have seen her name in the signature block."

Ashley shook her head. "I only came with you because Mrs. Harrison needed another woman to lean on."

"You mean to protect her from evil men like me who prey on innocent women like you." This was going nowhere fast. He rolled one shoulder to ease the tension knotted in his neck. "That's damned sanctimonious. Condemn a man before you have all the facts."

"I've heard every excuse there is." She ran her fingertips over her lips.

Tripp's cock noticed. Ashley had lush, pink lips and a perfectly indented Cupid's bow that drew his attention. She had a way of pursing them before she talked, like she needed to warm them up to speak. He wanted to warm them up.

"Give me one more chance to prove I'm innocent?"

Ashley looked away, studying the color poster of cat breeds on the wall across from the bench. "Just go see your family doctor, Mr. McClane, or make an appointment at the clinic. Do what you're supposed to do. Get a blood test."

"Better yet…" Tripp offered his last sure shot. "I'll introduce you to my damned sister. She's the one who submitted my name. Trish thinks it's funny to smear me every chance she gets. If you guys did a little research before you turned into judge, jury, and executioners, you'd discover the woman who listed me as one of her johns is Trish McClane, aka Trixie, Dixie, Ginger, or hell…" He ran a hand over his face. "I'm not sure what name she goes by now. But… hold on. I know." He pulled his wallet out of his workout pants' pocket and thumbed through his small collection of coupons and photos until he came across the one his mom had sent last Christmas. "This is her and that's my mom. Notice the resemblance? She's my twin. Look familiar?"

Ashley met his gaze then, those blues finally curious. But for the wrong reason. "You don't give up, do you?"

"Why should I? I'm innocent. I don't pay for sex. Never have. Not going to start now."

"And I'm not the person who treats people or collects this kind of confidential information," she snapped. "One of our doctors does. I'm just the public health educator, the one who gets to track down men like you when you don't respond to official notices."

"What notices?"

"The letters and emails the doctor sent. All the phone messages she left. You've never answered one of them."

"I've been out of town! Seattle, remember?"

"Most people can still access their email and cell phone messages when they travel. I checked the records. You've received plenty of both!"

He lowered his voice. "You just can't believe I might be innocent, can you?" Man, she was frustrating.

"Why should I?" She was up on her feet, her hands on her hips, and her lovely breasts heaving beneath the stiff placard of buttons on her boring man-shirt.

His gaze dropped to that prim line of plain white dots that left none of her neck showing between her buttoned-up collar and her chin. Long-sleeved, the dark cotton material was too thick to reveal the color or style of the bra beneath it. No sweetly pebbled nipples embossed the fabric. The thing's pockets were just as unrevealing, and those drab pants were a size too-large. She wore nothing to enhance her look. No lipstick, eye-shadow, earrings, barrettes, or bows.

Ashley's generic, gender-neutral get-up was probably her employer's fault, but her closed mind was all on her. What had happened to this bright, exciting woman to cause such a dark opinion of men? Was it all men or just him? Why did she dress like a guy? Was it because of her job or was she trying to blend in?

Tripp stopped trying to convince her of his innocence. Next step. Show her.

Chapter Eight

Once again, Ashley was sitting front and center in Tripp's monster truck. Her left hip and thigh were plastered against the very firm, very warm muscles of this bigger-than-life guy's right side. He was starting to grow on her, not because of his ardent declaration of innocence, but because he treated Barbara, a woman old enough to be his grandmother, so sweetly.

Before leaving the vet's office, Barbara had arranged for Chipper's cremation. Tripp had already promised he'd bring her back when the deed was done, to pick up her dog's remains. But when she'd selected a simple, inexpensive wooden container for Chipper, Tripp had slapped his credit card on the counter and told her to pick out a bigger, better remembrance chest, that it was the least he could do for that stinky little boy of hers. She'd actually smiled a tiny bit then. He'd put his arm around her, and for a moment, Ashley wished someone cared for her as much as he cared for his neighbor. His other neighbor.

Everything he'd done for Barbara today had been overly kind, gentle, and considerate, a trait Ashley didn't generally ascribe to most men. Her father, Bobby, had been one of those stay-at-home slackers who'd never broken a sweat a day in his life, not even at home. Her mother, Annette, and her mother's sister, Ashley's Aunt Karrie Lynn, surely did after they'd married the same kind of losers.

In her dysfunctional family, the women carried the full weight of providing for their families, while their husbands and live-in boyfriends did whatever they wanted, all day, every day. Which was why Ashley had worked hard to put herself through college. She'd refused to end up working a minimum wage job for the rest of her life, tied down to an egotistical deadbeat, like her mom and aunt had. Unfortunately, her degree in marketing hadn't translated into the life-sustaining career she'd hoped it would. Seemed everyone had degrees these days, especially in this super-charged, professional area of America.

Blowing out a sigh, she thanked her lucky stars she worked for the City of Alexandria. There was a glut of workers scrambling for employment these days. She was one of the lucky ones, and this job put her face to face with kids who needed vaccinations, women who needed mammograms or prenatal care, and a host of other free services her department provided. While she wasn't making the big bucks she'd once thought were important, she was making a difference. She hadn't realized until this job came along how big a bonus helping others could be. She always felt good after a hard day's work.

Her life was perfect. Well… almost.

Since Barbara had declined Tripp's dinner invite, they were now on their way back to the apartment complex. Country music played on his truck radio, offering a gentle background after the emotional day. Barbara said she needed a nap, that she was worn out. Her face was drawn, and she did look exhausted. Ashley worried about her being alone and made a mental note to check on her neighbors more often. All of them. Maybe even Tripp. Someday…

Cranking the wheel, he pulled his pickup into the first empty parking space in front of the complex's front entrance. But before he unfastened his seatbelt, Barbara opened her door and slipped off the high seat to the curb. Once on her feet, she turned around, tipped up on her toes, peered past Ashley, and said, "Thank you for the ride, Tripp. You kids have done enough for me. Now go enjoy what's left of the day. I'll be in touch."

"B-b-but—" he sputtered.

"But nothing. Go. Be happy." She shut the door firmly and waved through the window, then walked through the front doors with her chin up.

That left Ashley alone with the man she'd accused of having an STD. *Awkward…*

Running after Mrs. Harrison seemed like a good idea. But Tripp was staring straight ahead, his fingers curled around the wheel at two and ten o'clock. She scooted away from his side to the door and took hold of the door handle, not sure what to say or do next, other than tell him goodbye. Her other hand delved into her bag and wrapped around her trusty mace.

"I should go, too."

"If that's what you want," he replied noncommittally.

Oh, what the heck? She'd accused him of having an STD, not committing rape. Summoning what little gumption she owned, Ashley offered a quiet, "Or we could go somewhere and talk." *Just talk. Nothing else. Absolutely nothing else.* "Maybe have a cup of coffee." *Just coffee.*

Tripp turned those broad shoulders and looked at her then, his clear green eyes sincerely searching her face for motive.

"Not if you don't believe what I've been trying to tell you. There's no sense going anywhere with a liar, is there?"

She lifted her shoulder nearest to him, using it as a barrier. "I never called you a liar."

He said nothing back to her, just faced forward as if the car parked ahead of him was interesting.

"I, umm, I see a lot of crap at work," she explained. "Everyone lies these days. I never know who to believe."

"So you don't believe anyone."

She scratched her brow. *Well, yeah.* "It's easier that way."

"Might be easy, but it's cowardly."

Ashley hadn't seen that insult coming. But he was right. There was a day when she'd been brave and courageous, back when she'd first started college. Not anymore. If she wasn't in her safe cubicle at work, she was locked up behind solid wooden doors at home. She'd even bought a better, more secure, expensive, top-rated deadbolt for her apartment door. Installed it herself because she didn't want strange men, even installers of deadbolts or plumbers or maintenance guys or— anyone—inside her apartment. She'd tried that once. Tried to live like other professional women. Freely. Without worry. Carefree. Maybe even a bit brazenly. It hadn't worked out, and she refused to go through—that—again. Besides, she liked helping people, and her job offered plenty of safe opportunities to do so. Until last Friday…

"I guess it is," she admitted, "but—"

"It's safe," he finished for her. "You'd rather be safe than take a chance on trusting a guy you just met. Sounds kind of lonely to me, but I get it."

He still wasn't looking at her, which made it easier to say, "My life, my choice."

"Okay then…" He exhaled a drawn-out sigh that made her wonder how long he'd been holding his breath. "Guess we're done here. I told Mom I'd be by today. You'd like her, but hey. Wouldn't want you to have to walk on the wild side with a loser like me."

"I never called you a loser." Yet she had in a way, and she knew it. "Umm…" Ashley had no idea why she was still sitting in his truck. This wasn't a date. Yet she didn't want to end things this way, with him mad at her for doing her job, with her wondering what might've been if she'd taken the chance to get to know him. Not that there was anything going on between Tripp and her. There wasn't, and not all guys were creeps. Most of them, yes, but it was just possible that he'd told the truth. That his sister, what was her name? Oh, yeah, Trish. That she'd lied. It was possible. Make that highly probable. After all, street urchins weren't known for their honesty. It just seemed so bizarre, his sister naming him as one of her sexual partners.

"Does your mom like coffee?" she asked, watching him out of the corner of her eye.

He nodded at the windshield. "Mom likes everything and everybody. Her name's Andrea, by the way, but you can call her Andy. She'd like that. Hell, she'd like you."

"She would? Then, umm…" Ashley couldn't believe she was still sitting there. By herself. Without Mrs. Harrison as a buffer for protection, as if Barbara could protect anyone.

Ashley was on the verge of doing it. Being brave again. Taking a chance. Not running away. Until, right on schedule, her chest was too small for her heart and lungs. Inhaling took effort. Her ribs felt cramped and tight, as if her bra had shrunk two sizes too small. Something inside of her rattled like crazy.

It took everything she had to relax her left shoulder, lower it, and then turn enough to face him.

"W-what are we waiting for?" she stuttered breathlessly.

Truly, breathlessly. As in, without sufficient air in her lungs to make her vocal cords form those few words, to make them sound firm or loud, strong and confident, or—anything. Her heart was pounding behind her eyes, at the top of her head, even at the tips of all her fingers and toes. She was a coiled spring wound so tight that if she broke loose, she might tear the inside of this truck apart. Silly black dots danced at her peripheral, pushing her closer to the edge of control. The truck's walls were closing in. The windows weren't big enough or open wide enough. This was a mistake. Too early. Too soon. Too much!

"Because you still don't trust me," he said firmly, "and I get that, Ashley, honest, I do. You're a single woman, and women need to be careful these days. I've done nothing, yet you're unwilling to consider that the source of your information is the liar, not me. That maybe none of the men Trish slandered to get whatever drugs she needs to keep working the streets, did what she's accused them of. Trust me, I know my sister, and Trish would lie even when the truth sounds better. I know that's harsh, but do you honestly think hookers always tell the truth? Or is it just men you don't trust?"

"Men," Ashley whispered, swallowing hard, her trembling body and her heart at war with her common sense. But it only took once to be wrong. Which was why she worked in a nice, safe job for the city now. Also why she never went out at night, never left her apartment for anything but work, never dated and had no friends. Women's lib and personal freedom didn't mean anything if you let the wrong person into your safe place. All it took was once. "I'm sorry. It's my job to notify people who've been identified as possible carriers of... you know."

Tripp snorted. "See, you can't even say the words. You condemn people without a fair trial. You impugn their names, and I'll bet that info, right or wrong, gets stored in some deep, dark government file, doesn't it? Christ!" There went his hand again, up the back of his neck and over his head. Ruffling that pretty hair like a combine mowing over stalks of wheat in a field of gold. "If the government has it, the whole damned world can get it. Just what I need, more shit to deal with."

Panic whispered, "I can't do this."

He turned his head and looked closer at her. "What? Ashley? Are you—?"

Cranking that slick, sweat-covered door handle, she clutched her bag to her chest and exploded out of the truck. "I've got to go."

"Ashley, no!"

The curb was a long way down. She didn't make it very far. By the time her feet were safely on concrete, Tripp's big strong fingers were gently curled around her biceps. He was in front of her, holding her up. Not letting her fall. Not shoving or threatening. Just—there.

He crouched low enough to peer into her face, but she couldn't let him see her. Not like this. Couldn't let him in. She hated being vulnerable, couldn't let it happen again. Closing her eyes, Ashley bowed her head and raked her fingers through the ponytail now sagging at the nape of her neck. The knot let loose. Her hair was long and thick enough. It made a solid curtain to hide behind. Instantly, Tripp vanished from view.

"My God, you're shaking." He exerted just enough pressure on both of her arms, forcing her knees to bend.

It would be so easy to lean into him for support.

Never.

"You're hyperventilating."

Tell me something I don't know.

"On the curb, Ashley. Sit down, now," he ordered quietly. "Nice and easy. You're having a panic attack, that's all. No worries. I'll stay with you. I won't let you fall. Hold my hand. There you go. Just like that. Lean on me if you think you're going to pass out. Good. I've got you."

"N-n-noooo," she breathed, her blood galloping through her veins, her poor head about to explode, even as Tripp took her to the ground with him. The second her butt hit the curb, she took her hand back, crossed her arms over her knees, and buried her face in her shirtsleeves, mortified. It was happening again, and she was an idiot for thinking she could be brave. She should've stayed home, where she was safe.

"I hate you," she murmured.

"That's okay," Tripp answered easily. "I hate me too somedays. Like right now. Sure sorry I made you freak out. I press too hard sometimes, but I'm a guy, and I was Army. I'm used to giving orders, and I talk too much when I'm nervous, but you scared the shit out of me. I'm sorry. Take all the time you—"

"I was talking to myself," she interrupted, dizzy as heck, but not going to pass out. Not out here on the street, darn it. That would only put her at more risk. "Me. I hate me. That I can't do what I want to do when I want to do it. That... That this… I hate this. No matter how hard I try, I still end up making a fool of myself!"

Great, now she was on her way to full-blown hysteria. With Tripp's arm securely around both shoulders, she turned spineless. There was no longer any choice. She couldn't hold herself upright. Right on schedule, the tears drenching her face dripped off her nose. Then her chin. What a loser he must think she was. She wished the ground would swallow her whole.

Just that fast, Mother Earth complied. Ashley's heart stopped pounding. Everything turned black, as she collapsed into a puddle of nothingness.

A whispered, "Oh, fu-u-udge," breathed out of her.

Chapter Nine

"Ashley. Ashley!" Tripp anchored his arm under her and cupped the back of her head. She'd passed out. *Shit!*

"I'm so damned sorry," he said as he hit the remote on his key fob to lock his truck. Lifting Ashley's hair out of his way with his free hand, he searched for a medical alert dog tag around her neck that would explain her passing out. Finding nothing, he dug one-handed into her bag, hoping she carried an inhaler or something. Instead, he came up with that same cylinder of mace from Friday night. She probably carried it everywhere with her. That was why the bag. Great. She really didn't think much of him, did she? He'd deal with that bullshit later.

Damn Trish for being a flaming ass all the time! This was her fault. But he couldn't just sit around and wait until Ashley came to. Balancing her limp body against him with one hand at her back, Tripp situated her bag onto her stomach with his other hand. Then, easing an arm under her knees, he lifted to his feet and pulled her up with him. At the apartment complex entry, he paused long enough to dig his wallet out of his rear pocket, then waved it over the scanner, letting it detect the embedded code that allowed entry. After the door opened, he maneuvered Ashley carefully into the empty lobby. In several quick steps, they were inside the elevator on their way to the fourth floor.

"Faster," he urged the slower than shit contraption, watching the indicator light over the door blink at a snail's pace as it passed the second level and headed to third. Finally, the door opened on his floor. With long, urgent strides, Tripp strode past Ashley's place to his, sure that once he got her lying flat on her back on his couch, her lungs would relax, and she'd come to. Most people fainted from simple lack of oxygen. He kept his A/C set on low. The cooler air should help, too.

With Ashley still out cold and limp in his arms, he flashed his keycard at his apartment door's reader. The instant the lock disengaged, he kicked the door open and angled her into what was probably the last place on Earth she wanted to be. His place.

Butt-bumping the door shut, he crossed his living room to the couch and gently laid her down. Carefully, he lifted her head and finagled the strap to her bag out from under her hair. He set the bag beside the couch, within reach if she thought she needed to mace him when she came to.

His mom had stress-crocheted like a maniac while he'd been deployed. As a result, he had thick, plush afghans to spare. Tugging the camouflage-colored one with the black fringe off the back of his couch, he covered Ashley with it, in case the cooler air was too much. Then, carefully lifting her head, he eased another smaller, folded afghan under her for a pillow. She hadn't banged her head when she'd fallen, and she hadn't had a seizure. That much was good. But she might have a concussion. She'd been attacked only days ago, and she should still be at home resting, and—

Shit, this was all his fault. Blowing out a gut full of regret for being deaf, dumb, and blind to her panic attack, Tripp made a quick pass through his apartment to conceal anything that might connect him to his nighttime job. Finding nothing incriminating, other than dirty black clothes, which he had in abundance, he folded his long legs and sat on the floor, facing his unwilling houseguest.

Man, she was pretty, so innocent-looking when she was asleep. This woman was a hundred pounds, maybe. A little over five feet tall, but not by much. Peaches and cream skin. No freckles. No scars. No tattoos. No wrinkles. The laugh lines radiating out from the corners of her closed eyes didn't count. Glossy, straight black hair, and the bluest eyes. Not just blue, but dark, sparkling blue. Like sapphires in sunlight, they shone when she smiled. She was everything Trish was not. Which might explain Tripp's attraction to Ashley.

She was a breath of clean fresh air in his life, which until he'd seen her, had been full of combat and violence, either while on deployments or with Trish when he came home.

Tripp growled at his nearsightedness. He should've seen the signs. Because of what went down Friday night, Ashley had a dark secret, one that triggered panic attacks. Which explained why she hadn't answered her door until she'd heard Mrs. Harrison in the hall.

"Fuck," he cussed quietly. "She's scared of me. Me! The guy who rescued her. And all I did was make it worse until… God, I'm so dumb!" He raked his fingers over his head and down his damned stiff neck. "Mom always said I never listened. Guess she's right about that, too."

Andrea had also said Trish was headed for a lifetime of trouble. Wasn't that the truth?

Because he wasn't made to sit still, Tripp pushed off the floor and hurried into his small, adjoining kitchen. There wasn't much in his refrigerator, other than leftover Chinese takeout from two days ago and a six-pack of cheap beer, which was probably stale. His cupboards were as bare. But Bob's Best Pizza Oven was only a couple blocks away, and the jug of well water in his rented water dispenser had just been replaced. Ice water now, pizza later. Sounded like a plan. He'd order after Ashley came to.

In the meantime, Tripp ran to his room and changed into jeans. He knew he needed a shower. He'd been working out when Ashley had first knocked, but a shower could wait. Ashley couldn't. In his kitchen, he filled a glass with ice and water. Back at her side, he set the glass on the end table and ran the back of his fingers over her cheek. She had some color now, and her breathing was even. No fever, thank God. Just fear.

If a woman passing out because she was frightened didn't humble a guy, nothing did. Tripp folded into a cross-legged position, ashamed at how he'd spoken to Ashley. She'd just been doing her job. It wasn't her fault Trish had tagged him. Come to think of it, now he had a lead on his sister's whereabouts. That whole thing about twins having radar for each other was urban legend. The only thing Trish ever had radar for was his football buddies, or his paycheck. She had the uncanny ability of homing in on testosterone and cash, her two favorite mortal sins.

Moaning, Ashley lifted one arm and fluttered her fingers over her lips. Her shoulders lifted.

Tripp scooted back a foot to give her more personal space. He was the last thing she needed to see the second she opened her eyes. His chin dropped to the floor. He was twice her weight, and he was as rough a cob as any former soldier. He, of all people, should've known better than to badger a woman, even if he'd been right.

"Where… where am I?" Ashley asked sleepily.

"You're safe. You passed out. You're in my place." He looked up at her then.

Her head snapped to her right. "Your place?"

He put both palms forward. "Yes, ma'am. I wasn't going to leave you on the sidewalk."

Groaning, she covered her face. "I passed out? On the street? Oh, darn, I'm sorry."

"Don't be. Are you cold? Too hot? My mom's afghan might be too heavy. She likes to crochet. Think she's made enough to blanket the whole world by now. I can get you something else. Need a drink?" He reached for the glass of water.

"Where's my bag? I need my bag."

Of course, you do. "Right beside you on the floor. Might as well know I searched it. I was looking for something that might indicate if you had a medical condition."

"You looked in my bag?"

"Yup. Hope the expiration date on that can of mace is still good. Most become less effective after four years. Over time they lose aerosol and can't maintain enough internal pressure to overpower anyone." And he was talking too much.

The moment his fingers curled around the glass, Ashley pulled herself up and backed into the opposite corner of his couch. Her knees drew up into her chest, and Tripp recognized that for what it was. She'd created a barrier between them, like she'd done with her hair before. That was another one of her tells. She was still scared.

Tripp played it cool and didn't make eye contact. "Here. It's just well water," he told her, as he handed the glass over. "You're lucky I caught you before you hit your head."

Like a frightened animal, she reached forward just far enough to take the glass, then cowered back into her corner.

"You have PTSD," he told her gently but bluntly. "Like me, Ashley. Not sure where yours came from, but mine showed up the day a kid bombed a mosque in Kabul, Afghanistan. He killed eleven civilians. My squad and I were nearby, so we humped it over there and caught him before he could kill anyone else. I won't go into specifics, but what happened the day after, triggered something in my brain I still can't process. Don't know why. I sure can't explain how PTSD works. It's like one of those alien probes is stuck inside my skull. Every once in a while, something reminds me of him, and that probe lights up and pokes at me until I need to get the fuck away from everyone and everything." And now he was cussing.

"Like today?" Ashley asked quietly, her gaze on the water she still hadn't sipped.

"Nah, today was nothing special, except I helped Mrs. Harrison, and I finally met you."

She looked at him then, her blue eyes flat and dark, not a sparkle of her radiant inner glow in sight. "But you didn't want to go to coffee with me," she whispered.

"Yeah, well." He shrugged. "Guess I didn't think you really wanted to be seen with me."

"I'm not usually this bad."

"It's me, isn't it?" he asked earnestly. "I scare you."

She swallowed hard again. "No. Not you specifically. It all started…" She stopped talking, licked her lips, and whispered, "…a long time ago."

Tripp let that explanation be enough. If she didn't want to talk about what happened Friday night, fine with him. "You don't ever have to tell me anything you don't want to, Ashley. I'm nothing special. But it'd be good if you found someone to talk with. Someone who cares. Honestly, you keep your stress well hidden. I never would've guessed you had PTSD until you freaked."

Her head bobbed, and for the first time since she'd come to, a tiny smile curled the corners of her mouth. "I did freak, didn't I?"

"Yes, ma'am. Officially, you scared the shit out of me, and that's saying something. I've been to two county fairs and a goat roping, but I sure didn't see that coming."

"I'm usually very careful. I don't go out at night, and I don't go to unfamiliar places, and…" Her eyes widened as she took in his apartment. "I never take chances. But last week and today…" Her shoulders lifted. "I guess I thought I was stronger than I am."

She'd almost revealed what had happened Friday. Darn. Tripp wished she trusted him more.

"You're a control freak," he teased.

Actually, she was a victim. The attack Friday night had left a deep impression. A scar. But the problem with control freaks was the total impossibility of their self-assigned goal in life. Because life was not controllable. Shit still happened.

Chapter Ten

Desperate to escape, to reimagine herself, to at least transform the prison she'd created for herself, Ashley stepped out of her comfort zone and bravely asked, "Would you, umm, h-h-hold me?"

The brightness that exploded over Tripp's ruggedly handsome face was like the sun breaking through black clouds on a stormy Easter Sunday morning. "Yes, ma'am," he breathed. Not moving an inch, he just spread his arms wide and let her make the first move.

Which was the best answer. Ashley set the glass on the end table and, like a limp ramen noodle, poured herself off the couch. Cautiously, she landed in his arms, her backside on his crossed legs, and her heart beating like a frantic herd of wild horses. This might be the craziest thing she'd ever done, but she was so tired of being at the beck and call of the ugliness of *that* day. That other day. And now Friday night...

Once she settled, she wrapped her arms around herself. Tripp was much bigger-boned, and his legs were like sitting on crossed tree branches. Everything about him was so much harder than her, but those thick thigh muscles were warm and solid. Without saying anything, he wrapped his arms around hers like a blanket. He held her gently, as if she were a fragile package, which, at the moment, she was.

Ordinarily, she steered clear of getting this close to men she didn't know, but not once had she gotten a predator vibe from Tripp. He was big, but teddy bear big. And he was kind to stinky dogs and elderly women and—her.

While half of Ashley still held her breath, her other half looked up at the first man she'd taken a chance on in years. Everything about him was larger than life, yet she wasn't afraid anymore. At least, not scared witless, like she'd been when she'd passed out. How embarrassing.

He started rocking then. Slowly. His fingers were splayed on her back and her opposite shoulder, forming a solid circle around her. He'd turned into an impenetrable shield no one else could get through. Not even *him...* that other *him...*

At last, the frightened part of herself took a deep breath, then another. Her nose flared to inhale more of the masculine scent of his skin. The iron band around her lungs uncinched. She really was safe. She could breathe again.

"Believe it or not, I still have panic attacks, too," Tripp murmured confidentially. "It's not so bad now, but light a firecracker, and you'll see how fast I turn into a rabid dog. Foaming at the mouth and everything. Mom and me have a solemn pact. She doesn't allow fireworks near her house on the Fourth; I don't tear her place apart."

Ashley wiped her face on her crossed arms and listened as his belly expanded with a deep, manly breath.

"It's what happens to guys and gals who've seen combat. No big deal. I'm coping. A lot of them have it worse than me. I'm actually better now, but when I first came home…" He blew out a soft sigh against her cheek. "Things were pretty intense. You got someone to talk to? A counselor? Family?"

She shook her head. "No. Yes. I mean the doctor said—" Darn. She hadn't meant to let that slip.

"A doctor was involved, huh?" Tripp's arms tightened and his voice turned ragged, like he really wanted to do more than just talk. "That tells me whatever happened must've been damned scary, that you were hurt."

He hesitated as if waiting for her to elaborate, but there was no way she'd talk about either of her mistakes. Because that's what they were, and she was to blame for her two assaults. If she'd been smarter and more aware of what was going on around her, neither would've happened.

"You don't have to say another word," Tripp continued. His arms were solid, as big as her thighs. He was kind of like a warm, living wall that really could keep monsters out. "I understand how hard certain things are to talk about. When you're ready to ask for help, you're smart enough to ask. You'll get it. In the meantime, I'm here for you. Promise."

Those words… No. It couldn't be. Tripp was not her avenging angel. About the only thing he had in common with that guy was his size. Nothing else.

Pursing her lips, she focused on breathing slow and easy, like women in labor did. The worst of her attack was over. Because of what happened Friday, she'd have a monster headache for a couple days, sure, but eventually, she'd be okay. Once Tripp let go, she'd lock herself in her apartment, pull her room darkening drapes shut, and turn her music on. She'd light all of her nightlights. Peewee didn't mind. She was a responsible pet owner and a hard worker. She had plenty of sick leave, too. Maybe she needed to take another day off. Or two or three…

"There's lots of things I've seen and done that I don't talk about, either," Tripp said quietly. "I know how scared feels. I hate it. Trust me."

"You? You get scared, too?" She couldn't imagine what could frighten Tripp, but she was beginning to trust him.

"Oh, hell, yeah." By then his cheek was against hers. She relaxed into him. "Anyone who says they aren't scared when rocket-propelled grenades are coming straight at them, and IEDs are blowing up beneath their boots is a damned liar."

A cell phone vibrated from his jeans pocket. "Oops, sorry. That's my boss," he breathed into the side of her sweaty head. "I've got to check in. Don't go anywhere."

"Oh, that's funny," she tried to joke. "Not sure I can stand or walk straight right now, much less go anywhere." She pursed her lips and exhaled again. Slowly. Then listened to his polite conversation. Why not?

"Understood. Sure, Mark. The Bureau thinks it's the same guy?"

Brushing her hair out of her way, Ashley dared glance up at Tripp's handsome profile. He'd transformed into a stern professional, listening intently, and nodding to whoever he was speaking with. His brows were sharp and his green eyes shone as bright as broken glass. His jaw was tight, angular, and his lips were pursed, like he was thinking. Whatever was going on, it sounded serious.

"Damn. That's brutal. How many?" A tense pause. "How long has this creep been active?" Another pause. "And no one has any idea who he is?" Tripp glanced down at her and winked. "You bet. I'll be there in five. Might even bring a friend if that's okay."

She shrugged, not sure that she was ready to go anywhere. Until today, hiding out, taking time off, or crying herself to sleep was her proven cure when these awful panic attacks struck. She refused to use OTC sleeping meds and avoided prescription drugs. She didn't need the side effects. But for the first time in, well, forever, going somewhere with a man like Tripp sounded better than being alone with her bird.

"Yeah, yeah, smartass, I've got friends." He chuckled as his arm tightened around her. "Not all of them are in low places." He blew out a sigh. "You got it. Sure. See you soon." Tipping to one side, Tripp stuffed his phone in his back pocket and said, "I've got to go into the office. Won't be long. Come with me?"

Ashley pursed her lips and breathed out, expelling another tiny bit of the poisonous panic that had snuck up on her. That was what panic attacks felt like, poisonous gas. The key was in breathing properly to get it out of her system. Running a hand over her face, she met his gaze and admitted, "I'm a mess. Not sure I'm up for meeting anyone else today. Think I've surpassed my twenty-four-hour limit."

"Then let's get you over to your place," he replied easily, not a titch of coercion or condemnation in his tone. "I'm not leaving until I know you'll be okay." He lifted to his feet, taking her off the floor with him.

She leaned into his side once she was upright. Panic attacks took everything, her strength and her willpower. Tripp seemed to understand that. He hadn't let her go, had even pulled her under his arm and against his side to steady her, instead of letting her waver like a drunk.

There might still be a way to turn this day around. "I'd sure like to go with you, though," she said. Of course, then she had to huff out a quick breath to stall another rising tide of panic. This time, it was much smaller, and Ashley just plain didn't want to hide anymore. Not today. She wanted to be brave. If Barbara trusted Tripp, she would, too.

"Only if you're sure. TEAM HQ is only a few blocks south. I can run over and be back in under an hour. Then, I'll order pizza. That is, if you want to see me again."

He sounded so hopeful that Ashley couldn't resist. She took another slow breath, swallowed hard, then said, "I'll go with you, Tripp. Let me grab my bag." She didn't go anywhere without the mace in it. "On second thought…"

Things had to change, darn it. No longer would she live like a hermit in the dark. She wanted sunshine back in her life. Basking in the pretty green sunshine in Tripp's eyes was a great way to start.

She glanced over her shoulder at the man who'd stood by her. A gorgeous smile split his handsome face. Sparkles all but burst out of the dark centers of his eyes. "That's the first time you said my name. I like the way it sounds."

Oh, that. "I've been such a jerk. I really am sorry."

"So what?" he asked, smiling like a teasing little boy who'd just been handed an ice cream cone and might give you a taste if you were really nice to him. "I've been a jerk once or twice in my life. Forget it. I'll be right back. Just need to change into work clothes."

He returned a few minutes later, dressed in crisp black jeans, a matching black polo, work boots, and a leather jacket. He'd combed his hair and… *Dayum.* He'd shaved. The spicy, musky, male scents drifting off him were delicious.

Ashley breathed in the lusciousness of the incredibly sexy badass. She knew he was taller, broad-shouldered, and thick-chested, but all cleaned up? Tripp McClane was breathtakingly beautiful. No wonder he ducked when he entered most rooms. He filled doorways like they were picture frames, and everything about him consumed every last breath of air. A shiny, silver badge on his belt declared he was in law enforcement, which she hadn't realized until then.

"The TEAM?" she asked, not sure she'd read it right.

His head bobbed. "Yup. I'm an authorized private agent, not a cop. Alex Stewart owns The TEAM. Stupid name, I know. Ever heard of him?"

She cocked her head, thinking. "That name sounds familiar. Where did you say his business is?"

"King Street, across from the metro station. You'd like him. He does good work. Hires mostly vets. You ready to go?"

"Sure." Ashley left her bag where it lay, but slipped her keycard to the apartment complex and her apartment key into her rear pocket, before she took hold of Tripp's hand. It was so much larger and rougher than hers, and he was a good foot taller. Made her feel like a little girl.

"Where's your coat?"

She shrugged. "It's still warm. I won't need one."

"Are you sure? I've got a couple extra hoodies. You can sure borrow one."

"I'm fine. Let's go."

Back on the street, he helped her climb up into his monster truck, but not once did he touch her butt. Which was too bad. By then, she wished he would.

Chapter Eleven

Tripp paused when the elevator doors opened to TEAM HQ. He'd been so pleased to have Ashley along, he hadn't considered what entering a predominantly male office, where a bunch of aggressive, alpha-types worked, joked, and argued, might do to her. Also, because of what he'd done just a couple nights ago.

He'd turned the radio on during the drive over, to discover that those two young men had blabbed about the hate-crime that had nearly happened to them, and the strange appearance of a giant man in black who'd prevented it. How they would've died if not for him. How he'd appeared out of nowhere, then flown across the bridge like he had super powers. How he'd overcome five brawny bikers with his bare hands. How, when the fight was over and the bad guys were dead or dying—which wasn't true—he'd promised he'd always watch over guys like them.

As much as those two morons had embellished and fictionalized what really happened, they ought to go into journalism. Because Tripp didn't remember flying or promising or killing. Cussing, yes. Beating the shit out of a couple assholes, you betcha. But him a giant? Hell, no. Compared to some of the guys he worked with, like Mark, Zack, Lee, and Beau, he was a titch on the puny side. Plus, he hadn't killed anyone, not even in Seattle. Just gave them something, as in a few broken bones, noses, and fingers, to remember him by. But he had scuffed his knuckles over the weekend. His eye hadn't blackened, but he was sporting a butterfly bandage on his forehead. God help him if anyone asked what happened. He'd have to lie, and he hated liars.

He punched the elevator's close door button. "Maybe this isn't such a good idea."

"Why not?" she asked, while the car sealed itself for the ride back down to the street.

Tripp hit the hold button. "Because everyone I work with is former military, and they're mostly guys. Lots of big, dumb, loud-mouth Marines. A couple know-it-all Navy SEALs."

"Oka-a-a-ay..." Ashley pursed her lips and expelled a measured breath. "So, you're not throwing me to a pack of wolves. That's good."

"More like a herd of wild donkeys. Some of these guys can be real asses. A couple of the women are, too."

That made her smile. "Donkeys, really? Sounds like a fun office. I'll be okay."

"You sure?"

Ashley confirmed her conviction with a nod. "I deal better in group settings. It's the single situations where I freak."

"If I ever get my hands on the guy who hurt you—" Tripp didn't mean to, but he growled, wishing he could tell her who'd saved her, that he was the guy who'd showed up in time Friday. That for her, he'd do it again.

"Don't." She stopped his rant with a firm grip on his wrist. "Please. I don't want to talk about it."

Tripp knew then he'd overstepped her capacity to deal with what had happened, and that she liked when he complied without arguing. He hit the button and the door reopened.

"Okay then. Let's see what Mark wants. He's standing in for the boss tonight. Sorry, but I might have to park you at our customer service desk until I'm through talking with him. You'll be okay there. Mother doesn't bite."

"Everyone else does?" Ashley asked, the sassy sparkle finally back in her sapphire blues.

"Mostly they bray," he grumbled, steering her through a maze of walls, none more than three feet high, at the center of which loomed a tall bank of computer equipment and the customer service desk.

Connor Maher peered over his monitor and waved, his head tucked into the phone on his shoulder. Tripp gave him his chin. Ashley fluttered her fingers at him.

"You're new," a growly masculine voice said behind them.

"Hey, Beau," Tripp replied easily. "Mark called me in. Thought you guys would be in the Sit Room. Am I late?"

"Nah, he's still in his office talking with Director Chase. Guess the FBI needs an assist on a case they're working." He turned his gaze to Ashley. "Who's your friend?"

"Hello, I'm Ashley Cox," she said brightly, as she presented her hand. There she was again. The real Ashley Cox, Tripp's confident girl next door. "I'm Tripp's neighbor. We live in the same apartment complex."

Her fingers all but disappeared inside Beau's big, bear-like paw. "Nice to meet you, ma'am. Agent Beau Villanueva at your service. You need anything while you're here, you be sure to let me know. Just ask, and I'll come running."

Enough already. Tripp rolled his shoulder to shake off the green-eyed monster suddenly sitting there and poking the shit out of him. "Beau's one of The TEAM's best snipers, Ashley.

He also troubleshoots technical problems that pop up here in the office," Tripp explained, his right hand settling possessively at the small of her back, in case Beau upped his game and got friendlier.

It was a Neanderthal move, and Tripp knew it. He just couldn't help himself. Beau was built like a brick shithouse. Dark haired, dark-eyed, and Hispanic, he was one of those bulky, grouchy types who could turn on the charm at the drop of a hat. He shouldn't have grabbed her hand like he had, and he'd better stop smiling like he'd just found a delectable morsel. That alone was unlike the guy.

True, there was nothing to worry about with anyone here at TEAM HQ. Tripp knew that. Beau was happily married. Most agents were, or, like that dumbass Jameson Tenney, soon to be married. That was a mistake waiting to happen if Tripp had ever seen one. The guy was not only blind, he was marrying the first woman he'd dated in years, aka the boss's Protocol Officer, Maddie Bannister. They'd barely met a few weeks ago! What was Alex thinking, hiring a blind agent in the first place? And what were those two kids thinking? Love at first sight? There was no such thing.

Never mind that Tripp had just met Ashley. He sure as hell wasn't in love with her and yeah. He knew he had no right being possessive. He was as big an idiot as Jameson. Yet he couldn't help growling at Beau, who was still holding Ashley's hand, damn it. "You mind?"

The big guy flashed a toothy grin, then smoothed his free hand over the back of hers, almost like he was petting her. "I don't mind, but it sure seems like you do," he teased, as he finally released her. "Like I said, Ashley Cox, you need anything while you're here, just ask. We're all here to serve.

Can I get you a cup of coffee or a donut while you wait? I think there's some left in the breakroom."

"Thank you, no. I'm good," she answered, a little more breathlessly than Tripp would've liked.

What the hell was wrong with him? Again, the Neanderthal inside roared to the surface with a need to pound Beau's grinning ass into the floorboards. Fighting the urge, Tripp placed one arm around her shoulders, a definite caveman stamp of, *'She's mine. Back the fuck off or die.'*

Beau, damn him, winked. The prick knew precisely what he was doing.

"Tripp. Beau," Mother said from where she sat on her side of the counter. "Mark wants you two and Jameson in his office now."

About time. Tripp turned to the real technical advisor for The TEAM. "You mind if Ashley sits with you while I'm in with Mark?"

"The more the merrier," Mother muttered without looking up at him and with no hint of friendliness toward Ashley.

Jameson strolled up. "You brought a friend," he told Tripp, his hand already extended toward Ashley as if he could see. "Hi, Ashley, I'm Jameson Tenney, junior agent in charge of light bulbs. That's a joke, by the way."

How that guy got around the office as easily as he did still amazed Tripp. Except for the round-framed dark specs perched high on his nose, you'd never guess Jameson was blind by the way he moved.

"Nice to meet you, Jameson," Ashley replied evenly, shaking hands again. "You're visually impaired?"

"That's me, the token handicapped kid in an office of military geniuses. But I'm learning." Jameson lifted both shoulders and managed to look humble, a skill Beau ought to think about acquiring.

"Don't let him jerk your chain, Ashley," Beau muttered, cuffing Jameson's shoulder a solid one. "This guy's a former Navy SEAL. He's got radar none of the rest of us have. Like sharks and dolphins, he doesn't need to see to know which way to shoot."

"Oh, my goodness," Ashley gushed all over Jameson. "How do you do it?"

While he regaled her with a minute of humble deference meant to distract her from his disability, Tripp focused on not ripping the blind guy's jugular out and hanging him from the ceiling with it. Not that he would have, but—

Why was he so damned territorial all of a sudden? He didn't own Ashley. Hadn't even kissed her. Sure, he wanted to, but he'd barely touched her yet, mostly just to keep her from falling. Maybe that was it. She'd been scared of him, but she didn't seem to mind these guys handling her, and that bugged Tripp.

"Well, yes," she exclaimed. "I'd love to meet your fiancée for dinner. Tell me when and where."

Jameson asked her to dinner? Tripp ran a hand over his head, pissed that he'd missed the invitation. Jameson did have one of those cavalier guy-smiles that snared the ladies. Tripp had to give him that.

"Great. Let me check with Maddie. I'll be in touch." Jameson rapped his knuckles on the countertop. "Hey, Mom, how's Justice?"

Justice was Mother's hubby or boyfriend, Tripp still wasn't sure which, and he wasn't about to ask, either. Not as grouchy as she'd been since he'd been hired.

"Don't call me mom," she growled.

"But it fits you," Jameson replied innocently, his head cocked in that uncanny way he had when he was really listening. Which seemed to be all the time. The guy might be blind, but he was damned perceptive. It was almost as if he could read minds. "You take care of us guys and gals. We don't know what we'd do without you. You are The TEAM's mom."

"I am not," she replied haughtily.

"If you say so." He grinned and stepped away, then deliberately stage whispered, "Mom."

That brought Mother to her feet. "Damn it, Jameson! Stop calling me that."

Ashley tipped back on her heels. She was ready to run. Tripp latched onto her wrist before she could make a break for it. "Don't mind them," he whispered into the side of her head. "Jameson's just teasing. I'll be right back, then we'll go grab that cup of coffee, okay?"

"Sure, yeah. Okay." Ashley skirted cautiously around the counter. "But hurry back."

"You got it," he said as he bolted after Beau and Jameson.

Mark stood at his open office door with another guy as big, wide, and dark-haired as he was. Could've been his twin. The resemblance was uncanny. "Guys, FBI Director Tucker Chase. He called this meeting."

"This all you got?" Director Chase barked. "Three guys?"

Whoa, the sarcasm. Mark saved Tripp from jumping straight into a fist fight with this jerk when he replied, "These three will be more than enough. Come in. Take a seat at my table, guys. How's the little one, Tuck?"

That mellowed the bastard out. "Growing like a baby pig," he purred, his fatherly pride evident. "Mel says to tell you she needs another night out with Libby and your girls."

"Libby will like that. Okay, let's get started."

Chase changed back into an ass the second he took command of the opposite end of Mark's small conference table. He was dressed in the official black on black FBI attire, black tie stark against crisp white dress shirt. Everyone else was TEAM casual: black jeans, black TEAM polo, whatever boots or shoes they wanted.

Office scuttlebutt was that Chase had married Melissa McCormack, billionaire Jed McCormack's former daughter-in-law. How Chase had snagged the likes of her after Brady McCormack passed, Tripp had no idea.

Chase leaned in like the gorilla he was, braced his fingertips to the table top, and glared down at Tripp, Jameson, and Beau in turn. "Okay, guys, this is going to be quick and dirty, so listen up. We've got another serial killer in town. We're sure it's the same guy that struck two years ago, then went silent until last weekend." He snagged the remote to the big screen across the office, clicked it on, and—

"Holy shit," Beau breathed.

"Jameson," Mark said. "What we're looking at is a recent crime scene here in west Alexandria, along Interstate-395, I believe. Right, Tuck?"

"Yes. King Street junction." Chase clicked again. And again. With each click of that remote, he revealed one bloody death after another. All women. All in skimpy skirts pushed up over their hips, and glittery bras pushed up to their necks, where their throats opened into ghoulish smiles. Their arms and legs were spread wide, and each was displayed like a macabre, pornographic mannequin. There was no doubt the scenes had been staged. A single, long-stemmed, white rose lay across each woman's bloody, open mouth.

Tripp's heart stuttered into freefall. King Street extended westward from the Potomac River, through Alexandria for a little over five miles. At King Street Junction, it crossed over Interstate I-395. The junction was an organized snake's nest of declaration lanes that led to on or off-ramps headed in every direction but up. Coincidentally, King Street Junction, the Winkler Botanical Preserve, the free clinic slash Health Department, and Northern Virginia Community College, were all within walking distance of each other. The young men Tripp had rescued at the Preserve went to NVCC. Worse, any one of these women could have been Ashley. Or Trish. Where the hell was she?

"All bodies were left within the declaration lanes of King Street junction." Mark provided what Jameson couldn't see. "Are those southbound, Tuck?"

"Yes. All within this area." Chase pulled a laser pen from an inside suit jacket pocket as he brought up a map of the I-395 junction. The bright red light ran a circle around one of three small triangular patches of grass between the southbound and the declaration lane of the interstate, which Tripp knew was exit five to King Street. Three patches of grass occupied this quadrant of the busy junction. Three ramps ran between the grassy areas. The far-right off-ramp put a driver immediately west on King Street. The far-left off-ramp went beneath the King Street overpass, where it merged, either onto I-395 or circled back onto King Street. The third spur fed traffic from westbound King Street, across an overpass above I-395, then back around to the southbound on-ramp.

"Which may mean he lives somewhere north," Beau said.

"Which doesn't tell us squat," Chase snapped.

"But why that specific site?" Jameson asked.

Chase ran a hand over his head, "You tell me. It's out in the open where drivers from at least five different ramps and two busy highways could see him." He meant the frontage road and the interstate.

"Except they haven't," Jameson murmured, "have they?"

"Nope." Chase popped that P, giving it an impatient, exasperated ring. "Which means he's an arrogant son of a bitch."

Jameson tapped his index finger on the table. "Or he's thumbing his nose at APD and the Virginia Highway Patrol."

"But that's not where they were killed," Mark added. "This guy moves the bodies after the fact, then displays them where everyone can see them. Rigor and lack of blood at the scene verify that much. This is his stage. Damn. That's hard to look at."

"Three women," Jameson stated, not asked. He'd taken the corner chair nearest Chase, facing the screen he couldn't see. His head canted in what Tripp thought must be his much-touted *mad ninja* way. Junior Agent Walker Judge, another former SEAL, was the guy who'd recommended Alex hire this sightless agent. He'd coined the silly descriptor, said Jameson had *mad ninja skills*. Tripp had yet to see any.

"Yup, women," Tripp told his fellow agent. *Like them being female was a big surprise.* Then he asked Chase, "All hookers, right?"

The FBI Director's big chest heaved. "Yes, but what's concerning is the timeline. He's murdered two more women since eighteen-hundred hours Friday night. Total time between each murder, at least between each discovery, approximately twenty-four hours."

Oh, shit. Eighteen-hundred hours was six pm, civilian time. "He struck Friday night?" Tripp asked. "Are you sure?"

Stupid question. One of Chase's eyebrows spiked to the ceiling. "Of course I'm sure. He murdered victim number one early Friday, but waited to dump her body until right after dark, why?"

Because this creep had been in the same area, at the same time, as Ashley Friday night, possibly while Tripp was with her. And this crime scene was close to where Ashley worked. Too close. It could've easily been her in this ugly photo. His throat went dry at the frightening coincidence. He'd gone home that night, thinking he'd cleared the streets of danger, when he hadn't come close. The only comfort was knowing the bastard who'd assaulted Ashley was not this serial killer.

Tucker's fist hit the table, startling Tripp out of past mistakes and regrets. "You want to tell me what's going on, Junior Agent?"

Shaking the shock of this odd coincidence off, Tripp waved Tucker's attitude aside. "Just asking questions, shit." But bile welled at the back of his throat, and a hollow pit had bloomed in his gut. Saving others, even Ashley, didn't make up for the cold, hard fact that he'd failed these three other women during his late-night patrols. He should've been there for each of them. Why hadn't he?

"They were found by an APD officer, no doubt," Jameson said thoughtfully, his fingertips lightly drumming the tabletop in front of him.

"Yes, they were," Chase admitted tersely.

"The killer's taunting the police, which means he's escalating. He thinks he's smarter than they are, but he's most likely got an average IQ. Chances are he's handicapped. Killing women, demeaning them by displaying them, is his way of proving his masculinity, that he's just as good as a police officer. He wants the world to see that side of him, which is why I believe he's disabled, somehow. This guy doesn't want to be looked at. He wants, no, he needs to be seen without being seen. He's an introvert, but violently passive aggressive. I'm guessing he's shy around women, intimidated by them. Could our killer be a retired officer or a detective who was injured in the line of duty? Or someone who works closely with the police department? Maybe a consultant?"

"Spot on, Tenney," Chase replied gruffly. "Problem is we've looked at all APD employment records. Hell, we've even looked at any and all companies and their staff, that might have provided service to that office building. Haven't found anyone that stands out yet."

Okay, so that was another lucky guess, that the killer might be taunting Alexandria's police department just because he'd dumped a couple bodies in the middle of their stomping grounds.

"You're that profiler Alex hired?" Chase's dark eyes glazed over Jameson as if he found him wanting. Which Tripp certainly did. Could the guy even fire a weapon and hit something besides the broad side of a really big barn? Could he hit anything at all? Protect anyone?

"What else do you know about our killer?" Jameson asked without answering.

Chase huffed, then rolled one massive shoulder and loosened the knot in his black tie, as if he needed more air—or patience. He shot his next question at Mark. "Honestly, this is all the help you're going to give me? I've got a psycho in town, and you think dumping a visually impaired agent on me is going to—"

"The word is blind, Director Chase. Visually impaired is just PC speak. May I call you Tucker?" Jameson asked evenly, his face devoid of emotion, his round dark glasses now facing Chase. "And yes, I'm blind as the proverbial bat. So, ask me how I knew your victims are all female?"

Chase raked that same hand over his head. "Jesus Christ, call me shithead for all I care. I don't have time for this bull—"

"Excuse me, but I'd never disrespect another former SEAL by calling him names." Jameson leaned into the bigger, wider man standing across from him. "Asshole, maybe. Never shithead. I'll be honest, sir. It's in the tone of your voice, the way you and every other male around this table breathed while you clicked through those slides. But mostly…"

He paused and turned, aiming those dark spectacles at Tripp, almost as if he could see him sitting across from him. "It's in your heart rates. All of you. Decent men react differently when the victim is female. You're offended and disgusted by what you're seeing, which means each murder scene is brutal and graphic, because face it. We've all seen our share of death. Simple observation. Nothing magical or mysterious about it. I'm offended, too, but I'm missing the visual stimuli that makes a decent man stiffen with rage, makes him breathe hard, or stop breathing all together. Makes him sweat, crack his knuckles when he clenches his fist, so tight, he could scream. When he's angry enough to want to kill."

Tripp looked down at his white knuckles, blown away that Jameson had pegged him so accurately. "I would kill to protect women," he admitted quietly. "Any woman. Any child. Young men, too." *But especially Ashley and my mom. Okay, Trish, too.*

Jameson cocked his head onto his other shoulder. "Trust me, Tripp. I would, too, though I suspect your reasons are more… personal."

He paused, his nostrils flared, as if he could scent Tripp's real reason for wanting to put this mad dog down. As if he sensed Tripp's need to avenge the crime against Abdul Ikram, and Tripp's love for his stupid, missing sister. His sudden feelings for Ashley. He moved his fists under the table, in case Jameson could scent his sweaty palms, too.

"I pick up on things only an observant, dumb, blind man can, Director Chase." Jameson had turned back to Tucker. "Which is why I also know this murderer lives or works in the immediate area. This location means something to him. It's important, maybe because he can see it from wherever he lives or works. We're definitely looking for a male."

Man, that was the wildest guess. Tripp looked to Mark, expecting a quiet rebuff for Jameson's speaking to an FBI director like he had. But Mark was leaned back in his chair and smiling, one long leg sprawled alongside the table, and tapping the eraser end of a mechanical pencil on the tabletop.

Tucker's eyes turned black as sin. "You're the one who took out Lucy Delaney during that sting at Boston Harbor, didn't you?" he pointedly asked Jameson.

Tripp's neck snapped as he turned to face his friend. He'd heard about that risky, awesome take-down when he'd been in Seattle. "That was you?"

Jameson didn't answer that question, either. Just sat there tapping his finger.

"I never said you were dumb," Tripp breathed, in case this peculiar agent could read minds. *Now I'm worried I've completely underestimated you.*

"Think about it, gentlemen." Jameson addressed the room with the quiet resolute confidence Tripp had only witnessed a couple times in his life. Once in Kabul. Again with Alex Stewart. "I live in a world without color, light, or shadow. Also without the distraction of those visual stimuli. Because I'm blind, the universe opens up to me in ways it doesn't open to you. Trust me, I've worked my ass off to acquire these observation skills, but I also pay damned close attention. I focus on details others miss or might pass off as insignificant. Would I rather have my sight back? Absolutely. But I'm still useful, and I intend to end this motherfucker once and for all."

Finally. A king-sized curse from this meeker than shit agent. Tripp liked the sound of that. Guess a SEAL still lived behind that pretty exterior after all.

"And he can kick your ass any day," Mark added drily, directing that comment at Tucker. "Jameson is our resident Krav Maga expert. General Ben Amin trained him. Your own agent saw him fire those three shots into the precise location where Delaney was hiding that day, and I'll have you know that each of those rounds hit their mark. Check the ME's report. Jameson acted purely on muscle training and his uncanny sense of spatial awareness. That's what ended Delaney. She never expected a blind man would be the one to take her down. She thought wrong. Jameson works as hard now as he did active-duty. He might not be psychic, but he might as well be. He's as deadly as you, Tuck. Maybe more so."

That put the final nail in Tucker's *'this is all you've got?'* coffin. The muscles in his stiff neck worked as he swallowed whatever remark lingered at the tip of his tongue. Finally, he sat down and began working *with* The TEAM.

Chapter Twelve

The only reason he'd found her again so quickly was pure destiny. He'd simply followed the guy from his apartment in Olde Alexandria, and, just as he'd suspected, she was with the fool she'd called a hero. See? Patterns and promises and destiny.

He'd watched as the brute from Friday night's gallant rescue parked his equally large, yet unimpressive, truck at the curb. Unintelligent jocks tended to like big, big trucks. Penis envy and all. And bingo, his elusive little minx had fallen out of the truck into the brute's dirty hands. Which made him angry, that another man should touch her so brazenly. So intimately. But if there was one trait he excelled at, it was patience. After all, good things came to those who waited.

Which brought him to this bench in the King Street Gardens Park, a tiny triangle of green space caught between Diagonal Road, Daingerfield Road, and the ever-busy King Street. Where he could watch the comings and goings of everyone who entered that five-story, brick building across the way. The building where she was now.

A sliver of cool, deep, dark shade during the summer months, the park was known for its quaint touristy touches. It boasted a small sunken pool hidden within a massive hanging garden of climbing wisteria, the vine held up by an artistic rendering of stainless-steel pipes. The bricks underfoot supported the spiraling metalwork that, in turn, supported all those creeping vines and their ugly, dirty-purple flowers. It was said that George Washington laid out the streets that confined this little piece of history. Too bad he hadn't chosen better greenery when he did.

How he hated wisteria. Once it rooted, a man simply could not kill the tenacious woody weed. It had to be hacked to death, its roots poisoned, burned, hacked some more, then poisoned again. Even after all that, one could never be sure it was dead until the following spring. On second thought...

Maybe there was room in the world for the obnoxious plant. It wasn't completely unlike Ashley Cox. She had proven hard to kill as well. Hmmm.

This cold, metal park bench was a wretched place to watch the world go by after the sun set. But people watching was a lot like fishing. It took patience most didn't have the time nor the brains to develop. Most everyone these days wasn't intelligent. A wise man could bank on that. They just lived and lived and lived until... Oops, they didn't.

The way the metal arbor contained those twisted, wretched, woody branches, reminded him of cold, slimy snakes in a wire cage. Their flowers gave off a heavy, pungent stink. He much preferred cherry trees. Their blossoms were fragrant and sweet. Just like Ashley Cox...

A nasty curse caught his ear, then his eye. A tramp. A real slut, this time. Short, skanky leather skirt. Hard, mean eyes like all the others he'd entertained. She was crossing the street against traffic and in such a hurry. Stupid bitch didn't have a clue he was there.

A smile curled his lips. Maybe tonight wasn't about Ashley Cox after all. No matter. He'd found Ashley once. He could find her again...

Chapter Thirteen

"Sit," Mother ordered the moment Tripp stepped away with Jameson and Beau. "Ember's on maternity leave. Grab her chair. Everyone's working late tonight, which means we have to feed them. I'm busy, so you need to place an order for soup and subs."

"I can do that," Ashley answered cheerily. Might as well keep busy while Tripp was in his meeting. Like him, both those other men he'd left with were so darned handsome, either could've stepped out of GQ or off a Chippendale calendar. All the guys in this office she'd seen or met so far were that kind of polished and ripped.

"Thanks," the petite, silver-haired woman with the odd name answered. She pointed one lovely, manicured nail to the list of phone numbers below the edge of the countertop. "Dial nine to get an outside line, then call the *Soup Bowl* over on Prince Street. Number's right there. Here's the order." She handed Ashley an eight-by-eleven sheet of ruled paper with a couple dozen sub-sandwiches, chips, and soup orders listed. "Include something for yourself. Tripp usually gets a twelve-inch steak and swiss, salt and pepper with oil and vinegar. No tomatoes. Extra onions. If Harvey answers, tell him he still owes me a gallon of chicken noodle soup."

Ashley nodded as the phone rang in her ear. It took a few minutes to order, then to verify the lengthy list, but Harvey was a kick to work with. He seemed to already know the list by heart, and ended with a sassy, "Thank you, thank you! You tell that sweetheart, Mother, I'll send her two gallons of soup. One frozen for later, one piping hot for tonight. Tell her she still owes me a dance and a kiss!"

Ashley glanced sideways at the taciturn woman at her side. She danced? "Sure, I'll tell her. When will everything be ready for me to pick up?"

He all but squealed, "You must be new! I always deliver to my best customers. Give me forty-five minutes. I'll hurry. Tell Mother that, would you?"

Ashley passed the message along. "Harvey says everything will be here in forty-five minutes, and he'll hurry."

"Tell him it's about time. I'm tired of him being late."

Which Harvey overheard, judging by the delighted laugh at his end. "One lightning quick order, coming right up!" he declared as he disconnected the call.

"That man," Mother huffed. "Just like every other. All talk, no action."

Ashley wasn't sure what to do with that comment, so she placed the phone back into its charger and took a moment to absorb her new surroundings. The customer service desk seemed to be the central hub in this wide-open bay, dissected by three-foot walls and desktops of granite with polished steel accents. Each cubicle held one high-back leather office chair, two smaller wooden chairs, a credenza that ran the length opposite the doorway, and file cabinets. There were no walls for hanging pictures, but most desktops were cluttered with framed photos and personal items.

"He also said you owe him a kiss and a dance."

Mother clucked. "What I owe him is a foot up his ass. But just like every other man in my life, he doesn't use those two things flapping on the sides of his head. Don't know why the Lord wasted time putting ears on men. They don't use them. Name me a single guy who ever really listened to you. Humph."

Tripp came to mind, but Ashley opted for silent observation instead of active participation. Mother was as prickly as a porcupine.

"Men don't have any idea what we women go through for them. Take my boss, for instance. I've served, damn it, maybe not in the military, but I've worked as hard and as much as anyone on this TEAM. I've given my heart to these people. All of them! But what do I get in return? Nothing but more work and… and…" She turned away, but Ashley caught the covert index finger swipe under her nose. "He won't even consider my suggestions. Dumb ass thinks he knows everything. Never mind. Not your concern."

"This is a big office," Ashley replied thoughtfully, not sure what else to say. "I work for the city. We don't have anything as nice as this."

"And that's another thing. Alex is a good businessman, but foremost, he's a hard charging Marine. He wants to be out in the field, working with his men and women, not holed up here in meetings all day, or over on Capitol Hill, negotiating with senators and White House staff. I could do all that for him, and I'd be glad to, only… Sheesh. Why am I telling you?"

"Because you need someone impartial to talk to," Ashley said, as she leaned closer into this obviously upset woman. Working alongside Health and Human Services professionals, currently with Doctor Frankel, who oversaw the testing and treatment of STDs, including AIDS patients, she'd had some experience with distraught mothers and fathers.

Mother's eyes shot bright-blue daggers at her. "I hate when he calls me Mom," she hissed. "He thinks he's being clever, but he's not, and it… it…" There went that slender finger again, as her other hand delved into a nearby box of tissues and pulled several out. "Men!" she huffed.

"It hurts when we think no one understands us," Ashley sympathized, though she still wasn't sure why Mother found that nickname offensive. It wasn't much different than what everyone called her now. When Jameson said it, it sounded like an endearment, not a sting. "That was Jameson, right?"

"Yes, that's him, and I know he's not trying to be an ass, but…" She blew out another hiss. "He is. They all are."

Ashley found herself cocking her head the same way the agent in question had done moments earlier. Maybe that's what was going on. He already knew what Ashley now suspected, but didn't dare say. The word *Mom* was a trigger, yet he kept pulling it. Why? The only answer Ashley could come up with was that Jameson recognized the pent-up anger boiling behind Mother's temper. Was he purposefully goading her? Did he understand how close she was to the edge? More importantly, would he know what to do with her when she fell apart?

"I have PTSD." That was the last thing Ashley expected to confess when she'd tagged along with Tripp. Yet here she was, playing counselor to his emotionally distraught secretary. Giving it her best shot.

Mother hmphed. "Join the club. Everyone around here does. Even Alex. Damn him."

"Even you," Ashley dared breathe.

"Me? No, I most certainly do not, and don't you start on me. That's the trouble with everyone on this TEAM. They all think they're smarter than me, that they know what I've been through, and what I should do. But they don't. They don't know a damned thing about me."

Which, to Ashley, meant that Mother thought she was not only smarter than everyone else, but that she didn't need anyone. Which was just plain sad. Ashley tread extra carefully.

"I was attacked once," she murmured, swallowing hard as the memory came roaring back. Talk about a trigger. There was hers, a heart-stopping recollection that could still push her over the edge in a heartbeat. But this trigger had nothing to do with what happened Friday night. Not a thing. This attack happened two years ago. Yet she continued. Sometimes sharing helped others. "He said he came to fix the thermostat in my apartment. I was in college. In between roommates. Instead, he was only there to hurt me."

Mother stopped what she was doing. "Oh, you poor thing."

Ashley nodded. Yes, for a long time she'd been just that, a poor, poor broken little thing, afraid of her own shadow and scared to death of men. All men. But she'd taken advantage of the experts she now worked with. She'd gotten a referral for a good counselor, and she was earnestly working to not be the frightened puddle of fear she'd been after that awful moment in her past life. *Past* was the key she clung to. *That* kind of brutal event would never happen again. It couldn't. The statistics were stacked against *that*. Lightning did not strike in the same place twice.

Friday night was proof positive of that. Her attacker had just been a kid, a young man hooked on drugs. Not a malevolent killer like that other guy. Sure, the kid Friday night had cut her, but he hadn't meant to. It was the drugs. He was sick. He needed help, not the beating he'd ended up getting, and all because an angry angel had appeared out of nowhere and saved her. No matter what she thought about his brand of justice, she was alive today because of that masculine, potty-mouthed, handsome as heck, avenging angel.

Was she stupid or what? Ashley almost fanned herself thinking of the man behind that grease paint. Where was he tonight? Saving someone else? No doubt. He probably did that all the time.

"But I'm not a poor thing anymore," she told Mother, firmly shoving the more painful recollection of the two assaults into her past. "I still have panic attacks, though. Had a nasty one earlier today, but Tripp was there, and, umm… he helped me through it, and I guess what I'm trying to say is…" She'd lost her train of thought, so she reached out and took Mother's hand. "I don't know what happened with you. Heck, I don't even know why everyone calls you Mother. But I didn't get the sense that Jameson meant to be mean when he called you Mom. He doesn't strike me that way."

"He's not," she breathed, her voice so soft Ashley had to lean in closer to hear her. "He's sensitive and sweet, most days. He's thoughtful, and he always brings me something he thinks I'll like. Nothing big. Just knick-knacks. Junk mostly. Sometimes a flower. It's just that…"

Ashley braced for the words she already suspected.

"I don't want to be anyone's mother anymore. I had my chance, and I blew it. Then he makes it worse by calling me Mom."

Ashley swallowed hard.

"I lost her, and I'd give anything to have her back, and now Alex and Ember… They've got brand new babies and…" Her head dropped into her hands. "I don't know why I'm telling you this. I don't even know you."

"Kindred spirits," Ashley said softly. The office noises still clattered and murmured around them, but for a moment, she and Mother were sisters. "A smart person once told me that pain recognizes pain." And pain was pouring out of Mother. The worst kind, the loss of a child. A daughter. "I can't imagine anything worse than what you're going through," she said as she pressed her fingers around Mother's forearm. "But if you ever need to talk—"

"Who are you?"

Startled, Ashley looked up into a set of crystal blue eyes so sharp, they could've passed for lasers. If looks could kill, she had a feeling she'd already be drawn and quartered.

"Me? I'm nobody, just Tripp's n-n-neighbor," she answered breathlessly. Whoever this guy was, he was bigger than life. Dark haired with a hint of silver at his temples. Ruggedly handsome in a scary way. Stern, tanned, and tall, he towered over her. Dressed in a crisp, gray business suit, he looked like he could breathe fire, and burn the entire building down. Authority crackled around him like electricity.

"Alex?" Mother croaked, furiously wiping her face. "Damn it, what are you doing here? You're supposed to be with Kelsey. Wasn't her doctor's appointment today?"

Ah, so this was Alex Stewart. Tripp's boss. Oh. My. Heck. He was almost as beautiful as Tripp. Only darker. A whole lot darker, not in skin tone but in a predatory, I-own-the-world kind of way.

"Sasha, her appointment was this afternoon. It's evening. Already dark," he breathed, his gaze riveted to Mother and his face a mix of emotions Ashley couldn't decipher quickly enough. Remorse. Anger. Tenderness. Hate. Affection. All flashed across his countenance like lightning in a rolling thunderstorm.

One second, he was on the other side of the counter; the next, he'd grabbed Mother out of her chair, and she was glaring up at him. "Damn you, Alex," she hissed, her fists clenched on the lapels of his suit jacket. "I miss her! Just like you miss Sara and Abby! Is that so hard to understand?"

"I know, I know," he replied, his voice husky, his fingers splayed over her shoulder blades as he held on. "Grief is an ocean. You know that. One minute, it's a free, easy ride, and you're on top of the world. The next, it's a fuckin' tsunami, and you're drowning. Trust me, there are days I'm still drowning, Kelsey, too. Everyone who's lost a child feels the same way. The pain never goes away. You just have to hang on when it hits, and let the people you love in."

Ashley stuck her heels in the carpet and shoved her chair backward, away from the scene she had no business witnessing. This intimidating male cared about his secretary, but there was no satisfaction in knowing she'd guessed correctly, that Mother *had* lost a child. So, apparently, had Alex and his wife. What a way to meet the man who owned The TEAM.

The meeting Tripp was in must've been more important than he'd expected. No matter. Ashley knew her way home.

Chapter Fourteen

Tucker jerked the chair beside Jameson out from the table, turned it around, and straddled it. "So you think we're dealing with a male?" he asked, snapping his fingers. "Any idea what age? What he might do for a living? What's he look like?"

Tripp tipped his chair back onto its rear legs. Damned if he wasn't as surprised as Director Chase that Jameson actually had mad ninja skills.

"Age doesn't matter, sir," Jameson replied steadily. "Frankly, neither does this guy's appearance, though he's probably as ordinary-looking as everyone in this room. What can you tell me about his previous three murders? You said he struck two years ago, then went silent. Do you know that for sure, or is that a calculated guess? If not, let's check into all nearby states to see if they have unresolved murders that match this guy's MO. We should investigate prison sentences and release dates that fit his timeline. Military service records, dishonorable and honorable discharges, police officers who might've been fired or injured in the line of duty, who might hold a grudge against Alexandria's police force. Academy candidates, ones who dropped out or who didn't make the cut. Obvious indicators like those."

"Already did," Tucker answered. "Even had my team run over the crime scenes, looking for psychic hits. Usually Eden can pick up auras or psychic signatures or something. As far as—"

"Wait." This Tripp had to hear. "Psychic signatures? Auras? What kind of team do you operate? A bunch of ghost hunters?"

"They're really psychics, Tripp," Beau answered quickly. "Two are Level Tens. I didn't believe it at first, either, but these guys are good. You ever hear about Doctor Zaroyin? The mad scientist who came up with a way to mechanize living soldiers, but turned them into mindless drones instead?"

Who hadn't heard about Zaroyin? "You're shittin' me. He works for the FBI?"

"No, he's in a maximum-security federal prison for the rest of his life, but Isaiah, his son, works for me," Tucker answered without a speck of levity in his tone. If anything, his attitude had turned fiercely territorial, like he dared Tripp to say one more word against his team. "And he's damned good. So are Special Agents Eden and Ky Winchester, Tate Higgins, Keller Boniface, and Harper Kincaid. You got a problem with that?"

"No, sir, sure don't." Nonetheless, Tripp scanned the room, looking for any hint this was a joke on him. Or something. Psychic FBI agents? Really?

"Agent Chase, tell me about the recent murders," Jameson said.

Scowling, Tucker ran a hand up the back of his neck. "Same MO. Three women, all found in the exact same locations as his first three kills. The bodies were positioned like the originals. He staged them, right down to the white roses he put in their mouths. The only thing different is he targeted college students last time, prostitutes this time. Two years ago, he went after single women living alone. Never any in the dorms."

"He's reenacting those old murders," Beau muttered. "The sick bastard."

"Possibly," Tripp said, tapping his index finger to his bottom lip, wondering why the change. "But why students then, prostitutes now? Serial killers generally operate under specific MOs. If they take a trophy from one vic, they take one from the rest. Could it be this guy's not particular, just likes killing women?"

"No. That'd mark a significant shift in his MO, if—and this is just theory—he committed his earlier murders for the same reasons," Jameson said, "which we still don't know. Is there any similarity between the victims? Same hair color? Weight, height, anything?"

"The only things all six have in common is they were nineteen when he killed them, and all attended the same college," Tucker replied.

"Which college?" Tripp asked. "Where?"

"Northern Virginia Community College, here in west Alexandria," Mark replied. "And yes, I've already checked student rolls and teacher backgrounds for any correlation between the males on campus and the victims. Even dug into NVCC's maintenance employees, grounds keepers, and delivery personnel. Haven't found anything that stinks, yet."

"This creep take any trophies?" Beau asked.

Tucker nodded across the table. "You saw the crime scene photos. The bastard cuts their throats, then carves their tongues out, clean and neat. We haven't found anything yet to corroborate that theory. He used a razor-sharp blade, possibly a scalpel. There was one co-ed who got away two years ago.

Can't find her, either. Suspect she moved out of town and changed her name."

Tripp's gut clenched like his fist had earlier. "There were four victims two years ago? Three murdered, but one got away?"

Chase nodded glumly.

"Could she be in Wit Pro?" Mark asked Tucker.

"Witness Protection has nothing on her. We just know that two years ago, she checked into the free clinic after her assault. She was bruised and bloodied, but wouldn't submit to a rape kit. Said she didn't need it. Dumb asses didn't get her name or ID. Because it's a free clinic, they don't always demand identification before they treat someone. They have no written record of treatment, and all I've got is hearsay from the nurse on duty that night, a Miss Glenda Buckler. She retired last year, but according to her, the vic came in alone and left after the on-call doctor stitched her. Said she didn't need or want any more help. That she'd be okay."

"Which free clinic?" Tripp asked. "Where was she hurt? Why the stitches?"

"The one west on King Street." Tucker made a slicing motion across his neck. "Same type of cut to her throat. Took twenty-three stitches. Plus, a couple over her right eye where the bastard hit her. Buckler also said her forearms were bruised. She was scared to death. Buckler hated to see her leave. But her description of the attack matches the other three, all except for the way it ended."

"Isn't there at least a police report?" Jameson asked.

Tucker shook his head. "See, that's why I have Keller climbing through APD's files. There's no record of this assault anywhere. All he's come across so far is the name of the nurse, and all we've got is her word."

"Which is only hearsay," Mark murmured. "Thank God victim four got away."

"A fat lot of good it does for the other six," Tucker grouched. "If she'd at least given her name that day, we'd have someone to talk with. Christ, all we need is one gawddamned witness, and we could break this case."

"Can't blame a survivor for hiding," Tripp said thoughtfully. "She panicked. What woman wouldn't after being assaulted? At least she got the medical help she needed. That's what counts."

"She paid cash," Tucker hissed. "Five-hundred forty-four dollars. We don't even have a money trail or insurance records to follow. Shit."

Jameson cocked his head. "She was attacked during the day? Was every other attack at night?"

"Yes. All of them."

"Why did our killer change his MO? Or did he? Why carry out most of his work at night, then deviate that one time? Does time of day even mean anything to him?" Tripp asked, his heart on the timid woman he'd left sitting with Mother. Ashley'd had one helluva panic attack today, and she'd been scared to death Friday night. He could only imagine—

Exactly what he was imagining right damned now. Son of a bitch! What if she was the woman who'd escaped this same serial killer two years ago? What if Friday night wasn't the first time she'd been assaulted? It'd be the biggest coincidence in the universe, but her need to hide sounded eerily familiar. Those tells of hers fit a survivor of a vicious attack. Tripp bolted to his feet, needing to make sure that missing victim number four was not Ashley Cox.

"Hey! We're not done here. Where are you going?" Chase called after him.

"To talk with someone," Tripp yelled over his shoulder. Chase could wait. Ashley could not.

Shoving Mark's office door open, he flew down the short hallway to Mother's counter and ended up nearly running over her. "Where's Ashley?" he demanded.

Mother swiped a finger under her red nose. "I thought she was with you. I asked her to order dinner, but it already came and—"

That was no damned help. Tripp had no patience for Mother's attitude. Stalking past her, he took quick stock of the work bay. Most agents were laid back, eating sub sandwiches and soup. Talking. Taking a break. But no Ashley.

Out of that mess of men and women agents, Connor stood. "You lose someone, Tripp?"

"The woman I came with. You seen her?"

Connor jerked his head toward the elevator. "Think she left. You need help looking for her?"

Tripp didn't answer, just ran for the elevator, and stabbed level one. Why didn't she do what he'd told her?

Chapter Fifteen

Ashley blinked in surprise at the two men squared off across from her. Who would've guessed there was a boxing ring in the basement of an office building in downtown Alexandria? No wonder the guys upstairs were all physically fit. She'd intended to sneak away after that emotional scene between Alex and Mother. She'd used the restroom first, hoping no one would notice when she made her escape. But when she'd hit the call button for the ground floor, the elevator brought her here, to the basement. But what a basement.

Curiosity got the best of her. She stepped out of the car and into the most unexpected world she'd ever seen. A high ceiling extended throughout this level. All walls were a bright, glossy white, some darker where the lights weren't on. To her left stood a full fitness gym in muted darkness, complete with treadmills, recumbent bikes, elliptical machines, weight benches, barbells, an impressive set of heavy-duty weights, and other equipment she couldn't begin to name.

An impressive parkour workout course, complete with various sized wooden platforms, vertical beams, as well as horizontal beams that literally climbed one entire wall, filled the expansive, dimly lit room to her right.

She could smell the chlorine of a nearby swimming pool, but couldn't see it. Straight ahead, dancing on his toes inside a full-size boxing ring, with ropes, a bell, and everything, was

Tripp's boss. Alex Stewart must've come straight down while she was in the restroom. There he was, bobbing and ducking, dancing, and pummeling the heck out of the extra-large, bronzed, bald man in the ring with him. Neither man wore protective head gear, but the other guy was heavier muscled and a tiny bit taller than Alex.

Both of their white, short-sleeved t-shirts were darkened with sweat. Alex was in red boxing shorts, the other guy in black. They grunted like sweaty, angry bears, both hitting the other's chin, belly, shoulders, and, well, everything. Alex ducked a wide swing from his opponent that should've connected with his head and might've knocked him out. The other guy growled something she couldn't quite hear. But the sound of their leather gloves smacking all that skin and muscle like they meant to kill each other...? Ashley cringed at the pain they eagerly inflicted. How could men stand to do this?

Tripp's boss had the other guy in the corner against the ropes. It looked like Alex was winning, until the man ducked his punch. When Alex's glove skimmed the bigger guy's head, the guy's left glove came up under Alex's chin and nearly knocked his head off. Alex stumbled back, spit, and hissed, "Son of a bitch!"

How embarrassing. Ashley felt bad for Alex, him being the boss and all. She considered climbing back into the elevator. He didn't need to know she'd seen that. But he didn't go down, and he didn't slow down, either, not even to catch his breath.

Charging forward, Alex dished out a wicked volley of punishing blows. *Smack. Thud. Oomph, oomph, oomph!* Like a pissed-off panther against a hefty Rottweiler, he went bonkers on whoever the poor, poor other man was until the guy started laughing behind his raised gloves. "You had enough yet, Boss?"

"Damn it, Zack, you know better. I don't give up," Alex growled, and bam, bam, bam. He beat the crap out of his friend.

Zack still laughed!

At last Alex hissed, "Shit! Why can't I bulk up like you? Son of a bitch, we'll never be evenly matched. You're as solid as a bull elephant, just like when we were in the Corps."

"And yet you keep beating the hell out of your fists and face."

Just that fast, Alex dropped into a three-point crouch, kicked one foot out, hooked it around his bronze opponent's ankle, and knocked Zack off balance. He'd very nearly righted his much bulkier weight, when Alex was back on his feet. He charged and wrapped both arms around Zack. *BOOM!* He landed on his back, which made him laugh harder. Pushing Alex off, he leaned flat to his back, still chuckling. "Should've known you'd cheat, you dog. What happened to playing by WBF rules?"

"Thought those were just guidelines," Alex huffed while he slipped his gloves off, then leaned over and offered a hand to help his friend to his feet.

With a bounce off the mat, Zack cuffed Alex's glistening shoulder. "You still hit like a son of a gun. What's got you pissed this time?"

"Same BS." Raising one arm, Alex swiped it across his forehead.

"Mother again?"

"Yessss," he hissed. "Her ice princess routine is getting old."

"Then stop trying to bring her around. Let her go. She hasn't been happy since she came back anyway."

"Can't. Something's eating her. She needs us."

"Not sure that was ever correct, Boss. Dempsey's life and death proved it. Mother's a chameleon. She only shows what she wants us to see. You ever thought of limiting her access? Might be time to consider taking protective measures to keep the company safe."

Alex ducked between the ropes, then lifted the top rope for Zack to climb through. "Not going to happen," he said as he dropped to the floor. "I'm actually considering granting her more access. I've got a plan."

"You bought that property out west, didn't you?"

By then the men were standing in front of a floor-to-ceiling, wire storage shelf that partially blocked Ashley's view, stowing their gloves into an array of shelves. Each grabbed a white towel from the same open shelving.

Zack wrapped his around his neck.

Alex slung his over his shoulder. "Bought that place and the farm to the south of it last month. Already started building."

"How many acres?"

"More than enough for our needs."

"You burning through Pops Delaney's inheritance?"

The men paused to talk. They still hadn't noticed Ashley.

"Hell, no, that's blood money. If it goes anywhere, it'll go to the Police Officer Family Survivor's Fund. They need it. I don't. My attorney's working the details. Let him figure a way forward."

"Sounds like you've got big plans for The TEAM's future."

"I do. We've outgrown Alexandria. With the Seattle office closed, it's time to reorganize all assets and focus on the disciplines we do best."

"Like what?"

"Like the work Beckam and the guys do for the homeless vets over in the District. Like what Mark and Harley do in Afghanistan. What you, David, Walker, and the others are doing in the Far East."

"You're going international?"

"We're already international, Zack. The TEAM's a major world player. Because our reputation's solid, President Adams asked me to consider working closely with him. I'd like to discuss a plan to move forward with you, Mark, Harley, and David, first thing tomorrow morning."

"You're considering putting Mother in charge of all things tech-related, aren't you?"

Alex shook his head. "Not just tech related, more like technological innovation. She's got the talent, and I believe her biggest problem is she's stymied. It's time she has enough staff and resources to challenge that big brain of hers. I have ideas for covert warfare that I want off the drawing board and implemented before Christmas. She can do it. I know she can."

"Seriously? Will the new digs be ready by then?"

"Hers will. I've got workers working on the rest of the foundations now."

"Well, good. We outgrew this little bunker a long time ago."

"That we have."

Ashley took a step backward into the security of the elevator car, wishing she were anywhere but eavesdropping on Tripp's boss again. She had no business overhearing this conversation, either. Too bad the elevator pinged extra loud the second she moved, as if it were motion-activated or something. Which it probably was.

Both men's heads came up, and she was caught. Breathlessly, she ducked inside the car and slapped the close-door button a couple times. "Get me out of here," she whispered.

"Ashley Cox? Is that you?" Alex asked as they headed her way.

"Y-y-yes?" she whispered, her throat gone desert dry. Determined to get away, she hit that darn close-door button one more time. Why wasn't it working?

"Wait up!" the extraordinarily large man named Zack called out.

"W-w-why?" She hit that stubborn button one last time. Okay, that made her the world's biggest chicken, but Alex and Zack were both big guys, big-chested, and sweating like draft horses. They blocked her way and filled her entire view. They took up all the air and, with it, her ability to think. They were everything she was afraid of—they were men. Their only saving grace was that Tripp worked with them, and for Alex, and maybe...

Too late. Alex clapped a palm across the metal doors just when they'd finally decided to close. "Do you box?" he asked, jerking his head toward the ring.

"M-m-me? B-b-box? Oh, no. I-I-I…" *Sound like an idiot.* She cleared her throat and proclaimed, "I'd never hit anyone."

A big, toothy smile lit Zack's face. "Too bad. I teach self-defense to most TEAM wives and a few of their kids. I could show you a couple moves. Let me know if you're ever interested."

"No!" popped out of her mouth like a speeding bullet. "I mean..." *I can't believe I'm going to say this but,* "Self-defense? Really? You'd teach m-m-me? But I'm... short." She really meant to say a woman, but these guys seemed to think anyone could learn to stand up for themselves. Even kids.

"Thought maybe that's why Tripp sent you down here," Alex muttered. "Want a tour?"

"Ok-a-a-ay," Ashley replied, the tremor in her voice hard to tamp down. But this was Tripp's boss, and he'd just whipped Zack's butt, and... She was so frazzled she lost her train of thought.

"Women need to be able to defend themselves, Ashley," Alex said evenly. His voice had changed from clipped and precise to calm and mellow, almost as if he knew she was ready to bolt. Smart man. She was. "Especially these days. We teach handgun safety and conceal carry classes, too. Tell Tripp to get you registered, and my wife will be glad to take you to the range one of these days and—"

"No, thank you. Err..." *What'd he say?* Ashley cleared her throat again. "Your wife shoots?"

He nodded, those razor-sharp eyeballs quartering her and taking stock. Measuring her. A smile breached through that critical-looking face. "You remind me of her. Kelsey had never touched a pistol before she met me, but she carries now, even at home. She teaches a conceal carry class at her place of business, too. You'd like her."

"Kelsey's already back to work?" Zack smoothed his towel over his head, blotting the rivulets of sweat running into his eyes.

"Sure. She takes the baby and Lexie with her. Raymond's Place runs a daycare, and with all those vets working for her, she's got it made."

Draping his towel over the inked sleeve on his massive shoulder, Zack shook his head. "That woman's unstoppable."

The laser glint in Alex's eyes softened even more. "That she is."

"Who watches your dad while she's working?"

"I hired a live-in caretaker. Mel seems to like him."

"Didn't think he liked anyone these days."

Alex grunted. "You've got that right."

"Tripp didn't send me down here," Ashley murmured. These guys didn't seem worried she'd overheard them. "He's still in his meeting, and I didn't want to be a bother, so I was on my way home. But the elevator brought me down here instead of to ground level where I thought I was going, and…" *And I'm rambling.*

"Come on, Ashley," Zack wheedled. "Let us give you at least one good self-defense skill while you're here. Who do you want to take down the most, me or this big-mouthed boss of mine?"

Taking down either of these behemoths wouldn't be good business for Tripp. She'd never. Not that she could anyway. Her head shook with hard and fast tremors of denial. "Not me. I can't—"

"Oh, yes you can!" a familiar voice boomed from the door marked STAIRS to her far right. "I'll show you."

"Tripp!" Thank goodness he showed up.

He set a quick pace to her rescue. "Here you are," he breathed into the side of her head as he gave her a half-hug. "I've been looking for you. These old guys bothering you?"

"Hey," Zack groused. "I resemble that."

"Oh, no. Not at all. I—"

Tripp reached out and grabbed Zack's little finger. He dropped to his knees and his towel fell to the floor. "What the fuck?" he yelled.

"Lesson number one," Tripp told Ashley calmly. With a twist of his wrist, he bent Zack's finger farther back. "When faced with imminent attack, act fast and decisively. Go in fast, hit hard. Never let them see you coming."

"Payback's a bitch, junior agent," Zack growled up at Tripp.

"You see, even the smallest fighter can leverage a much larger opponent, simply by getting the jump on him or her," Tripp said without glancing at or answering the man groveling at his feet. "It's all about knowing where to strike to get the most leverage, and where your opponent's weakest points are. Fingers are easy targets, but in a close-up fight to the death, they're not enough. Fight for keeps, Ashley. Fight to kill. Gouge your attacker's eyes, punch the heel of your palm into his nose, or make a good hard fist and punch his throat. Knee his balls, kick, scream, whatever you have to do to stay alive. Just do something before he lays a hand on you. If nothing else, scream. Second rule: never give up. Even when all hope seems lost, when he thinks he's got you down, endure to the fuckin' end."

"Tripp's right. Every second counts in death struggles," Alex added, his blue eyes fixed on Ashley and completely ignoring Zack, who was growing more miserable by the second. "The universe never stops moving or changing. The worst thing anyone can do is to give up when help might be just around the corner."

"Exactly." Tripp cranked Zack's little finger even farther back! The poor man's sweaty face was wrinkled in agony. He looked like he was about to cry. Ashley wanted to cry for him. "Case in point. Zack Lennox here, a big, tough guy who weighs close to three hundred pounds, didn't see this coming. Yet here I stand, making him sweat, on his knees, just by tweaking his pinkie. I don't intend to give up until he does. Want to try?" He offered Zack's much larger, but still twisted baby finger, for her to take.

"No!" she replied adamantly, her heart in her throat for what Zack was going through. "You're hurting him."

"No, I'm not," Tripp answered even as he looked down at the man on his knees and asked, "Am I hurting poor widdle you?"

"No, damn it, you ass. Let me up."

Which nearly made Ashley smile. Of course, Zack would say that. Men didn't usually admit they were hurt when a woman was around. "You've made your point, Tripp. Let him go. Stop picking on Zack."

"Aw, am I picking on you?" Tripp teased, as he released Zack's finger.

Zack jerked his hand away, shook it, and for some reason, Alex took a full step backward. Just in time. Without so much as a whisper, Zack barreled into Tripp, and the fight was on. In seconds, he had Tripp pinned flat to the floor, his massive forearm across Tripp's windpipe. "You think you can take me, smart ass?"

Ashley stepped alongside Alex. "Make them stop. He's hurting him."

"No, he's not," Alex answered, both arms crossed over his chest. "Watch."

Tripp's face turned red. Ashley bit her bottom lip at the sweating male pretzel sprawled before her. It certainly looked like Tripp was in trouble. His eyes bugged out. He wheezed. Sweat dripped off the ugly face Zack was making at him. But the second he eased back just a tiny fraction, Tripp twisted his body and bent one leg, then stuck his other knee up into Zack's groin.

"Pressure points," he whisper-gagged at Ashley. "It's all about making the most of your attacker's pressure points. With one good kick, I can now knee this big boy in his—"

"Like hell!" Zack rolled off Tripp.

Tripp was now sucking in air like a fish out of water.

"Damn, for a minute there, he had me," Zack admitted as he looked up at Ashley. "He could've broken my finger, remember that. Might does not make right. Men who assault women are generally bullies and cowards. They're weak. They think because they might be physically bigger and male, that women are easy targets. Now you know better. If you ever find yourself up against some jerk..." He stuck his chin at Tripp. "Surprise the hell out of that son of a bitch and prove him wrong."

"Eyes, nose, throat, balls," Tripp rasped. He was sittings cross-legged, looking up at her with a crazy smile.

"But the best defense for an untrained woman," Alex interrupted, "should always be to scream bloody murder and run in the opposite direction. Know your surroundings at all times and never get into a car with someone you don't know.

Don't look for trouble, Ashley, but don't be afraid to knock it on its ass if it comes looking for you. Now, about weapons training… Tripp, get your lazy ass off the floor."

"Yes, Boss," he replied, as he bounced to his feet and extended a hand to help Zack up.

Zack slapped his offer away. "From a place you'll never see, asshole, will come a sound you'll never hear."

Ashley didn't get the joke, but Tripp and Alex both laughed.

"Get this woman a weapon," Alex ordered. "Teach her how to shoot. That okay?" he asked, turning those icy blue lasers back to Ashley.

"Yes," she admitted. "I'd really like to be able to defend myself." *Because hiding under the bed when I'm scared sucks.*

A big sweaty arm landed around her neck. "You bet, Boss," Tripp replied. "Right after Ashley and I have a little talk."

Chapter Sixteen

Tripp steered Ashley away from his boss and Zack and into the waiting elevator car. The second the doors closed, he asked, "Why didn't you wait for me?"

"Because you were working, and everyone was busy, and I didn't want to be a bother."

"I thought we were going out for coffee after I finished here?"

She looked up at him. "You don't need to babysit me, Tripp. Besides…" Her voice trailed off.

"Did Mother say anything to you? Was she rude?"

Ashley blew her hair out of her eyes. "She's seriously depressed. Did you know she lost a child? I'm not sure when. Recently, I think."

"I had no idea," Tripp murmured, wondering how she'd come to that bit of gossip. "That explains why she's difficult to work with. I've been bounced between here and Seattle since I was hired, but every time I needed something from her, she's been difficult. I usually work with Beau. He's just as smart, without the attitude."

"Try being kind to her for a change and don't call her Mom. That's a huge trigger for her. I'm not sure why Jameson keeps calling her that. Do you?"

"Sure don't, no." *Because I mind my business at work, and I've got enough family drama of my own to worry about.* "Hey, listen—"

"Alex and his wife lost a baby, too. You're surrounded by people with PTSD."

Ashley was certainly full of personal TEAM information, but Tripp needed answers. "Okay, stop. This is all good gossip, but—"

"Oh, it's not gossip. Mother had a little breakdown while I was sitting with her. She told me about losing her daughter. Then Alex showed up and told her to hang on, that everyone who's lost a child feels like they're drowning some days. That he and his wife Kelsey were still drowning, too. Your boss and his wife lost a child, Tripp. Isn't that awful?"

Tripp nodded but said nothing. Things in the office were making a little better sense now. Alex's obsessive-compulsive attention to detail might've come out of his need to make sure no one else died on his watch. The loss of a child also explained Mother's bitter comebacks at the drop of a hat. The way Alex and Mother seemed to tolerate each other some days, then hate each other the next morning. The way Mother snapped at Jameson. Alex seemed to have a handle on his grief, but Ashley was right. Mother was still drowning. That was the perfect descriptor.

Tripp felt like he and his mom were drowning in his sister's drama. How could he even begin to help someone like Mother, who wouldn't let him close enough to ask a simple question? Better question, what did Jameson know about Mother that no one else did? He wasn't usually an instigator, yet he seemed to be taunting her even after she'd told him in no uncertain terms to stop calling her Mom.

The elevator was nearly at The TEAM's floor. "You've been busy," he murmured.

Ashley looked up at him. "I just listened, that's all. And I ordered soup and sandwiches, too. You've got a foot-long steak-and-swiss waiting upstairs for you. Soup, too. I didn't get myself anything because I didn't want to impose. Would you mind sharing?"

Such an innocent question for a woman who, only this morning, couldn't stand to touch him.

He licked his bottom lip and changed the subject. "Where'd you go to college, Ashley? Were you ever…?" He never got the rest of the question out. The moment he said the words, he knew he'd ruined the rest of the evening.

Ashley's eyes widened with something that looked a lot like fear. Not surprise. Her pupils dilated, squeezing the sparkle out of the sapphire blue. Her breath hitched. She took a step back from him. One hand clutched the top buttons of her shirt, as if she needed to hold it together. As if it might suddenly be torn away. Or off. But the worst physical reaction? She dropped her lashes and seemed to shrink into the woman he'd met Friday night.

Damn it, he'd done it again. Common sense sometimes took a full minute to engage. Tripp was, after all, one of those hard men who'd stood in the dark of the darkest nights and done what most other men would not. He'd seen and done too much, though sometimes, he felt as if he hadn't done enough. Like now.

A flaming spark of *'Shit, damn, maybe I shouldn't have asked anything,'* slapped him upside his hard, Army head. The convo ground to a sudden stop. He swallowed hard, huffing through a throat that refused to comply, trying not to see

Ashley's lovely face superimposed on the victims in those gruesome crime scene photos in Mark's office.

She retreated to the opposite corner of the elevator and went as still as a church mouse, not looking at him. Ashley planned to bolt the second those doors opened.

Shit. Tripp sucked in a belly full of regret, managed to finally swallow, and reached a hand to her. "Come with me, Ashley. Please," he said evenly, needing her to give him a way out of the mess he'd created. "We need to talk. In private." His throat was so damned dry, he sounded like a toad croaking.

The car doors slid open, and there stood that son of a bitch Jameson, his head cocked as if he'd known precisely where Ashley would be. "Ashley?" he asked a helluva lot more calmly than Tripp had. "May I speak with you in private for a minute before you go?" And he'd given her a way out. Said she could go. Tripp had to admit, Jameson was a smart guy.

She stared up at him, trembling like a sweet, innocent doe caught in the crosshairs of a hunter's scope. Her nostrils flared, and the pulse spot in her throat quivered.

Tripp looked to Jameson for more help. Could he sense how badly Tripp had messed up? Had he anticipated Ashley running out of the elevator for the stairs? Sure seemed like it. God, what didn't that guy know?

Jameson held out his right hand and fluttered his fingers, as if he knew where she stood. "Come on, kiddo. Just for a minute. Tripp, would you like to join us?"

Yes, gawddamnit, his inner Ranger roared. But he replied more evenly, "Sure. Maybe you can help us with a case we're working, Ashley."

"Me?" she squeaked, her pretty blues wide and glistening. Finally, she looked at him.

Tripp wanted to kick his own ass. Once again, he'd frightened her by charging full-speed ahead without thinking. His rough-and-ready style might work in combat and on the streets at night, but it sucked boulders in relationships. Not that he had a relationship with Ashley, but—

"Yes. You do," Jameson whispered, so damned quietly that Tripp wasn't sure he'd heard the guy right. Had he just answered Tripp's unspoken question. Was he clairvoyant?

"Yes, Jameson and I would like to talk with you, Ashley," Tripp admitted more easily once his lungs filled with air and his head with cool, calm enlightenment. Since the moment he'd seen her, he'd known Ashley was different, that she was tiny and timid and special. It was time to admit that much, at least to himself. He punctuated that calm affirmation with the exclamation point of his most sincere smile.

Her eyes lit up when he did that, which soothed him more than she could possibly know.

Mark, Director Chase, Beau, and several agents were now gathered around the customer service desk, watching Jameson usher Ashley away from them, toward the opposite hallway.

"I'll make sure Tripp keeps it short, Mark," Jameson said. "We'll be right back."

Tripp held his hand out to Ashley when she rounded the corner, but Jameson intercepted him with the ease of a jungle cat and pulled her into his side with a firm, "You'll be fine, girlfriend. I've got you."

Girlfriend? Like hell! You've got her? Shit, damn, and son of a bitch! It was a struggle keeping his inner Neanderthal on its leash, with Jameson taking control of his girl—err, ahh, neighbor—as smoothly as he had. Who the hell did Jameson think he was?

Walking behind the visually impaired agent, who seemed to know a helluva lot more about women than most sighted guys, was one hell of an endurance test. Tripp rolled his neck, not sure why Jameson was getting on his last nerve. The guy was engaged. He'd seen him with Maddie. They adored each other. But he was… So. Damned. Smooth!

Chapter Seventeen

Tripp's friend Jameson was as calm as he was expressive. They were mismatched bookends, both seated kitty-corner from her at one end of the conference table, both in TEAM black, and both handsome. But where Tripp was deeply tanned and sandy-blond with a definite windblown, rough-and-ready look, Jameson was dark-haired and as neat as a pin. He'd even interlocked his fingers on the table in front of him, when he'd taken his seat. They were both dressed business casual, but Jameson had yet to capture the essence of the word. If anything, he was James Bond elegant, even in jeans. Although scruff shadowed his jaw, Jameson appeared more focused. Intense. Controlled, but in a kinder, gentler way than Tripp. Even his dark hair was under control, parted, and combed like a choirboy's.

Tripp did casual like a scruffy tomcat on the prowl. He was reactive, make that, over-reactive. Everything he did seemed based on intense emotion. On his heart.

Still not sure why they wanted to talk with her, Ashley splayed her sweaty fingers on the table top to calm her jittery nerves. She needed the strength emanating from the cold, hard granite, as well as a barrier between her and the guys, to keep that sneaky panic attack at bay. Wow, this one had come on suddenly. Poor Tripp had only asked where she'd gone to college. It wasn't as if he'd asked, even hinted about what happened *that day*.

The opposite wall was one huge, floor-to-ceiling window facing the sunset. The King Street Metro Station and the George Washington Memorial Masonic Temple loomed over busy autumn traffic to the west. The King Street free bus had just lumbered out of the metro parking lot. She wished she were on it.

Jameson's calmness instantly set Ashley at ease. She'd settled down the moment he'd pulled her into his side. Tall, dark, and handsome, he leaned over his interlocked hands now, his face turned toward her. "Ashley, I meant what I said. This won't take long. You can leave any time you choose. Just say the word."

"W-w-what'd I do?"

Tripp rested his hand on the back of her chair. "Nothing. Sorry if my question startled you." He cleared his throat. "Just want to ask something in private. That's all. Nothing to worry about."

"Why was everyone looking at me?"

Jameson's face cracked into a sincere, open smile that made it easier for her to breathe. "We do come across like gangbusters once in a while, don't we? Sorry about that. But the FBI has asked us to assist them in a murder investigation, and we're on a short suspense. Stop us if we get too personal, okay?"

She nodded but then said, "Sure," when she remembered he couldn't see. "Have you always been blind?"

He shook his head. "Nope. Lost my sight courtesy of a stinky, little donkey and two deaf boys taking a joyride in the middle of the Afghanistan desert." His right hand skimmed the dark shadow on his jaw. "My SEAL team and I were in the middle of a firefight. Couldn't let those kids get themselves killed, so there we were, chasing after the donkey those boys were taking a joyride on."

"I didn't know that," Tripp muttered, his brows furrowed and his face turned to his partner.

"Never mind. It was a stupid question," Ashley breathed. "Of course, you weren't born blind, or you wouldn't have been a SEAL."

Jameson nodded. "I still am. A SEAL, that is. Anyway, after a couple of us guys charged out to save those boys, little Eeyore got scared and set off a string of buried IEDs."

"Improvised explosive devices," Tripp translated.

"Oh, no." Ashley didn't want to hear the rest of this story.

"Oh, yes." Jameson's lips pinched. "The ISIL soldiers we were fighting had set the perfect trap. They knew Americans wouldn't let those kids die. Guess we're dumb like that. Lost two friends and two perfectly good retinas that day. But let's talk about you. Where'd you go to school? You are from around here, aren't you?"

"Yes, I grew up in—"

The door slammed open, banged into the wall, startling everyone.

"Boss?" Tripp cranked his head around. "Oh, it's you."

"Director Tucker Chase," Jameson said calmly, gesturing to Ashley. "May I introduce Tripp's neighbor, Ashley Cox?"

The fierce-looking guy with black eyes and dark hair, the same one who'd glared at her from Mother's counter, growled, "Nice to meet you, Ashley Cox. Guys, APD has another vic. Move out with me or sit tight, I don't care. But I'm leaving now."

Wow, he was rude. Ashley stood because Tripp and Jameson did.

"We're going with you," Jameson replied. "Ashley, we'll be back later to talk with you if you don't mind."

"Move it!" the rude man bellowed. "Hustle! I'll be in the garage, waiting. Be there in five, or I'm leaving without you."

"Go. I'll be fine," Ashley told Tripp and Jameson, fluttering her fingers to make them hurry and leave.

"Stay here," Tripp ordered, but then he added, "Please," more gently.

She gave him her best smile, then watched them race after Director Chase. A flurry of activity followed them. More men. More urgent chatter. These people took their jobs seriously, and she liked that. By the time she walked into the hall, the office was quiet, and Tripp was gone. So were Mark and just about everyone else. Two agents, a man and a woman she didn't recognize, were the only ones still at their desks. Even Mother was nowhere in sight. Sandwiches lay half-eaten. The debris from their late dinner over-filled the trash can beside the customer service counter.

Ashley drew in a deep breath, proud of herself for having taken her first successful step back to normalcy. She'd done it. After two long years, she'd finally cracked the shell she'd been hiding in. She'd left her apartment, and she'd done it at night. Okay, so she'd had another tiny, sneaky panic attack, but she was feeling better now.

The agents still in the office were engrossed with whatever was on the huge monitor behind Mother's desk. She wasn't there, so Ashley figured, why not? She'd meant what she'd told Tripp. She didn't need a babysitter, and she didn't want to sit around until he returned. He had important work to do. She was in the way. It was time to go home.

Chapter Eighteen

Tonight sucked. Another murdered hooker, from what APD dispatch relayed. An elderly couple out for their evening walk found her on the walkway behind the Chinquapin Park Rec Center. Same MO. Same bloody scene. APD cordoned off the area.

Tripp's gut had churned enough while he and Jameson geared up in The TEAM armory before charging to the scene. Tucker had left without them, the ass. He was already on-site, asking terse, pertinent questions, gathering names, times, and details. A man in an ankle-length winter coat, had to be APD's crime photographer, snapped photos from all angles of the scene, the shadowy surroundings, even the boisterous onlookers. Some gawkers videoed him and Jameson as they walked to the death scene. Others had their backs to it so they could capture selfies, 'live-on camera.' Which, no doubt, would be on YouTube within minutes.

Disgusted to the depths of his warrior's soul at the crass antics, Tripp headed for the heart of the scene, to the poor woman who'd been murdered. He'd never understand this new generation. Refused to try.

"Steady," Jameson murmured, toggling his white cane back and forth on the lawn ahead, his chin up and his nose in the air. It was as if he could scent where they needed to go. Without Tripp saying anything, Jameson had zeroed in on the location of their target, inadvertently tapping Beau's leg when he passed by.

"Hey, guys," Beau muttered when he looked up and saw them. "It's bad. Real bad. This one's not much older than us."

Most hookers these days weren't. Seemed as if women started working the streets younger every year.

"We've seen *real bad* before," Tripp replied, elbowing his way to where Tucker now stood over the vic with his hands on his hips. Damn, he was an arrogant son of a bitch.

The big guy glared at Jameson when he and Tripp cleared the police tape, and that pissed Tripp off. Tucker Chase might be an FBI director at the Bureau. He might run the only FBI psychic team. But Jameson was a TEAM agent, damn it. That made him a brother, and brothers stood together. Tucker could take his high and mighty SEAL attitude and shove it where the sun didn't shine.

Reaching his free hand out, Jameson grabbed Tripp's elbow, which was annoying, but okay. Tripp got it. The blind guy needed help getting through the crowd of APD officers, detectives, and EMTs, as well as the over-active photographer.

"Coming through," Tripp announced, until he and Jameson were finally within gagging distance.

Beau was spot-on. Gruesome was too generous a word. The woman lay face up. She'd been brutally beaten. Her face was hamburger. Her throat had been cut, and there was so much blood on the grass under her. Beside her. Everywhere. For the most part, she was still dressed, but her tiny leather skirt was torn. Oddly, four EMTs, two on each side of her, were working furiously to save her.

Tripp couldn't believe it. "She's alive?"

"Yes," Tucker replied grimly. "The old guy interrupted our killer in the act. He's a Vietnam vet. Scared him off with his Smith and Wesson. His wife called 9-1-1 while he started first-aid. If not for them, this vic would be on her way to King Street Junction."

Tripp glanced sideways at the older couple, separated now from each other. Both were silver-haired, each talking with different officers. Tripp pegged them both close to seventy years old, but they looked spry and bright-eyed. That was good. They'd be credible witnesses.

"She's fighting to live," Jameson murmured, his dark glasses focused downward as if he could see and hear the victim. "Do we know her name?"

Tucker shook his head. "These gals don't carry more than a shittin' tiny purse big enough to hold a couple prepackaged baby wipes, maybe a few bills. Lipstick. Stupid shit like that. But no ID."

"Did our Good Samaritan get a good look at the killer? Are we sure it's the same guy?" Jameson asked.

"For hell's sake, look at the vic's throat, you moron. What do you think?"

Tripp didn't answer, but Jameson couldn't see to *look at the vic's throat*, damn it. And Tucker knew that. He needed to back off.

"Tell me what you see, Tripp," Jameson said evenly. "Lend me your eyes. What are we looking at?"

"Blood," Tripp replied as he crouched alongside one of the EMTs. Jameson crouched with him, then hooked a hand over his shoulder. "Adult female. Weight, maybe a hundred pounds. Five feet tall. Throat's been cut. Fingernails are bloody and broken. Looks like she fought back." Except… "No…" breathed out of Tripp. "It can't be. No-no-no!"

He shrugged Jameson's hand off, then batted it away when Jameson couldn't leave well enough alone and grabbed his jacket sleeve. The few fingernails not broken on this vic were painted a garish, flat black—Trish's signature shade. The tarnished pewter ring in the shape of a coiled snake with green glass eyes on her right hand cinched what he didn't want to believe. Middle finger. Her continual fuck-off to him. To her mom. To the world.

"Shit, no, no, no," he hissed, as the universe narrowed down to the ravaged woman bleeding into the ground in front of him. "It can't be her. Shit, damn, and son of a bitch! No!"

But it *was* her. His obnoxious twin. Trish McClane.

Tripp leaned forward, desperate to cradle what was left of his sister, to protect her from the gawkers and reporters. From every gawddamned one! No one had a right to—

Jameson caught him. Held him tight. Held him back. "I've got you, brother," he growled, his voice hard, and his hand on Tripp's shoulder so damned steady.

"Get the fuck off me, Tenney!" Tripp roared, elbowing Jameson hard in his ribs, ready to fight to protect what little he had left of his one and only sister. His twin, for God's sake! "You're not my brother. Can't you see? That's my sister, gawddamnit! Tripp and Trish, that's us. That's who we are. Were! We were born minutes apart and…and…" He forgot what he'd needed to say. Of course Jameson couldn't see!

"I know, I know," Jameson replied gently, his head bowed, but his fingers still holding on. "You can't touch her, Tripp. Not yet. We have to follow protocol, or we'll never catch the man who did this to her. Let the EMTs and police do their job first, then—"

"But it's…it's her. Can't you see?" He couldn't help asking that stupid question! "I can't just leave my sister here, Jameson. Not like this." He couldn't think straight. God, his mom! This would kill her. How could he face her, tell her that Trish had been attacked and nearly killed? That she might still die? It'd been hard enough that she'd disappeared like she had, that she'd ever thought hooking was smart or sexy or worth the cash she made from selling her body. Her soul!

"I'm not going anywhere, Tripp," Jameson said as firmly as ever. "I might not be your flesh-and-blood brother, but I've got you."

He needed to shut the fuck up! "You've got nothing," Tripp roared, pissed that this guy kept saying his name like he knew anything about him or his sister. Like they were friends. They weren't! "You can't even see her! What do you know?!"

"I know death is a cheating, motherfuckin' bitch with no heart," Jameson murmured, his voice so low Tripp had to shut up to hear him. "It doesn't ask permission, and it doesn't care who it takes or how. It just takes and takes and—"

Tripp whirled on his knee, cocked his fist back, ready to knock the shit out of Jameson's sanctimonious big mouth. And he would have. Could have easily pounded the blind guy, who'd just hit the nail in his heart on its gawddamned head, until—Tripp caught the sparkle welling behind the bottom rim of Jameson's dark glasses.

Tripp's bluff and bluster evaporated into the cold, thin air. *Shit.* This awful scene had impacted more than just him. It was killing Jameson, too. For the first time since he'd hired on with The TEAM, Tripp liked the mild-mannered guy.

Lowering his fist, Tripp leaned back on his butt, and sucked in a deep breath. Swallowed. Looked at the bloodied body of the once-upon-a-time innocent little girl he might never get to argue with, tease, hug, or worry about again.

Gawddamn her. Why couldn't Trish have made different choices?

Watching the medics work on her was hard on his heart. They'd stuck two IVs into each arm, one saline solution, the other blood. Which meant the trauma to her throat was so critical that a local doctor was on duty, right here, working alongside the EMTs to save her life, maybe prepping her to be life-flighted to the nearest trauma ward. Most EMTs didn't stock blood. It was too hard to store and had a short shelf life. But the guys and gals that flew Air Med did. They were affiliated with specific hospitals and saw more trauma. The truth hit Tripp like a knock-out punch. Trish might not make it this time.

God, he needed a miracle.

He wiped away the bitter tears he hadn't realized were dripping down his cheeks and off his chin. Looking closer, it registered how profound Jameson's grief was. His cheeks were wet, and that made Tripp think of his poor mom. Andy had a soft heart. But mostly, Tripp wished it was him lying on the grass instead of Trish. Because that was how Andy would take this death. She'd be losing her baby girl, and somehow, Tripp thought that would hurt his mom worse than her losing him. He'd been a warrior. She'd been prepared to lose him. But Trish? God, Andy had spent nearly all these past years trying to save Trish.

"Come on," Jameson urged gently, his arm now crooked around Tripp's neck, his elbow under Tripp's chin. Not strangling or squeezing, just blocking him from moving further into the horrific scene and taking over. Just holding him back. Like the brother Tripp never had. Like the father he'd never known. Funny how little things, like why his dad had died young, mattered when the world fell apart.

"The last thing I told her was I was working, I was busy. I didn't have time for her," he confessed through blurry eyes. Somehow, knowing Jameson couldn't see his meltdown helped. He'd said that years ago. Hadn't heard a word from Trish since the day Ikram was murdered. What a fucked-up world, that murder and blood connected people, families, and days like it did.

"She knows you love her," Jameson whispered. "Focus on that. Think of the good times you two had together. That's what'll get you through the next couple days."

Tucker Chase was crouched beside them by then, his fingertips stuck into the ground for balance, the other hand flat against Tripp's sweaty shoulder. "Your sister?" he asked kindly.

"Yeah," Tripp choked. His heart pounded so hard, he could barely cough the word out. "Trish McClane. My twin. She took off from Mom's house a week ago. Maybe just five days. Mom and me looked everywhere for her. Talked to everyone who might've seen her, who might've known her. I'd just come back from Seattle and..." Tripp bowed his head at the tragedy in his life and let his tears fall. He had no pride. "My poor damned mom."

"I'll go with you to tell her." The gentleness in Jameson's voice was heartbreaking.

Tripp stared at the dew-laden carpet of green that stretched from beneath his knees all the way to the blood bath beneath Trish, wishing miracles were real. That she'd flip him the bird with that reptilian ringed finger. That she'd wake up cursing, calling him profane names, telling him to fuck-off, to mind his business. That she'd—

God, that she'd just keep breathing.

Out of nowhere, Alex Stewart was there kneeling with him. Jameson, Tucker, Mark and Beau were standing over him. Connor stood nearby with his wife Izza, both TEAM agents. Some other guys and gals Tripp didn't yet know were there too, but he could tell they were former military. He was surrounded by a wall of warriors, not able to see his twin when the EMTs transferred Trish to their gurney. Nor when they loaded her in through the gate of the waiting ambulance, or when they roared away, lights flashing, siren screaming… just like his heart.

"I'll need information," Tucker said quietly. "Whatever you can tell me about your sister and when you last saw her. Who she worked with. Her girlfriends. Her daddy. Her madam. Details like that. Anything you can think of. Whenever you're ready, Tripp. Tomorrow morning'll be fine."

"To be honest," Tripp declared hoarsely, "I haven't seen her in years. We had a falling out when I was deployed to Afghanistan. I was in the middle of a mission, and she… and she…" Was on an entirely different mission, one fueled by anger and self-hatred, one that just might've gotten her killed. Tripp stopped talking. That his sister had sold her body for drugs, juice, or fuck, whatever, said it all.

"No worries," Tucker said calmly. "You think of anything, give me a call."

The crime scene photographer had moved closer into the death scene, still taking pictures of what little was left. When he bent over and snapped a close-up of the sticky, bloody grass where Trish had lain, Tripp lost it. Breaking out of Jameson's hold, he bounced off the ground and onto his feet, fighting mad that sacred ground could be violated so quickly, so gawddamned easily!

"Get the hell out of here! You stinkin' ghoul! She's a human being. She deserves to be treated with respect and dignity!"

The guy straightened, lowered his camera, and stared straight at Tripp. "You're her brother?"

"Yes, and I'll kick your dumb ass if you—"

"Right on!" some fool from the idiot gallery yelled over the top of Tripp. "You tell him, buddy! Kick that guy's ass! Go on, you can do it! Punch him out. Break his gear! Bust him up!"

Damned if the vapid audience gawking with that loud-mouthed asshat didn't clap, whistle, boo, and cheer for a fight. A slew of other inane, boisterous arguments and opinions on the subject roared to life. God, people were dumb. Tripp had almost forgotten they were there.

Another brave asshole shouted to the photographer, "Don't just stand there and take it like a pussy. Fight back! She was a worthless whore! A slut! She deserved what she got!"

Tripp's pistol sprang to his hand. These disrespectful sons of bitches needed to be taught a lesson. But, just as quickly as he drew his weapon, he landed flat on his back, the wind knocked out of him, not a dozen feet from where Trish had lain. Jameson had taken him down with a full body slam, locked a forearm across his neck, this time with the intent to choke him.

Someone else wrestled the weapon out of Tripp's hand. Shit. That was Alex. Tripp never had a chance to aim, much less shoot one of those sons of bitches. Not that he would've. But he wanted to. Despite everything she'd done, Trish deserved someone in her corner here at the end, and that person was him, gawddamnit! She could like him or not, he was her brother, by hell, and he would defend her to the death.

"Focus, Tripp. Think, damn it," Jameson growled down at him, those dark glasses somehow still in place. "A brother's first job is not to waste time on losers with big mouths and little brains, which is precisely what those people are. A brother's first and only job is to track his sister's killer. Hold it together. Trish is this bastard's first mistake. She survived. She's going to live. Nothing helps a murder investigation better than a credible witness."

"Are you sure she's gonna live? Did you see her?" Shit, Tripp kept talking like Jameson had eyes that worked. How the fuck could he know anything?!

"No, I can't see her, but you can. You saw. She's in the best possible hands, isn't she?"

"Yes, but... It's just that..." Trish had been hurt so horribly. There was so much blood.

Tripp choked, glaring up at the smart guy behind those dark, round lenses. Jameson looked a lot meaner up close. "Are you sure? She's gonna live?"

"With a brother like you in her corner, hell yeah."

God, he needed Jameson to be right. To really know more than he did right then. "But someone needs to pay," Tripp told his new friend through the tears welled in his eyes. "You have to help me. I have to make sure the guy who did this dies."

"I get that, buddy. Let's make sure the right bastard pays, though. Everything else here is just noise. It's hot air and a sickening sign of our times. Let it go. The only one who matters from here on out is your sister and us finding the chicken shit that tried to kill her. Tried, Tripp. Tried and failed. Copy that?"

"Yeah, yeah…" God, he was glad Jameson was there. Tripp grabbed hold of his buddy's wrist. "I get it. I do. Copy."

"Then let's get your mother. She needs to be with her daughter. She needs you too, man."

"Yeah. Mom. My mom. Damn…" Tripp turned back to the crime scene, blinking hard, hating himself for not being there when Trish needed him most. Him, one of the Army's best snipers. Alexandria's gawddamned vigilante!

"Do we know where they took her?" Jameson asked Alex.

"Alexandria Surgical Center. It's not far from here. I'll drive."

"Need to swing by Tripp's mother's place first. She'll need a ride."

"Copy that. Let's go."

Tripp blinked, wishing he could've seen Trish before the medics took her away, wishing he could see her now. But it was too hard to see through his tears.

Chapter Nineteen

Ashley was on her way home. Why not? She knew Alexandria like the back of her hand, and Tripp was right. Their apartment complex wasn't far from his office at all. In fact, it was just a few blocks to the north, maybe ten at the most, and the evening was perfect for walking. What did she have to lose?

From the metro station in the west to the Potomac toward the east, King Street was a lovely tourist area, one of her favorite haunts during the day. Crossing Diagonal Road to King Street Gardens Park, she inhaled a deep breath of the fresh evening air. She'd almost forgotten how autumn in Virginia brought warm, sunny days that ended in crisp, cool nights. It was a jacket weather kind of night. There were clouds hovering low in the sky.

The chance of an early snow spiked excitement in her blood. A good, short walk would keep her warm. There were plenty of people on King Street. She hurried out of the shadows of the quaint little park to join them. There was nothing to worry about. Not anymore.

Heading east took her past the Hyatt Hotel on her left, Hampton Inn on her right. Then a wealth of bookstores, antique shops, and the ever-constant big box stores that had slowly encroached on Alexandria's quaint persona. She couldn't imagine living anywhere else. People were friendly here, and the street was always filled with the lovely aromas of Indian curry, Spanish cumin, the cold Potomac River, and seafood—all her favorites.

As she passed a string of professional offices, a hair salon, and another antique shop, Ashley set a measured but quick pace for herself. Fall used to be her favorite time of year, and she'd always enjoyed walking, catching glimpses of other people's lives and celebrations through their front room picture windows. Thanksgiving and Christmas were the best times to take long strolls. People had families over then, and sometimes, an observant walker might catch a glimpse of turkey dinners and festive tables covered with feasts, or of Christmas trees and happy kids. She loved spying from the sidewalks of her travels, on families who obviously loved each other. Those homes had always seemed to glow more golden at those times of year. For the last couple years, she'd missed these walks and that glow. It was time to get her life back to normal.

She paused at the corner of King and Patrick. Murphy's Grand Irish Pub lay three blocks east. They had the best cinnamon bread pudding in the world. She would know. That and their Irish coffee were a treat she'd given herself after work. But only during daylight hours when it was safe. Which was why she was out walking by herself after her narrow escape Friday. There were still plenty of people around.

Days were getting quite a bit shorter now, and the sun had set. Still, it was a beautiful night, and her apartment was a mere seven blocks North, then three East. She could do this. Easy.

Without the cumbersome messenger bag flapping against her thigh, she turned northward, feeling lighter. Freer, if that was even a word. Her heart started skipping, and she was a girl again, carefree, with a boyfriend. Well, at least with a very handsome neighbor. A few blocks farther down, she hugged herself and spun a silly circle in the middle of the leaf-strewn sidewalk.

Ashley laughed. Out loud. The thick, gnarled branches of the giant maple tree in the yard she was passing, had spread a magic carpet of burnished red, orange, and yellow leaves for her. On nights like this, it was easy to believe the world was safe and perfect and good.

She wondered about that meeting she'd almost had with Tripp and Jameson. What was it about? They'd all but dragged her into that conference room. She'd reconnect with Tripp first thing tomorrow morning, after she checked on Mrs. Harrison. It seemed more respectful addressing her formally instead of calling her Barbara. But darn, it'd been such a busy day, she hadn't thought to ask for Tripp's cell number. Come to think of it, she hadn't given her numbers to Mrs. Harrison, either.

A tiny breath of autumn's chill breathed over the bare skin on the front of her neck. She brushed it off, not going to let anything ruin this walk home. She'd left her bag at Tripp's place. No matter. He'd bring it over once he finished today. Unfortunately, her cell phone was also in that bag. Her mace. That thought wiped the smile off her face. She had no way to phone for help or protect herself. Not like that mace had helped Friday night, but that vulnerability rattled her best intentions. Maybe it was time to step up the pace and do a little speed-walking.

Fortunately, her keycard and her apartment key were safe in her rear pocket. All she had to do when she got to the complex, was bump her butt to the scanner, which would scan her keycard, and she'd be inside and safe, almost home-free. Not that she was worried. She wasn't. It was just time to get off the street.

As if the universe conspired against her, a breeze kicked up more leaves as it whined through the bare branches overhead. The friendly night turned spooky. It started to sprinkle. Then rain. Then downpour. The hoody Tripp offered sure would've come in handy.

Shivering, Ashley hurried. If she'd really been smart, she would've also kept a credit card in her rear pocket; she could've called a taxi then. Not that she would have, not with her phobia about men. Unknown men. Dangerous men. But she could have, and that was all the positive reinforcement she needed to lengthen her stride.

In minutes, the rain turned Ashley's hair into slick, wet ribbons that clung to her back and forehead. Her clothes were soaked and she was cold. Ashley swiped her dripping bangs out of her eyes.

The street was darker the farther she walked from the bright business lights of King Street, through more residential porch and street lamps. Her imagination turned paranoid. Every passing car could hold a potential kidnapper. Worse, a murderer. Each house turned into a drug hang-out. Each barking dog, a vicious Rottweiler, or a crazed, slathering Pitbull, all champing at the end of their tire chains to take her down. To drag her into the bushes. To hurt her…

Like *he* had.

The flashback blew through Ashley's thin veil of confidence like a tornado whipped through clothes on the line.

Two years ago. Almost to the day. He'd come to install a new thermostat, or so he'd said. She'd been in her second year at the local community college, a single woman living alone in a refurbished home-turned-apartment.

It was the affordability of the small, older home, and attractiveness of the clay-tiled roof and creamy stucco walls, that had cinched the deal for her. The house itself was immaculate; boasted two up, two down. Her studio apartment had been at the rear of the second level, overlooking the back lawn turned into a parking lot. She could've seen the college dorms from her bedroom window, if she'd stood on a stool. Her only other window had faced the side of the neighboring house. Not much to see there.

She'd been between roommates. Her first mistake...

She'd known the instant he'd shut the door behind him and stood staring at her without saying anything that he'd lied. It was in the way he'd spread his legs and crossed his arms over his narrow chest, blocking her exit. The way his bag of tools dropped to the floor, like he'd never needed them. Because he didn't. They were just props. His way in.

He wasn't bad-looking, but neither was he particularly good-looking. Ordinary. Nondescript. Short. Light-brown hair combed straight back. No facial hair, acne, piercings, scars, glasses, or visible tattoos. Khaki shirt and matching pants. Nothing in his appearance labeled him cruel or frightening. If anything, he was the definition of bland, two short sticks on a chunk of walking oatmeal.

His eyes were what she remembered. They were the lightest gray, almost bluish silver, like two puffs of frozen breath in winter. Like cigarette smoke, the promise of death when inhaled. Lethal, if it touched you.

Ashley had run to her kitchen and grabbed her one and only steak knife from the dish strainer beside the sink. He was on her by then, had one hard arm crooked around her neck and a fist full of her hair. He'd jerked her back against his front and slapped the knife out of her hand. She'd sucked in a panicked breath to scream. But he'd clamped a sweaty hand over her mouth, rubbed his nose into her cheek, and asked the words that haunted her, "Wanna play, little girl?"

"No!" she told her nightmare, fighting to keep him out of her head. "I didn't want to play then. I don't want to play now." Out of habit, her right hand skimmed her thigh, missing her messenger bag. Swallowing hard, she began to run. Her simple black walking shoes slipped on the soggy, wet leaves that, just moments ago, had made the night beautiful. She nearly fell but spread her arms in time and righted herself.

The memory rolled on.

He'd shoved her to the floor and punched her when she'd cried out. He'd caged her under his smelly, unwashed body, locked between his knees, on the floor beside her daybed. He'd just sliced the buttons off her shirt and used her knife to do that. He'd straddled her hips, had spread her shirt open, drooling down on her like a pig. She'd been hysterical and crying, staring up into those ghostly, unfeeling eyes, her arms trapped at her sides. He'd licked his lips. Then reached behind his back and produced a long thin blade. A fillet knife.

Ashley had freaked. She'd managed one short squawk before her intruder slammed his dirty, sweaty hand over her mouth again. He forced her chin up and pressed the knife into the soft skin under her jaw. "Bet you wanna play with me now," he'd told her, his pupils bigger and blacker. "But you're like the others, dirty and proud of it. Skanks who think you can rule the world."

That was when Mac, the real maintenance man, had pounded at her front door and called out, "Hey, Ashley! It's me, Mac. I'm here to replace your thermostat like we planned. Just finished old man Toone's. You're gonna like it. It's easy to program. Even I can do it, and it comes with a remote."

Her attacker had glanced over his shoulder at the door, momentarily distracted. Desperately, carefully, she'd snaked one arm up from her side.

The creep turned back to her and hissed, "Mac likes you and you like him. You'll play with him, but not me."

She'd blinked hard then, trying to recall if she'd ever seen this guy before. Had they ever met?

Mac knocked again. Louder. "Open up, young lady. Time's a-wasting!"

Her killer was antsy by then. "Make one sound and I'll kill your fuck buddy!"

Frightened out of her mind, Ashley had grabbed his free hand and bit his thumb. Hard! As long as she could stand the dirty thing inside her mouth. Until he'd slammed his other fist into her forehead, and she'd thought her brain exploded.

"You can't get away from me," he'd hissed. Like the sick dog he was, he'd trapped her arm again, then dropped his nose into the corner of her neck where it joined her shoulder. He'd stuck the flat of his nasty tongue on her skin and licked a long, wet trail up her neck, onto her cheek, and into her hair.

She'd been dizzy, sure she was going to die. Closing her eyes, she'd cringed under the vile assault, too afraid of the knife to call out to Mac or bite again or—do anything. He'd sniffed her, licked her, his other hand still plastered over her mouth, and her heart climbing up her throat.

By then, he'd cut her, up high, under her chin. He'd hit her again. Punched her face. Her mouth, nose, and neck were bleeding. But Mac's arrival must've spooked him. That was the only way she could explain why he'd suddenly jumped to his feet, grabbed his bag, and ran out her front door.

By then, Mac was gone. So was the creep. He'd even taken his fake tool bag.

Ashley had locked herself in, then went to her bathroom and wrapped a towel around her neck. Her throat hadn't been cut through, just sliced deep enough to bleed. Later, when she'd stopped shaking, she'd called a cab and went to the free clinic to get stitches. The doctor there had wanted her to go to the police, but she'd refused. She'd been too scared. Besides, the assault was her fault. She hadn't locked her door.

That was when she'd moved to her current apartment and invested in an expensive deadbolt.

Were those footsteps behind her? Was someone following her? Was it—*him*?

Ashley didn't dare turn around to look.

"God, no," she scolded herself, her breath a frozen stream of vapor that shone white against the dark night. The vapor seemed to glow tonight, probably because she was sweating and scared. "I'm not scared," she lied to herself. Why admit it and make matters worse? Denial could be a darned strong friend to have in your corner when memories of past attacks whispered too close for comfort.

Ashley threw her heart into making it the last two blocks to her apartment. All she had to do was get inside the lobby, and she'd be safe.

Run, run, run, her paranoia prompted.

"I am," she answered back, her elbows cocked at her sides, her feet pounding the wet, treacherous sidewalk like machined pistons. Home. She was going home where she could lock her door and turn on her music and drown herself in a big mug of hot chocolate. Where she'd be safe. While she shivered and shook until every last wave of panic subsided. Until she knew for certain her trustworthy deadbolt was latched, her windows were blocked and locked, and that she could keep everyone out!

"I can make it," she promised as the deadly chill of the latest attempt on her life invaded her lungs with terror. Her sudden burst of frantic energy attacked her side with sharp clenching pain. Copper lifted up the back of her throat. But that was what running for your life did to a person. These pains were nothing compared to—

Run!

In panic, she turned her thighs into pumping machines of speed and fury and pounded the wet pavement home. After Friday night, she'd sworn she'd never be vulnerable again. Yet, here she was. Alone. At night. In the rain. Without her phone or her mace. She should've stayed at Tripp's office like he'd asked. She wished she had.

The oddest sensation that someone was watching her, shivered up her spine like an icky, sticky spider. There was no way she could run faster. She'd already given her all. All she could do was endure to the end of this miserable rainy night, hit that lobby door, and get inside!

At last. Ashley turned the corner. Her apartment was just three blocks away. But she was out of air, could barely suck in a breath. And she was dizzy. She ground to a cold, sweaty stop at the corner, put her palms to her knees, and risked a quick glance behind her.

A dark vehicle with its headlights off was inching along the curb on her side of the street. A stocky man in a long gray trench coat was walking on the other side. Both were heading in her direction. That was all she needed to see.

Ashley sprang headlong into the hardest run of her life. Only three blocks left. She could do it. Why had she ever thought she was brave enough to walk home alone? Never again!

Chapter Twenty

Ah, look at her run. Good form. Long legs. Great stamina. She must've taken track sometime during her miserably short life. Well, good for her. This one was already wet. She was going to be so much fun. And to think he'd followed that other skank when he should've stayed the course and tracked this one.

Lesson learned. Let Ashley Cox think she was safely home. That's when he'd strike and strike hard. Wouldn't she be surprised to see him again? Might do things to her he hadn't done with the others. Might let her linger while he… played.

Tonight had been unusually full of coincidences. First, running into that other slut. Then, discovering the slut's brother was the same hero who'd captured Ashley's attention Friday night. There was a certain pleasure in knowing he'd hurt that alleged hero as deeply as he had. Then… making it back to that cruel, cold bench just in time to see Ashley Cox venture into the dark all by herself. That had been the biggest coincidence of the night. He'd had to drive like a bat out of Hell to get back to King Street in time, but he'd made it. Which told him that destiny ruled nights like this one, else the stars wouldn't have lined up as precisely as they had.

It wouldn't take long now.

While he followed his panicked prey, he ran his tongue over his bottom lip in anticipation, imagining all the ways he would make her scream. Mmmm, mmmm, yes. He adored the way she'd cried and whimpered the last time. She'd been shocked when he'd cut her. But pitiful noises were not what he needed. He was more into the scorching adrenaline rush coursing through his blood when a woman screamed. After all the trouble this woman had caused him, he was due the small satisfaction of playing outside the box, so to speak. He could keep her for days. Maybe even make her come while he bled her dry. Yes, that's precisely what he would do.

But for now…

He needed somewhere to accommodate the noise this sneaky bitch would make. The blood. Because there would be screaming and bleeding. Crying. Pleading. Some place nearby, close and convenient, would be perfect. Something close to the river would be better. Rivers made body disposal so much easier.

Look at that. She was headed to the multi-unit apartment complex ahead, the one surrounded with pine trees. Thousands of tiny white lights decorated those trees, but there were also shadows where a man could hide. Okay, good. Let her get inside. No need to hurry the inevitable.

Silly girl. Ashley Cox wouldn't escape this time. He'd make sure of it. Everything he needed to get the job done, he now carried with him. On fortuitous nights like this, his trench coat might make him look like a secret agent. In fact, he knew it did. He'd seen the way people looked at him with deference when he wore it. They wanted to be him. They were envious. Maybe even intimidated.

Too bad for them. It was his disguise, and if they came too close, they'd quickly find out that its many loops and hidden pockets hid a wealth of not-so-nice surprises.

He stopped in front of the double glass doors his prey had just scampered through. Interesting. Entry required some kind of access card, which he didn't have. That might be a problem.

The informative yellow plastic tripod standing inside the door declared the lobby elevator wasn't working. Which meant Ashley Cox was right then running up flights of stairs to her apartment. Probably sweating. Breathing hard. He closed his eyes at the thought of all that luscious panic wasted. Imagining the sweet sounds of her panting, crying, or screaming—he wasn't choosy—he closed his eyes and recalled the way she'd smelled the last time he'd had her. Almost had her.

Some flowery scent, sweet and rich, mingled with the natural sweeter scent of fear. What. A. Rush. *A man could live forever on those vivid, sensual memories. The smell of a woman's sweaty body when she fought back was a powerful aphrodisiac. If he worked her just right, it was enough to unman him. But when she bled and cried and couldn't get away no matter how hard she tried… He was a real man then. A supercharged superhero. If people only knew the power that came with killing.*

Hmmm. Wonder which floor she lived on. Which room?

As luck would have it—and luck was a large part of everything he did—an ordinary man in coveralls entered through the door marked Do Not Enter *at the far side of the lobby.*

He rapped on the plate glass window to get the unlucky guy's attention.

"Can I help you?" the idiot asked through the lobby door he'd just—luckily—opened.

"Why yes, as a matter of fact, you can," he replied as he stepped inside the lobby. *"I just moved to Virginia, and I'm in the market for an apartment. Is there a very long waiting list here? Or are there any apartments available now? May I take a look around?"* It never hurt to ask.

"Sorry, man, but this is a secure complex. You can't just come into these buildings and look around. See that number over there?" The foolish man pointed at the cardstock taped to the door. *"Call it and talk to the manager. He'll know if anything's available. Not my job."*

He glanced quickly at the posted notice before he swung back around and stuck a finely-honed shiv into the guy's gut. Like the professional he was, he rammed it higher under the unlucky guy's ribs, tearing the flesh, muscle, and organs in between. Making sure the guy didn't suffer now that he was dying. That wouldn't be fair.

"Secure, huh," he growled in disdain, his gloved hand now out of the body, wet and dripping. *"We'll see about that."* Because it was almost time to play again, and nothing would get between him and Ashley Cox.

Chapter Twenty-One

Tripp called Mother's number from the Surgical Center. The moment she answered, he asked, "Could you please arrange for someone to drive Ashley home, or call her a cab? I need to stay with my mom. I'm not going to make it back for a while."

"She already left. I heard about your sister. Is that where you are now, at the hospital? How's she doing?"

"Yes, we're at the Alexandria Surgical Center." He held off sharing anything more personal with someone who didn't seem to care. "What do you mean, Ashley left? I told her to stay put until I got back."

"Guess she doesn't think you're her boss. What else do you need?"

Tripp ran a hand over his face, wondering how Mother could sound so cold at a time like this. "Never mind. I'll find her myself."

He disconnected the call, afraid he'd say something he'd regret. And worried. He didn't have a way to contact Ashley. She'd left her purse at his place. At the time, he'd thought that meant she'd trusted him. But wherever she was now, she didn't have her phone or her can of mace.

Quickly, he thumb-dialed Mrs. Harrison and asked her to check on Ashley for him. He was fairly sure they hadn't exchanged phone numbers yet. Could she please knock on

Ashley's door, then call him back and let him know she was safe?

"Sure, but what's going on? Where are you?"

"I'm at the hospital. My sister's in emergency surgery, and I can't get away."

"Oh, no, I hope it's nothing. It wasn't drugs this time, was it?" Mrs. Harrison knew about Trish.

"Not this time." He went for distraction instead of admitting the horrid truth. "Please hurry. Call back as soon as you can. I'll be waiting."

"I most certainly will."

The contrast struck him hard. Here he was asking a favor from a woman who'd suffered her own personal loss today, yet who was on her cheerful way to do him a favor. All because his selfish sister had continually put herself in harm's way, for the fun, the thrill of it. It was hard not to want to wring Trish's neck, while, at the same time, he desperately needed her to live.

Like he had since they'd arrived at the scene of her assault, Jameson was sticking close on his left. Alex, Mark, Tucker, Beau, and several other TEAM agents were sitting with him in the main waiting room outside surgery. His mother sat worrying her rosary beads at his right.

"That girl's going to be the death of us both, Tripp." Andy didn't mince words, and she didn't waste time on tears or feminine dramatics. She'd been down this same road too many times. After a while, a person, even a mother, grew numb to other people's death spirals. Even their daughter's.

"She sure ran into the wrong john this time." Just once, Tripp wished his mother would've said no, and let him handle the mess. But moms never did what was best for them. They always showed up when their kids needed them, and they always got their hearts broken when they did.

The longer Tripp sat, the more TEAM agents showed up. After several long hours waiting for news from the surgeon, the only agents missing were those from the Seattle office, the ones on assignment, and The TEAM task force against human trafficking, now somewhere in the Far East. Zack and Beau should've been with them, but they'd stayed stateside to assist Mother. Tripp wondered if they got hazard pay for that.

But mostly, he watched the large, closed double doors at the end of the hall that declared, **Do Not Enter**. The ones hospital personnel in gray scrubs ignored.

His poor mom. She'd already been through so many different levels of Hell with Trish. Searching the length of the East Coast for the know-it-all, runaway teenager after they'd first moved. Faithfully reporting her missing daughter to APD every time Trish took off. Problem was, it'd happened so often that Andy knew most local police officers by name these days. She even took homemade cookies to the local precincts because she knew how hard they'd tried to locate Trish, and how hard their job was.

Then there were the various detox and rehab centers that had cheerfully taken every last cent of Andy's meager savings, promised the moon, but in the end, couldn't contain Trish's demons any better than her mother could. Add to that all the halfway houses, back alleys, bars, and drug houses Andy and Tripp had searched. The filthy streets and dirty park benches. The worst dives across the Potomac River...

Yet Andrea had never given up. Tripp wished she would.

He looked down between his boots at the generic, easily-washed and disinfected tiled-floor. He'd given up on Trish long ago. In Idaho. She'd been an embarrassment then. Still was. Yet here he was… God, he was just as bad as his mother.

Andy patted his clenched hand on his thigh. "My turn to get coffee. Would you like a breakfast biscuit or two?"

"No, Mom. Stay put. Let me do that for you," he told her, squeezing her slender hand in return, wishing he could save her from whatever prognosis still lay ahead. It couldn't be good, not with all the blood Trish had lost.

"Nonsense. I need the walk. It'll do me good. Sitting here and worrying is eating me alive. You stay here with your friends. The cafeteria's not far. I won't be but a minute."

Alex sprang to her side, his arm cocked for her to take. "May I accompany you, Mrs. McClane?"

She smiled tiredly up at him but accepted his assist. "Thank you, yes. It's not a long walk, Mr. Stewart, but this is a big place. I may need help finding my way back."

"That's what I'm here for, ma'am," he replied respectfully.

"Your friends are too kind," she told Tripp before she walked into the hall with his boss.

Tripp turned his head and asked Jameson quietly, so no one else would hear, "You ever wonder that if you'd died, maybe someone else would've lived? Would've wanted to live? You know, because the universe is all about balance, and at some cosmic level, your death, no matter how it came down, might turn a wayward person around? Might make them think? Make them care less about themselves and more about others? What they put others through? Make them consider doing something decent with their lives for a change?"

Tripp didn't expect an answer. His question was more rhetorical and desperate, than earnest. Truth was that Trish had been born selfish, while he'd stepped up and had always taken care of his mom after his dad had died. Even as a little boy, he'd been the responsible half of the pair. Trish had been the selfish princess with a rhinestone tiara stuck up her entitled ass.

Jameson took a long, slow sip of the bad hospital coffee left in the paper cup in his hand. He'd been quiet since they'd arrived after the ambulance. Had only asked Tripp what he'd needed when they'd sat down together and began this vigil. But the guy seemed to have his life figured out. Tripp needed some of that inner calm.

Jameson shifted the cup to his left hand and ran a finger under the lower rim of his dark glasses. "When I first lost my sight, yes. I wondered why them and not me. I lost two good friends in that firefight, but I've had a longer time to deal with my survivor's guilt than you. I know now that mess was the perfect trifecta designed by ISIL to kill American soldiers. It took me a while to realize that, in order to move on, I had to put the blame where it belonged. Saving those little boys' lives was not a mistake. My buddies and I made the best moral decision that day. We chose the high road, Tripp, something I strive to do every day. In a way, the universe does balance. It took two Navy SEALs, sure, but it left two children alive and…" He set the cup on the table beside him. "We do the best we can, when we can. Do you think sacrificing yourself when you were in Afghanistan would've somehow saved your sister from making bad choices now? Is that what you're asking?"

"Maybe." Tripp dropped his chin and went back to counting the tiny black flakes in the square tile between his boots. He'd come up with twenty-six each of the last five times. An even number. Like thirteen sets of twins. That had to mean something. He just didn't know what.

He'd never understood why Trish had acted out as a teen. Why she'd changed so drastically when she'd turned fifteen. He'd been a football jock, a local hero in a way, even back then. Engrossed in the game, the comradery and the plays, basking in the adulation, he'd never missed a single game or a minute of practice. Hadn't dared. Playing football and running drills with his coach and his team had been his out, his way of dealing with missing the father he'd never known. Mom still loved Boone McClane, said she always would. That everything would've been better if he'd lived. But he hadn't. A weak heart claimed him before his twin babies turned two. Except for the photos Andy still displayed around her house, Tripp didn't remember a thing about his dad.

But in their sophomore year, Trish had flipped a switch and went from being his best friend, to being the most popular girl in high school—for all the wrong reasons. At fifteen, they'd already been headed in opposite directions. She'd cut him out of her life, and after too many screaming rants against Andy, he'd cut Trish out of his. Nobody badmouthed his mom.

Sitting there in the busy, quiet, stillness of another stark raving family tragedy, a man tended to think of things like heaven and hell. If either had anything to do with just rewards, or if both were mankind's weak attempt at understanding Karma. He'd read somewhere that men created their own heavens or hells by the way they lived. If that was true, Trish was in for an eternity of fiery damnation. So was Tripp, but for different reasons.

Yet even as he thought that, Tripp knew better. Andy believed in a loving Heavenly Father, one who always forgave his sons and daughters. One who loved them unconditionally because He was the wise One, not mankind. In the grand eternal cosmic scope of things, mankind was just a bumbling celestial infant. Not perfect. Not even close to it. Prone to make the ugliest, worst mistakes possible before enlightenment finally dawned inside his hard, empty skull.

"I couldn't save Ikram, and I can't save her," he told the floor. "I was the man standing closest to Ikram, and I lived nine months in the same womb with Trish. I was born first. I even came into the world holding tight to her ankle. I literally dragged her kicking and screaming into the light with me. That should mean something. I wasn't going to leave her behind, even then. But I did."

Jameson's palm landed on Tripp's shoulder like a firm, warm rock. "That's the best and worst thing about choices. We each get to make our own. We also get to live with the consequences. I saved a donkey once. Look what it got me."

Tripp glanced at Jameson. Saw the tiny smirk barely twisting his lips. Also saw the dark glasses, and knew there were two unseeing eyeballs behind them, side effects of the risk he'd taken to save children he hadn't known. Like it or not, Jameson had come to The TEAM already a legend. He didn't swagger and boast like a lot of SEALs did. He was nothing like Tucker Chase, another SEAL. He just did his job, and he was quick to pitch in. Like now.

"You're humble for a SEAL, you know that?"

"Is this a contest?"

"No, but—yeah. In a way. She's my sister. Me and Mom are all she's got. Of all the people in the world, I should've known what she needed. I should've been able to keep her from hurting herself."

"Says who?"

"Says me."

Jameson shook his head. "It doesn't work that way, and you know it. The same fire that hardens steel, melts butter. Simple physics. Doesn't matter who we came into the world with, who our parents are, or what circumstances we were born into. It's never about the fire that burns us, only the fire within us. Only what and who we truly decide to be. Only what choices we make during the hours, days, and years, hell, the minutes we're given."

He was right. Tripp did know that. His mother used that iron and butter analogy often enough. It didn't help, but it did explain how Trish fought against the very things he'd fought for.

"You want the best for your sister," Jameson continued confidentially. "I get that, Tripp, but you can't make her be good. Nobody can."

"Tell me something I don't know."

"She's had the same opportunities as you. I can't imagine your mom being kind to you, but cruel to her. No, somewhere along the line, she intentionally chose the path she's on, and you have to believe…" He ran a hand over his head, ruffling the perfectly straight part that always made him look like an altar boy, something Tripp had never been. "You have to believe that she's doing the best she can with what she's got to work with."

"Yeah, well, what she's got to work with is shit."

"Is it? Or is it a shit ton of experience that will eventually, hopefully, benefit her or someone else in her future? Maybe someone she'll love more than she loves herself. Maybe a child?"

Tripp turned to really look at Jameson. The guy was totally serious that Trish could ever love someone more than herself. "That's easy for you to say. You don't know her, and you're not the one cleaning up behind her or watching my mom cry and pray and—"

"People can change," Jameson interrupted quietly. "Don't give up on her, Tripp. It's not over until it's over."

Which reminded Tripp of what he'd told Ashley. *Second rule: never give up. Even when all hope seems lost, … endure to the fuckin' end.* Who was giving up now?

Thank God, a stern gentleman in scrubs, his mask loose under his chin, shoved through the door marked **Do Not Enter**, and saved Tripp having to admit Jameson was right.

"Who here is related to Trish McClane?" the man called out to the crowded waiting room.

Tripp jumped to his feet. "Me, sir. I'm her brother. My mom will be right back."

Beau was already half out the door. "I'll go get her. Sit tight."

"Come with me," the doctor ordered Tripp. "I'm Doctor Pitt. We need to talk."

He jerked his head at another closed door across the hall, which ended up being a small family counseling room. Shutting the door, he crossed his arms and leaned against the doorjamb. "Your sister is on her way to ICU. I'm the thoracic specialist who was called in to repair the damage to her throat. How she survived having it cut, as deep as it was, is beyond me. Next she'll face spinal surgery, a procedure that will hopefully repair the extensive compression fractures she suffered."

"She broke her back?"

"No, the man who assaulted her caused severe damage to her spine. Doctor Smith, the spinal specialist on staff, will be in as soon as he can to discuss the procedure, her care, and a way forward. She'll need lengthy rehabilitation."

"But she'll live?" Tripp had to know before his mom returned.

"It's hard to say this soon, but I believe so, yes. The guy who assaulted her crushed her larynx. I believe he attacked from behind, grabbed her head, and twisted. He just didn't twist hard enough to kill her. I've repaired what I could, but her vocal cords are damaged. She may never talk again. You need to be prepared to deal with that. Also..." He jerked his head at the closed door and growled, "She's got cervical cancer that'll most likely require a hysterectomy, three different STDs, she's malnourished, and what the bloody hell is she using?"

"Anything she can get," Tripp admitted somberly. "Probably H. She used to live with my mom. That's what she used then. Wait." He pulled the health notice Ashley had given him out of his back pocket where he'd put it after he'd changed into his work clothes. "She was at the free clinic a couple days ago. Here. And yeah, that's my name on her list of possible infected partners, but I would never."

Doctor Pitt's brow spiked when he came to Tripp's name. "You're clean?"

Tripp bristled at the implication. "Yes, sir, and I can prove it. She's done this crap to me before. Thinks it's funny. It's not." He was glad Andy hadn't returned yet. She didn't need to know this, too.

"How long has she been working the streets?"

"Years. Since she was a teenager. Before she dropped out of high school." Christ, this was humiliating.

"There are programs—"

Tripp put a palm up. "Been there. Done them all, Doc. Trust me, Mom and I have tried everything to turn Trish around."

"Some people only learn the hard way," Doctor Pitt muttered.

"And some people never learn." Tripp's cell phone buzzed in his pocket. "Excuse me, sir, but I have to take this."

Doctor Pitt waved him to go ahead, then hurried out the door.

"Mrs. Harrison?" Tripp asked as he stepped into the hall and aimed for the waiting room.

"Ashley's not answering. I knocked, Tripp. I knocked really loud, but I don't think she's home."

"Okay, thanks."

"You're welcome, young man. I slipped a note with my name and phone number under her door. The minute I hear anything, I'll call you. I'm sure she'll be home soon," said his neighbor, the eternal optimist.

"Thanks again." Tripp disconnected the call. He still had to relay the news about his sister to his mom. At least Trish was alive. But where the hell was Ashley? "I have to go," he murmured to Jameson, afraid to leave, yet needing to run. "Mother said Ashley left HQ a while ago, but she isn't home yet."

"Maybe she stopped for dinner or decided to—"

"No. She's not like that. I need to find her. Call me the second my mom gets back."

Jameson looked at Tripp long and hard. Rather, he looked in the right direction. "Don't give up on her."

"Not happening." Tripp didn't know who Jameson meant, Trish or Ashley. But something was wrong. He could feel it. He ran for the nearest exit.

Chapter Twenty-Two

With her heart clawing its way out of her chest like a crazed squirrel, Ashley stifled a shuddering breath and waited. Just her luck. Once she'd burst into the complex lobby, thinking she was home free, she discovered the elevator was out of order. She'd run up four flights of zig-zagging stairs, and now stood at the heavy fire-door between the fourth and fifth floors. Listening. Afraid to breathe too loudly in case the person climbing the stairs behind her might hear. Just as afraid to step into the hall in case someone was there. She was positive someone had entered the lobby after the first-floor fire door closed behind her. She needed to be sure that person, whoever he or she was, exited on a lower level. Frightened that he or she might live another level up and have to pass her, she held her position.

Whoever was climbing the stairs below her now tread quietly. Stealthily. Couldn't be Mrs. Harrison. She'd said she was tired and was probably in bed by now. Not Tripp, either. He'd be running, taking those steps two at a time. Then who was it?!

Did she dare break cover? Her key was tight in her hand. She could make it. Cautiously, she peered over the banister and down the stairwells. No one was there. Yet someone still climbed upward. She could hear them. Step by step. Drawing closer and closer. The paralysis of blind, dumb terror kept

Ashley frozen in a Freddy Krueger nightmare of her own making. One where all monsters and murderers were omniscient, victims were stupid—like her—and where bad guy always won.

Not. This. Time.

Scared witless, she flung the heavy fire door open, ran into the hall, and flew past Tripp's door. Twenty steps farther would bring her to her apartment. She could make it. Until she fumbled her key and it fell. Crouching, she grabbed the darned thing, but stabbed it so hard, it slid beneath her door. No, no, no! Only a tiny brass edge showed.

She could still hear pounding footsteps in the stairwell. Going up or going down, she couldn't tell. She had to get that key!

Using just her sweaty, trembling fingertips, Ashley took a shallow breath and focused on pulling the rest of her key out from under the door. Oh, no! Had the elevator just pinged? Was it fixed already? She was shaking so hard. Only the tiniest corner of her key showed now. She couldn't risk taking a quick glance in either direction. Only getting that key!

At last! Thank God! The sweating skin of her index fingertip sealed to the tiny brass tip showing. She had it! Jumping up, she stabbed her key into the lock and the trusty deadbolt turned. Just in time. With her head about to explode with panic, Ashley burst into her apartment, and slammed herself inside. Almost. The darned door didn't close!

Her gaze hit the tip of a big, black boot stuck in the doorjamb. "Stay out!" she screamed, as she slammed the door again. Then again. As hard as she could. She wouldn't go easy!

Peewee was all fluffed up and shrieking his lungs out by then. She'd scared him. He'd spread his wings and was flapping like a windmill, no doubt stomping his clawed feet, too. Birds did that when they were threatened. They made themselves bigger, acted tougher and braver, when they were anything but. Like Ashley. She'd been living a lie, and now she'd die.

A voice. Out in her hall. Someone was growling. The killer! He'd found her! A wide, manly hand reached in through her door and—

BANG, BANG, BANG! went her door on that jerk's arm! "Leave me alone!"

Peewee shrieked along with her. His raucous squawks drowned out everything. Even her.

That awful hand turned into a thick, leather-covered, muscular forearm. Then an elbow. The door opened wider with every inch her killer gained.

"Why are you doing this to me? Who are you?" she cried as this unknown monster forced his way into her apartment.

Peewee shrieked louder. Waking the dead. More feathers scattered. Ashley had no choice. Breathing hard, she stepped back, as with one hefty *OOMPH!* She let go and the invader was inside her home.

"D-d-don't do this," she begged, unable to tear her gaze from the hulking shadow of a man, dressed all in black, back-lit by the hall light. "Help! Someone—!"

That monster's hand reached for her wall switch. Not her. And...

Click. There was light, and there was Tripp. Not—*him. Oh, God. It's Tripp.*

Real concern panted Tripp's beautiful face. He reached a hand for her to take. "Ashley, it's me. Honey, don't cry, it's just me."

Stuffing her key into her rear pocket, she fell into his outstretched arms like a walking puddle of sweat and fear and—yeah—PTSD. It was killing her! Trembling like a kite in a stiff wind, she nuzzled into his neck, needing every last bit of those drugging male pheromones pouring off his skin. Needing him.

"I thought… God, I thought… I'm scared that…" *You're going to think I'm insane!*

"Shhhhh. Shush, honey, I've got you now. I'm here," he murmured, his hot breath in her face the solid conviction of a man who would kill for her. "What's making all that racket?"

"Peewee. It's just Peewee. My poor little boy." *I scared him, too.*

Hurriedly, she ran to the large cage by her window. Peewee sat with his beautiful, peach-colored feathers ruffled, his crest flared high and wide, and squawking his beak off. A dozen or more large flight feathers lay scattered on the floor. "My poor baby. Quiet, please," she urged her sweet companion even as her heart pounded to be let out of her ribcage. She'd really made a fool of herself this time.

Reaching inside the cage door, Ashley stroked his crest, then under his outstretched wings until he calmed. "Sorry, little guy," she told him as she checked his water and food bowls, then covered the cage with his blanket, as much to settle his nerves as to settle hers.

Tripp was standing behind her by then. He pulled her back against his wide, warm chest, his arms the steel protection she desperately needed. His warm breath was so darned welcome on her sweaty cheek.

"You're soaking wet," he murmured. "Sorry I deserted you. Really thought I'd be back sooner. Thought you'd wait for me."

"No, I... I... I..." Ashley didn't know what she meant to say, only knew he was there now. She was safe, and no one could hurt her. If anyone had even been following her to begin with. She still wasn't sure. That was the trouble with panic attacks. They blinded a person, and logic was the first thing they stole. Common sense didn't hang around much longer. But fear surely did. If her heart pounded any louder, the noise it was making would scare the whole world.

"You're here," Ashley told Tripp, earnestly fighting her imagination as much as her panic. But still afraid to look at him and let him see her. "That's what m-m-matters."

Turning her around, he pressed her body flat against his, one broad hand between her shoulder blades, the other tangled in her wet hair, cupping her head. Holding her up and holding her tight. Keeping her from falling apart.

"You... you probably think... I mean..." *Man, what* do *I mean?* This was getting old. She didn't want Tripp to think she was crazy, too much drama, or too much trouble. Because she was. Heck, if PTSD didn't kill her, her wild imagination would.

Without saying another word, he stooped low and slipped one arm under her knees, then picked her up and walked to her couch. Down he went with her on his lap, folded inside both his arms, the top of her head under his chin. He reached under his arm and withdrew a really big gun, which didn't surprise her at all. If anything, that gunmetal gray weapon he'd just set on her end table brought a sure sense of security to her apartment. Tripp knew how and when to use it. She was finally, totally—safe.

Ashley shut both eyes, ashamed at how seriously out of control this day had gotten. She focused on breathing slow and thinking smart. Tried to remember why she'd even started running. What scared her? Shadows? Figments of her imagination? The wind in the trees? The rain? Or had someone really been out there? Man, it was hard to know for sure. Harder to relax. Two panic attacks in one day took a lot out of her.

"Was that you behind me on the stairs?" She had to know.

His voice rumbled deep and low under her ear. "Didn't know you were ahead of me, but yeah. Elevator's broke. I was in a hurry, so I hit the stairs."

Wow. Tripp could be quiet. And she was a fool.

"I think I s-s-scared myself," she admitted breathlessly, her nervous head bumping against the underside of his hard chin.

"Who's the guy who said the only thing we have to fear is fear itself?"

Her cheeks puffed with a heartfelt gust of relief. "I have no idea. Roosevelt? Churchill?" *Who cares?*

Tripp was doing it again. Understanding. Somehow absorbing the sharpest edge of her panic. Sharing the terror she'd kept hidden for too long. Ashley squeezed her eyes tight, relieved but feeling stupid. "I think I could write the book on fear, title it *'How to Scare Yourself for Dummies.'* My head always hurts after these attacks."

"I'll bet. You're not going to pass out on me, are you?"

Lifting her chin, she looked up at him. Couldn't miss the sincere glint in his emerald gaze. The way his eyes tracked her lips. The way her body arched into him. "I don't think so, but I did think you were someone else when I couldn't get my door to close."

"I'm just me," he murmured, his voice a velvet purr. "Who'd you think I was?"

"Never mind. It's just me. I get nervous and—"

His head tilted a scant millimeter to his right. Instinctively, hers canted as well. They were breathing the same air.

"Tripp?" she asked, wondering how that bottom lip of his would taste.

"Ashley. Please," he growled softly, the tip of his tongue sliding back and forth over that lip. Making it shine. "It's been one helluva day. May I kiss you?"

She'd never been asked before. "W-would you?"

Tripp closed the distance between their breaths and mouths. Softly. Carefully. His lips brushed over hers, filling her with the tenderness of a worthy male.

Ashley lifted her free hand and cupped the hard angle of his jaw. Then brushed the pad of her thumb over the bristly whiskers shadowing it, matching the strokes of his tongue on her lips with the strokes of her thumb on his jaw. Then his cheek.

He asked without asking, the tip of his tongue softly licking the crease of her sealed lips, lighting an invisible fuse between her mouth and her core.

Breathing hard, Ashley granted him a way forward. Just a tiny step into an uncharted ocean. Just a kiss. Just the wildest risk she'd taken in a long time.

Tipping her back into the muscular crook of his arm, Tripp cradled her while their tongues began a slow exploration.

She licked at the slightly sweet taste of coffee on his mouth, but along with it, her nose inhaled the faint sting of antiseptic and the mellow, dark spice of his skin. The scents of musk and male crowded out the last of her fright.

She was a woman. He was all man. Hungrily, she breathed him into the empty cavern of her lonely heart. Ashley had kept herself separate and in hiding for so long. She wanted the sunshine that glowed in this man's gorgeous eyes. She wanted to be free again. To live!

Tripp knew what he was doing. Manfully, he lifted a hand from her arm to her neck and threaded his fingers into her hair. A husky growl moaned out of him as he took over and deepened the kiss.

Ashley canted her head to reach more of him. So he could have more of her. There was no way she could ever have all of him. This was her breaking point, the line in the sand her attacker had drawn years ago. The barrier between her living free and hiding scared. As badly as she wanted her life back, she knew the second Tripp touched her breasts or asked for more than she could handle, she'd freak. This foolish daydream had to stop. She eased back, broke the kiss, and ended the fairytale before it broke her heart.

He took the separation well, moved his mouth to her forehead and pressed a breathy, fervent kiss there. Which put her nose in his chin. Breathing in all those salty, sexy, masculine pheromones helped her whisper, "I've never been with a man before."

He didn't laugh, didn't even smile. Just eased far enough back from her face to let those sexy greens melt deep into her soul. "And I've never been with someone like you, Ashley. You're so beautiful, so damned good."

Ashley took his head between her trembling fingers, needing him to know he was wrong. Licking her lips, she took a deep breath and closed her eyes. Honesty was going to hurt.

Chapter Twenty-Three

Tripp watched Ashley suffer through whatever was troubling her. He'd seen plenty of frightened people before. She was that pretty fox in a trap, with no way out but to chew its foot off. So, he gave her a way forward. "I'm not pushing. Whenever you're ready."

Besides, he already knew what she'd gone through. A woman didn't survive an assault like she had Friday night without a few night terrors.

When her head came up, two bright, shining orbs of teary self-recrimination stabbed his heart. But he also read guilt in those pretty eyes. Which pissed him off. She wasn't guilty for what happened Friday night, damn it. It was bad enough that society blamed females for the heinous crimes committed against them, and the automatic guilt they assumed. That damned scarlet letter A. She didn't need to blame herself.

He'd heard the lies and outright bullshit before. If *they* hadn't been in the wrong place at the wrong time, *they* wouldn't have been raped. *They* shouldn't have gone to their favorite restaurant or bar alone. *They* shouldn't have smiled at the wrong guy. *They* were out at the wrong time of day or night or week. *Their* skirts were too short, *their* hair too long, or *their* walk too suggestive. *Their* hips too wide, *their* breasts too voluptuous or too small or what-the-fuck-ever.

But the worst one yet, spoken by mothers and fathers, police officers, counselors, and judges alike: *'Boys will be boys.'* And a boatload of other male-privileged bullshit that allegedly defined women in general—not the fuckin' creeps who violated them. That was what created repeat offenders, the juveniles who'd bragged about assaulting females, then got off on reduced plea-bargained sentences, only to do it again as adults.

"Maybe someday," Ashley answered, her voice so damned timid, it hurt his heart.

Once again, a deep, raging primal need to exact bloody, heart-rending revenge on her Friday night aggressor all over again filled Tripp's being. To avenge Abdul Ikram, another lost soul who'd never stood a chance in this world where *'might made right'*. Thugs and bullies everywhere used innocents for their own vile agendas. Whether to overthrow governments or just to prove they were bigger and meaner, it was the same ugly story. The world was full of predators. All that stood between them and innocent lambs were highly-trained shepherds like Tripp. Which was why he hunted at night.

Yet Ashley wasn't as helpless as she believed. Yes, something had frightened her tonight. She may even have scared herself, like she said. But she'd been magnificent when she'd walked up and slapped that stupid health notice in his face this morning. What the hell happened since then? Was it him? Had he scared her that badly? Just by standing up for himself?

He had to know. "Where'd you go to college?"

She made a funny sound in the back of her throat, like she couldn't swallow. Or she was choking.

When she didn't answer, he told her what he could. "That's all Jameson and I wanted to talk with you about earlier, kiddo. After your panic attack this morning, combined with the crazy serial killer we're after, I had the craziest notion..." He shook his head at his own stupidity. "Call me paranoid, but I jump to conclusions sometimes."

"What serial killer?" she asked, her voice soft and timid.

He swiped a hand over his face and chin, not wanting to worry her more than she already was. But she might as well know. "That's why I met with Mark and Director Chase. Two years ago, there were three murders in Alexandria, all committed by the same guy. The victims were college girls, and the FBI believes the killer's active again. Director Chase thinks he's re-enacting his first murders, only this time, he's going after prostitutes." *Like my sister...*

Tripp caught the sigh that breathed out of Ashley. The way she seemed to relax at that news was interesting. Peculiar, but interesting.

"Anyway…" He cleared his throat. "The reason I asked what college you graduated from, is because the first three women this jerk stalked and killed were coeds at Northern Virginia Community College, and…" *Shit, should I even tell her what I thought? She'll think I'm crazy for sure then. Here goes...* "Anyway, I thought you might've been one of his victims. Guess one woman got away from him. She went to the free clinic, which is right near where you work. But they never got her name, and she refused a rape kit, and I thought maybe that woman was you. I just wanted to make sure it wasn't."

He scrubbed a hand over his head. What were the odds? Astro-fuckin'-nomical. Like, out of this world, not even remotely possible. It sounded crazier by the second, even to him. "Never mind. Forget it. Like I said, I tend to overreact sometimes without thinking. I do that a lot."

Although, something she'd said earlier today came back to him. When he'd asked if she had someone to talk with about what happened Friday night, she'd distinctly sputtered 'doctor,' but then snapped her mouth shut, as if she'd said too much. Were they even talking about the same thing?

Tripp looked closer. Was he right after all? Had she been assaulted before Friday? Was she the missing fourth victim? He stopped talking. It was Ashley's turn.

The silence between them stretched. He watched her pulse flutter in the hollow of her neck, making him sorry he'd pressed her. Until at last, closing her eyes, Ashley blew out a ragged sigh and scraped her fingernails over her forehead, another unconscious tell she employed when she was worried.

He leaned into the side of her head. "Whenever you're ready, kiddo. What I'd like to know now, is how you've come so far and done so much with all this baggage dogging you?"

"I told you. *'How to Scare Yourself for Dummies.'* I'm that dummy. I could write another book on that stupid confidence builder: *Fake it 'til you make it.* Whoever came up with that line is an idiot. It doesn't work so well." She finally met his gaze. "Least, not for me."

"You mean that bright-eyed, confident… what'd you call yourself? A trained…?"

"A trained public health educator. I call people—"

"Idiots, you mean. You call idiots like me," he teased.

She nodded, but admitted, "I don't believe that notice anymore. Like you said. It's not true, and I'm not notifying anyone else until I can verify what we've been told. I need to do some fact-checking first."

"Thank you," he murmured. "But are you telling me that beautiful, trained, public health educator, the amazing woman who has the audacity to march out of her apartment every day, with her head held high, and who smiles at the world like she loves everyone in it, is a fraud?"

Ashley's lips pursed, then twisted to one side of her mouth. "Yeah. That's me. I'm the world's biggest fraud."

"Oh, no, you're not, and you're not a victim, either." Tripp took careful hold of her jaw, his fingers laced over her ear and into her hair. He tipped her quivering chin up with his thumb, until Ashley had no choice but to look at him. "Trust me, honey, I've seen victims before, and you're nothing like them. You're a winner. A survivor. You *are* faking it, and you *are* making it. So what if confidence doesn't come back in a day or one month, or even in a year? What you think you're lacking, you've made up for in courage. In bravery, girlfriend. That's what they call people who march out of their homes and away from their families for war. They're heroes, because even when they're scared as fuck they're going off to die, they do it anyway. They're called brave, Ashley. It takes a shitload of courage to do what you've been doing. Can you do it for just one more day?"

"You called me girlfriend."

Out of everything he'd just said, she'd picked up on that. "That's what you are to me, Ashley. I mean after today, what should I say? *Hey, you?*" Tripp was trying so hard to make her smile again.

Those beautiful sapphire eyes blinked. "I get up extra-early," she murmured, "just to talk myself into going to work.

Every day, I look in my mirror, and I tell myself I'll be okay. That I can do it. 'Course I never leave my apartment until everyone else is going to work, too. I don't go into elevators alone with guys, and I don't let men into my apartment. I'm very careful. Same way at five o'clock, but in reverse. I travel home in crowds, Tripp. Never alone. Until tonight." She licked her bottom lip. "Won't do that again."

"Yes, you will. I have faith. You and that can of mace will go far."

There it was. Finally. A real smile. "Does being scared count as being brave?"

Tripp grinned. "I've got news for you. Every last one of us soldier-types is scared shitless sometimes. Deep down, we're just boys doing men's work. Now talk to me. Tell me what you can, and I'll tell you what we know."

"That fourth woman…" Ashley's bottom lip disappeared behind her top teeth. "Sh-sh-she… she, umm, didn't get away. He's the one who got scared. He just l-l-left."

Hot white rage exploded inside Tripp. "You *are* the fourth victim," he rasped, his throat so damned dry, he could barely speak. *Shit, damn, and son of a bitch! I was right. I knew it!*

"Yes…" She forced another noisy swallow. "I left my door unlocked one afternoon. I was expecting Mac. I had a late class, and at that time, I didn't have a roommate. I was alone. He just came in like he owned the place. At first, I thought h-h-he just had the wrong apartment but… Then he grabbed me. He kept asking if I wanted to p-p-play." Her voice trailed away.

"The bastard," Tripp hissed, so damned angry he could barely see straight. But he refused to frighten Ashley now that she was talking. It took a few seconds, but he came to his senses and toned the angst-filled rhetoric down. But she'd been assaulted—twice! Two gawddamned times! "Sorry, kiddo. Go on. Tell me what you can. I'll be quiet. Who's Mac?" *Until I find that fucker and rip his head off!*

"Okay, umm, well then…" Ashley trembled, she was so nervous. "Mac was the maintenance guy where I used to live. It was an older home near the college. We'd arranged for him to replace my thermostat, only… that other guy came. He didn't look like a r-r-rapist. I mean, he didn't have tattoos or piercings or scars, anything weird I could see. He wasn't particularly ugly, but he wasn't what I'd call cute, either. He looked boring. Normal."

"What color hair and eyes?"

"Light-brown hair, but weird gray eyes. Light gray. Like fog."

"How tall was he?"

"About my height. Ordinary build. Not muscular or handsome, like…" Her gaze dropped when she said, "…like you."

She blushed the prettiest strawberry pink, and for some stupid reason, Tripp's all-male body sucked in its gut and flexed its muscles. Not on purpose. It just happened. Reflexively. Like blinking and breathing and thinking of Ashley. Of breathing in the sweet scent of her hair and feeling the sensational softness of her skin beneath his fingertips.

It was time to move. They were still sitting together on her couch. Trying not to be obvious, he eased her off his lap and set her next to him. Tripp kept one arm around her shoulders, and he hoped—man, how he hoped—she hadn't noticed what was going on under his zipper.

"Anything else you can remember? Like how old he was?" he asked, wishing he sounded like Joe Friday, the emotionless cop from those old time *"Dragnet"* reruns. Instead of the sometimes baritone, sometimes tenor, sixteen-year-old jock he was sure he'd just devolved back into.

His physical reaction was expected. Instinctual. Typical male response to a pretty woman. Tripp couldn't help it; he had no more control over the bad boy in his pants than he had over the chill in the autumn air. But his emotions were something else. They were all over the place. One minute he was pissed as hell. The next, so damned tender and worried for her that he wanted to cry at all she'd lived through. By her damned self!

He ached to keep her as safe as he was going to keep Trish from now on. Wished he'd already killed the pricks who'd hurt both of them. And Tripp *would* kill them. On the job or during his late-night shift. With every quiet explanation out of Ashley's mouth, every last inch of him hardened into a lean, mean war machine. His knuckles couldn't clench any tighter. The guy who'd hurt these women would pay. In blood and guts, by hell.

Real men stood up for women. Period. That was how he'd been made, raised, and how he would die. A defender. Never a coward. Never a bully. Okay, so he had a full-blown hero-complex. He *had* been an Army Ranger, damn it. That's who he was.

"Did you hear what I said? Tripp? Hello." Ashley was looking up at him again, that same soft glow in her eyes, her fingers lightly tap-dancing on his wrist to get his attention.

"Ah, excuse me. Sorry, no. I ahh…"

"Please don't be angry with me."

"I'm not. Why would I be?"

"Because I didn't do what you wanted."

"So? You're a grown-assed woman. I'm not the boss of you." Damned if he didn't hear Mother coming out of his mouth.

"But if I'd stayed at your office, none of this—"

Tripp covered Ashley's lips with his whole mouth, just closed his eyes and swallowed any excuse she might come up with. Two things were abundantly clear. Ashley Cox was that one in a million, and he wasn't going to let her blame herself.

He kept this kiss wet but quick, ending it with a throaty purr that came out of nowhere. "I need to visit my sister and mom tonight. Trish is still at the hospital. Come with me?"

Ashley looked up at him a little cross-eyed, which made her sexy as hell. "Umm, w-w-what?"

He loved that he'd put that star-struck hitch in her voice and the just-been-kissed shine on her lips. "Come with me. Mom'll love to meet you. She needs someone in her corner."

Ashley's fingers drifted through her hair, pushing it away from her face and over her shoulders. "Umm, sure, I guess. But what happened?"

Oh, that's right. She didn't know. Tripp gave it to her straight. "I think the same guy who hurt you two years ago attacked my sister tonight. She's been in emergency surgery, which is the only reason I left. Trish is going to live, but she's got some serious trauma to deal with and—"

"And you didn't say anything to me until now?" Ashley nearly shrieked.

Thump. Poor Peewee fell off his perch again.

"Relax. Mom needs some good news and, honey…" He pressed a kiss to Ashley's forehead. "I think that good news is you."

Ashley's fingers fluttered back to his chest. She'd snuggled into him, even kissed him before, but this was different. This was a woman reaching out to a man, intentionally touching him, up close and personal. Her fingertips glided over his shirt. Up his collarbone. Lighting a wave of heat and appetite beneath them.

Tripp's hands curled around her biceps, and he pulled her close. There would be no one-and-done with a woman like Ashley. While that had always been his take on the women he'd partied with before, something else was happening here. Until this moment, he'd thought he'd known Ashley's future. It included children, a white picket fence, and a good man in her life. Some Plain-Joe who'd always put her first, who'd work a nine-to-five job, and take the family to Disneyland once a year. It included her big, pink bird and her safe job. What it hadn't included was a vigilante.

Keeping his distance and his true identity had made perfectly good sense until she'd touched him. Her sweet fingers were laying claim to him. Time held still. Peewee stopped squawking. Tripp stopped breathing. The only sound in his head was the rhythmic ba-bump of his heart valves opening and closing, the heady rush of blood in his veins, and the reflexive, involuntary movement of life. In him. In Ashley. Around them.

The rest of the world fell away. There was only Ashley and Tripp. Just one more kiss. Another taste. That was all he wanted. But one more kiss wouldn't be enough, and he knew it. He wanted Ashley in his bed and beneath him. Tripp leaned into her, every move a calculated hope that he was doing this right. That he wasn't scaring her.

Trembling with what could've been the same need—but obviously wasn't—she eased out of his hands. "Uh-uh. Your mom needs you," she whispered, her breath still soft and warm against his mouth. "I'll stay here tonight."

"But I need you," he growled, his body going up in flames at the scent of her skin and hair. At the taste of her.

Ashley kissed him then, a sexy, wet meeting of lips and tongues that promised there would be another kiss. Tripp kept it hot, but quick. When he ended the kiss, they were both breathing hard, but he knew Ashley was right. Andy needed him tonight. Maybe Trish did, too.

He had to get back to the hospital. "Promise me you'll be okay?"

Chapter Twenty-Four

In the end, Tripp only left Ashley because tonight wasn't an appropriate time for her to meet his mother, not with Trish still in surgery. Andy could only handle one trauma at a time, and if things went sideways with Trish, Tripp didn't want Ashley there. Besides, she was ten shades beyond exhausted. She promised she'd be ready to go the next morning. He stood outside her door until he heard her deadbolt click into place.

The Alexandria Surgical Center wasn't far away. His truck was parked and Tripp was back with his mom and his TEAM within twenty minutes. Not much had changed. Alex sat with Andy, his wife Kelsey at her other side. Which was damned thoughtful, Kelsey being there. Everywhere Tripp looked he saw friends, empty and half-full paper coffee cups, and plenty of empty fast-food wrappers. He took the chair across from his mom. "Any word?"

Her eyes and nose were red. "Doctor Smith is in with her now. He came and talked with me first, but he said we should go home. That this kind of surgery will take hours. But I don't want to leave, Tripp. I'm staying."

Kelsey held Andy's hand sandwiched between hers. "I told her she's entitled to stay if she wants. She's Trish's mom, and moms know what's best."

Tripp could've seriously kissed Alex's sweet wife for her fierce loyalty to a woman she'd just met. "I agree. I'm here now. If you guys want to go—"

"No." Alex shook his head. "It doesn't work that way. You stay, we stay. We're family, and we're here to serve. What do you need?"

"My mom could use a room and a bed," Tripp answered quietly, staring at Andy. "We've been down this road before. She won't leave until—"

"Done," Alex interrupted, his cell phone already in his hand, as if he had the world on speed-dial. "What else?"

Tripp had no idea. "Mom? What—?"

"Nothing for me. A miracle for Trish would sure be nice, though." She ran the tip of her tongue over her top lip, then turned to Alex. "Can you do that, too? Can you make my baby want to live?"

Tripp could've cried at the beseeching tone to her question.

"No, ma'am, I'm sorry. I'm not in the miracle business," Alex said kindly. "But I know people. Let me see what I can do for Trish." Pushing his palms to his knees, he lifted to his feet, winked at Kelsey, then strode into the hall with his phone at his ear.

Within minutes, a young man in scrubs entered the room and zeroed in on Andy. "Are you Mrs. McClane?" he asked gently, his brows raised.

"Yes, that's me," she answered, her voice as weary as Tripp had ever heard.

"I'm Thane Roberts, your family advocate," he said. "The hospital has rooms available for families of trauma patients. You must be exhausted. Come with me, ma'am. I've got just the room for you. It's near the chapel, and it's quiet. You'll be able to rest."

"I'm not leaving."

"I'll go with you," Kelsey told her. "At least you can freshen up there, then we'll come right back."

Andy buried her face in her hands and cried. Tripp looked away. It never got easier, but hearing his mom beg Alex for a miracle gutted him.

"Mom," he said, his voice hoarse from his own pain. "I'm here now, and I'm not going anywhere. Go with Kelsey and grab some sleep while you can. We'll rotate shifts. When you get back, it'll be my turn." *Like we've done all those other times.*

She made a strangled noise. "You always say that, but I know you, and you never sleep when you should. You're as bad as me."

"Or as good," Jameson murmured from where he sat with Mark and Beau. "Don't worry, Mrs. McClane. There are plenty of us here for you and Tripp. Let us help. Get some rest while you can, and I'll make sure Tripp gets some shut-eye when it's his turn."

Andy nodded, but Tripp could see the signs. She was already running on empty, the cumulative effect of Trish's destructive lifestyle. "Well, okay then. I'll try. Ready?" she asked Kelsey.

"Sure," Kelsey answered easily. "This way, with the two of us, we shouldn't get too lost."

She had her arm around Andy when they walked into the hall with Thane. Tripp could've bawled at the kindness everyone had for the mother of a guy they barely knew. He'd bounced between Seattle and Alexandria over the last two months, and his nightly excursions hadn't fostered any close friendships. Until now.

Alex walked back into the room and took the seat across from Tripp. "I called in a few favors. The best thoracic surgeon and spine specialist in the country are at your disposal. They can both be here tomorrow. Second opinions never hurt."

"Thank you." Tripp nodded, nearly struck dumb at his boss's reach and generosity. Physicians of that caliber would be pricey, even for second opinions. But Tripp would find a way to pay for it all. Trish deserved a second chance.

The hours ticked by. Midnight came and went. His mom returned with Kelsey when the sun came up. She must've talked Andy into sleeping. Andy looked rested but as weary as she had last night. Beau and his wife, Doc McKenna Fitz, returned with baskets of home-cooked breakfast and industrial-sized thermoses of coffee and juice. Kelsey made sure Andy ate, then stayed at her side, chatting about kids and babies and the joys of motherhood. It was good to hear Andy chuckle over the happier times before Trish derailed.

At last, after hours of waiting, a nurse appeared with news that Trish was out of recovery and had been moved to the ICU. A tired Doctor Smith was waiting there to discuss her prognosis with her family. Only two family members at a time were allowed to visit her. Ten minutes per visit. Six visitors per day. Which would never be enough time for Andy to spend with her only daughter.

Tripp held out his hand to her. "Come on, Mom. Let's go see Trish."

After they checked in at the Intensive Care nurses' station, they were redirected to a family counseling room. Doctor

Smith was much younger than Tripp expected. Tall and dark-haired, he was built like an athlete. Had to be close to seven feet tall. Broad, muscled shoulders but trim at the hips. Long-legged. And grinning.

Tripp took the seat across the table from him. "Basketball?" he guessed.

Smith's tired eyes lit up as he stretched a long arm to Tripp. "Yes, sir. Gonzaga U, power forward, twenty years ago."

"The year Gonzaga went to the Sweet Sixteen?" Tripp asked, shaking the guy's big hand. And instant rapport was born. He'd seen those reruns, too. A man who could handle a ball like Tripp had seen Smith do during those long-ago NCAA college playoffs, had to be the best doctor for Trish.

Doctor Wesley Smith proceeded to prove just that. He offered no judgment on Trish's lifestyle or choices, just gave Andy and Tripp what they needed to keep on keeping on. At the end of his simplified version of what had been a full night of delicate spinal surgery, he stood, reached a long arm across the table, and took hold of Andy's hand. "Trust me, Mrs. McClane, your daughter will walk again. Yes, this surgery was complicated. Spinal compression fractures always are. I fused six of her vertebrae, and she'll need to manage her pain for the first month or so, but she's going to pull through this. You'll see. Normal recovery time is six to twelve weeks. I'll be glad to give you the names of a couple excellent care facilities that specialize in critical-care patients like her. They'll get her up and walking in no time."

Tripp didn't dare say anything, but damn. The dollar signs were adding up.

"But her neck. I mean her throat. Won't she need to recover from throat surgery first?" Andy asked.

Doctor Smith's dark-brown eyes lit up with enthusiasm. "Which she's doing right now, as we speak. The days of keeping patients with spinal compression fractures in bed, while they turned into vegetables, are long past. I've already assigned her own personal physical therapist. After a short stay in a rehabilitation center, Gracie Fox-Armstrong will go home with Trish and stay with her until she's not needed. She'll teach your daughter how to meet her goals and stay the course. Gracie works at one of those facilities I mentioned. She's a doll. It's exciting, isn't it?"

Tripp ran a rough hand over his hard head. "Feels more like hell on steroids."

Smith turned those bright dark eyes on him. "I understand your sister survived a heinous attack last night, is that right? That she's lucky to be alive?"

Tripp nodded, not going to out Trish any more than she'd already outed herself.

"As her primary homecare specialists..." Smith's gaze rolled from Tripp to Andy and back again to Tripp. "It's essential that you two believe this is an opportunity for Trish, not an impossible obstacle she'll never get over. It's a second chance. Focus on what I just said. She's lucky to be alive. Let that be the mantra you start and end each day with. Prove it to her. Make her believe she's the luckiest person in the world. That she can do it. Because she most definitely can."

"Kind of like 'if you believe it, you can be it?'" Andy asked.

"*'Fake it 'til you make it,'*" Tripp muttered what Ashley had said. Only with Ashley, miracles seemed doable. Real possibilities. But with Trish…?

"Exactly!" The excitement in Smith's voice was palpable. "Your daughter *is* lucky to be alive. Will the next year be tough? Absolutely. Will it be worth it?" He grinned with all the energy of a kid on a sugar high. "That'll be up to you."

"And Trish," Tripp added, but without the hopped-up faith in a woman who'd crapped all over her family—most of all, her mother—that this stranger had.

But Andy seemed encouraged and hopeful, and Tripp wouldn't rain on her parade. Yet he couldn't help but think: *Here we go again.* False hope followed by crushing disappointment, Trish's modus operandi. Her everloving MO. Too bad Smith had no concept of her track record. It was easy to believe in miracles when you weren't the guy in the foxhole fighting through yet another one of Trish McClane's shitstorms.

Andy must've picked up on his gloom and doom. She reached over and patted the back of his hand. "We can do it this time, Tripp. I know we can. You're home. You'll help me, won't you?"

"What kind of question is that?" he groused. "Of course, I'll help. You're my Mom. That's what I do."

"How about Trish?" Smith asked, those damned bright, brown eyes too sharp, maybe even all-seeing. Like Jameson's.

Discouraged or not, Tripp gave his words right back to him. "She's lucky to be alive."

I hope Mom believes that line of BS, because right now? I sure don't.

Chapter Twenty-Five

After she checked the peep-hole and unlocked the deadbolt, Ashley opened her door to a pale, depleted version of the man who'd left her last night. Tripp's face was lined with fatigue, worry, and defeat. He stared at her, his crystal green eyes devoid of his usual enthusiasm for life. Even his hair looked limp.

"Do you have to go right back?" she asked. Pulling him into her place, she shut the door, snapped the deadbolt in place, and locked them in.

"Not right away. She's out of spinal surgery, and she'll be in ICU for a few days, maybe more. She's still out cold. Mom's with her, and everyone else is still there in case Mom needs anything, but I just..." He shrugged out of his leather jacket, then the double holster she hadn't realized he'd still been wearing. Huh. Two black pistols. The holster went over the back of her couch. Both pistols went to the top of the hutch over her antique, Amish roll-top desk.

His heated gaze rolled over her like a steamroller. She'd dressed to meet his mother this morning, in her comfiest jeans, a lavender knit top with a cowl collar, and running shoes with purple laces. She still didn't have her messenger bag or her phone. They were in Tripp's apartment. But she had him; she'd be safe without them. Err, not that she'd ever *had* Tripp, but the thought was certainly tantalizing enough to make her palms sweat and her heart flutter. "But you can't stay," she told him.

"I shouldn't." His lashes lowered. He ran a hand over his face, ending at his chin. "I'm just so damned tired. Mom and I have been cleaning up after Trish for so long..." Exasperation groaned out of him. "Yet here we are again. Working our asses off so she can shit all over us again. But mostly on Mom. She's always carried the brunt of this... this mess."

Ashley clamped her hand over his wrist to pull him into her kitchen for coffee or something. "Are you hungry? I've got—"

"No, thanks. I'm so damned caffeinated, I couldn't sleep if you drugged me." With a gentle tug, he pulled her into his arms. "You're what I need right now. Just you."

Ashley melted against his thickly muscled chest, content to listen to his heartbeat. To feel his nose in her neck and his breath on her skin. To know he was safe. No matter when or what, Tripp always smelled of wind and leather.

Her fingertips fluttered over his collarbones, from there, they slid up his neck. She looked into the dark eyes of a hungry man staring down at her. Any hint of green in his pupils had been swallowed by black, and she was caught in a tantalizing, paralyzing trap.

Ashley lifted to her toes and, without taking her eyes off him, kissed his prickly chin. Her arms looped around his neck, which put her breasts on his chest, where he could touch them or kiss them. She wasn't afraid anymore.

"You need to sleep. At least take a nap," she told him, but her voice came out ragged and needy. Breathless.

Tripp's head slanted. His gaze slipped from her eyes to her mouth. "No. I just need you."

He'd turned his back to the window. She'd already opened her room darkening curtains for Peewee; the sunlight streaming behind him cast golden light into the room. He looked like an angel, backlit with all that gold. Fierce and powerful, but broken. Tired of fighting the world, of fighting his sister's demons.

Yet he was nothing like the fallen angel from Friday night. That guy had been frighteningly powerful and brutal in the justice he'd dished out. He'd offered no quarter to the man who had assaulted her. But Tripp had only ever been kind and sweet. Gentle with her and Mrs. Harrison. Now he needed someone to pour a little kindness on him.

They stood there on the edge of forever, both suddenly breathing hard. Wanting.

"I'm not afraid of you, Tripp McClane," Ashley whispered daringly.

Something dark shifted through his eyes. "Maybe you should be."

Her heart started pounding, but she sucked up her fear and gave his sentiment right back to him. "No. Not of you. Never you." Glancing over her shoulder, she said, "My bedroom is that way if you… if you…" The suggestion caught in her throat. Darn. Just when she'd thought she could act tough, she couldn't. It took all of her courage to finish the invitation. "If you'd like to lay down for a while."

A sad smile curled his bottom lip. "With you?"

She nodded, bobbing her head, too afraid if she said anything else, she'd make a bigger fool of herself. Never in all of her twenty-some years had she been the aggressor. Not that she was now, because she hadn't the nerve to be that kind of strong or pushy. But this man needed her, and she wanted to give back a fraction of what he'd given her. She wanted to make him smile.

Trembling, because she'd never done this before, Ashley took the first step into the unknown, reached for his hand, and then tugged him along behind her. Not that Tripp resisted, because he didn't. But because doing this, taking control of this one thing in her life, was important. She needed to be the leader. It was her home and her bed and...

Oh, fudge. What if he rejected her invitation? Her heart stuttered to a full stop. But no. She wanted this man, and she was pretty sure he wanted her. Else why had he come back?

As if he'd read her mind, Tripp reached one arm around her shoulders, the other under her knees, and carried her into her room. With every step closer to the bed, her heart danced a perky salsa up her throat. Ashley tipped back in his arms and smiled, just before he tossed her onto the bed.

"Nice place." he growled as he settled a knee between her legs. "Are you sure this is what you want to do? I mean, I'm still me, and—"

"Yes, you," she told him earnestly, her arms hooked around his neck again.

He'd settled over her, his elbows alongside her head and his legs between hers. "Ashley," he breathed, his eyes searching her face, her neck, and the low V of her collar.

"Tripp," Ashley whispered, licking her bottom lip, her body weeping at the weight and heat of the magnificent male holding her down. But not hurting her. To move past that horribly frightening day in her past, she reached behind her back and tugged her top over her head and off.

His eyes widened, then fell to her lacy, violet bra. Her closet might be full of more manly clothes than feminine attire, but she knew how to make herself look attractive.

It must've worked. Tripp's tongue just made a quick swipe over his bottom lip. "You're beautiful," he said with awe.

"Hands," she ordered, not turning back now. "P-p-please put your hands on my… my…"

"Breasts?" he asked, his voice low and incredibly husky, and his gaze still hot on her bra.

"Yes. Them." The darned tremor in her voice had to go, but if she didn't do this now, she'd never get past that other day.

Then, because he hesitated, she grabbed hold of the big hands he'd placed alongside her head and moved them to where she needed them. The second his palms flattened on her bra, a wave of fear crashed over Ashley. She closed her eyes, scared, but wanting this so darned bad, she could've cried. Enough was enough! She was tired of pushing everyone away, especially Tripp. Ashley wanted this, darn it. She wanted him.

"You're trembling," he told her.

"Yes, well…" Opening her eyes, she looked up at the man she'd once accused of despicable things. "I've never done this before."

His head cocked. "Ah, yes. You're a virgin," he breathed.

"I know that makes me a unicorn. A freak. I just wasn't ever one of the in-crowd. I've never belonged or wanted to be popular or—"

"You're not a freak, Ashley Cox," he interrupted, his voice a low, sexy growl. "If you ask me, you're one of the rarest women in the world. I just never…" His top teeth scraped over his bottom lip again. "But me? Are you sure I'm the guy you want to do this with?"

"Yes. You, Tripp. Now." That almost made her sound bossy. Man, she wished she were.

Carefully, as if he were handling something breakable, he cupped her bra. His fingers settled gently over the girls she'd kept hidden, bound tightly, and restrained for years.

"I won't hurt you," he breathed, the spark back in his sexy green eyes.

"I know, b-b-but you need to know that this is as f-f-far as he got. By then he'd cut my neck, and I was bleeding, but he never... he never..." Fudge! It was happening again. Paralyzing panic stole her breath and—

Tripp dropped his mouth over hers and breathed for her. All tongue and heat and desire, with one lick he swept the stranglehold of too many lost days and dreams away. The frightening moment in her past lost its grip, as Ashley lost herself in the giving and taking. For the first time in two years, she was a woman again, and Tripp was the man she wanted to give herself to. Right here. Right now.

Instinctively, her hips arched into him. The smart, sassy woman she wished she'd been throughout all of this wasted time took over. That black polo had to go. Hungry now, she dragged the hem of it out of his jeans. Lifting to his knees, he stiffened his arms to help her pull it over his head. It flew like batwings to who-cared-where.

This man's chest was so much more than she'd expected. Wide and solid, coiled muscles rippled when he moved. Sparse chest hairs declared he was all male, but those shoulders... Those arms.... She licked her lips at the meal hovering over her.

Tripp's bottom lip caught in his teeth. His eyes sparkled with passion. She'd seen that exact look somewhere else, but where? Too bad she was too busy to focus on that trivia question now. Tripp had just climbed out of bed and peeled out of his boots, jeans, and—

Oooo, black boxers, sexy long legs, and those muscular thighs…

She was in heaven. Anxious to get her hands all over him, Ashley hurried and toed her running shoes off, then kicked them to the floor. She did the same with her socks and then, wiggled out of her jeans. But the moment she lifted her butt and hooked her thumbs inside the elastic band of her violet bikini panties, Tripp put one big hand on her belly and growled, "Uh-uh. No, you don't. Those are mine. All mine."

Every feminine muscle in Ashley's body clenched at that erotic declaration of male ownership. A delicious shiver rolled up her spine and danced across her shoulders, making her wiggle even more. "Okaaaaay," she demurred, her heart kicking into a cartwheeling handstand, three backward somersaults, and ending with a perfect, ass-waving, two-point landing.

Hormones roared through her like an electrical current. They were a matched set. He was still in his underwear, too. She was down to her panties and bra. His eyes skimmed over her nakedness. The lust stamped on his face was priceless. Man, Tripp was so beautiful, she wanted to cry.

He settled between her legs, his long legs hanging off the mattress this time. He lowered his head and fervently kissed her belly button, his tongue slick and warm and swirling into that divot, his breath a gentle tease on her sensitive skin. His morning scruff tickled and scraped while he tasted her tummy.

She'd turned into a quivering, needy bowl of *Jell-O*. She wasn't exactly sure what to do with his big male body to make him happy too, but was sure going to give it—him—her best shot.

Ashley laced her fingers over his head and into his hair, loving the lush, cool feel and thickness of it. Her body had a mind of its own. Her hips bucked into his chin, as if offering him everything. But when he dipped lower, when he smoothed his hands under her ass, lifted her hips, and nuzzled her panties—there—she froze. There? R-r-really?

Lifting his chin, Tripp looked up and across her stomach at her the second she stopped breathing. "One of these days," he purred, his fingers slipping under the elastic waistband of those silken panties. "We're going to get creative, you and me. But not today, Ashley. Today is all about you. Only you. When you're ready. But until then…"

His big, warm hands slipped inside her panties and cupped her bare ass, peeling the panties off and down her legs. Instead of throwing them like she had his shirt, he stretched one arm and set them on her nightstand. Then, lifting to his knees, he climbed up her body and settled between her legs again. That beautiful erection settled hot and thick against her bare skin, her throbbing core. Almost right where she wanted it.

Ashley's heart was pounding so hard by then, she was sure he heard it. It was happening. What if she did this wrong?

Planting his thick arms alongside her, Tripp skillfully maneuvered one hand behind Ashley's back and unlatched the eyehooks that held her bra in place. "Tell me if you want me to stop. Just say no. One word. That's all. I'll stop. I promise."

"I'll never tell you no," she whispered, her eyes locked to his. Ashley knew her breasts were larger than most women's. She'd often thought they were the reason she'd attracted the attention of *that man* two years ago and the drug addict Friday night. But until this morning, Tripp had only seen her in frumpy man shirts. Which was why she'd worn lavender today. She wanted him to see her as a woman. But what if he didn't like them? Or her?

Ashley lifted to her elbows. This time, she didn't close her eyes, but watched while Tripp carefully slid the loosened bra straps over her arms, then tossed it over his head with a wicked grin.

She smiled carefully up at him.

His eyes darkened with lust. His breathing hitched as he took in an eyeful. Her breathing did, too. But when he dipped his head and put his mouth over her breast... When he suckled her entire nipple into the slick, slippery heat of his tongue and mouth...

Her head fell back, and Ashley stopped worrying. She was definitely doing things right. The sweetest flame licked up the inside of her legs as he sucked and nibbled. She widened her knees, needing more friction. Needing Tripp. Instead, she got a roaring inferno that started deep inside her core. Felt like he'd lit a bottle rocket.

The bubbling flame exploded into bright white shards of lightning that flashed, so hot and so bright, she shattered. Incredible pleasure rippled through her. Over her. She couldn't breathe or think. Could only enjoy the scintillating sensations rolling through her blood. Her veins had turned into conductors of the most intimate electricity, that her fingertips buzzed. Her nipples were hard as rocks, but as sensitive as butterfly wings.

Too soon, the fireworks faded into stars, and she was falling with them. But what a rush! Ashley drew in a panting breath, effervescence still popping under her skin, her core drenched with a need for more Tripp. He'd done that to her. And she liked it.

"Fudge," she huffed, her chest rising and her bare breasts still happy in his very capable hands.

He grinned down at her, the handsomest smile splitting his tired face. "The first time should always be the best."

If she'd died and gone to heaven, right then and there, Ashley couldn't have been happier than she was inside Tripp's arms. "Is it always like this?"

"It can be," he replied. His cheeks ballooned, as he blew over her wet nipple. She shivered, and of course, the needy little beggar perked right up, turned hard and sensitive. He ran the tip of his tongue over it, then turned his attention to her other breast, lighting some kind of connection between it and her core.

Ashley held onto his broad shoulders while tremors of delight raced over her. It was happening again. She was coming undone at just the touch of his tongue. "Tripp, I'm… Wow, I'm… I think I'm… doing it again."

"Then fly," he commanded gruffly. Adding fuel to her fire, he slid one hand down her body and slipped one finger inside of her. "Fuck! You're so tight. I know you can do it."

She could. She did! Ashley flew so sweet and so high, the heart-stopping intensity of this second orgasm rocked her world and stole every last breath. Tears brimmed, even as she blinked them away.

"You're so ready for me," Tripp murmured, his voice guttural and deep. He lifted his head. He was watching her now, his eyes dark forest green, his pupils blown. "But if we go all the way, it's going to hurt. This is your first time, and I'm afraid—"

"Don't be afraid," she whispered. "Please, Tripp, don't be afraid. I'm not, and I don't want to hide anymore. Not from you."

The hunger in his eyes softened, but this man was thinking too much. Ashley cupped his angular jaw in her hands, loving the soft brush of scruff under her fingertips. The tenderness glimmering in his eyes was so much more than she'd experienced or had ever believed a man capable of. Until this moment, they'd all been users and losers. Braggarts and bullies. Or indifferent professionals, like her boss.

Could this tremendously high, weightless feeling be love? Probably not. She'd given up that pipe dream long ago, after watching her mom work her heart out for nothing but to get up the next day and do it all over again. Nothing good had come out of her mother's sad relationship, except for Ashley. Whatever she did with the rest of her life, she refused to live one more day being afraid. No. More!

"Are you sure?" Tripp was biting his bottom lip again, scraping his top teeth over it. Worrying it. Adorable, simply adorable.

"Yes," she told him. Feeling brave, she slid one hand between their bodies and past the waistband of his boxers. "I'm darned sure, Tripp. Let's do this."

Chapter Twenty-Six

Damn, he was tired, and if he'd been smart, he would've been asleep by now. But Tripp couldn't help grinning at Ashley's courageous declaration to *'do this.'* What man could resist an invitation like that? Not him. But when her fingers circled his cock without hesitation... When she tightened her grip... He purred like a damned tame housecat. She'd known what she was doing. She'd planned to seduce him, maybe not this morning, but today. Unfortunately...

"I've got no condoms with me," he had to tell her. "Don't suppose you have any handy."

"I... I..." Her head bobbed, and there was that sultry smile again. "As a matter of fact, yes, I do. I'm the outreach coordinator for the Health Department, remember? I've got free samples." She made that sound like she'd just solved world peace.

He fell, right then and there, into the prettiest, most sincere, sapphire blue pools he'd ever come across. There was no way to catch himself or stop the freefall. For the first time in his life, Tripp was in over his head. "You do, huh?"

"Yes, I do. At least, I'll give some away if I ever notify someone face-to-face again. They're in the other room. I have a whole box!" She sounded so damned pleased with herself.

He grinned at the sassy woman in his arms. Everything about her was different now. From her feminine clothes and shoes, to the sexy as fuck underwear he'd peeled off her. She'd even left her hair loose and was wearing a titch of lipstick and blush. Which she hadn't needed. Her lips were plenty swollen and wet, the loveliest shade of just-been-kissed pink, and after two orgasms, there wasn't one part of her body not blushing.

"You want me to get them?" she asked.

"Yeah, sure. I mean…" Her body was thrumming with need that, suddenly, Tripp's wasn't exactly feeling. He dropped his face between her breasts and breathed. Just breathed. God, it had been a long, hard day and night. The scents he loved best, cherries and Ashley, filled the cracks in his heart. The cracks he'd known were there, but hadn't truly allowed himself to acknowledge until then. "No. Let's… Why don't we just lay here for a minute longer? I don't want to rush this," he murmured into her sweet, soft skin. "I need a few minutes of just this. Just you."

"Okay, sure." Ashley settled back into the pillow and ran her fingers over his head. His damned hard head.

Something strange and wonderful was happening here in her bed. Something he didn't know how to deal with. Everything had changed. Him. Ashley. The world. The feelings he'd stuffed down into his soul, the ones he'd honestly thought he'd never have to deal with again, were back. Making him wonder if the wiser men and women of the world weren't right. If there wasn't more to life than just the revolving door of slams, bams, and thank-you-ma'ams of fast, hard fucking. Especially with the tender woman in his arms.

Yeah, he'd been a horny beast as a kid. What teenage boy wasn't? He'd used girls and tossed them aside. Why not? Every football star, especially good-looking, buff linebackers, had plenty of sex thrown in their faces. From their first Friday night win to the day they graduated, were injured, or left the sport, high school football stars were stalked, bribed, and titillated by offers of free sex. And yeah, he'd indulged. Why not? They'd offered, and he'd snarfed down every last sweet thing that came his way, a couple of their mothers, too. He hadn't been old enough, nor wise enough to understand anything about self-control, the unique sanctity of virginity, or how precious the gift of a good woman was back then.

He'd been a damned cocky jock, a walking, talking stack of vibrating testosterone, puffed up with too many 'atta-boys' and swamped with undeserved hero-worship. He'd been a stupid kid. Just seventeen. Not even a real man. Certainly, no hero.

Tripp knew the difference now. Heroes were the unseen men and women who'd fought and died fighting for their countries. It honestly didn't matter which country, either. The second any person put their wants and needs aside, the moment they picked up their country's banner and fought for something bigger than themselves, they were the real Friday night winners. Every overpaid sports celebrity, even Hollywood's finest, were so much less. Had they given their blood? Had they lost their lives? No. They were only concerned with ratings and the illusion of being more important than they truly were.

Heroes were the invisible people, like Ashley. Men and women who would never lead others into battle or into dark alleys. They were just regular people fighting their own private hells, who got up every day and convinced themselves to keep going and keep trying. To keep pasting on smiles they might not feel, even as they marched off to jobs they might be over-qualified for, or searched for wayward daughters who'd curse them when they found them. Who'd curse them for loving them. *Like Mom.*

As much as Tripp wanted to show Ashley a really good time this morning, the stress of the last couple days was a hard mountain to climb. He nuzzled his nose deep between her luscious breasts. A couple tears eked out of his tired eyes. What a loser.

Until her slender fingers threaded into his hair and settled around his head, her fingertips against his scalp. "Hey," she breathed softly. "What's wrong, honey?"

Honey. She called me honey. That cost Tripp another tear, and he honestly didn't understand why he was this emotional. He was no pussy, damn it. He was a man, and he… and he...

Fuck, I've got feelings. That had to stop.

"Not a damned thing," he lied, turning his face to the side, wishing he were a better man even as he used her breasts for pillows. That he deserved this woman. "I'm just happy, Ashley." *Truly happy. Finally.*

"Sure. Stay right where you are," she replied, her voice soft and loving, her arms wrapped around his head now.

He knew it, that thing he was feeling. He was utterly, hopelessly, for the first time in his life, in love. Not just in lust. He'd found what he'd been searching for all these years. Tripp just didn't know what to do with it. Scare her off by professing true love? Take her now while she was wet and willing, but still so innocent and way too giving? Before she understood what he'd only just figured out? That she was worth a hundred greedy, grasping men like him. Or should he let her go and live that perfect white-picket fence dream?

Tripp had no business thinking what he was thinking, and he knew it. She would always be the angel; he'd always be the sinner. He was so fuckin' tired.

Chapter Twenty-Seven

What do you do with a naked man who's fallen asleep in your arms? Simple. Ashley bowed her nose into the top of his head, smoothed her hands over his shoulders, linked her fingers behind his neck, and kissed his hair. That was all. Tripp had finally let go. She could tell. The second he did, the hard knots in his shoulder muscles relaxed. His body was limp and heavy. She couldn't remember ever feeling so privileged in her life, and thankful that she'd called her boss and had taken the rest of the week off.

Tripp's needs were paramount to everything else. The first, obviously, sleep. Then sex, hopefully. Maybe a shower. And lunch. For sure lunch. He needed to keep up his strength. It was difficult not staring at the expanse of naked man spread over her. His broad back that narrowed to a trim waist and a taut ass and long legs. He'd dipped most of his face between her breasts. Warm steady breaths now feathered over her skin.

But what a sight. Every last ropey muscle over his shoulders and down his back and arms, his biceps, even his forearms, were thick and heavy. Gnarled veins stretched under his bronzed skin. He'd been in Seattle. Not much chance he'd gotten that deep tan there. Which meant he'd gotten an awful lot of sun when he'd been deployed. Which also meant he hadn't been home very long. His skin was still so dark, and sun-kissed highlights in his hair shone through the darker blond strands. White and gold, a perfect combination.

She loved the feel of him, so she let her palms drift anywhere they wanted to go. His skin felt different than hers, thicker maybe. Rougher in some places. The smooth expanse of muscles beneath it were definitely more solid than hers. Of course. He was all man and a soldier. He'd trained to be tough.

Grunting in his sleep, he wrapped one big arm around her waist, scraping his fingers between her back and the mattress, until he had her caught. Not like she minded. His back didn't feel chilly, but just in case, she snagged the sheet he'd tossed aside when this adventure in bed began. Tugging it up, she covered as much of him as she could. Mostly his bare back and butt. Not his long legs.

He settled into her, sighing.

Ashley was happier than she could ever remember being. There, squashed beneath a sleeping giant of a very warm man, she'd found peace. It hadn't seemed possible at first. She'd made assumptions he'd proved were foolish and wrong. Tripp McClane had grown on her. He'd snuck under her radar, under her skin, and into her heart.

It was happening. She loved this man.

Chapter Twenty-Eight

He knew where she was now, and he knew who she was with. The big, tough guy with green eyes hadn't left her place since he'd knocked on her door early this morning. He was still there. What were they doing? Fucking each other's brains out? How terribly predictable. Damn him. But he'd soon get his comeuppance. By the end of the day, that big, brave, tough guy would be sniveling like a baby for leaving her alone and unprotected.

He wouldn't have gotten this far if he hadn't taught himself how to break into homes and hotel rooms, how to pick locks and pockets, to lighten a woman of her wallet long enough to find out where she lived or worked. It had never been about stealing money, only essentials, like the master keycard to this entire apartment complex now in his pocket. He hadn't wanted that guy in the lobby's money. Not at all. To prove it, he'd left the unpilfered wallet with the body. It was true. Dead men didn't tell tales.

The next step? Get Ashley Cox. He was so very close to her. So near and so quiet. She'd never see him coming, but come he would. He shut the door across the hall from her apartment, locking himself in where he could keep an eye on her. The goal was so near, he could almost taste it. Her. For Ashley Cox, he could wait. He'd already waited two years.

What was another hour or two? And then, they'd play. Oh, how they'd play.

Chapter Twenty-Nine

His phone chimed like the fuckin' bells of Notre Dame, startling Tripp out of a dead sleep. That ringtone indicated a hunchback from work was calling. Possibly Alex. Surely, a troll just as annoying, whoever it was.

Tripp groaned and rubbed his face in the fragrant mounds of womanly flesh he'd fallen asleep on. He was in breast heaven. His nostrils flared and his cock was ready for action. Thank fuck. Until his damned phone pealed again. Louder, like the thing was pissed off. Tripp sure was. What bad timing.

"Where's my phone?" he groaned into Ashley's sweet, fragrant skin.

"It's wherever your pants are." She was smiling. He could tell by the glow in her voice.

"Yeah, well..." Tripp arched back onto his haunches, careful not to crush or pinch her. He would've found his pants and his phone if... he hadn't stopped to take in the delectable feast spread in front of him. Her hair was mussed, black tendrils of silk laced around her head and spilling over her shoulders and the pillow. Her breasts were marked and wrinkled from some big moose who had, apparently, fallen asleep in her arms. She'd tucked her legs together when he'd lifted up. Which was not what he wanted. He'd love to see all of her, but they were still in the early stages of... whatever was happening between them. If she needed more time to feel comfortable with him, she'd get it.

He'd never slept better, but neither could he resist. Leaning onto his forearms, he watched her eyes widen as her gaze scrolled over his shoulders to his bare ass, now raised high behind him. Well, let her look. Her naked body was one helluva fine sight to wake up to. His hands landed on her pillowy breasts and—

The damned phone rang again.

"I have to answer that," he said, his fingers tapping her soft breasts. He needed more time with his woman. More awake time.

"You do," she murmured, her eyes extra-large, extra-dark this morning.

Ring, ring went the damned phone!

Lifting his ass off the bed, Tripp jumped to his feet and went in search of his pants, which were slouched on the floor at the end of the bed, his boots still in the cuffs where he'd toed out of everything. Fumbling, he snagged his cell and answered Jameson with a terse, "McClane here."

"I hate to tell you but—"

"Another body?"

Ashley lifted to her elbows, watching and listening.

"Yes, but if this was our perp, it's his first male victim. Same MO. One sharp cut. One red rose. Tongue missing. Sure feels like his work, but I can't tell for sure. Where are you?"

"At Ashley's," he didn't mind saying. "Why?"

"Because this body was found an hour ago, one block east of your apartment complex, in the green space between the on-ramp and northbound GW Parkway." The George Washington Memorial Parkway.

"Jesus. That's just a block away."

"Yes, and this kill's fresh. Rigor hasn't set in. Don't know if you want to join us, but I wish you would. He left a bloody body bag this time."

"Which explains how he's moved the other bodies."

"Most likely. It's pretty rank. Don't think he's ever hosed it out between vics. The ME is here, and FBI forensics just arrived. Just thought with your sharp eyes, you might see what these guys are missing."

Tripp read between the lines. *You mean, what you're missing.* "Chase still being an asshole?"

"He's certainly focused." Jameson's weariness came loud and clear through the connection. "He's called in his psychics. Thought you'd want to meet them, too. I've got to say, they are an interesting group. I like them."

Tripp shot a glance over his shoulder. Ashley had just gotten out of bed, and he had the best view of her bare supple back, the two dimples above her lush, heart-shaped bottom, and two long legs that might soon—he hoped—take him all the way to heaven. Just not now. Damn it!

"Sure, yeah, I'll be there," he replied, running a hand over his bedhead. "Give me ten to grab a shower." His eyes slid back to Ashley. "Or twenty."

She'd slipped into the cutest pair of light-tan boy shorts and a white t-shirt that didn't hide a thing. When she looked over her shoulder and smiled his way, he told Jameson, "Make it a half-hour, give or take a few—"

"No, I need you here now. I need your eyes, damn it!" Shit, he was testy.

"Okay, yeah. Sure. On my way. Be there in five." Talk about bad timing.

A murmured, "Thanks," breathed over the connection before Jameson ended the call.

"I have to leave," Tripp told the woman he was beginning to have serious feelings for.

"Okay." Her pretty face was as bright as Sunday morning. "I'll fix coffee and send you off with a travel mug. Sugar? Cream?"

And you? Tripp licked his lips at what he was leaving behind. The sweetest, rarest sugar, the richest cream. And he was a hungry man. But the business of murder victims would always come first. Especially if Trish, like Ashley, was one of this bastard's failed kills.

"Black," he told her, then went in search of his shirt. Quickly, Tripp dressed in yesterday's clothes and this afternoon's wrinkles. His mom might mind how he looked, but this was the job. Activating his cell again, he saw that he'd slept a solid three hours in Ashley's arms. Sweet.

Tucking his phone in his rear pocket, he snagged her silk panties off the bedside table, tucked them into his pocket and followed her into her kitchen. The compact room was a mirror image of his. Their shared wall housed the plumbing. That put their kitchens and bathrooms back to back. From her kitchen door, he could see her entire place.

The master bedroom shared one wall with the bathroom. The other space was divided between an open entryway with a beige tiled-floor, an open great room with floor-to-ceiling windows and deep blue carpet. A smaller bedroom was situated across the great room from the master bedroom. Room-darkening panel curtains graced all of Ashley's windows. They were open now. Peewee's wrought iron cage stood in the center of all that glass. Guess he needed to see out more than she did.

She'd decorated her apartment in feminine soft pastels, mostly peaches and powder blues. His was decorated in round-tuits, as in he was going to decorate when he got around to it.

Tripp kept his exercise equipment, his gun safe, and his spec ops gear out of sight in his spare bedroom. The door to Ashley's was open. Inside, a cozy brass daybed with a quilted mauve blanket stood along one wall, a long table and chair, with a gooseneck lamp on the other. Two small, plastic toolboxes were open beside the lamp, both revealing four removable shelves of stackable trays. A couple trays were lids up. Looked like a work bench. She had tools?

"You have a hobby?" he asked, as she handed him a tall, black metal to-go cup.

"Beading." She shrugged it off as if it were no big deal. "I sell beaded purses, belts, and bookmarks online. I'll show you sometime."

Tripp set the cup on her coffee table, then pulled her into his arms. "I don't want to leave."

Ashley came easily, looking up at him as if he really were someone, her hands on his chest. "I don't want you to leave, either, but you do important work. Go. Find the guy who's killing women. I hope he's the same one who hurt me, then it'll finally be over."

Her eyes were clear today. Brighter than he'd seen them before. He hoped he was the reason for the confidence shining there. "Plan on meeting my mom later if we can swing it. That okay with you?" he asked as his hands skated down her back and over those sexy boy shorts and the plump cheeks within them.

Her head bobbed. "Of course. I'll be here."

He sealed that promise with a kiss. Three other little words tripped up his throat, but Tripp swallowed them. He was not the settling down kind, so, he told her instead, "Don't go anywhere. Stay inside."

There was that smile again. "Did you forget who you're talking to? It's me, remember? The best-selling author of *'How to Scare Yourself for Dummies.'* Trust me, I'm not the go anywhere type. You go. Do what you do best. Save the world."

She made him feel like he could do exactly that.

Easing out of Ashley's embrace, Tripp snagged his holster and slid it over his shoulders. He retrieved his pistols from her desk. Racking each slide, he ensured both had a round chambered, then tucked those babies under his arms where he could easily reach them. He slipped into his leather jacket next, concealing the fact that he could and would end the fucker now killing women in his town. That was what Alexandria had become, Tripp's town.

Unlocking Ashley's deadbolt, he puckered his lips and pantomimed a kiss to her, then closed the door behind him. He waited for the click of her deadbolt engaging. *Good girl.*

Only then, did he head out to do what he did best. Hunt.

Chapter Thirty

It was time. At last. The green-eyed gorilla had finally left Ashley Cox's apartment. He'd stood there with his head cocked long enough before he'd left, though, as if he were listening. But then he'd nodded once and strode to the elevator. Obviously, he'd waited until his little girlfriend locked herself in for the day.

Like that would keep her safe? Hardly.

He licked his bottom lip, his gut already filled with the gnawing, razor-sharp need that ruled every move. Couple that with the giddy anticipation of the tears and terror that lay ahead, and...

He palmed his junk to keep it from getting ahead of the game. He was primed for a very good day, but patience. He needed patience.

He liked this part of the game. There was so much to look forward to. It was like Christmas Eve. The expectation! His heart skipped a beat at the thought of all the afternoon would bring. The shrieks. The joy! The pain. The screams! It was enough to make a man come in his pants. But first...

He needed to surprise her. Yesssss... This part of the game was the best. Surely, Ashley Cox would agree. It wasn't like she'd have a choice, would she?

Chapter Thirty-One

She was a woman in love, and Ashley knew it. She'd done something outrageously bold this morning. She'd made love, well, almost. But she had initiated her first ever, honest to goodness, sexual encounter with Tripp, and she'd had two orgasms! How wonderful was that?

Sharing a sweet, intimate encounter with him had brought her world into clearer focus. He'd been so gentle and giving. The poor guy had been dead on his feet, yet still he'd given her a morning she'd treasure forever. If only they'd had more time. She was falling hard for the gentle giant of a man, and she had no way to stop herself. For the first time in her sheltered, boring, timid life, Ashley was in love, and it was spectacular.

Floating on air, she twirled silly, lazy circles across her living room floor, her arms lifted like wings, and her heart on that handsome devil who'd just left. She'd told him she'd be here when he returned, but wouldn't he be surprised? Because she was done being a loser and a coward. A scaredy-cat. Ashley wanted her life back today. She used to have dreams. Well, hello world, today, because of Tripp, she started dreaming again.

Pulling off her tank top, she slipped back into her violet bra. She'd seen Tripp's eyes light up when he'd first seen it. She intended to blow his mind when he returned, and she met him at the door dressed in nothing but sexy underwear. A shiver ran over her shoulders. She'd never dared do anything so naughty before.

With a quick, backward glance at her closet full of boxy man shirts and loose pants, she made a mental note to go clothes shopping. Today, she'd dressed for success. Violet success! But work first, play later. Snagging her bathrobe, she covered herself, then hurried back to her kitchen and went to work.

Grinning like a silly woman in love, Ashley pulled the frozen chicken breasts she'd bought on sale last week out of her freezer. They went into the microwave to defrost. Besides beading, she dabbled in cooking. She wasn't sous chef caliber yet, but she knew her way around her kitchen, and she was fixing her specialty this morning, chicken and dumplings. It'd be the perfect comfort food to take to Tripp's poor mom. The last thing she needed to worry about was what to eat or where to go for dinner.

After washing the thawed chicken in her kitchen sink, Ashley patted the pieces dry and placed them in her already-lined-for-easy-clean-up crockpot. She poured an entire carton of chicken broth into the mix, added an array of delicious spices, turned the pot to high, and busied herself tidying up what little mess she'd made. The chicken breasts would be tender and ready for shredding in a couple hours. By then, she'd have celery and onions chopped, ready to be tossed into the mix. In the meantime, she'd slice and cook several carrots to be added later. When they were tender, she'd turn the crockpot off and strain the broth. It wouldn't take long to thicken it into rich chicken gravy, and shredding crockpot chicken was simple.

Then, prest-o, change-o, back into the crockpot the aromatic stew would go. Dumplings were as easy as—she snapped her fingers—that.

Hmmm. Maybe Mrs. Harrison would like a serving of chicken and dumplings, too. Good thinking! Ashley had more chicken in her freezer. She could make enough for Tripp's entire team. Happily at work in her kitchen, she started humming some commercial jingle. She couldn't wait to see the look on Tripp's handsome face when he came back and she opened her door. What a great, sexy day to be alive!

Chapter Thirty-Two

Most people thought deadbolts made their homes impregnable. They couldn't be more wrong. Deadbolts were as easy to break into as locks on bank vaults—if you knew how. Which he did. Pulling his well-used set of lockpick tools from one of the many deep pockets of his trench coat, he dropped to a knee. The final game had begun, and he was going to win.

Good thing he always carried this unique set of lock pick tools. Deadbolts were all designed with inner pins, but some with more difficult-to-pick spool pins. The trick was to get past the deadbolt's inner workings, do it right, and do it fast. A deadbolt had to be picked counter-clockwise. Pick it clockwise and you were a fool. Game over. Go home and jerk off in the shower.

First step: Concentrate. He slid a tiny tension wrench into the lock's aperture. With his right hand, he maintained the right amount of tension, while he inserted one of his many rakes in his left hand, just over the wrench. Deftly, he manipulated the rake in and out, one-by-one pushing the inner pins to their up positions.

Next step: Take a breath. Quick glance right. Quicker glance left. Make sure you're still unseen. Keep working.

His diamond pick came next. Then a lifter. He raked each pick with delicate precision, adjusting the tension wrench as needed. But slowly. Carefully. With every cautious breath, the universe narrowed down to the genius—him—and this one final game.

He cocked his head to listen, both to the pins inside the lock, and for sounds of life on this floor. There were four apartments on each level. He now knew the one directly opposite Ashley Cox was vacant, but in need of new flooring in the bathroom. An older woman occupied the one up the hall, next to the vacant apartment.

But imagine his surprise when he'd broken into the apartment next to Ashley Cox and discovered a photo of the gorilla, who he now knew was Former Army Ranger Tripp McClane. My, my, but his blonde smiling mother didn't look old enough in that picture to have a son his age, nor a daughter as nasty as that slut he'd left behind the Chinquapin Park Rec Center.

That had been a damned close call. He'd almost been caught and attacked himself. The murderous light in that old fart's eyes and the way his wife had screamed when they'd seen him and what he'd done to the tramp, had nearly unnerved him. Like a novice, he'd panicked and run. The old bastard had a gun. Jesus, people these days!

But now that he'd settled down, he wondered about the sheer coincidence of it all. The destiny. Brother? Sister? Mother? All caught in the same trap as Ashley Cox? How sweet this particular game was ending. Andrea McClane might just bear looking into… as soon as he was done playing with Ashley Cox.

Maybe this wasn't the endgame after all, but the match point to the more-deadly game with an Army Ranger. What would that sound like? The scream of a trained soldier when he found his girlfriend and his mother displayed on the gameboard of death? Without any way to tell what happened to them or who tortured them. All games ended in death. Surely a warrior understood that. If Tripp McClane didn't now, he soon would.

At last, all pins were up. Time to break the lock. Enter his specialized locksmith drill. Inserting the finely machined tip into the lock's aperture, he squeezed the sensitive trigger. The keyway spun as surely and as quietly as planned. Mission accomplished. No deadbolt could keep him out. Once again, Ashley Cox was vulnerable. Accessible.

Patiently, he stored the tools of his trade, lifted to his feet, and swept the flapping sides of his trench coat behind him. It was time to play—for keeps.

Chapter Thirty-Three

"What do we have?" Tripp called out, as he ducked under the streaming, yellow FBI tape surrounding the latest crime scene.

Several police and city cars lined the opposite side of the street, where he'd parked. A dark gray EZ-up had been constructed over the scene. The ME had already removed the body, but white privacy sheeting still draped three sides of the pop-up tent. APD detectives and police officers were on-site, doing their thing. As were a few local reporters. No surprise there. Vultures always showed up when there was blood.

Cocking his head, no doubt with the frequency of his ninja radar ears turned up extra-high this afternoon, Jameson already faced the direction Tripp had come from.

"Here!" he called out, waving Tripp over. Jameson didn't have a clue how to dress casually. Back at the hospital, he'd been in TEAM black like everyone else. This afternoon, he was 'business professional'. Gray suit, matching gray tie, white shirt, thick-soled, blavck work shoes. No doubt he carried at least one pistol under that jacket. How the hell did a blind guy coordinate his wardrobe as well as this guy did? Jameson had to be as OCD as Alex. That actually made sense.

Four heads turned at Tripp's boisterous approach, three male agents, one very lovely, blonde female agent, all with FBI shields on their belts. Director Chase intercepted them the moment they'd headed toward Tripp. By then, Tripp was already with Jameson.

"Chase has been on my ass since I arrived," Jameson murmured under his breath. "He's antsy as shit about this murder."

Tripp shot the asshole in question a glare over his shoulder. "What's his problem? Besides his big head?"

"I get the impression he's frustrated that his folks can't peg our killer, that maybe we can."

"We can?" Tripp leaned in closer. "What do we know that Chase doesn't?"

"That there's enough forensic material in that well-used body bag to nail this son of a bitch. We were first on the scene. Alex has the county ME on speed-dial. He signed off the evidence trail with the ME. That's when Chase called FBI bullshit. Claims this is his crime scene, that he's got total jurisdiction, not Alex."

"Then why'd he ask for a TEAM assist?"

"Agent McClane! Hello, Agent McClane!" The blonde FBI agent called, as she approached with long, elegant strides on his six.

"Here," he answered, lifting one hand to acknowledge her.

She was a looker. Long-legged and lean, dressed in black like her buddies, she made that suit look a hundred percent better. Long, golden curls ruffled in the breeze, creating a gentle wake behind her. And right behind that wake, another agent followed on her six. Sandy-haired and built like a brick shithouse, he had her beat by a good foot in height. Maybe a solid hundred pounds in weight. Straight spine. Erect as fuck. If he wasn't former military, Tripp was a fairy godmother.

Jameson commenced introductions while they were still in transit. "Tripp, FBI Special Agents Eden and Ky Winchester. Winchesters, my friend and teammate, Tripp McClane."

"Ma'am." Tripp extended a hand to Eden when she was within reach.

But damned if the male-half of the duo didn't grab his hand first, a grin cracking his ugly face and his grip crunching Tripp's fingers. "Tripp McClane! My God! How the hell are you? Never thought I'd see you again." Ky laughed, his unmasked voice full of crystal-clear joy. "Though I'm pretty sure I didn't see you last time we met, either. Man, you're a sight!"

Tripp cocked his head. "Do I know you?" he had to ask, as he manned up and gave that bone-cracking handshake his all. Whoa. Ky was no pushover, and those weren't fluffy shoulder pads under that black FBI get-up. He was as strong as a fuckin' ox. Plenty of upper body strength. Wide damned shoulders and a thick neck that looked like he power-lifted.

By then his two buddies had also circumvented their boss and were headed his way. Chase stood there with his feet spread and his hands on his hips, glaring as his team walked away from him. Well, let him glare. There was no I in this TEAM. Apparently, he hadn't gotten the memo.

"Probably not, but you're one of the guys who rescued me and a couple other soldiers outside of that private prison south of Kabul," Eden's husband declared proudly. "I was on my way to the USMC morgue, but I made sure I got the names of everyone who was there that night. You helped save my life, man. I was blind and beat to shit, b-b-but, d-d-damn…" Ky's amber eyes brimmed and his lips pinched. "Thank you so g-g-gawddamned much for being there," he stuttered. "I'm so d-d-damned glad to meet you in person."

Tripp found himself pulled into a mighty, suffocating bro hug. He damned well recalled the barely alive Marine he and his team had found that ugly night outside Kabul. Army had never worked so well with the Corps as when both were on the same search and rescue missions. Tripp just wished he'd been the one who'd ended the sadistic bastard who'd operated the shithole Ky had escaped from. But someone else had the privilege of killing the Taliban banker. Scuttlebutt was that guy was one of the Taliban's own snipers. Interesting.

"My husband was only on his way to the morgue until I convinced him to stay alive for me," the pretty blonde added. Her arm looped through Ky's cocked elbow. She patted the bulky biceps that stretched his black suit jacket sleeve to the max.

He beamed down at her. "Yes, you did, Eden. Sorry. I should tell you," he said to Tripp, "we're the FBI's one and only psychic team, but—"

"But we can't read shit off a gawddamned thing this bastard's touched," the behemoth who'd just joined Ky growled. "Agent Tate Higgins at your service. Ky's told me a lot about that night. Good to finally meet you, McClane." He reached a bear-sized hand forward, and Tripp expected another death match, the kind all former military exacted upon meeting members from a different service.

The rule was simple. Whoever blinked or whined first bought drinks for the house. Tripp had usually gotten drunk those times, but he wasn't so sure about that outcome today. Tate was a big guy with large, work-roughened hands. Dark shaggy hair. Darkly tanned like most guys and gals who'd served too long in the Middle East. And a grip that wouldn't quit.

But neither would Tripp. He gave until Tate's ugly face cracked into a toothy grin. "You're all right," Tate muttered when he gave up the win. "Almost as good as your buddy there."

Tripp had to glance at Jameson. "Him?"

Jameson lifted a shoulder, as usual, and said, "Krav Maga. I never lose, remember?"

Which made Tripp laugh. "Yeah, whatever."

By then, the fourth agent had joined the FBI psychic threesome. He stuck out a much more slender, elegant hand and announced, "Agent Isaiah Zaroyin at your service. Pleased to meet you, Agent McClane. It's a privilege to be able to work with you."

So, this was that mad doctor's son, huh? Tripp took hold of Zaroyin's hand, surprised to find more physical strength in his grip than he'd expected. Zaroyin was the Christopher Reeves version of *"Superman."* Tall, dark, and handsome. Slender, but strong in a better-looking package than Ky, Tate, or Tucker. And smart. Isaiah relinquished the handshake first and stepped back into line behind Ky and Eden. Guess he didn't feel the need to prove he was bigger or better. But then, he'd never served in the military, either. Tripp could tell.

"So, you guys are all, what? Mind readers?" he asked, half-expecting one of them to reach over and pull a coin out of his ear.

Ky's better-half smiled. "Some of us can read minds, yes," Eden replied, her pretty green eyes twinkling with mischief. "But each of us came into the FBI with different psychic skills. Mine are more long distance, which is how I was able to reach out to Ky in Afghanistan from my home in Virginia. Tate has an affinity with most animals, and—"

"All except alligators and crocodiles," he piped up. "Bears, dogs, and everyone else. Even snakes and birds. Just nothing left over from '*Jurassic Park*.'"

Interesting word-choice: *Everyone else* instead of anything else. Tate identified more closely with animals than people. Tripp liked him instantly.

"Eden and Isaiah are the only Level Tens in the States," Director Chase bragged, now that he'd caught up with his people. "Isaiah's got skills not even he can explain."

Isaiah cleared his throat. "And Tucker's skills are coming along just fine. He's a fair mind reader and getting better every day."

Tripp ran an appraising eye over the guy with the biggest ego. Tucker? A mind reader? He'd have to see that to believe it. Call him skeptical, but yeah. Not falling for all this BS.

He turned to Ky Winchester. "And what do you do?"

Ky shrugged and pointed to Eden. "I'm married. What do you think? I do whatever she tells me to do."

That bought a few laughs and loosened the mood. Even Chase smiled.

"He reads people," Eden explained. "Not their minds, their auras. He can tell you things about yourself you might not even know."

I doubt that.

Her lips turned up with a sunny, wide-open smile. "You'll see. Let us hang around with you for a day, and you'll see."

Tripp had to look twice at Eden. *Did she just read my mind?*

She winked.

She did! Tripp ran a hand over the back of his neck, disconcerted as fuck!

"Boss, I know we've got a case to work," she told Tucker. "But may I?" she asked Tripp, her small right hand already reached out for him to take.

"Sure, why not?" He accepted her gracious handshake, expecting it to be brief and gentle. Instead, he got the ice-cold stare of a woman who could see right through him. Time stopped. Eden blinked in quick, jerky succession, like she was processing data he hadn't meant to share. Hadn't known how to share. Jesus. She was inside his head. He could feel her. Couldn't stop her, though. Didn't know how.

"Stop," Jameson commanded, his voice sharp and curt. "Eden, break the link. Now!"

She blinked again, shook whatever had just happened off, and released Tripp's hand, which by then, was sweaty as hell.

"I'm... I'm sorry," she breathed, sinking to the ground. Ky slipped an arm around her waist before she hit the dirt.

"What the fuck was that?" Tripp hissed, shaking his fingers to get them to stop humming. Felt like Eden had just electrocuted him. Even his head buzzed.

"Sorry, Agent McClane. It happens," Ky answered calmly, as he turned his attention to his wife. "You okay, hon?"

Her head bobbed forward, and all those blonde spirals fell over her face. She was shaking, and Tripp was damned well-shaken. Sorry didn't cut it. "What the fuck just happened?"

Isaiah stepped between the Winchesters and Tripp. "It's called transference, Agent McClane. Apparently, you have, for lack of a better word, some intense *shit* going on in your life right now." Isaiah cocked his head in that same curious way Jameson was prone to do. "Sometimes that shit is too much for one person to hold, much less hold back. It transfers, automatically, to the nearest receptor, which this morning…" He nodded at Eden, whose rose-colored blush had been replaced by gray pallor. "…is the first FBI psychic ever, Eden Winchester."

"She read my mind?" That sounded a lot like invasion of privacy.

"No. Actually, your overloaded mind reached out and dumped itself into Eden. She can read minds, yes, but that's not what happened this time. She's not able to block spontaneous transference yet. We're all learning how to handle our talents, but we've still got a long way to go."

"How do you even know what happened to me?"

"He's our psychic over-watch," Tate answered, his hefty arms crossed over his chest. "He keeps track of the rest of us. All the time. He always knows where we are."

"What is he, God?" Tripp snapped out.

"Let it go," Jameson breathed. "The same thing happened when I shook her hand. Guess I've got unresolved anger issues related to my loss of sight. Like that's a shocker."

"You do?" Tripp asked, damned surprised that this suave, cool, collected guy wasn't as perfect as he appeared.

"To clarify…" Isaiah held a hand up for attention. "The same thing has happened with nearly everyone from your TEAM, Agent McClane. Eden shook their hands. Their minds threw everything down, like yours just did. You're all open books, which is why we want to work with you. We can read you, so we trust you. That, and each of you brings a different skillset to the job at hand."

"Skills we just don't have," Ky added, his arm still securely around his wife.

"So what did my mind tell you?" Tripp studied Eden. "If we're all transparent, why can't you read the killer's mind?"

She was leaning into Ky for support, and he had that whole protective, male vibe humming. Tripp didn't need to be psychic to see that. Eden's lashes fluttered. He couldn't help feeling sorry for her. She looked as bad as Tripp felt.

Ky met Tripp's question head-on. "Mind dumps are confidential, Agent McClane. Come see us at our office sometime, and she'll tell you everything. But as far as our killer's concerned, some people have natural mental blocks we don't yet understand how to get through. Psychic ability is not a one-size-fits-all scenario. Tate's the one who taught the rest of us how to block psychic babble. He grew up knowing how to do that. It came natural to him. Now we're figuring out how to get through natural mental blocks. Do you know how?"

"Err, me?" Tripp shook his head. "I'm not psychic." *Or crazy.*

"It's not crazy, Agent McClane," Isaiah said.

"Stop reading my mind, damn it."

A knowing smile curled the corners of Isaiah's big mouth. "Sorry. It's a lot like learning to walk. Once you start, it's hard to slow down. Next thing, you're running."

"Try," Tripp ordered dryly.

Isaiah nodded, but the guy grinned, as if this was all a game for him. "Imagine waking up one day, and suddenly, you're able to hear what's going on in every person's mind within a ten-mile radius of your bedroom. That's when my psychic gift manifested. I was a teenager, and thought I was crazy, a freak. It wasn't until I met Tate a couple years ago, that I learned how to filter the excess noise out of my head."

"It's called tuning," Tate added with a shrug of his big shoulders. "No big deal. I grew up knowing how to tune down the noise and zero in on what's important. It's easy once you know how."

"But none of you can read the perp's mind?" Jameson asked.

Ky shook his head. "Correct. Which is why Tucker's fit to be tied. Eden's able to pick up psychic impressions off people's clothing, sometimes from an item that meant a lot to them."

"Like a doll or a purse. A shoe," Tucker added grimly, his arms crossed over his chest.

"She works like a bloodhound?" Tripp asked.

"In a way, yes," Ky replied, still holding onto his wife. "Eden's psychic gift acts very much like a bloodhound when it picks up scents from clothing or in the air. But we've already gone over the other crime scenes. Trust me, she's been on her hands and knees with her fingers in the dirt this jerk walked on—"

"The same dirt his victims bled into," she added quietly.

"And we've got zilch," Tucker ended, his exasperation loud and clear. "I've got the best team in the whole United States, and we can't get a feel for this one crazy bastard."

Tripp was dying to ask Eden what she now knew about him that he didn't want in the FBI's possession. Like the identity of the vigilante. Or anything about Trish. The instant that insecurity ghosted through his mind, she looked straight at him. She knew everything. Damn. She was on to him.

He shrugged that annoying development off, rolled his shoulder, and grumbled, "This is all real interesting, but I came here to investigate the crime scene." *Not to get cross-examined over something I'll never admit.*

"Right this way," Tucker quipped. "Wouldn't want to disappoint anyone from *The TEAM*." He colored those last two words with enough sarcasm to choke a horse.

"Smart thinking," Alex's deep baritone rumbled behind Tripp and Jameson.

"Alex," Tucker replied with a tinge of embarrassment.

"Tuck," Alex bit out, his sarcasm on full power.

Tripp turned sideways as Alex approached. "Hey, Boss. Just got here. What do we know?"

Like the rest of his TEAM, Alex had dressed in jeans, a TEAM polo, work boots, and a light jacket to cover his double holster and the SIG Sauer pistols he always carried.

"Can I ask you something first?" Eden directed that question at Tripp. Her eyes were green like his, yet more than just green. It wasn't so much the color of her eyes or the size of her pupils, which seemed bigger and blacker than everyone else's at the moment. It was more the way she used her eyes, as if they were high-powered microscopes, seeing far deeper than everyone else.

Tripp felt like a bug pinned under glass for closer inspection, maybe dissection. Damned unsettling. Swallowing his guilt for what she probably knew about him, he shook his head, needing to stay focused on the current crime. "Sorry, no. Only got time for our serial killer or the victim. We got a name yet, Boss?"

Alex, Tuck, and the others were walking up to the scene. Jameson was hanging back with Tripp, when a soft, warm hand settled over his forearm. Tripp looked down at Eden. It was her hand and her touch burned. "The victim is Tommy McMurray," she told him.

His breath caught. "Tommy? Are you sure? He's the maintenance guy for my apartment complex. Fuck! And you're just telling me that now?"

"I didn't know you knew him until I shook your hand, but our connection was so strong, I almost passed out. Go home, back to your apartment. I'll drive. My car's—"

Tripp grabbed Jameson's elbow and ordered, "Truck, now. Keep the fuck up."

He had to get to Ashley.

Chapter Thirty-Four

Peewee shrieked again. Poor boy was probably tired of being ignored. Ashley had been in the kitchen baking and cooking since Tripp left. She'd just put the finishing touches on the peach cobbler she'd whipped up to go with the chicken and dumplings. Some days were all about comfort food, and one more sprinkle of cinnamon sugar would make this cobbler her best yet.

"Shush, sweetheart, I'm coming," she called out, dusting her palms on a nearby kitchen towel, as she checked the crockpot one last time. The carrots and shredded chicken were now drowning in rich gravy. The second she lifted the lid, she closed her eyes and took a deep breath. Her apartment always felt more like a home when she baked or cooked.

She'd set three casserole dishes with lids on her counter, one for Tripp's mom, one for Mrs. Harrison, the other for Tripp. He was running on empty and would need a decent dinner. As soon as he returned, she was feeding him, then bedding him. She couldn't wait to get him back in her arms and her hands all over him. It was her turn to make him feel good.

Tossing her robe over the back of her kitchen chair, she grinned at the lightness in her step and the silly jingle in her heart. Man, she was happier than she'd been in a long time. What was that saying? *'Today is the best day of the rest of your life?'* Well, it was true. She knew what she wanted and the metamorphosis began with her. Right now.

"You look better than I remembered."

That creepy voice jerked her head up. *It's him! He's inside my apartment!* That was why Peewee was squawking and beating his wings. The poor bird's crest was standing on end. He was scared. *And I'm in nothing but my underwear!*

Ashley crossed both arms over her chest, her mind jitterbugging back two years to *that day*. A burning wave of humiliation climbed up her neck at what this creep had almost done to her then. What he'd gotten away with.

His eyes were the same eerie shade of gray. Spooky, like a ghost lived inside him. His gaze slid over her nearly naked body like ice water, dousing all those wonderful homey feelings, turning them into terror.

"Looks like you're finally ready to play," he purred.

For the third time in two years, Ashley faced a killer. Poor Peewee still flapped his wings and screamed. Feathers and dust flew everywhere. She wished she could scream as loudly, but every drop of saliva in her throat had evaporated. Her lungs were working extra hard, but she wasn't getting any air. No potty-mouthed guardian angel would drop out of heaven this time.

"Shut that shittin' bird up," her nightmare ordered, "or I'll wring his neck and gut him."

"Okay, okay, s-s-sure," she stuttered, her poor heart banging against her ribs. How stupid that she was only wearing her bra and panties.

"Did you think I wouldn't find you?"

Here we go again. Ashley's fingers trembled, as she kept an eye on her would-be killer, while she side-stepped to her poor baby's cage and covered him for what would be the last time. Peewee didn't need to see what would happen next. She couldn't do that to him.

"Answer me, Ashley Cox. Want to pla-a-a-ay?"

Cringing at those familiar words, she closed her eyes, speechless. Hopeless.

Until Tripp's words came back to her. *'When faced with imminent attack, act fast and decisively. Go in fast, hit hard. Never let them see you coming.'*

But I'm scared and he's got a knife.

'Eyes, nose, throat, balls…'

And you were supposed to teach me how to shoot.

'Eyes, nose, throat, balls…'

Ashley glanced sideways at the monster in her home. The trench coat made this creep look professional and mysterious, the knife made him look evil. But he was still short. Average weight. Average build. Not anything like Tripp or Jameson or his boss. His trench coat was stained and dirty. The hems of his jeans were ragged. His pea-green running shoes were muddy, the laces frayed and dirty. His gray eyes weren't as scary as they'd been the first time she'd seen him. He was nothing special. He was ordinary.

'Fight for keeps, Ashley. Fight to kill. Gouge your attacker's eyes, punch the heel of your palm into his nose, or make a good, hard fist and punch his fuckin' throat. Knee his balls, kick, scream, whatever you have to do to stay alive. Just do something.'

Fudge. Okay. Deep breath. Tripp wasn't there, but Ashley was beginning to think she might just stand a chance. That she could live through this attack.

'Might does not make right. Men who assault women are generally bullies and cowards. They're weak. They think because they might be physically bigger and male, that women are easy targets. Now you know better. If you ever find yourself up against some jerk... Surprise the hell out of him and prove that son of a bitch wrong.' Those were Zack's words in her head now. Tripp's friends sure wanted her to live. They made defending herself sound doable. But she'd never hit anyone before in her life. Ever. Could she really keep this monster from hurting her?

The jolt came out of the blue. She wanted to live. This guy intended for her to die. To borrow Tripp's salty vernacular... *No, fuckin' way.*

Ashley might not be able to keep this guy from hurting her, but this time, she could hurt him back.

Still facing Peewee, she curled her fingers around the apple wood perch she'd intended to put in his cage the next time she cleaned it. Terry Chandler had brought several hefty branches to work the last time he'd trimmed his trees, after she'd told him how cockatoos were voracious wood-chewers. Most extra branches were stored in her spare bedroom. He'd given her enough applewood to last Peewee a couple years, and he'd trimmed them all to the perfect length. Applewood took Peewee longer to chew. It was a hardwood. The would-be perch was dense and smooth. It felt really good in her hand.

She clasped it against her chest. Her heart was still climbing up her throat, but her grip was solid, and she meant to fight back, even if it killed her.

"Game time," the creep who thought she was still a timid little waif said. "Get your ass over here."

Even his voice was nothing special. More whiny than masculine. A pitch too high to be dominant. Nothing like Tripp's gruff baritone or his boss's husky bass. Ashley closed her eyes, shaking with fear. This jerk wanted to play? She was ready.

Ashley faced the creep with Peewee's perch in her sweaty hands, her heart a flock of scared hummingbirds fluttering up her throat. "Who are you?"

His face wrinkled into a snarl. "Your worst nightmare."

How cliché? This girly guy wasn't much bigger than she was. She could take him. So what if he had a sharp knife? She had a perch that she'd turned into a club, and it was longer.

Ashley raised it over her right shoulder and charged. She screamed like a banshee. Peewee screeched along with her. The jerk turned sideways. Good move. She bashed the bat into the side of his skull. His cheek shifted over his teeth like a loose rug in the wind. Spittle flew out of his mouth. Was that a tooth? Man, she hoped so.

"I'll kill you for that!" he bellowed.

"Get out of my home!" She hit him again on the upswing. That blow wasn't as strong. It landed too high on his shoulder.

"Why you fuckin' bitch!"

She battered up again, her club cocked like a baseball bat over her shoulder. But she'd gotten in too close. If she'd had more room to swing, she could've knocked his head off. Instead, his fist snaked out and hit her chest. Dead center. He knocked the wind out of her.

Ashley stumbled, shocked at the pain sucking her breath away. Black shadows danced at her peripheral. She'd landed on one knee. He was still a man and bigger; she was still learning how to fight. He came at her with his knife raised next.

She stuck her club into the carpet and used it like a walking stick, needing to get back on her feet.

He kicked it aside and shoved her to her back.

Fighting for her life, Ashley rolled to her side and wrapped her hand around the perch, not that she could swing it. But not letting it go, either. This was war, darn it!

He was on her, weighing her down and straddling her hips. His hands on her neck, choking her, his thumbs digging into her throat.

Ashley wasn't stupid enough to think he'd set his knife down to strangle her. With one hand still on the club, she slapped her other palm to the floor, needing to locate his knife before he did. Needing with all her heart to stab this creep in the eye!

Hissing, he cocked an arm back and slapped her. The force of that hit knocked her head to the side. Fudge, that hurt! She lost her club. So much for finding his knife.

"You're all alike!" Her attacker spat saliva into her face. "Conniving, lying bitches. Every last one of you!"

"Yeah, well, you're an ass!" she yelled back at him. Two years ago she would've cowered. Not today.

That slap must've dislodged something in her brain. The guy Friday night had said he'd just wanted oxycodone, but he'd sat on her and called her a slut, too. What was wrong with men these days. Slut? Bitch? Were they all threatened by strong, intelligent women? Not that she was in any position of strength at the moment, but—

The ass slapped her again!

"Ouch! Stop it, you jerk!" she cried, her attacker blurry and possibly bleeding, if those dark spots on his face were what she hoped they were. If they were, that meant she'd drawn first blood. It was hard to know for sure with all the black dots dancing at the corners of her eyes. The possibility that she really could win this battle powered Ashley's confidence.

Grunting, he lifted to his feet, reached down, and grabbed a fistful of her hair.

"Let me go!" she ordered.

He didn't answer, just twisted her around and dragged her to her door, the carpet on her nearly bare backside burning her skin.

Terror rolled up Ashley's throat when he stopped to pick up his knife. This guy was the serial killer everyone was looking for, the one who'd nearly killed Tripp's sister last night.

"I'm going to kill you!" Poor Peewee shrieked along with her. All that noise should attract someone. Anyone!

"No, you're not," the killer replied as he opened her door and dragged her into the hall. Then, as if he'd forgotten something, he stopped, twisted his fist in her hair, and told her, "You're not going to live long enough to do anything but scream and cry. Now shut up!"

Instead of fighting his hold on her hair, Ashley reached out and grabbed the club while she could still reach it. "You won't get away with this."

He dragged her farther down the hall. "That's what they all said. But this time, we won't be interrupted, and you won't get away. We're going to play the rest of the day, and trust me…"

They were nearly at Tripp's door. What was he going to do? Drag her down the stairs? Her stomach lurched up her throat. If only Tripp were home!

"I'm not moving you like I did the others. Not this time. This is personal. Your boyfriend's gonna cry when he finds what's left of you. Like a pussy-whipped, helpless, little boy who wants his mama, he's gonna scream and rage, but it'll be too late. By then, I'll have played with her, too."

She didn't understand. "What do Tripp and Andy have to do with anything?"

"She's his mother. He's her only son, isn't he? Don't you get it?"

"No. Explain it."

"The freak's in love with his mother!"

"So?" Ashley jerked to her side, fear for Tripp and his mom hammering at her nerves as she struggled to escape. "What's he ever done to you?"

"He made me look bad!" Her killer stopped dragging and turned to look down at Ashley, her long hair still knotted in his fist. His gray eyes were flat and unfocused, like he was looking through her to somewhere else. "I didn't know she was his sister. She was just there, in my way. But it makes sense now. It was destiny. She was there for a reason, because she led me to him, and he led me to you. If you think about it... if you really stop and take the time to connect all the dots... me finding her... me following him... me killing him for taking her away from me... for loving her... me finding you on the street where he works... in the dark... me following you all the way home..." The jerk ran his tongue over his bottom lip, like he was savoring something. "Just imagine what he'll do when I play with his mother like I'm going to play with you."

"You can't hurt her! No! What's she ever done to you?"

"She loves him! Don't you get it? Isn't that enough?"

Ashley dug her bare heels into the carpet, but it was no use. She couldn't reach him with her club. Just one good hard hit, that's all it would take. "No, I don't get it. Damn you, I don't know the rules of this stupid game. Explain them to me!"

At Tripp's door, he finally let go. Her head dropped to the floor, as his full weight settled onto her hips. He tipped forward, his ugly lips nearly touching her nose, and something small but hard as a rock grinding into her pelvis. She closed her eyes in horror at the thought of being tortured while he jacked-off.

"There are no rules to the game of love, Ashley Cox. You just need to scream how much you love me, when I tell you to, if you still can. Not like anyone will hear you because there's no one else on this floor but us. Trust me, I checked. It's just you and me and—" he ran his tongue up her cheek "—it's time to play. On your knees, bitch." The tip of his knife nicking the underside of her chin. "First move is yours. You're going to crawl into your boyfriend's apartment and beg me to love you. Bring your little stick with you. You'll need it."

Chapter Thirty-Five

The son of a bitchin' elevator was down again! Like a heat-seeking missile, Tripp changed course and aimed for the stairwell. The second he jerked the door open, ready to run, Mrs. Harrison stumbled out and all but fell into his arms.

"Oh, Tripp. I'm so glad to see you," she said, patting his chest like he was a good boy while she caught her balance. "Is Ashley with you?"

"No, ma'am, she's not," he replied, taking polite hold of her biceps and setting her aside.

"Oh, that's too bad. I've been listening to some old records this morning, and I'm afraid I had the volume up too high. Maybe I upset her bird. It's certainly making a lot of noise. I thought—"

"Peewee's screeching?" At this time of day?

"Yes, it's been going on for a while now and—"

"Sorry, ma'am. I've got to run." Tripp didn't have time to explain. If Peewee was upset, something was dead damned wrong at Ashley's place.

Inside the stairwell, he looked up through the ceiling of zig-zagging handrails.

"How many floors up?" Jameson asked at his side.

"Four. Keep up."

"All the way," was the last thing Tripp heard, as he cleared the first and second floor landings. At the third, he damned near pulled his arm out of its socket when he attempted to jerk the door open. The son of a bitch was locked! How could that be? Mrs. Harrison had just come through this door and down those stairs. Suspicion climbed up Tripp's spine. He was missing something.

"Stand back," Jameson ordered, his weapon, a damned sweet .44 Magnum, already in his hand. Holding Tripp back with his other arm, Jameson ran his fingers over the door. As soon as he located the keyhole beneath the stainless-steel handle, he fired once.

BOOM!

Tripp didn't have time to be amazed at the fuckin' loud noise that weapon made or this blind man's crazy ninja skills. He ran to Ashley's place at the opposite end of the hall, his ears ringing and Jameson on his ass. The second Tripp hit her wide-open door, he knew he'd been had. He glared at the elevator, walked over to the damn thing and punched the down arrow on the exterior control panel.

"The son of a bitch works! It was never out of order. He was here!"

Jameson still stood at Ashley's doorway, his pistol near his cheek, pointed up. "Let's make sure she's not home. I'm going in. You should, too."

"Make it quick," Tripp snapped, his pistol in his right hand, regret a sucker punch to his gut. He'd left Ashley alone. With a bird! He should've left one of his pistols. Why'd he need two?

Tripp hit the emergency stop button inside the elevator car, then made a hurried, cursory run through Ashley's place. With every step, angst choked the shit out of him. That there'd been a struggle was apparent. The careful array of items on her antique desk was scattered. The killer must've picked her deadbolt; Ashley was smart and paranoid. She would've checked her peephole if he'd knocked. The aroma of something cooking filled the air. She must've been in the kitchen when he'd surprised her. Poor Peewee looked like a fluffball of powdery, spiked feathers. His blanket and a shitload of down laced the floor in a wide circle around his cage.

Tripp took a minute to calm her pet as much as he could, "Settle down, big guy. I'll find her, I promise."

But Peewee wasn't buying that line any more than Tripp did, and he was nowhere near calm enough to fool himself, much less the bird. With one last nod at her upset baby, Tripp stalked to her door, needing to run. But when he saw the bloody smear on the inside of the doorjamb, he lost it. "Gawddamnit! He's got her!"

A hard hand landed on his shoulder. "Then let's end this motherfucker," Jameson growled at his six. "Going down?"

"Hell, yeah."

A second later, Tripp was inside the car, his foot tapping, his blood running hot with the need to get to Ashley before this bastard hurt her again. "He locked the fire doors, took her down in the elevator, then set the maintenance sign out to throw us off the trail." *And it worked like a fuckin' charm! That son of a bitch!* "Come on, Tenney. Move it!"

But Jameson had paused. He cocked his head like the steady, thoughtful man he was. "No. Wait. He thinks he's smarter than us."

"And he very well might be! Get in! Jesus, move your ass!"

"First tell me what you see."

Tripp was half out of his mind with worry. "I see an asshole holding me up! Get in or I'm leaving without you!"

"Blood, Tripp. Is there any blood inside the car? On the inside of the door. On the walls? Anywhere? Droplets? Spatter? Spray?"

"Blood? Here?" Oh, yeah. Tripp's brain flashed back online. He took a deep breath and stifled his panic, then scanned the floor, the walls, the ceiling. Everything. He hit the emergency close-door button, looking closer. No more mistakes. Ashley needed him to be smart. He swallowed past the hard knot in his throat and reopened the doors. "You're right. Not a drop of blood in her."

Jameson stood with his arms braced on each side of the elevator, his head cocked to the side. If Tripp hadn't known better, he'd swear Jameson could see something no one else could see. "That woman downstairs, do you know where she lives?" he asked quietly.

Tripp stuck his chin toward the other end of the hall. "Mrs. Harrison, sure. Across the hall from me. My door's the far one on your left."

"Think," Jameson whispered. "This guy just gave APD a shitload of evidence in that body bag. But he's smart. He knows it'll take months to sift through and analyze the mess he left behind. It'll be a good year before we get DNA matches to anyone in the system, if we get results at all. If our guy's even in IAFIS. He knows that. He's taunting us."

IAFIS stood for the Integrated Automated Fingerprint Identification System that fell under the jurisdiction of the Federal Bureau of Investigation. Right in Director Chase's backyard.

Tripp swallowed hard. "Get to the gawddamned point."

Jameson nodded down the hall, that monster weapon of his pointing the way. "He's still here," he whispered. Then in a louder voice, he declared, "Call it in, McClane! No one's here. He got away again."

Tripp played along. "Shit, damn, and son of a bitch! Why's this asshole always one step ahead of us?"

"I'm beginning to think he's smarter than the rest of us."

"I'll kill him if he hurts her!" Tripp poured all his rage into that very real threat. "Gawddamn him. He's dead. He just doesn't know it yet."

Jameson pressed his index finger to his lips, then crept stealthily toward Tripp's place. "Check the apartment across from Ashley's," he whispered. "Let's cover all bases."

"You think she's in my place?" That made no sense.

"I think she's still on this floor."

Okay then. Tripp shut down his need for revenge and followed Jameson's calm lead. He didn't know who lived across the hall from Ashley. Had never cared. He did now. He leaned his ear against that door, praying for some sign that she was still alive. A whimper. A thud. Any damned thing!

Nothing. He swallowed hard, his hand to the doorknob as all those gruesome crime scene photos flashed through his mind. Bowing his head, he finally realized how much he stood to lose, that he might never see Ashley alive again. That he might've already lost her.

'Not Ashley,' he prayed silently. *'God, I... I love her. I do. If you're as good as my mom believes you are, then save Ashley!'*

With one hard kick, Tripp was inside what turned out to be an empty apartment. He made a clean sweep through the wide-open floor plan. Found nothing.

Back in the hall, Jameson crouched at Mrs. Harrison's door, his ear flat against the wood. He'd just beckoned Tripp forward when another hand landed on Tripp's shoulder. Alex wax there. Tucker Chase, Eden, Ky, Isaiah, and Tate stood behind him.

"Damned elevator's out," Tuck groused.

"Quiet!" Tripp hissed. "Fucker's still here. He just wanted us to think it was out."

Eden whispered, "Any reason why Ashley's in your spare bedroom closet?"

Tripp's heart stuttered. "Thank fuck!" he hissed, at last believing in psychics. "You can't read the killer, but you can read Ashley? Is she okay?"

He and Jameson stepped away from Mrs. Harrison's door.

"Yes, she's bleeding, but she's pissed off, too. She's got a club, Tripp, and right now, she fully believes she's going to die. That she's got nothing to lose. He hurt her, but she hurt him first. She's thinking of beating him to death the first chance she gets."

Tripp did a neck-snapping double-take. "My Ashley?" *My timid, little Ashley?* Yeah, okay, so he'd just outed himself, and he'd seen Alex's sharp eyes widen when he did. But who cared? Not Tripp. He had a woman to save.

"Yes, your Ashley," Eden piped up evenly. "We have to do this carefully. We still can't read him. We don't know what he's doing right now. What if he's prepared to die? What if he has a bomb in there or a boobytrap?"

Tripp hadn't thought of those scenarios.

"He doesn't," Jameson answered. "This man's in over his head this time, and he knows it. Last night's murder was a panic kill. He had a plan, and Tommy McMurray got in his way. Our guy over-reacted and lashed out when he should've taken a step back and rethought his strategy. If he thinks he's cornered now, then this is his finale. His swan song. He won't be taken alive."

Tripp didn't like the sound of that. "You think he'd blow himself and Ashley up?"

Eden shook her head very deliberately, side to side. "No, Tripp. From what I'm sensing in Ashley's mind, this guy wants you to suffer first."

"Why? I don't know him."

"Then why's he in your place?" Tucker asked.

"How the hell would I know?" Tripp looked to Eden for that answer.

"That I don't know, but Ashley's afraid what he might do to you and your mother. That's why she's going to confront him."

"He wants you to watch while he hurts Ashley," Jameson added. "That's where he gets his power. He believes hurting women makes him a man. He believes he's still in charge, that he's all powerful."

"Which he sure has been," Tucker groused.

"Until now," Alex said. He'd been uncharacteristically quiet.

Tripp turned to his boss, a USMC scout sniper of legendary skill. "Are you thinking what I'm thinking?" Elite teams who'd worked together for too many operations were oftentimes linked with an uncanny sixth sense that put them on the same wave-length and made words unnecessary. Only Tripp hadn't worked closely with this legend yet.

But Alex had picked up on Tripp's intention. His cell phone was already in his hand. "You or me? Your call."

"You. I'll give you fifteen to get over there and set up."
Because I need to be the first one in. I need to save my girl!

"Only need seven."

Tripp dug his earbud and cell phone out of an inside jacket pocket. "Then seven it is," he said as he set the timer on his cell and tucked his earphone in his ear. "Sync in three, two—"

"Done." Alex returned his cell to his jacket pocket and placed an earbud inside his ear.

"Stay frosty, Boss," Tripp told Alex. *And please be as good as everyone says you are.*

Again, with the stoic head nod. Alex left the way he'd come. Like a deadly, quiet ghost.

Tripp huffed a hard breath through his nose, his composure rattled. This was it, then. Ashley's life was on the line. Stepping up to his door, he inserted his key, not assuming anything and needing to make sure it worked. Nothing happened. Tripp tried again, pushing into the door, as if more weight would do the trick. "Shit. Something's blocking my door."

Damned if the only blind man on the floor didn't step forward and ask, "What do you need?"

"You got any C-4 breach charges on you?"

Jameson's head kicked back. "You sure think I work miracles, don't you?" he asked quietly.

Tripp gave it to him straight. "Fuck yeah, brother. I know damned well you do." He fluttered his fingers. "Just need one. Hand it over."

The grin that cracked Jameson's face was priceless. More so when he tugged what looked like a small black container out of an inner jacket pocket and produced a neat cube of the off-white plastic explosive. "I've got blasting caps and det cord, too," he murmured as he produced the rest of what Tripp needed from different pockets. In seconds, the lock to his door was packed with the right amount of C-4, wired, and ready to detonate. The way forward wouldn't be blocked long.

"Move your ass, Alex," he whispered.

Of everyone in that crowded hallway, Tripp didn't expect the confidence builder that came from Tucker Chase. "He won't let you down, Agent McClane. Stewart's a fuckin' rock."

Tripp's head snapped to the big guy's jet-black eyes. "Step back," he ordered. None of them had once asked what he and Alex were up to. Not that Tripp would've explained. Guess they really were psychic. He fingered the scrap of silky underwear in his pocket. Alex had one damned minute to get his ass in position.

Chapter Thirty-Six

Ashley didn't know how much longer she should wait to attack again, or if she needed to. The jerk who'd kidnapped her was quiet. Too quiet. She wasn't sure where he was, if he was even in Tripp's apartment anymore. She'd hurt him. She knew she had. Maybe not enough to stop him. He'd thought he could just order her to crawl, and she'd fall apart like the weakling she'd been before? Guess again.

She'd fought back. Hard! Yes, she'd crawled, but once he'd slammed Tripp's door behind her, he'd kicked her ass. That sent her sprawling face first into the carpet, right on top of her club. Thinking fast, she'd rolled to one side and…

WHAM! Up came the sawed-off end of that perch. She punched it straight into the jerk's face, hit his nose, and dropped him to his knees. She knew now she should've beaten the shit out of him once she'd knocked him down. But adrenaline had gotten the best of her, darn it. Like a scared ninny, Ashley had jumped to her feet and run into Tripp's guest bedroom, instead of back out into the hall and down the fire stairs. Her killer hadn't followed her yet, but he would. Why else had he moved her out of her place?

To trick Tripp, that was why. He wouldn't think to look for her here. She knew how he operated. Tripp was emotional and reactive. He'd be frantic to save her. His mind might be firing on all eight cylinders, but his heart would be driving every last one of his decisions.

Ashley worried for Tripp's mother, for Mrs. Harrison, too. Had this guy already hurt them? Was that why Mrs. Harrison was so quiet? The racket Peewee made had drowned out her screams for help. There was no one coming this time, and she knew it. Tripp was out doing his job. Unless she was injured, Mrs. Harrison was too elderly to be any help. She couldn't fight a flea anyway. That left everything up to Ashley. If she wanted to live, she'd have to fight for the right.

Her lip and nose were bleeding, and her scalp stung where the creep had jerked patches of her hair out. But nothing was broken. When she'd resisted being dragged up the hall, she'd felt the arsenal of sharp shapes and edges inside this creep's trench coat. They had to be weapons or tools of his diabolical trade, which was why she hadn't dropped her club. No way. She didn't understand why he'd let her keep it. Maybe he'd thought he could easily take it away from her? Use it on her?

His craziness panicked Ashley. Fudge, she was trembling so hard, she could barely breathe. If she wanted to attack first, she'd soon have to give up the safety of this closet and move into the open. To effectively fight back, she needed more space to swing her club. Tripp's closet was so full of boxes and guy stuff, there was barely room to hide. The man sure had a lot of exercise and weight-lifting equipment. Plus, that monkey-bar thing in his spare room, fastened to two walls and running over the ceiling between them. What was he, a big kid with a secret playground in his apartment?

Her pulse pounded like a thousand hammers through her veins. Noisy hammers that made it hard to think. Harder to hear what her killer was doing out there in Tripp's living room or kitchen. If he was still there. She'd have to choose her defensive position carefully. Let him come to her. Let him stumble over those barbells and weight sets, those big round things with handles that lay between her and the door.

The jerk had a bloody nose now. What was he up to, treating his wound? Aww, poor creepy asshole baby! Ashley took a perverse twinge of satisfaction in that possibility. She refused to be assaulted without fighting back this time. She *had* to do something, now, while he thought she was scared and he was safe. Before he came at her with that knife. She had to act!

As quietly as possible, nearly without breathing, she cracked the louvered closet door open and stepped into the cluttered guest bedroom. It was now or never. Whispering Tripp's second rule and her new mantra, "Never give up. Never give up. Never," Ashley knotted both hands in a death grip around Peewee's perch.

It would've helped if she'd sounded more like Tripp and less like herself. Because here in his apartment, she would make her last stand. Here, she would fight to the bitter end to live and to save Tripp's mom. Or die trying.

Chapter Thirty-Seven

It was now afternoon on a godawful Tuesday. Tripp had never worked any ops with Alex Stewart, but he'd heard the office gossip. The man was a fuckin' god who'd started The TEAM from scratch after he'd left the Corps on a hardship discharge years ago. That must've been when he'd lost the child Ashley told him about. Made terrible, tragic sense.

The time left for Alex to be where he needed to be? Ten damned seconds. Then five. Everyone stepped back from the door. Swallowing hard at all the ways this could go wrong, Tripp counted down, "Three, two—"

The breach charge detonated without making much more noise than a husky, *PFFF-Whump!*

Tripp kicked his door in, both pistols up and ready, and there… across the room, standing in the breeze-blown sheers at his shattered picture window was—APD's photographer?! He was the killer? Worse, the bastard had one arm cocked around Ashley's neck and a twelve-inch knife in his other. He had that blade stuck under her chin. Why was she just in her bra and panties?

"You!" Tripp spat, aware that Jameson, Tucker, Eden, Ky, Isaiah, and Tate had crowded into the room behind him. That everyone could see every last piece of Ashley.

"Yeah, me!" the guy crowed through swollen, bloody lips. "How dumb are you, soldier boy? Three bitches? Most guys can't handle fuckin' one!"

Tripp had no idea why he'd said three. Didn't matter. *I'll kill him.* "What have you done to her?"

"Nothing but punch me and drag me," Ashley answered hoarsely, her plump breasts crushed under his arm and her nipples on display. "I hit him, Tripp. I fought back, but then I... I lost my bat." She must've meant that hefty branch on the floor.

"And you're just in time to watch her die!" The bastard tightened his elbow, squeezing off her words. "Drop your guns! All of you!"

He thought he was in charge? No one dropped a thing. Little did this asshat know that an alpha killer now had the back of his head lined up in his crosshairs. Tripp didn't have a clear shot, not as twitchy as this guy was. Neither would Alex, the way the photographer kept bobbing behind Ashley, unintentionally keeping her head within the same crosshairs. Alex had better be a gawddamned good shot.

Looked like this jerk had been in one helluva fight, though. His nose was a bloody mess, and he was breathing hard. Despite the silly paper towel plugs he'd stuffed up his nostrils, blood dripped steadily down his lips, chin, and neck, onto his trench coat. One eye was swollen nearly shut. But he was the guy with the milky gray eyes Ashley had described. Guess he'd gotten more than he'd bargained for this time around.

"How you doing, babe?" Tripp asked her, trying to exert calmness, even as acid poured into his gut at how frightened she looked.

Ashley stood there trapped, with too much skin showing and shaking like a leaf, her bare back and almost bare ass to the creep's front. She was barefooted, too, but she hadn't stepped on the broken window glass yet. Her feet weren't bleeding. Both hands clenched the guy's forearm, her elbows pointed out. She was fighting his stranglehold. "I hit him, Tripp," she wheezed through the pressure on her throat. "Like you told me to do. I wasn't going to let him—"

"She thinks she's a tougher bitch than the others, but she isn't!" The photographer's arm clamped tighter around her neck, cutting off her words. "Never will be! Won't live long enough to do more than go splat!"

"I'm tougher than you'll ever be," she ground out, her knuckles white against his coat sleeve. "You're a coward. That's why you hurt girls." Lifting one knee, she angled her foot and kicked his shin with her heel.

The jerk winced.

"Shhhhh, Ashley. Not now," Tripp ordered gently. *He's already crazy. Don't make him throw you out that window.*

"Shut the fuck up!" APD's cameraman snarled, spitting blood out the side of his mouth. One of those nasty paper towel plugs plopped to the floor, making him look just plain pathetic. "Don't you idiots get it? They're all mean, greedy bitches, willing to step on anyone who gets in their way. They don't know a thing about the game of love! Enough about them! It's my turn to play!"

Still keeping Ashley in a stranglehold, he fisted his knife at a hard, right angle under her jaw, the tip pointed up. At this rate, that blade would pierce her tongue and palate on its way to her brain. She'd be dead in seconds. The killer cast a quick glance at the tattered sheer curtain flapping in the breeze behind them. He was over-the-top agitated, unpredictable as fuck. A thin line of blood ran down the blade to the handle. He'd already cut her!

Tripp knew what he had to do. *Rein it in. Tone it down.* For Ashley's sake. Before he forced this maniac into action. Fighting for composure, he showed the killer his pistol, held it up and sideways to prove he meant what he was saying. "How about we talk? Just you and me. Let the lady go. This is me bargaining in good faith. See? I'm putting my weapon down. Guys, everyone get out of here except—"

"How 'bout we see how good this bitch flies?!" the photographer screeched over Tripp. His eyes were drug-addict bright, more black than ghostly gray. He was definitely hurt, breathing hard, and favoring his right foot. But in two shorts steps, he could still throw Ashley out the window. "Wanna see if you're quick enough to save this one like you saved that other bitch? Huh, do ya?"

"What other bitch?" It dawned on Tripp then. The bastard was talking about Trish. Tripp's pistol never reached the floor. It flashed back on target. It was time to end this one-sided negotiation with a man who didn't deserve to live. Alex had better be ready. "Drop, Ashley! Now!" Tripp bellowed. "Hit the floor! Get out of my way!"

She obeyed, just closed her eyes, and turned into limp deadweight. The photographer couldn't hang onto her. He fumbled his knife trying to keep a grip. The second her head slipped down past his chest—

PEW! From a place he never saw, came a sound this bastard never heard. Alex's round hit true. At the same time, Tripp fired, tearing a hole in the photographer's throat. Then—

BOOM! A fucking cannon roared over Tripp's shoulder. Right next to his ear. Could only be Jameson's .44 Magnum following through.

Dead man standing. The bastard's body stilled in a macabre flash of exsanguination. With both ears ringing, Tripp charged for Ashley before APD's photographer could take her with him. Tripp had her in his arms by the time the killer's lifeless body flopped backward through the empty window frame.

"Jesus H Christ!" Tucker Chase snarled from somewhere far away. "You guys think you got him?"

"Had to make sure Tripp didn't miss," Jameson countered easily, his voice just as muffled.

"Him miss? At this range?" Tucker scoffed, his voice as distant as Jameson's. "Alex already wasted the prick. How the fuck do you even own a pistol, Tenney?"

"Easy. I qualify. Why didn't you fire?"

Tripp was barely able to hear, but he couldn't hold back a smile, listening to the Neanderthal FBI director argue with the inestimable Jameson Tenney, blind sniper extraordinaire. Jameson had only done what any decent soldier would've done. He'd simply covered his buddy's ass and made damned sure the HVT was down for good.

Peeling out of his jacket, Tripp covered Ashley's bare body. While she hiked her bra into place and shivered her arms into the too-long sleeves, he zipped the damned thing up all the way to her chin. No one needed to ogle his woman like he knew they were. Men! What a bunch of animals.

Once she was snug inside his jacket, her breasts covered and most of her long legs out of sight, he placed his hand on the knife wound under her chin.

"You need this?" Jameson came to Tripp's rescue, a palm-sized bandage in his fingers. How the hell did he even know Ashley'd been cut?

"Yeah, man, thanks," Tripp answered, taking the bandage. "Sure do."

"Tripp," Ashley breathed into his neck. She'd burrowed back under his chin, her fingers ice cold, and the rest of her a one hundred percent quivering female. "Don't let me go. P-p-please, hold on tight to me."

"Never. I've got you, kiddo. Just tip your head up a little, so I can take care of that cut," he replied, his heart pounding like a mother at how close he'd come to losing her.

While Jameson crouched silently at his side like a bodyguard with his head up, sometimes tilted, sometimes not, Tripp peeled the sterile bandage open. "Battle scars," he told Ashley. "You should be proud. You're a bona-fide badass now."

Despite his shaky fingers, Tripp managed to press the sticky bandage under her chin. The knife cut was small, not deep, thank God. Better yet, most of the blood and gore from the photographer's head painted the wall behind her, instead of her.

But shit, damn, and son of a bitch. Enough was enough. Three fuckin' times she'd been a target! What the bloody hell?!

"J-j-just like l-l-last time." Hiccups racked Ashley's slender shoulders when he had her snuggled back in his arms. "He just came right in. Only this time, he unlocked my deadbolt, Tripp. Can you believe that? I thought I was safe, but I never really was. I was in my kitchen, but then I heard

Peewee squawking, and when I turned around, and I… and he…"

"You fought back," Tripp said more calmly, needing her to settle down before she launched another panic attack. "That's all that matters. Focus, babe. Breathe in, breathe out. You just realized you're stronger than you thought."

"I am!" The poor woman's teeth chattered. She had enough adrenaline thrumming through her tiny body to power the entire state of Virginia.

Jameson landed a solid palm on her trembling shoulder, then squeezed. "You got quite a few good licks in this time, girlfriend. Good for you. You hurt him. He was in trouble before we arrived. I could tell by his voice."

Ashley snorted the most unladylike snort, as she peered around Tripp's arm up at Jameson. "I-I had to. He was gonna kill me. I used Peewee's new perch. He didn't think I'd hit him, but I showed him."

"Yes, you did," Tripp purred, so proud of her that tears blurred his vision. "But why'd he drag you out of your place and into mine?"

"He didn't think you'd look for me here," she murmured, snuggling back under his chin. "I was so scared. He said he was gonna hurt your mom, too. But the first chance I got, I swung that perch, hard. Once I used it like it was a pool cue, then like it was a baseball bat. I hit him!"

"Homerun!" Jameson crowed. "Your fighting back like is what gave us enough time to get to you."

"I j-j-just did what Tripp said." She tipped back far enough to look up at him. "G-g-go in fast, hit h-h-hard. Never let him see me coming. And never give up. But he punched my chest, and he slapped me, and…" That explained her fat lip. Even as pumped as she was, Ashley was falling apart. Her cheeks were puffy and red, and tears spiked her eyelashes. She latched onto his biceps. "He was gonna kill me, Tripp. In your place. He was doing it to hurt you."

That made no sense. "Why?"

"Because he said Trish had been out there for a reason the night he attacked her. That she led him to you, and you led him to me."

"He admitted he hurt Tripp's sister?" Jameson asked.

Ashley's head bobbed. "Yes, and he said you made him look bad, Tripp."

"Shit," Jameson muttered. "That crowd did some hardcore taunting that night."

Tripp shrugged. "So what? Someone called him a pussy. Told him to fight back." Which APD's photographer hadn't been able to do with Ashley. Brutalizing women was bully work, best done in the dark, by weak men to weak women. It wasn't fair fighting. The bastard could dish it out, but he couldn't take it once his victim fought back.

Truthfully, Tripp had lost track of the guy once Jameson had knocked Tripp on his ass at his sister's crime scene that night. After Alex had relieved him of his pistol. He'd had Trish to think about then, not some employee who should've been thoroughly vetted by Alexandria's finest.

Ashley burrowed deeper into the folds of his jacket, hiding her face. He knew she was crying. "That guy hated you, Tripp," she murmured sadly. "He saw you the night he hurt Trish. He wanted to kill you for loving her, and, I don't know how, but he knew you loved your mom, too. He said there weren't any rules in the game of love."

"Crazy bastard," Tripp muttered, as he dipped his chin to the top of Ashley's sweaty forehead.

Peewee was finally quiet. Tripp had a feeling that Special Agent Tate Higgins was behind the silence since he was no longer in sight. Tucker Chase still roamed the entire apartment, searching for evidence, which was downright disconcerting. Tripp didn't need Chase finding his face paint and jumping to conclusions about a certain vigilante.

"Director Chase?" he asked, hoping to distract the FBI director on the prowl. "Want to bet you'll find photographic evidence inside this guy's home that will tie him to every murder he's ever committed? Maybe others we don't know about?"

Tucker nodded. "Already got a man on it. The second Isaiah gets back to me, I'll let you know what he found."

"Do we have a name?" Jameson asked.

"Doug Driscoll. He was APD's crime scene photographer, which gave him all the inside information he needed. Also helped him escape notice. Hold on. Here's Isaiah now." Tucker cocked his head the same way Jameson always did. Was Tuck listening to Isaiah? Sure looked like it. His eyes were unfocused, as if he were watching something far away. "Driscoll's been with APD a little over two years. Lived in Atlanta before that. He's got… shit! Do not enter until Tate arrives. I'm sending back up, Isaiah!"

What the hell?

Tucker broke whatever psychic connection he had with Isaiah, shook his head, then turned to Tripp and hissed, "Driscoll's got a gawddamned shrine inside his place. Photos of dozens of victims, all female. But the largest is a blurry shot of Ashley in the center of what looks like an altar."

"How do you even know that?" Tripp asked, pressing Ashley more firmly inside his jacket, wishing he could absorb her to be able to always keep her safe. "Isaiah couldn't have gotten to Driscoll's place already. He just went downstairs. It isn't humanly possible."

Tucker tapped his index finger to his temple, that far-off gaze back in place. "Oh, good to know. You're right. Carry on." Tuck turned to Tripp. "False alarm. Isaiah isn't at Driscoll's apartment. It's in Arlington, but he's still downstairs with the body. Isaiah doesn't need to travel to investigate crimes like you and I would," Tucker said, with something that sounded like pride in his tone. "Trust me. My guys are the best."

"He can tell all that just by being with a dead body?" Unfuckin'-believable.

"By reading that body, yes. Isaiah's a Level Ten." Tucker said that like being a Level Ten explained everything. "You'd be surprised what he can get out of a dead man's mind if the death is recent."

"So this is what psychics do," Jameson murmured. "Interesting."

Tripp needed more than psychic babble. "And Eden and Ky? Where'd they go?"

Tucker stuck his big square chin at the shared wall between Tripp's and Ashley's apartments. "They're next door with Tate. He's our Doctor Doolittle. He'll see to it Peewee's taken care of for as long as you need, ma'am," Tucker told Ashley. "These two apartments are now crime scenes. I'll let you know when you can move back in."

"Thank you," Ashley replied. She'd wrapped both arms around Tripp's waist. He could feel her fingers spread across his back. One cheek rested over his heart. And Tripp stopped worrying about what Tucker might find that could link him to the vigilante. Ashley was alive. That was all he cared about.

He dipped his nose into the silky depths of her hair and inhaled. Cherries and Ashley. His two favorite flavors. It had finally happened. He'd fallen, too. Into Ashley. Into love.

"You're a damned fast learner, woman," he murmured, a healthy load of adrenaline still working its way through his body. "I'm proud of how you handled that rat bastard."

Tilting her chin, she looked up at him. "You saved me." Tears of relief washed down her pretty face. Her lower lip quivered. "If you hadn't gotten here when you did, if you hadn't fired when you—"

"Uh-uh, that wasn't me. That was Alex from the next building over. He fired the first shot. Jameson and I just followed up with double taps to make sure the bastard couldn't hurt you again."

"Alex? Your boss?" She turned to look over her shoulder. "Where's—?"

"Here," Alex replied gruffly from the doorway.

Man, he was a sight for sore eyes. Long, lean, and every bit the gunslinger his TEAM claimed he was. Alex shouldered past Director Chase, with a damned fine sniper rifle in his right hand. A Springfield, if Tripp wasn't mistaken. Looked like one of those rare as hell, big-assed, Israeli, sniper rifles. If it was, it'd bear the Star of David behind its scope mount. That baby had to go for around four K. *Sweet.*

"Good job, guys. Ma'am." Alex nodded respectfully to Ashley. Sirens screamed from the alley below. "Tripp, get your woman somewhere clean and quiet. She's been through enough. Does she need a doctor?"

Ashley's hands tightened around Tripp's waist. "No. I just need Tripp."

Alex never batted an eye, just sent him a silent signal to do whatever she asked.

"I'll get a room close to the hospital," Tripp told her. "If you change your mind, the ER's just around the corner. You good with that?"

"You'll stay with me?"

"Try and stop me."

"Could we visit your mom, too?"

"You bet."

Alex turned on Tucker. "You need anything more from my guys?"

"No need for you or them to stay. My team and I witnessed how everything went down. We'll clean up here. Might be good if you paid me a visit in the next couple days, though. Details, you know."

"I can do that," Alex answered, shouldering his rifle, the strap as worn as the weapon.

Eden ducked into the apartment doorway with a cheery, "I'll accompany you into your place so you can change clothes and pack an overnight bag, Ashley. Whatever's in your crockpot, it smells divine."

"I was making chicken and dumplings for your m-mom," she told Tripp. "That's what I was doing when he, when he—"

"Do you think it's done?" he asked, trailing a finger down her cheek, needing to distract her.

"It should be. I just needed to make dumplings, and they're easy."

"Mom'll understand if we don't get to the hospital tonight."

Something incredibly stubborn shimmered through Ashley's soft blue eyes. "But she'll be hungry, and she needs to see you."

Yes, she probably was, and of course, she did. "But I need time with you." *Just you, damn it.*

"Oh," she said quietly. "I was kinda hoping you'd say that. Let me grab a change of clothes. I'll be right back."

Chapter Thirty-Eight

Ashley stayed snuggled inside Tripp's warm jacket on the drive to the hotel. At least she'd been able to change into jeans, a gray Henley, and running shoes before Eden officially declared her entire apartment a crime scene and off limits. The afternoon had turned into evening, and for the first time in years, she wasn't afraid of the dark. She felt lighter. Freer. The cool night air even smelled sweeter, and there was music in the song of Tripp's truck's tires on the street. The lights of businesses and homes passing by twinkled. Sparkled. And to think, this all began with her staying too late at work. Friday night seemed like a lifetime time ago.

The burst of adrenaline from her third near-death experience had dissipated, leaving her exhausted and limp. But alive. And this time, her living was not just because some potty-mouthed guardian angel had materialized out of nowhere and come to her rescue, as if she were some helpless weakling. Uh-uh. She'd fought back! All by herself, as in she'd really, really meant to hurt that Driscoll guy. Tripp seemed to know him, but the last time Ashley had seen those pasty gray eyes had been two years ago. Two long years of hiding and being afraid of her shadow. No. More.

Inhaling a belly full of confidence, Ashley let it ease out of her on a sigh. She wasn't afraid. She wasn't weak nor helpless, either. The third time was the charm, and she was going to take Zack up on his challenge to teach her some self-defense moves. Because next time, if there ever were a next time, she was going to kick ass and do it better.

With that decision made, she relaxed. The warmth and scent of Tripp surrounded her, lulling her to sleep. The next thing she knew, he was sliding her across the seat and out of his truck.

"Are we there?" she mumbled sleepily.

"Yes, ma'am," he breathed. One arm slipped under her knees, and he lifted her off her feet.

"I can walk. Put me down."

"Hush. I like carrying you."

"Oh, well then." Ashley snaked one arm around his neck, touched at his gentleness.

"Jameson wanted us to stay with him and Maddie tonight. Guess they just bought a big house and have plenty of room."

"Hmmm. Maybe another time."

"Eden called while you were sleeping. She offered to take the chicken and dumplings to Mom and the gang. I told her you'd like that."

"But I haven't made the dumplings yet."

Tripp tipped her full weight onto his thigh, balancing her while he unlocked the hotel parking lot exterior door with a keycard. Hmmm. Where'd he get that?

"Eden made the dumplings, said she couldn't let your gift go to waste. She and Ky are already sitting with Mom. So are Alex and his wife, Kelsey."

"That's so nice."

"Yeah. I like Tucker's people."

"You'll have to introduce me another time. I was too busy to care about anyone but you." Ashley yawned. "I'm so tired."

"My thoughts exactly. You need sleep and we need to be alone. Privacy, coming right up."

"Did you already check in?"

"I did. Didn't want to wake you."

By then, he was striding confidently through the hotel. Normally, she would've buried her face in his neck, in case they came across another guest. Not anymore. This was her life. She wanted to see every last second of it.

Besides, there was something extremely comforting about being carried by this man. His chest muscles rippled under his shirt, and not once had he groaned at her weight. He wasn't breathing hard. But she was. The size of this man and his sheer sense of self, excited the femininity in her. Made all of her girly parts stand up and take notice. Even her toes.

Once on the elevator, she stole a quick glimpse of his profile. Again, something about him felt familiar. As did being held by him like she was... The way his top teeth scraped his bottom lip when he was thinking…

"It was you. You were there Friday night, on the sidewalk outside the Health Department." She cupped that stubborn, scruffy jaw and forced Tripp to look at her. "You're my guardian angel. You rescued me."

He chuffed. "I'm no damned angel."

"That's exactly what you said then. Oh, my goodness, I'm right. It *was* you!"

"Seriously?" He'd stopped at a hotel room door and again, jostled her as he unlocked it. "I think you've got me confused with some nut roaming the streets, looking for trouble."

Ashley tipped into Tripp and whispered in his ear. "No. I don't think, I know you're the man who saved my life. You're my guardian angel, and I love you."

He stalked into the room and kicked the door shut behind them. "Love me? Nah. You don't mean that. It's only been, what—?"

"Long enough," Ashley murmured against his cheek, her eyes closed and her nose working overtime. He was leather and wind, exactly who she thought he was. "How could I not love the man who's come to my rescue again and again? The guy who taught me how to stand on my own feet, but insists on carrying me?"

Time was standing still, and Tripp was holding his breath. But Ashley didn't care if he admitted it or not. This was her gift to him, total acceptance of the man he was. Did that make her a fool like her mother? Possibly. But from the start, Tripp had won her heart, and she needed him to know. She loved this potty-mouthed angel. He didn't have to love her back, and he didn't have to admit to anything. After this past weekend, he didn't have to do more than exist.

She wiggled out of his arms at the foot of the bed and toed off her shoes. "You showed me how to live, Tripp."

The heated light in his green eyes told Ashley she was onto something. Slowly unzipping her jeans, she shimmied out of them and tossed them to the built-in dresser. "Because of you, I'll never be the timid, little mouse I've been all my life." Her voice turned hoarse, but when Tripp ran his tongue over his bottom lip, she did it again. "It's true. You made me the woman I am today." Off came her Henley shirt, over her head and onto the dresser.

He took a step closer, his pupils like full black moons.

Ashley traced a fingertip along the top line of her bra, watching him watching her. "I'm not a little girl who can be bullied and made to cry or made to hide. Not anymore. All because of Tripp McClane."

Reaching both arms behind her back to unsnap her bra was Tripp's undoing. Before she could reach the hook-and-eye, he clutched her waist and tossed her into the middle of the king-size bed. Ashley laughed, but she wasn't done seducing Tripp. Rolling to her side, she crawled on her hands and knees to the edge of the bed where he'd come to a full stop. He might've carried her there, but she meant to show him just how empowered she was.

He looked down at her, still and silent, his hands on his hips, as if he didn't know what to do.

Ashley lifted to her knees in front of him, loving the uncertainty playing across his handsome face. Was her big, mean, guardian angel frightened? Of her? How amazing was that?

She had to ask, "Are you afraid of me, Tripp?"

Chapter Thirty-Nine

"Ah, that would be a damned big no, ma'am," Tripp replied gruffly, as he stared down at the woman he thought he knew. Until now. It'd only been maybe twenty minutes since he'd set Ashley inside his truck and fastened her seatbelt. She'd been compliant as hell—then. The drive to this hotel hadn't taken long at all, but something had changed between there and here.

She'd said she loved him. Loved. That one little word. Not that he hadn't heard it before, because, he sure as hell had. From high school cheerleaders and sometimes, from their moms. From Army-wife wannabes and tag chasers who hung around Army forts, taverns, strip clubs, and bars. But the honesty in the way Ashley said it made a man stop and think. And for once in his adult life, Tripp was really thinking, not just acting on impulse or marching out to do his duty to man and womankind.

Love… That's what had been happening between them since Friday night. Incrementally, like an inch worm, it had opened his eyes, and he'd fallen for Ashley. It didn't feel half-bad or contrived, not at all. If anything, this thing with her felt more real than anything he'd felt for any other woman.

Her eyes were glittering like a feline on the prowl tonight, a very sexy feline with a fat lip and a mark of courage taped under her chin. She might've taken a few licks, but she'd beaten that photographer like a pro. With a stick! While he had a knife! Tripp couldn't have been prouder. He just hadn't expected the sensual predator vibe coming from Ashley now. Confidence looked hot-damned-good on her.

He liked the jut of her shoulder blades as she stalked him. The sway of her barely clad hips and the way her full breasts filled her bra. He loved the clear view of those breasts cupped in purple, like an offering. Her hair drizzled over her shoulders and down her arms, like black silken fingers. Her dark lashes fluttered, and if she licked her lips one more time… Tripp ran the heel of his palm down his belly and over his zipper. *God, help me.*

Shrugging out of his holster, he called her bluff. If this woman wanted to play, then play it was. His pistols went on the nightstand, his holster to the floor beside it. He toed out of his boots, then unbuckled his belt while she watched. The boots and belt went beside the bed with his holster.

Ashley had settled cross-legged in the center of the duvet, her lips wet and glistening, her eyes wide-open, as she watched. Not in a million years had he planned to put on a strip show, but there he was, peeling his shirt off, her eyes following every move. He saw how she wiggled her butt, shifted, and crossed her legs when he tossed his shirt over his head. How she ran her fingers through her hair, then fluffed it off her shoulders and down her back. He loved how her pretty eyes widened, when they skated over his bare chest and down his belly, with what looked like sheer delight. How she licked her lips…

Like a damned teenager, every muscle in Tripp's body flexed at the approval shining in her eyes that, right then, were more black than blue. Her being aroused like she was, damned near did him in.

Before he had the chance to make a move, she lunged and grabbed the waistband of his jeans. With her thumb, she flicked the brass snap open and arched up into him, her lips lush and glistening, ripe for the taking. Ashley rubbed her breasts, still encased in purple, up his belly to his chest.

Tripp tipped his forehead to hers, his hands cupping her shoulders. His nostrils flared, drawing in the sweet scent of her arousal. Eagerly, she worked his zipper. At this rate, he'd be finished before they even started. That wouldn't do.

He straight-armed the woman who was supposed to be his quarry. That was how this always worked in the past. He played the hero in charge. The woman played the coy, shy, demure, helpless female. Ashley had certainly been all that before. Yet with every blink of her big, expressive eyes, his blood boiled hotter. This wasn't playing. The whole idea of an aggressive female in his bed, turned this night into something he hadn't expected.

"Scoot back," he ordered, as he cupped those lush, soft mounds of womanly flesh and strummed her nipples through the purple lace. They turned hard and tight at his touch. He was already hard as steel. She moaned, the perfect accompaniment to the unbidden groan in his throat. Man, what she did to him.

"No. You scoot back. This started in my bedroom, and I'm still in charge."

Damned if a grin didn't crack his face at her sass. "You're in charge, huh?"

She nodded, no sign of the demure woman she'd been before in sight.

Tripp let go and stepped back a full foot. "Okay then, tell me what you want me to do next."

All that brash feminine bravado shimmered with hesitation. "Don't stop that," she told him. Reaching for his hands, she pulled him back to the edge of the bed, then wiggled, as she placed them right back where they'd been.

Ah, she liked his hands on her body. He re-engaged happily, cupping those soft, sweet babies, his thumbs rubbing over the lace until her nipples were once again hard-as-diamond tips. He was looking down at her. She was looking up at him. Breathing hard. Her chest heaving. Still not experienced enough to know what came next, but so damned beautiful. She was breathtaking. Heart-stealingly perfect.

"What now?" Tripp asked, his voice turned to gravel and his blood on fire.

"I... I..." Ashley bit that damned bottom lip, already glistening and swollen. "Kiss me," she ordered.

"Where?"

"Ahh..." A sigh breathed out of her as she pointed at her mouth. "Here."

He bent over her, still palming her breasts, his knees against the mattress. Tripp kept the kiss chaste and brief, teasing this lovely wannabe-dominatrix, who didn't have a clue how to order a man like him around.

"Not like that," she huffed petulantly into his face. "Like you did this morning."

"You mean when I did this?" He sank to his knees on the floor, leaned forward, took firm hold of her hips, and tongued her navel. The scent of her surrounded Tripp, and he was lost in a haze of silky softness and feminine pheromones. Closing his eyes, he kissed and nuzzled, let his nose and mouth feast their way up her stomach and between her succulent breasts. His nostrils flared at the scent of her womanly warmth. And Tripp wanted more.

Her palms settled on his shoulders. "Yessss. Just... like... Oh, fudge. Yes... That."

He meant to take it slow. After a lifetime of neglect, Ashley needed to be in charge. But with one taste of the cherries on her skin, the fuse was lit. He pushed her bra up to her chin and nibble-kissed sloppy, wet kisses over those succulent breasts, then tipped her flat to her back and climbed onto the bed beside her. His hands landed on her waist, and his heart fell at her feet. Tripp swallowed the tip of her breast, then suckled, drawing that nipple deep into his mouth. Stretching it. Tugging and nipping. Making her moan.

Ashley's hands cupped the back of his head, holding him to her. She'd untangled her long legs when she'd fallen back. Best move ever. Ashley's eyes were closed, and her cheeks were red and feverish. He had just the thing for that temperature spike.

By then her breasts glistened from his mouth. Running his palms over her hips and down her legs, he took gentle hold of her ankles and pointed her toes to the ceiling. Which put her entire body in one of the most erotic positions known to man. On her back. On display.

Tripp leaned back to get a good look. Her hair was mussed. Her lips were wet. Her sapphire eyes were bright, shining with lust. Her nipples were wet, her long legs were stiff, and those damned boy shorts and that bra were in his way.

He didn't want to scare her. He was a big guy. Heavy as a tank. Broad. Built for football and combat. Made to be in charge. But she was a tiny, slender thing. And he needed out of his pants. He'd dressed commando. His boys were dying to meet her girls. They couldn't take much more of the zipper's teeth chewing at them.

Without waiting to be told what to do, Tripp hooked one hand around both of her ankles, and reached his free hand behind her back. With her bra unlatched, he smoothed his free hand under her ass and kept going, until those cute boy shorts were on the floor.

She slipped her bra straps off her shoulders and tossed it away.

Tripp situated his knees at her delicious butt cheeks. He spread her legs again, wider this time. Beads of sweat trickled down his temples and between his shoulder blades at the self-control this luscious view cost. His cock was begging for freedom. But he was still in jeans and this was her show.

"What now?" he breathed huskily.

Moaning, Ashley tossed her head from side to side on the pillow. "Take your darn pants off, Tripp. I can't reach them like this, and you know it. Stop teasing. Make love to me. Just do it."

Thank you, Jesus!

Tripp lifted off the mattress and stripped. In record time, he retrieved the strip of condoms from his pocket, suited up, and was kneeling back between her long, stiff legs. His hands cuffed her ankles, and her toes were once again pointed at the ceiling. This was his new favorite position.

"I'll go slow," he told her, beads of sweat dripping into his eyes and his heart on fire. "All you've got to say is—"

"Oh, for Pete's sake, will you shut up and kiss me?" Ashley whined.

"Yes, ma'am," he replied. This position would give him every last inch of her. She was ready, but so inexperienced. Shifting over Ashley, he squeezed her ankles, as he thrust his hips between her legs and began breaching her core. Slowly. So slowly. He slid just the tip of him inside, letting her body adjust to his girth, to this intimate intrusion. Tripp allowed time, sweet time for her to accept him as slick ridges met hard, heavy steel. That steel shank sank deeper as, millimeter by millimeter, he fed himself to her, until she bucked her pretty ass up off the mattress and growled for more.

Her impatience made Tripp smile. He let Ashley take over. Reaching around him, she latched her fingernails onto his ass and slammed him home. Filled herself up. She whimpered. He groaned. For a meek little thing, Ashley had just joined them to the hilt, in heat and in blood. In heart. Hot damn.

Tripp pursed his lips at the slick, fiery heat of their union, then growled at the sudden shock of their coming together. Sparks crackled up his spine and danced down the insides of his legs. But he refused to hurt her. This woman deserved to be handled with kid gloves her first time. He tipped his torso away from her, needing her eyes. "Look at me," he ordered.

Ashley blinked up at him, her lashes spiked. "It's okay. I knew it would hurt. Just don't stop." She squirmed against him, moving him around inside her body.

"We need to take it slow, honey. This is all new to you. Hurting you was never my intention."

"I know, I just…" Her gaze shifted to something over his shoulder.

He tipped forward, spreading her legs wider, but without sinking in deeper. He settled his forearms alongside her shoulders. "Relax. We're not here to set any records. Let me show you how good this can be."

"I... I..."

"Look at me, Ashley." Tripp cupped her jaw, rotating her head until she blinked and looked at him. "I'm not afraid of you, and I sure as hell don't want you to ever be afraid of me. You did just fine. We don't have to do anything, okay? Let's explore. Let's get to know each other better."

"You make it sound easy." She was still blinking, and he knew damned well her sensitive folds had to be stinging from the blunt head still embedded deep inside of her.

"It is easy. Slow and easy," he said, easing out of her slick heat, then just as slowly, easing back in, but not going in as deep. "It's like dancing. You lead, I'll follow."

She arched her hips, meeting his gentle thrust. "I like that."

"See? No pain. You're so ready for me. The wetter you are, the easier."

Her hips began to arch in rhythm with his thrusts. Each time he went in a little deeper. Each time she met him with more force. Tripp took over from there, easing in and out, giving her body time to acclimate to his girth. Watching pleasure replace the worry lines on her face. Looking down between her legs, he noticed everything.

When she finally relaxed completely, his body turned into a giant, feral piston, striving to please her, pushing for more. Deeper. Then deeper still. Ashley growled, their mouths still sealed together, their tongues tangled and mated like their bodies. She was talking to him, saying something with her mouth full.

He'd never felt anything so intense or this perfect before. Tripp tipped away from her pillowy breasts just enough to see her. "Yes, ma'am?" he huffed, his back already arched into another thrust.

There were tears in her eyes. Man, he loved this woman. He was so screwed.

"Do it," she ordered, her bottom lip quivering. "I'm not going to break. Fuck me, Tripp. Harder."

Whoa. He never expected that word out of her mouth. Another side to this amazingly complex woman. Ordinarily, he'd get right to it. Never in his life had he refused an invitation like that. But he couldn't. Not this time. He came to a full stop.

Because this wasn't just fucking. Something else was going on here, on this bed, in this rented room, with this woman. It was that *something else* most of the guys in Tripp's office had with their wives. This was that *forever thing* he'd been resisting ever since he'd seen Ashley fighting for her life on the sidewalk just last Friday. This wasn't another lookie-loo hook-up. This was that elusive, intangible *more* staring him in the face, daring him to get close enough to get burned. To finally invest in a life that mattered more than playing hero after dark.

"Where'd you hear that dirty word?" he asked gently, his momentum blown and his wits scattered. Not that he hadn't fucked plenty of times before. He had. But hearing it from her mouth...? Reducing what they were doing to—that? Somehow cheapened everything.

She stilled. "Did I do something wrong?"

"No. Not you. But that word..." He didn't dare repeat it. He wouldn't give it power. "That's not what we're doing here tonight, Ashley. I hope you know that. That crap happens on TV, on all those bed-hopping soaps. That's what shallow people do. They're all cheaters, losers, and users. But us..." He let his words trail away, not quite ready to jump into forever. Yet there he lay, with a woman beneath him who meant more than any other he'd ever taken to bed. For the first time in his life, Tripp wasn't sure what came next.

He cleared his throat and told her to, "Look down between us. What do you see?"

Ashley tucked her chin and did as he asked. It was so damned sweet the way she bit her bottom lip at the sight of his body sealed tightly inside hers. "Umm, us. We're... together."

"We most certainly are." Tenderness welled in his heart at her total lack of sophistication. Man, the world was a rank, dirty place, and he had no doubt she'd heard that word plenty growing up. So had he. But Ashley was everything that ugly word wasn't. Even now, with her legs spread for him, with her breasts slightly chewed, her nipples definitely wet and well sucked, she was still pure and holy. She was light and love—everything he was not.

"We're making love, Ashley," he told her, his voice gruff and his throat dry at the precipice he seemed to be standing on. "I've got to tell you, I've done the other enough to know that this..." He arched his hips into her. "This is honest to God the first time I've ever made love."

Yes, love, damn it. Tripp was as bad as Jameson, and he knew it. Falling in love at first sight. Thinking of forever after only knowing this woman a few days.

Ashley blinked those big expressive blue eyes up at him. "I think you love me," she whispered.

Did he dare take that last step? "I think I want to get to know you better."

'Chicken shit,' his heart whispered.

'Fast thinking!' his randy cock crowed. *'Now get on with it.'*

So, he did. Like the big, mean guardian angel Ashley believed he was, Tripp gave her his all. He didn't dare say the L word, but he proved it by taking her with soft, loving thrusts. For this very first time in her life, Tripp made the gentlest, truest love. He took her step by cautious step. Slow and easy. When at last she moaned his name and her legs stiffened…

When her body quaked, and she scored his shoulder with her fingernails…

When Ashley lay shattered in his hands, like the fragile piece of perfection that she was…

Only then did Tripp close his eyes and allow his release to blow through his body. He didn't chase it this time. Didn't need to. Not with this woman. It just roared through him like a hurricane. Because Tripp was in love, and he damned well knew it.

When the act of what was most definitely love, was complete… When he bowed his head to her sweaty forehead and breathed in the sweet, musky scent of their lovemaking, worshipping her, wanting her still… Tripp knew damned well that fucking could wait for their next go around. Maybe later. Maybe never. Because Tripp couldn't imagine a time that he'd ever want to just fuck Ashley. Did. Not. Compute. He'd found her, and he would cherish her forever. Together or not, from this day forward, he'd find a way to watch over her. Somehow.

Maybe he was the elusive guardian angel she thought he was. Maybe he wasn't. A tear slipped out of the corner of his eye at the thought of giving her up, of letting her go. But that was what guardian angels did. They never hung around; they hovered, unseen, but always nearby. Close enough to rescue. Never intrusive, yet ever ready to protect and serve. In the shadows. Like him…

Chapter Forty

Ashley couldn't believe she was crying. After that! After finally making the most beautiful love with her fierce guardian angel, she fell apart. Sticking her nose in his neck, she wrapped her arms around him and sobbed. Just sobbed. She'd never felt so treasured, nor so loved before in her life. So special. Like she was truly important. Like she meant something to him. So what if Tripp hadn't said he loved her back. That wasn't why she'd said it to him. There were no words to describe the depths her broken, battered heart had plummeted before she'd met this man. Just as there were no words for the soaring height her soul had reached now. She'd flown! Because of Tripp, she'd found heaven, and it was inside his arms and against his chest.

Tripp rubbed his massive palms up and down her arms and waist, still holding her as if she were fragile, which, apparently, she was. How had he known that? At last, she swallowed her emotions, licked the tears off her lips, lifted her chin, and faced him.

He bowed his head, looking down at her. In one swift rollover, he was on his back, her hands were on his chest, and her legs were splayed over his hips.

"Hey," he murmured, his deep voice rumbled through her tender, sensitized skin between them. Not one part of her wasn't still singing. She'd become a bundle of live wires, his hands on her hips and his thumbs on her tummy the only things holding her together.

Ashley half-murmured through her tears, half-choked at the mixed feelings pouring out of her. "You must think I'm crazy, crying like this."

Tripp had the best smile. When he was happy, it covered his entire body. Even his cock twitched between her legs.

"Not at all. But I do think you've been holding a lot of hurt inside these past couple years. I know you said you've been to a counselor, but we've got a pretty neat lady at the office you could talk to. Her name's McKenna, but we call her Doc Fitz. I talked with her a couple times when I first hired on. She's Beau's wife. You'd like her."

"I might do that." Tipping forward, Ashley crossed her arms under her chin and flattened herself onto Tripp's chest. A counselor was the last thing she wanted to talk about, but first… "Don't think just because I said I love you that you—"

"It's only been a few days. I just need to—"

"It's okay if you don't love me, Tripp," she insisted. "That's not what love is about. It doesn't make demands, and it's not quid pro quo. It just—" her shoulders lifted "—happens."

"Damn it, listen to me," he growled. "You're emotional right now. You're overwhelmed. You don't know what you're saying. Besides, I'm not the marrying type, and you deserve someone better than me. But I—"

"Who said anything about marriage?"

He cupped his hands to both sides of her head and pulled her up his body, closer to his face. "Let me finish, woman," he muttered, then kissed her and sucked the air out of the room. His was a kiss of fire and passion, a mind-melding clash of lips, tongues, and teeth. By the time Tripp finished devouring her tonsils, Ashley had forgotten her name. He ended the kiss by bumping his forehead to hers. "I want to see where this thing between us is going."

"Oh," she squeaked breathily. "But you don't have to. I mean, we only just met and—"

"You really don't know how to make friends, do you?"

Friends. The word stung more than she expected. Was that all she was? His friend?

"I… Me? No, I…" He'd flustered her with that one word. Ashley hadn't wanted Tripp to feel pressured. She'd been trying to offer him a way out, but now that he'd taken the offer, was she just a friend with benefits?

She gulped so hard that her swallow got stuck in her throat. Was he right? Did she know how to make friends? Short answer, not really. She'd closed down years ago, long before that creep had ever broken into her college apartment. With her mom's transient lifestyle, she'd never lived in one place long enough to find or make real friends.

One did not garner personal power or self-confidence from a childhood caught between a self-serving, narcissist father and a self-effacing mother. If one wasn't badgering, bullying, and belittling his only child, the other was stuck in denial, always defending the man who'd never worked a day in his life. Ashley knew now that her parents were forever half of a nauseating, codependent whole. The false narrative she'd grown up with had left her confused and forever uncertain.

Until she'd left home, Ashley had been batted back and forth like a badminton birdie, in a game she hadn't been able to win. Simply because children didn't understand their parents' twisted, messed-up adult relationship rules. Ashley's determination to leave home, to be independent, and to get away from her mother's idea that self-martyrdom was any kind of happily-ever-after, had come crashing down the afternoon of Driscoll's first assault.

He hadn't taken her virginity, but he'd surely taken her momentum, her freedom, and her dreams. He'd taken her tiny shred of self-esteem, which hadn't been much. He'd stolen her confidence and, indirectly, her life.

Was that her problem? Had she been so worried about her personal safety, that she'd never let anyone close enough to love her? Well, duh. Why go looking for more pain? Why not shut the hard world out and buy a bird who adored her? If she couldn't make friends, how could she expect to keep a lover?

Suddenly, Ashley was back at square one, on her way to a lifetime of cloistered anonymity, the invisibility enjoyed by victims the world over. Only… she knew better now. Driscoll hadn't taken anything. Uh-uh. Just because her one and only role model, her mom, had turned victimhood into a fine art, that didn't mean Ashley had to. Driscoll hadn't stolen anything. Ashley had freely tossed her independence and confidence out the door with him when he'd run off that day. She'd made the choice, not him, and it had been the wrong choice. Safe? Yes, sort of. But not really. And it had been stifling the heck out of her ever since.

All along, keeping safe had been an illusion. Safe wasn't behind deadbolts or bigger locks. Driscoll had proven that. Safe was that cocky, brash something Tripp carried with him wherever he went. He cared about people enough to put himself in danger protecting fools like her. Safety was in being prepared, trained, and strong. In knowing who you were before you stepped off your doorstep each morning. In relying on yourself, instead of a stupid deadbolt.

How pitiful she'd been, quivering behind black-out curtains like a scared rabbit in its hole. No. More. She, Ashley Cox, had challenged a serial killer with nothing more than her bird's perch today, and by heck, she could do it again.

Leaning his torso up into hers, Tripp pressed his warm lips to her forehead. "I'd like a year to date you, Ashley. A year to fall in love. If that's what this feeling between us is, I want time to get it right." He bumped his hips between her thighs.

"Want to know what gave you away?" Ashley asked slyly, needing him to back off the love train and focus on something else.

"Gave me away?"

"You know what I'm talking about." She dropped a big wet kiss on his mouth, ending it by nipping his bottom lip. "You're my angel. You can't fool me."

"Trust me, I'm no angel."

"Yes, you are." Ashley shook her head, denying his denial, as she tossed her hair over his face. "You bite your bottom lip just like he did. You'd smeared grease paint on your face and neck, and you wore a black beanie to conceal your hair. But it was you. I'd know your voice anywhere."

He opened his mouth to argue, but she cut him short. "Never mind. I want you to teach me how to shoot and defend myself. I'd like to know my way around guns, and I want a conceal carry permit. Could you teach me parkour? That's what those bars on the walls and ceiling in your extra bedroom are for, right?"

"I intended teaching you to shoot," he muttered quietly. "But those bars are for pull-ups, not parkour. There's a good parkour course at work. Jameson would be a better teacher for that.”

“I think I’d like to learn how to box, too. Zack said he’d teach me.”

Tripp trailed the back of his fingers down the side of her face, then traced the pad of his thumb over her lips. His eyes had gone dark emerald. The barest tip of his tongue peeked over his bottom lip. “You don’t have to do everything at once, you know.”

“No, but I have to do something. Hiding sure hasn’t helped me, has it?” Her poor heart fluttered with hope, followed by the tiniest frisson of dread. Tripp was going to do it. Say it. He was going to tell her he loved her.

Instead… “I need to run over to the hospital,” murmured out of his mouth. “Come with me?”

“Umm, yeah. S-sure,” Ashley stuttered like the disappointed star struck fool she was.

Was this how it started? That thing called codependence? With her needing more than he would ever be able to give? Was she falling for a guy who was more like her father than she’d thought? Was she more like her mom than she’d dreamed?

But she wanted to meet Tripp’s mother. So, Ashley nodded, swallowed hard, and shoved her needs back and away, down where they apparently belonged. They’d certainly lingered there long enough, like all of her adult life. Ha. What a joke. She wasn’t an adult. She was just her mother’s daughter.

Chapter Forty-One

Tripp tucked his wrinkled shirt into his wrinkled pants. He'd showered alone, which he hadn't expected, not after making love the way he and Ashley had. She'd gotten quiet and had politely declined his invitation to join him.

But what the hell could she expect? Him to declare undying love after knowing her less than a week? Sure, there was a definite physical attraction between them, a powerful magnetism he couldn't deny. But adrenaline was a potent aphrodisiac. It messed with people's heads and their hearts. Everyone knew that, and this had been a week full of some hellacious adrenaline spikes. He hadn't been thinking any clearer than she had. So what if he'd come close to saying the L word? Not that he didn't love Ashley. Tripp knew damned well that he did. But he wasn't the right man for her. From the first moment he'd seen Ashley, he'd known she was an angel, that he'd always be the sinner. When it came down to it, he loved her enough to let her go.

As if things weren't strained enough between them, someone had posted a video to YouTube. Since it claimed to have been taken in Alexandria, the local news stations were airing it. Wasn't that just special? The poorly shot clip of him had already garnered thousands of views and comments. Also, a terse invite to the inner sanctum of Alex Stewart's office, first thing come morning. That ought to be fun.

Ashley sat at the end of the bed, staring at the TV on the credenza across from her, watching the grainy image of an unidentified man dressed in black defending a homeless Vietnam War vet over the weekend. Tripp watched himself toss those two punks into the Potomac again, like the garbage they were. He was proud of what he'd done. Those kids deserved what they'd gotten, and the old guy they'd slapped and kicked around, deserved a helluva lot more than just one night in a homeless shelter. But he'd been thankful for the assist. Grumpy, but thankful.

That was what kept Tripp on the streets after dark, grumpy old men and stupid young guys. Women who thought they were safe when they weren't. Honest hard-working people who'd lost track of time and stayed too late at work.

His glance strayed to Ashley. She'd popped in and out of the shower after he'd finished in the bathroom. Her wet hair was now braided and curled into a shiny, tight knot at the back of her neck. She was back in jeans and her light gray Henley. His jacket lay like the child of divorced parents, bereft on the bed between them.

"Would you like to stop and grab something new to wear before we go see Mom?"

She shook her head. "No thanks. I don't have any cash with me. It's in my bag, and my bag is…"

Still at his place. "No worries. My treat." Knowing her need to be in control, he back-pedaled on that offer. "Or you can pay me back."

"No, Tripp. I'm fine," she insisted, her voice as tight as that braid. "Let's just go."

The dreaded *fine*, pure poison in conversation with any woman. Trish had certainly used it enough. In her language, it meant, *'fuck off.'* With Ashley, it most likely meant, *'Leave me the heck alone.'* Which somehow, made Tripp feel worse.

Unlike Trish, Ashley deserved a white picket fence, a cute little family, and security, not a guy like him. Tripp was a driven loner, still more GI than civilian. Still prone to over-the-top PTSD issues, he'd proven over and over that he was as rough as a cob and short-tempered. Hell, his family was nothing to be proud of. He refused to give what he didn't have to offer. Ashley deserved more. End of story.

"Come on, then," Tripp said as he lifted to his feet, his arm stretched out to her, his fingers fluttering for her to take his hand.

Ashley stood, but kept her hands to herself. "Let's go."

Well, damn. It'd been a long time since Tripp had to deal with the cold shoulder. Sucking in a gut full of tolerance, he gestured toward the door. Words were no longer necessary. There was nothing he could say that would make this night better. Maybe he'd take Jameson and Maddie up on that offer after all.

The hospital was just a couple blocks up the street from the hotel. Tripp called his mom for Trish's room number, after he parked his truck in the attached parking terrace. The elevator ride up to Intensive Care was quiet. At the ICU nurses' station, he checked in and asked about his mom. One of the nurses said she was with Trish's doctor in the family room across the hall. Shit. What now? Go in alone? Drag Ashley into a private and potentially embarrassing family discussion?

Tripp didn't want to see his mom without Ashley at his side. Not that he needed her to save him, but her being a woman would surely help Andy. Taking a chance, he wrapped an arm across Ashley's shoulder and pulled her into his side. "You don't have to do this if you don't want to."

For the first time since she'd refused his invitation to shower together, she looked up at him. "Shut up, Tripp. I'm here for you, and I'm here for your mom. Get over yourself."

God, he wanted to kiss the hell out of her all over again. Ashley had developed one helluva backbone these last couple days. She was… He damned nearly swallowed his tongue. She was too good for any guy, not just him. But he sure as hell didn't want to be the guy who lost her to someone else. Who wasn't smart enough to hold onto her.

"Thank you," he whispered, as meek as he'd never been in his life. He was the jock, the super star, the one everyone cheered and adored. Yet this tiny elfin princess had shot an arrow through his self-inflated opinion of himself, past his grandiose ego, and straight into his heart. The damned thing hurt like she'd torn it open with that prickly spine of hers. Could he give her up? Could he let her go? Tripp wasn't sure he could be that selfless anymore. Or if he'd ever been. Bombastic. Arrogant. Dumber than shit. Those descriptors rang true. But selfless? Not so much.

Gathering his courage, Tripp palmed the family room's door open and ushered Ashley inside, his hand possessively on the small of her back. He couldn't help but notice how tiny her waist was, how his larger hand dwarfed her. Or how his mom's tired green eyes, the same color as his and Trish's, lit with joy when she saw him, but mostly when she saw Ashley.

Andy jumped to her feet, ever the gracious hostess, even at the worst of times. Like all women, she ran a quick hand over her hair. "Tripp! Who's this pretty thing?"

"Hi, Mom. Sorry I'm late. This is Ashley Cox. Ashley, meet Andrea McClane."

Ashley reached her hand forward, but just like he knew she'd do, Andy brushed it aside and pulled her into a hug. "You're the one who made that delicious chicken and dumplings," she murmured into Ashley's ear as she squeezed her tight. "Thank you so much for thinking of me and Tripp's friends. It was so good. Everyone wants your recipe."

Every damned thing about his mom was always sincere. Tears sparkled at Tripp's peripheral. He wiped that shit away. Guys didn't cry.

"I'm glad you enjoyed it, Mrs. McClane," Ashley replied quietly. "I love comfort food. I hope the soup helped you feel better."

"Oh, it did, and it was such a nice surprise. Tripp's guys have been taking good care of me, but home-cooked meals are always the best. It isn't every day my boy brings a girlfriend to meet me. In fact…" Andy rolled her eyes. "This is a first."

She offered Ashley the chair at her right and nodded for Tripp to take the one at her left. "Please, sit down. Join us." Andy made it sound like a good thing. "Doctor Smith is just about to explain my daughter's transfer into a nearby rehabilitation center, Ashley. He's her spine doctor. Doctor Pitt just left. He's her thoracic specialist. You might not know this, but she was attacked a couple nights ago, but she's going to make it, isn't she?" Andy aimed that question at the ever-smiling Doctor Smith.

"Already?" Tripp barked. "You guys are moving my sister already? Christ, has she even woken up yet?"

Doctor Smith shot him a big, wide open grin. Man, the guy had as square and big a chin as Tucker Chase, with teeth as straight and white as any guy on a toothpaste commercial. "Of course not. We need to make sure she's stable before we move her, but she's showing excellent progress. Aren't you excited?"

Tripp ran a hand over his head. It hadn't even been a full day yet. What was there to be excited about? Staggering hospital debt? Trish's eat-shit-and-die attitude in his face every damned day for the rest of his life—if she were totally disabled? Andy being run ragged to please a daughter who'd never once in her life cared about anyone but herself?

His gaze dropped to the tabletop in front of him. Funny how it looked like real wood, but it wasn't, was it? It was laminate on chipboard with a shitload of glue holding them together. One hundred percent fake. Like the hope Smith was dishing out.

"Tripp, honey?" his mom asked, her much smaller hand settling warm and so damned strong on his wrist. "I need you in this with me all the way. I know it's a huge responsibility, but we can do it. Together. We can save Trish's life, maybe even turn her around. I know we can."

Tripp swallowed his concerns and stiffened his spine. Andy already believed; now she needed him to jump on the faith train with her. He just didn't know how. But he could pretend. Anchoring the pad of his thumb at his temple, he swiped his fingers over his forehead in frustration. Here we go again.

This wasn't a simple mom and son outing staring them in the face. This was his messed-up twin—another one of her disasters in the making. Ever since he'd been old enough to work, he'd supported his mom and sister. Come hell or high water, he'd sent most all of his Army paychecks home, so

Andy could focus on helping, finding, or rescuing Trish. So his mom wouldn't have to worry about where her next meal was coming from, or whether she had enough money to pay rent and utilities.

Tripp would have to work overtime for the rest of his life to pay Trish's hospital bills—if he still had a job after his meeting with Alex tomorrow morning. Her rehabilitation would be costly, and she'd require months of that. He'd rarely see his mom or her because there wouldn't be enough damned time in the day to work his guts out *and* help his family. Andy'd be the one stuck tending to Trish's physical and emotional needs, day in and day out. Tripp would be the one stuck paying the bills. Again, gawddamnit. Cleaning up Trish's mess for the rest of her sad life. However long that was.

"I take it you haven't talked with your boss yet?"

Tripp looked down at Doctor Smith's much larger hand now clamped over the top of Andy's hand and Tripp's wrist. "No, sir. Sure haven't. But tomorrow, first thing, I get to do that."

Smith peered at Tripp from beneath his brows. "Mr. Stewart's a good guy, isn't he?"

Everyone knew that. "He's a good shot, too." *And he's going to kill me tomorrow, bright and early.*

Smith drew in a deep breath, then blew it out slowly through pursed lips, like he was debating what to say next. "It's not my place to tell you this, but…"

Shit, what now? Tripp honestly couldn't see a light at the end of this godforsaken tunnel. Not this time. Trish had done it to him and Andy again. Through all her wrong choices, she was still stomping the shit out of the only two people who'd ever loved her sorry ass.

Tripp pulled away from Smith's unwelcome touch and kicked his chair back from the table, sick at heart for his mom most of all, but too damned worn out to care about his twin.

"I think you should know that…" Smith ran his tongue over his bottom lip. "You and your mom aren't alone in this endeavor."

Tripp glared at the doctor. "Excuse me?"

"It's true." Smith's head bobbed. "I'm going to tell you something I wouldn't ordinarily share. It's not confidential but…" His eyebrows lifted to his hairline. "Here goes. Mr. Stewart's paying your sister's medical costs. All of them. Even her rehab. Anything else she needs. He's already called in two of my esteemed colleagues for second and third opinions. Do you believe that?" The man just could not stop smiling. "Trust me, Trish is in the very best hands, so are you and your mom."

Unbelievable. "No kidding?" Tripp asked, at the same time Andy shrieked, "He what? No. Mr. Stewart can't do that. I won't let him." She turned on Tripp. "You have to stop him. Tell him no."

Tripp didn't know what to say. "But Mom, he's my boss, and once he makes up his mind to do something…" *Telling Alex no won't go over too well. It's the right thing to do, but damn…*

"It's not his burden to bear." Andy tipped her head into her hands, her shoulders quaking. "It's mine."

Tripp rested his hand between her shoulder blades. Man, her heart was pounding. So was his. "It's ours, Mom, not just yours. Don't cry. I'll talk to him, and we'll figure a way forward."

She turned her teary eyes on him. "Promise?"

Not fair. He never could resist his mom when she cried. "Sure," he said, patting her back to keep her from falling apart. "I have a meeting with him first thing in the morning. I'll talk with him then." *And then I'll file for unemployment.*

Ashley turned her pretty blues on Andy. "I'd let Alex help. I've seen his workplace, and…" She glanced at Tripp out of the corner of her eye. "I heard him telling his friend about some land he just bought, and how he has great plans for his TEAM, and…" She swallowed hard. "One gift never diminishes another, Mrs. McClane."

"But we're talking a lot of money here," Tripp argued.

She met his eyes and raised him one. "Sounds to me like Alex has more money than he knows what to do with. Don't make him feel bad by rejecting his kindness. That's not why gifts are given, to make someone else feel bad. I've only just met him, but if he wants to do this for Andy and Trish and, err, you, I'd sure let him."

"Where did you find this gem?" his mom asked, her eyes bright with unshed tears.

"At the corner of King Street and forever," Tripp murmured, his heart stuck up so high in his throat, he could barely breathe.

"So, it's a go then? You'll accept Mr. Stewart's gift?" Doctor Smith asked, his enthusiasm for Trish's recovery off the Richter scale again.

"I'll have to talk with him first, but…" Tripp stalled. His mom's pride and self-respect were on the line. They were all she had left. He refused to trample her wishes the way Trish always did. "I mean, Mom and I will talk with Alex." He leaned into her and kissed her cheek. "You asked my boss for a miracle, remember. This might be it."

Tripp thought back to the night he'd found Trish after her assault. He'd asked for a miracle then, too. Jesus, could Alex really be the answer to that hastily uttered prayer?

Andy turned to face Tripp. "But I never meant for him to be so... so..."

"Generous?" Doctor Smith offered the seemingly innocuous word, that was right then choking the shit out of Tripp. His boss was doing this for him? For his mom? Trish's care would run into hundreds of thousands of dollars. What did a guy say to a gift like that? *No? Yeah, sure, thanks?* Tripp couldn't come up with the right words.

Ashley wrapped an arm around Andy's shoulder. "Maybe Alex Stewart is your guardian angel in disguise. We all have one. I know I do. Alex must be yours."

"I don't believe in angels anymore," Andy sputtered. She was blinking, trying to keep her composure. "And I never meant for anyone to do this."

"Here you go, Andy." Doctor Smith handed her the box of tissues from the credenza behind him. "It is a huge monetary gift, and, of course, accepting it would be hard. I understand that, but Alex Stewart is one of our biggest donors. He and his wife built the new pediatric intensive care unit upstairs. Trust him. He's only doing this because he can, and because he cares."

Tripp knew damned well that his boss cared. Else why did he absorb his agents' health insurance costs like he did? Talk about benefits. Alex gave The TEAM the best of everything. But this? Tripp stuck both hands in his pockets, trying to wrap his head around accepting that great of a gift. His right hand fell into the silken nest of Ashley's panties. His eyes shot to her tender features. She'd just given him one helluva gift, yet he'd held back. Hadn't said the words she needed to hear.

While Andy blew her nose and dabbed at her eyes, Ashley's sapphire gaze drifted over her shoulder to him. "I believe in guardian angels, Mrs. McClane," she told his mom while she looked at him. "They're as real as devils, only they show up when you need them the most. Be kind, Andy. Let Alex be kind, too. You get to give him a gift just by accepting his offer. Give him a hug next time you see him. Bet he'll like that more than anything else."

Tripp bowed his head, a smitten, but foolish, foolish man. If he were alone, he'd pull those panties out of his pocket and bury his nose in them. He licked his bottom lip, shocked at how hard his heart was thumping in his chest, like it wanted out of its cage, right damned now.

He shoved his chair back. "Mom, I, umm…" *Have got to get the fuck out of here.* "M-m-nom," he choked. "Stay here. Talk to Doctor Smith. I'll be right back. Just need a minute with… Ashley?" Tripp stretched out his hand, daring her to refuse him this time. "Please?" he begged, needing whatever the hell she had that made her tougher than anyone he'd ever met.

For God's sake, every time she'd been knocked down, she'd gotten back up, and that was something to be damned proud of. She was that dog-tired boxer in the ring, the one nobody ever bet on. The one everyone, even her own parents, expected would lose. She was the long shot. The underdog. She'd been backed into corners all of her life. Bloodied and sweating and about to drop. About to give up. But here she was, still going strong. Stronger…

He'd known that same hopeless feeling, the panicky what-ifs that went with fighting the world. It was one hell of a desperate alone-time, when a person's mettle was truly tested. When it had just been him against the odds. Those times were when he'd truly known what he was made of. When he'd had to pull every last ounce of resilience up from the deepest part of his gut to keep fighting, just to keep trying. To stand.

Yet Ashley had done that all her life, and she'd done it alone. She wasn't a loser, by hell! She'd relentlessly fought on and fought back. She thought she was a coward? Guess again, little girl. This woman was a lot braver than some grown-assed men he'd served with.

Her tender analysis of Alex's magnanimous gift had knocked Tripp right out of the ballpark. Sloppy tears perched on the rims of his eyelids, ready to drip down his damned face. This was another one of those alone, what-if times. Alex's stepping up like he had was like someone taking a beating for Tripp. Someone purposefully stepping into the line of fire. Sure gave that old sniper saying, *'From a place you'll never see, will come a sound you'll never hear,'* a different meaning. Because Tripp had never seen this coming.

"Please, take my hand," he asked again. *So I can stop embarrassing myself.*

Silently, Ashley lifted to her feet and reached for him. Tripp grabbed onto her fingers like a drowning man grabbing onto a lifeline and pulled her into the hall. Like a man gone crazy, he pinned her against the wall the second the door closed behind them. "You," he groaned into her surprised mouth. "I want you. Only you."

He kissed her hard, grinding his lips into hers, breaching her mouth with his tongue, spearing her the way her words had just speared his heart. He'd always thought he knew so much, but he didn't, not really. Sure as hell not about what mattered most.

Thrumming with worry, Tripp ran both hands over Ashley's shoulders and down her arms, then back up again, needing to absorb this woman. If only he could. He cupped her delicate jaw between his big, rough hands. Hands that had dealt out death and justice wherever he'd served. Yet not once had he accomplished what she just had. Not once had he seen through all the crap in life, to the heart of it, the real reason for living and fighting. It wasn't about serving justice or revenge. It surely wasn't about making people pay for their mistakes. Life was about giving back. It was about service and pure, simple love. Which, apparently, his badassed boss understood a helluva lot better than he did.

"Ashley," Tripp breathed into her mouth. "I'm sorry. You're right. God, you're so much braver than me."

"I am?" she mumbled around his lips.

"I am such an idiot." Tripp couldn't hold back the passion storming his soul. But he didn't want her to see him crying, either. So he hid it by kissing her.

"You are," she whispered sweetly into his mouth. But then she bowed her head and told the floor, "I don't know what to say anymore."

But he did. "I love you, Ashley. I know it's crazy, it doesn't make any sense, and it's too soon, but—"

"You're emotional right now. You're overwhelmed. You don't know what you're saying."

Damn it, she'd just tossed his words back at him. Tripp knew he was losing ground. "Yes, I do. I knew it last Friday. B-b-but it was happening so fast. Too soon. I mean…"

Shit, damn, and son of a bitch! He couldn't believe how badly he was screwing this up. But the thought of losing her, along with the weight of Alex's enormous gift, and what Trish's critical condition was doing to his poor mother… God! Ashley was right. Everything was too much! He was overwhelmed, but he finally knew what he wanted.

Tripp wiped the back of his hand over his eyes and took a deep breath to settle his nerves. "I love you, woman, and I want to date you," he breathed. "Is that asking too much?" And there he was again, stressing Ashley out, making the desire of his heart sound like an accusation instead of a promise.

"Date? Just date?" she asked. But when she leaned into him and placed both palms on his chest, he knew she'd forgiven him for being a man.

Tripp trapped her lush, warm body against his, his arms crossed behind her back, his hands in her hair, and his fingertips unraveling that damned tight braid. "Yes, date. You're right. It has been a rough couple days, and I am emotional. But that's who I am. I cuss too much, and I can be one hell of an ass. I don't think things through, and sometimes, I follow my heart instead of my brain. But I finally know what I want. At least, I know what I can't live without, and it's you, Ashley. It's you. I love you and I'm keeping you."

There. He'd said it, and somehow, that heartfelt declaration smoothed over the troubles of the day, like water poured over dying plants in the desert. At last, the crimped wonder of all that ebony silk cascaded over his hands and tumbled through his fingers and back into his life. Tripp could breathe again. Cherries and Ashley, his life blood.

He got it then. He knew. Somehow, between him and his mom, and, God bless him, Alex, things would work out. Trish would be okay. Well, as okay as she ever could be. Tripp knew he could look his boss in the eye tomorrow morning and not feel like a poor relative or a charity case. All because Ashley believed in Alex's kindness.

But she needed to know what she was getting into. He took her head between his hands, tipped her chin up with his thumbs, and told her, "I'm not an easy man to live with. Nearly every penny I make goes to my mom and Trish. I never knew my dad, and there are days I wish I didn't know my sister. She's a vampire, a drain on my mom and everyone who comes into her life, and she'll suck the life out of you, too. She's a user in every sense of the word. Not just booze and drugs, but people, Ashley. Men especially. You don't need someone like me and my family dragging you down. I come with a shitload of crap and—"

"How do you know what I need? What I want?"

"Look at me, for Christ's sake, just look at me." He bent his knees to peer into her eyes. "What do you see?"

Ashley lifted her hands to his face, her fingers stretched into his hair and her thumbs on his cheeks. "I see your mother's gorgeous green eyes and her blonde hair. I see her strength and her devotion to you and Trish. I see her love." Ashley inhaled a deep breath. "It's written all over you, Tripp. I see the most beautiful man I've ever met, and he comes with a wicked sense of honor and pride, which he got from his mom. I see a man who spends most of his days and nights helping people who can't help themselves."

"I do love my mom," Tripp admitted, wishing he didn't sound like such a crybaby loser.

"And you love your sister. Even Driscoll could see that. That's why he wanted you to suffer. You have everything he didn't. Why are you so angry with Trish if you don't care about her? Why'd you send money home when you were in the Army?"

She had him there. "She's my twin," Tripp answered quietly, the truth, as hard as it was, finally faced. "She's a pain in my ass, but, yeah. She's my sister."

"And you love her."

"I do." Tripp took a deep breath of the luscious sweetness that was Ashley to her core. "I want you beside me for the rest of my life. I know it's too damned soon, and I wouldn't be surprised if you've changed your mind about me, but I love you and—"

She lifted onto the tips of her toes and swallowed every last one of his fears.

Chapter Forty-Two

Ashley leaned into Tripp's side on the short drive back to the hotel. After they'd walked Andy to her room and made sure she was settled in for the night, Tripp had all but dragged Ashley out of the hospital to his truck. He had to be as exhausted as she was. The minute she got into their room, she intended to find a phone number for Tate Higgins, to ask how Peewee was. Poor bird was probably scared—or not. Funny. She hadn't worried about her baby until now. What kind of bird mother was she?

Tripp cranked the wheel into the hotel parking lot. At this time of night, all the close parking stalls were taken; he had to park in the rear lot. But there was plenty of overhead lighting, so Ashley didn't think twice about their quick walk to the secure side door, not with the grip he had on her hand. Opening the door, he bent over and scooped her over his shoulder.

"Tripp!" she exclaimed from her upside-down view of the hallway and lobby. "Put me down."

"No, ma'am," he answered, his fingers splayed over her backside, holding her in place, and her hair flouncing over the backs of his long, lean legs. "You wanted a guardian angel, you've got one."

"What will people think?"

That earned her a gentle smack on her ass. "You should know by now that I don't care what anyone else thinks. Only you, Ashley. You're all that matters to me."

At least no one was in the elevator on the way up. He didn't put her down. Just tapped his fingers on her butt while *Muzak* played, until the doors opened. A man and woman stood there waiting to go down. Oh, darn. Ashley buried her face in the back of Tripp's leather jacket, embarrassed to death.

"Umm… Excuse us," the man said with an amused hitch in his voice.

"My goodness," the woman exclaimed, her tone more cheerful than his. More excited. "Looks like you two kids are going to have a good time tonight."

Tripp didn't reply, and Ashley was mortified that her butt was all of her they'd seen. "Put me down," she ordered as soon as the elevator closed.

"No, ma'am," he growled, his long strides eating up the distance to their room, his big hand still warm on her butt.

Electric sparks shivered up the back of her legs. Damn. He hadn't really touched her yet, and she was coming undone, just from the terribly erotic display he'd made of her. What the heck?

"Hurry," she mewed, needing more than just that hand on her ass.

That earned her another smack, only this one stung. And that was all it took. Her legs stiffened. Ashley grabbed hold of his belt, arched her back, and moaned like a cat in heat, as the craziest, hottest orgasm exploded up her spine. Like a fountain, it ripped through her and into the stars. What he did to her!

Tripp had the hotel door opened and closed, and her on her back on the mussed bed in no time. "Jesus Christ, you're so—"

"Kiss me! Now!" She grabbed that big square head of his and all but chewed his lips to get at his tongue.

"Where? Kiss you where?" he mumbled around her determined mouth.

"Everywhere," she breathed, her body on fire with scintillating aftershocks that threatened to morph into another orgasm if he didn't hurry up and... "Do something!" She'd turned into a wanton alley cat that craved being petted, stroked, and tasted.

Tripp had her out of her clothes in a heartbeat, his face between her legs, and his hands behind her knees, pushing her open, making room for his broad shoulders, and...

Oh. My. He knew what to do with that tongue and those teeth. Ashley growled at the intense pleasure assaulting her body. She was rocket fuel, and he was the spark she'd needed to blast her into the universe. Into life. Her butt muscles clenched as it happened again. Ashley's fingers delved into his hair as a blinding light roared through her. The heat! The rush of coming!

Suddenly, his hips were cradled between her legs, and he was inside her body. So, so deep. So big. His hands were on her breasts, his fingertips pulling and pinching her nipples. With every thrust of his hips, with every push and slap of their naked flesh together, her body clenched like a wild cat ready to pounce. And then... It got better.

"I can't wait," she ground out. "Come... come... with me."

"Always," he breathed, his body so big and heavy over hers that it blocked the lights and the world and—

"Yessss," she hissed, then cried, "Tripp! Yes, yes, yes!"

"Ashley," he breathed, and with one more deep, grinding thrust, he roared a few cuss words, then flew with her. And they really were starlight. Quick, bright meteors that burned together before they crashed softly to Earth.

She panted through her pursed lips, undressed and undone, so in love with this man that she fell apart and cried again. Tripp was everything, her springboard and her jumping off point, her beginning and her ending. He was her launchpad. Her tether and her anchor.

Tripp huffed in her face and asked, "You know Jameson?"

Ashley stared up at her wild, crazy man. "Really? You want to talk about him now?"

The sexiest, devil-may-care grin cracked Tripp's rugged face. "Hell, no. Just wanted to tell you that he asked Maddie to marry him within days of meeting her."

"Why's that important?"

Tripp smoothed a hand over her cheek, wiping her tears away and tugging a strand of hair out of her mouth. Tipping forward, he closed the distance and pressed a warm, wet kiss to her sensitive lips. My gosh, they felt swollen.

"Because they're getting married the first of the year. Crazy shit, love. It shows up when you least expect it, doesn't it?"

"Like guardian angels?"

Tripp leaned his head back and roared. "Okay, okay. Like guardian angels. You're right. I'm the guy who interrupted that losing fight you were in Friday night. That was me. Are you happy now?"

Ashley loved the strength in the cords of his neck. The whiskers he hadn't shaved when he'd showered. The musky, male scent of his skin all over her. "I'm always happy when I'm with you. Especially after we make love."

Her big mean guardian angel peered down at her with love shining in his bottle-green eyes. "Move in with me? I mean, after we buy our own house, which we should do as soon as we can. Like the first thing tomorrow."

"Are you sure?"

"Never been more sure of anything in my life."

"How long should we live together?"

"Long enough to grow old?" Tripp said with an endearing smile.

What else could Ashley say but, "Deal."

Chapter Forty-Three

Alex could be damned formidable. Downright scary. The man wasn't a big bruiser like Mark Houston, Zack Lennox, Beau Villanueva, or Tripp. He was more of a hard-as-nails, straight-up, in-your-face, wiry, street fighter. He wasn't blustering thunder, but Tripp knew damned well he could bring the rain. Alex was the number one legend in The TEAM, and he knew how to lead from the front, instead of pushing his troops from the safety of the rear. The man had seen more combat than any other warrior in both the East or West Coast TEAM offices.

But after working with the guy to save Ashley from Driscoll, Tripp wasn't intimidated. He settled his butt in the chair beside Alex's tidy desk, kicked out one long leg, and made himself comfortable. "You wanted to see me?"

Staff meeting would follow what Tripp knew would be a one-on-one butt-chewing. But he'd been disciplined before, Army style. This couldn't be any worse.

"At ease," Alex said, even though he sat ramrod straight in his upholstered leather executive chair, those laser eyes of his raking over Tripp from his head to his booted toes.

Tripp met the man's gaze and raised him one. "Good job taking Driscoll down yesterday, Boss. Great shooting."

"Thanks for working with Tucker's team. They can be…" Alex thumbed his clean-shaven chin like a prizefighter between rounds. "…challenging."

"It was Eden who located Ashley, or we would've been chasing our tails, what with that elevator out-of-order ruse."

"Driscoll thought he was smarter than you."

Interesting word choice: *you.* Not *us.* Alex knew how to play the game.

"He damned near was, but Jameson sensed he was still on my floor." Tripp always gave credit where credit was due. There was no I in TEAM. No asses, either.

"We need to talk." Dipping his hand into the pencil drawer at the center of his desk, Alex withdrew a single folder and tossed it across the desk.

Thumbing the file open, Tripp faced several high-res, black and white action shots of… Shit. Himself. Whoever'd taken the photos was good. All were high-clarity. Good angles. Taken from both Seattle and Alexandria, each shot showed his profile or his face. He couldn't deny the truth. These shots were all of him.

Going for broke, Tripp slid the eight-by-eleven glossies onto Alex's glass-covered desktop and arranged them in chronological order. The line-up started with the shot taken the night he'd rescued that five-foot-nothing woman from those thick-headed morons on Pike Street in Seattle. It ended with the shot of him tossing those punks into the Potomac River, after they'd roughed up a harmless, down on his luck, Vietnam vet. Once he'd lined up the evidence, all photos faced his boss. Tripp asked, "Now what?"

Alex leaned back in his chair, interlocked his fingers behind his head, looked at the ceiling, and said, "You tell me."

"Whoever took these shots is good." Okay, that was lame.

"The integrity of traffic and security cams has come a long way."

Which meant either Mother or Beau had busted their asses accumulating this specific intel. One or both of them must've scoured hundreds of miles of security footage to locate these few specific sightings. Also meant if Alex had this intel, someone else could put two and two together.

"Technology…" Tripp breathed. Gotta love it and the computer geeks behind it. Damn them. They'd caught him.

Alex had the stone-cold eyes of a sniper. Didn't blink. Didn't speak.

Tripp chewed the inside of his lip, not wanting to fight his boss, but he refused to apologize for doing the right thing. If Alex had these shots, he also knew precisely what transpired before Tripp stepped in. "You want me to resign? Is that what this is about?"

"Did I ask you to?" Alex shot back.

"Then what? Do you want me to quit fighting for justice? Me to stop hunting bastards after dark? Me to let good people get raped or beat, while everyone else looks the other way? What?"

Leaning his elbows onto his desk, Alex tented his fingers into a damned stiff-looking steeple. "I want you to decide who you're going to work for, *Junior Agent*. If this is what you do…" He spared a quick glance at the photos. "…you're on your own. Go for it. I don't employ vigilantes, but I promise you, I will hunt them down."

"Despite the obvious fact that, without me, these victims could be dead?" Unbelievable.

"No one gets to play cop, judge, and executioner on my watch."

Tripp wanted to ask, *'Then why aren't you out there saving innocent folks with me?'* But he sensed another big, fat 'but' coming up. So, like Alex had before, he waited.

"If you want to circumvent the law," Alex said, "I know someone who runs several black ops teams. You'll fit right in."

That didn't sound like a compliment. "Who?"

"Senator Sullivan, Texas."

"He the man who went to bat for Walker Judge?"

Alex shook his head. "No, that was me. If you go to work for Sullivan, you'll make good money, but you'll be overseas more often than not. Might work out better for you. Think about it."

Not if he had to leave Ashley behind. Tripp held his breath.

"But if you want to work for me..." Alex made that sound like a threat. *Here it comes...* "The son of a bitchin' night hunts stop now."

"Like hell!" Tripp's shoulder muscles flexed and his nostrils flared at that pompous demand. "Then who'll be there when the police haven't shown up yet, and shit's still going down?" He stabbed his finger at the photo of the poor blonde in Seattle. "They had her half-undressed and backed against a brick wall when I stepped in. You think she cares who saved her, the police or me? You think her husband or her three kids care?"

Lifting with deliberate grace to his feet, Alex leaned over his desk and stabbed the photo taken deep within the Winkler Botanical Preserve. "Do you have any idea who the young man you saved last Friday night is?"

Tripp looked down at the shorter of the two kids, the one who'd called him a hero. "Of course not. I don't check IDs when I'm working. Would you? I just do what I should. All I heard was a couple names in a biker bar and the location of an upcoming beatdown. Spencer something-or-other. I acted on that intel, located the boys, and it's a damned good thing I did because…" Tripp lifted to his feet and faced the man who could destroy him with all this evidence. "I saved that kid and his buddy, and you know it! Those bastards went after them with chains and tire irons. They would've died that night if not for me. Sure as fuck didn't see *you* there!" That came out a little stronger than he'd meant it to.

Alex shrugged off the underhanded accusation like it meant nothing. Never even blinked. "The name Spencer Nantz ring a bell?"

Oh, shit, damn, and son of a bitch. That wimpy kid was Spencer Nantz? The son of the newly appointed Secretary of State Karen Weatherford Nantz, wife of Calvin Nantz, the Ambassador to Israel? Ms. Nantz was also the only daughter of Ashley Weatherford, the entrepreneur who owned the largest construction company on the entire East Coast.

As if wealth or status mattered to Tripp when he was doing his job. "So? He's still alive, isn't he?"

"Yes, and his mother is hellbent on locating the man who saved his life. Trust me, she has the power and the means to find you." Alex's leaned forward. "She wants to publicly thank the idiot. How long do you think it'll take after she outs you, before you're arrested and charged? Or badgered by every son of a bitchin' news outlet for interviews?"

Crap. Pursing his lips, Tripp stared down at the photo of the little shit who should've kept his mouth shut. He couldn't blame Spencer, though. This wasn't his fault. It was his. He was the idiot. "Then why's he just going to NVCC?" Tripp asked more calmly. "Why isn't he at Georgetown with all the other rich kids?" *Or Harvard? Or Yale?*

"Because he chose to stay with his friend, the other young man you rescued."

Tripp sank back into his chair. Closing his eyes, he pinched the bridge of his nose. "I was just doing what's right."

"You're too emotional, Tripp. You go off half-cocked. You need to think a helluva lot longer about all possible consequences before you spring into action."

"Which is why no one else ever does anything! Jesus!" Inside, Tripp seethed at the thought of leaving vulnerable people to fend for themselves on the mean streets of America. It wasn't right. And… But… "What about Abdul Ikram! He was just a kid! He…" Tripp blinked at the memories pouring out of his big mouth, but he was helpless to stop them. "He murdered him, Boss. Don't you get it? He murdered Ikram right in front of me and a couple dozen witnesses. But did anyone else care?! Did anyone do a gawddamned thing to stop that rat bastard from killing a kid?!"

Alex cocked his head at the outburst. Just that fast, the predator stalking Tripp turned into something deadlier. "What about Abdul Ikram?" Alex asked gently. "Who murdered him?"

Alex's voice was so damned calm, Tripp wanted to puke. If only Alex would fight back! War he knew how to deal with, but this steady, logical assault on all that Tripp held dear kept coming out of left field. The air in this spacious office was suddenly so damned thin.

"That pompous ass, Anwar Khan, the Crimson Fuckin' Sword of Allah!" Tripp roared, his entire body overheated and sweat running down his back, between his shoulder blades. "Anwar Khan. Yeah, him."

Yes, forever—*him*. Tripp pursed his lips and blew out a breath to slow the pounding panic filling his head. Shit, he was making a fool of himself, but the damned cat was finally out of the bag, and now Alex knew what drove him. *That day. That poor teenage kid.* Of all the atrocities Tripp had witnessed overseas, Ikram's cold-blooded murder would forever stand out like a big, black, fuckin' monster filling up the blurred backstop of everything else.

Pursing his lips, Tripp blew out a gutful of air, wishing he'd stayed in bed with Ashley, and that he'd kept his mouth shut. Almost wishing he'd never taken on the righteous cause of being Alexandria's only vigilante. Because, damn it, Alex was right. An honest, hard-working vigilante couldn't help anyone once he was outed. Not in this day and age.

"How'd you get these photos?" Tripp asked meekly, wishing he'd brought his hard-assed boss another cup of the high-test brew from the breakroom's overused, beat- to-shit coffee-maker. Alex had yet to rip Tripp's head off. That had to mean something.

"That's beside the point. You were in charge that day, weren't you? It was your responsibility to hand over the prisoner."

Tripp nodded. "Yes, and I fucked it up. I should've stopped Khan. I should've saved Ikram. He was just a kid. Instead—"

"Instead, nothing. There was no way you could've stopped Khan. We can't save everyone."

"I know that, Boss, but shit…" Tripp ran a tired-as-hell hand over his stubborn head. There was no way he'd tell his boss about the nightmares from that day.

"Abdul is why you hunt at night."

"He's why I do a lot of things." *Like cry, rant, and forever need to stop cruelty before it takes over the world.*

"That explains things," Alex said quietly. "Do you still want on my TEAM?"

"On," Tripp answered without hesitation. There was no vigilante without a job. Hell, there was no more vigilante either way, with or without a job. Not with the Secretary of State looking for him.

Alex took his seat. "I'll take care of Secretary Nantz. From now on, you're in charge of my newly established Civilian Anti-Terrorism Team. You'll work with the Commandant of the National Guard, but you'll answer directly to me. Your focus will be working with the local police, not behind their backs. You'll organize civilian community outreach officers to assist victims of crimes, train other civilian professionals to report low-level crimes, like ATM burglary attempts, muggings, and vandalism in vulnerable neighborhoods and in unlighted parking lots. Or outside the local Health Department," he said pointedly. "You'll set up civilian patrols to report credible threats overheard in biker bars, not to act on them, damn it."

"What if the police can't arrive in time? Am I…? Are we supposed to sit on our thumbs and just hang around and watch?"

Alex glanced at the photos. "You didn't use firearms defending any of these people."

"I didn't want to kill anyone."

"And yet you got your point across."

"So…" Tripp ruminated a second. "We can rough up the thugs we find in commission of crimes, just not kill them?"

"Physical restraint is legal in the prevention of any violent crime. But notice I said *restraint*. It does not include beating alleged assailants with your bare hands." Alex's gaze flashed to Tripp's knuckles, which were still plenty bruised and raw. "Your civilian team will be one of many being established across the country. Stronger, more organized local teams are President Adams' way of supporting our country's police departments. They're stretched thin these days. I'm delegating the Virginia and District Civilian Anti-Terrorism Team to you. You'll provide local police offices with a volunteer army of highly-trained civilians who are knowledgeable and physically capable of standing up to bullies. The TEAM has a good reputation in this country, Tripp. Don't fuck it up."

"You're putting me in charge? Just me?"

"You're the first vigilante I've ever had to deal with. This is me, dealing with you."

Tripp was certain Alex had just called him a dumbass. "So basically, I'll be doing the same thing I'm doing now, except with your authority, more people, and…" He cleared his throat. "…more restraint?"

"No, you'll be in charge of men and women who, like you, aren't willing to stand by and watch our country crumble," Alex snapped. "You know damned well how easily evil triumphs when good men choose to do nothing! Your people won't have the authority to arrest or shoot anyone, but they can be the eyes and ears of local law enforcement. They can prevent idiots from damaging property or harming innocent bystanders. Choose your team wisely. I did."

Your people. Tripp liked the sound of that. Made him feel like he belonged to something bigger than himself again. "I can hire former military?"

"And physically able civilians capable of serving and following orders. Can you do that for me?"

For me. Tripp recognized Alex's request for personal commitment. Swallowing hard at the faith this fierce man had in him, Tripp nodded and almost replied, *'Yes, sir.'* But that would've landed him in a steaming pile of shit. He caught himself in time and said, "You bet, Boss."

And a more loyal motherfucker had never been born.

This was Alex's true talent, getting badassed former warriors to follow him into Hell and back. Damned if he hadn't just finessed Tripp into accepting one helluva lot more responsibility and a fuck ton more work. Precisely what he needed.

"Boss, Mom's really struggling over what you've done for Trish," Tripp segued quietly. "Would you have time to meet with her later today?"

Alex settled back into his chair like a contented beast, the ice in his blue eyes not as sharp as earlier. "For you and Andy, anything. Let me know when she can make it here, or I can go to her."

"Ahh, err, no." Tripp cleared his throat. This man just kept giving, and that open-door policy of his was damned humbling. "It'd be better if she came here. Andy needs a break, and… Thanks for everything you and your wife have done for my mother and sister. Trish might not deserve it, but—"

"We'll never know that for certain, will we?" Jumping to his feet, Alex grabbed hold of Tripp's hand, his grip a damned

USMC vise that would've brought tears to Tripp's eyes if they hadn't already been misty." Every second counts in death struggles, Tripp. That's just the way it works in our business. Now get the hell out of my office. Staff meeting's in five."

Chapter Forty-Four

Alex folded his trim, athletic frame between the armrests of his executive chair in his Situation Room, straightened his tie, and watched his TEAM take their places around the oversized, black walnut conference table. Ember and Rory Dennison were still on family leave after the birth of their little girl. Walker Judge and his wife Persia were in East Asia, along with David Tao and several other operators. They were working a highly illegal, covert op to intercept yet another child smuggling ring running underage girls between Cambodia and China. Sex trafficking had become the twenty-first century's blackest plague. No country was immune, not even America.

Two of his three senior agents arrived first. Mark Houston took his place at Alex's right side; Harley Mortimer took the chair to his left. Tripp nodded when he followed Jameson in, pulling Alex back to the reason for this staff meeting. When the last to enter—Mother—took the only available seat beside Jameson, Alex lifted to his feet and began.

Sliding a poster in Braille of all upcoming changes across the table to Jameson, he opened with, "As you know, I've closed our Seattle office. Those agents are relocating to the East Coast as we speak. But we can't accommodate that kind of growth here in Alexandria any longer. A new TEAM Headquarters is under construction in far western Virginia."

"Are all of them moving out of Seattle?" Izza Maher asked. "Even Cassidy?" Izza had begun her TEAM employment in Seattle, but moved East when she'd married Connor.

"Yes, Cassidy and Jude accepted my offer," Alex replied. "Last I heard from Murphy, all but twelve agents are coming with him."

Murphy Finnegan and Roy Hudson had been Alex's first senior agents. Both resigned at the same time, but Murphy had re-upped, after retirement proved boring.

Alex activated the big screen on the wall behind him, and stepped to the side to let his TEAM absorb the blueprint of their future. "We're moving this January, and this is where we're going." The overhead map displayed five major buildings under construction in a large tract of land in western Virginia, plus three buildings already completed. "The two large outbuildings are barns." He highlighted them with his laser pointer. "This one is where Harley will oversee the breeding and training of work and comfort dogs; the other's for Maverick's therapy horses."

Between Maverick's horses and Harley's dogs, Alex was establishing a safe haven where returned vets could rehab among warriors who understood what they'd been through. The cottages for those men and women hadn't been built yet, but the barns were already occupied.

"My monsters can't wait to move," Harley added, his hazel eyes bright with excitement. The monsters were his rambunctious twin boys.

Maverick lifted one hand from the table. "And Kiri's got another batch of kittens if anyone's interested. Just offering." His daughter operated her own cat rescue operation, and he operated *Everyone's a Cowboy*, a local therapeutic riding program for special needs children. Maverick had agreed to expand it to include veterans. Alex agreed to carry the cost of that expansion. In his mind, it was a total win/win. Maverick needed the therapy that came with riding those big horses more than he realized.

"Put me down for two," Zack spoke up. "Song and MiKi have been nagging Mei to let them have a cat. I figure, the more the merrier."

"With your two Pitbulls?" Mother asked snarkily.

"Sure," Harley chimed in. "Introduce them carefully, and they'll be friends for life."

"Hmmpf," Mother grumped. "I doubt that."

"That's because you haven't seen Fluffy and Moo Moo recently. They sleep with LiLi, *in her bed*," Zack emphasized, "which is why my other girls want cats. They want something to cuddle, too."

Fluffy, a brindle, and Moo Moo, a black and white, were the Pitbulls in question. He'd gotten them after LiLi's abduction, more for Mei's peace of mind than his girls' protection. Alex didn't doubt they would take down anyone stupid enough to go after one of Zack's girls, but they were the sappiest protectors Alex had ever seen. Well, except for his TEAM. The men sitting around this table could be pretty damned sappy, too.

Alex continued. "The smallest outbuilding…" He used a laser pointer again. "…is the on-site TEAM clinic. Doctors McKenna Fitzgerald-Villanueva and Libby Houston, along with registered nurse Judy Mortimer, have agreed to operate the clinic, part-time at first, full-time as needed."

"Hey, Boss, we got a decent offer on our old colonial last night," Mark announced. "Libby's really looking forward to working with The TEAM. DC life has worn her down."

"I'm damned glad she opted to join us," Alex remarked.

"I can't wait to work with her again," Doc Fitz added. "With Judy, too. I adore those women."

"Judy's just as thrilled," Harley said.

Beau Villanueva and his wife, Doc Fitz, already lived in the vicinity of the new TEAM HQ, as did Alex, Maverick, and Renner Graves. But for others, the move would be a major disruption to their lives. With Taylor Armstrong's help, Mark and Libby had recently finished restoring one of Northern Virginia's old colonials. With five kids and a practicing physician for a wife, this move wouldn't be easy for Mark. Yet he and Libby had wholeheartedly concurred with the need for TEAM expansion when Alex broached the idea to them months ago. He'd admitted the root of the move was his need to spend more time with his family. Like everyone else's, his two children were growing up too fast, not to mention that his father's mental faculties deteriorated more every day. From now on, Alex intended to maintain a lighter touch on his TEAM. He wasn't retiring, but it was time he became the family man he'd always wanted to be.

All major directors were now selected and on board with his dream. This meeting was where the few remaining delegations would be made and hopefully, accepted. He wanted his people to be as excited as he was about their future. After a few minutes of silence, Alex divided the screen, like Beau had shown him to do earlier, and brought up another window beside the first. This one listed each new department he was creating, along with the director who would manage it.

For the most part, he'd maintained his current chain of command. His senior agents were still Mark, Harley, and David. But he recognized his aging workforce. Married men with families had different needs, and active ops were for youngsters. He'd assigned responsibilities according to those individual strengths.

Mark would now manage International Operations, not including East Asia. Zack would oversee those, while David managed The TEAM safe house there. Harley would handle the newly established K-9 program, and it hadn't taken much for Maverick to agree to manage the Equine Therapy program.

Lee Hart had agreed to stay on as full-time Physical Fitness Director. When he wasn't on active missions, Jameson Tenney would teach parkour and Krav Maga, his specialties. Ember Dennison, when she returned from family leave, would manage the new on-site shooting ranges, all weaponry, certifications, and The TEAM armory. Alex had purposefully removed her from Mother's oversight. Ember deserved a change.

"What's Technology supposed to mean?" Mother asked, an edge to her question.

And here we go...

Alex used the laser pointer to circle one of the few unfilled directorships. "It means I want you as my Director of Technology. You're the genius. You know what it takes for us to get our jobs done."

She huffed, her fake fingernails clattering on the tabletop. "Sure. Yeah."

Clenching his jaw at her indifference, he kept going. "At the moment, it's an empty design lab, Sasha. As Director, you'll select your team of technicians, and you'll determine what equipment you need. You'll be able to—"

"You nixed all my TEAMwear concepts."

"Just the nanny-cam items. They were redundant."

TEAMwear was an integrated collection of spec ops outerwear she'd designed. It came with networks of monitors hidden within the fabric and heads-up displays of the goggles. The original objects had been to monitor heartrates, temperatures, etcetera, much like the high-tech suits astronauts wore. But Alex refused the daily workload that much minutia had dumped in his lap every day. Bottom line, he didn't micro-manage. Mother had yet to appreciate that concept.

"They could've saved lives," she bit out with a slight head swagger.

"A smart man delegates responsibility, then gets out of his people's way and lets them work. I trust my people."

"Them. Not me."

Son of a bitch, she was determined to make this all about her. So be it. Alex stared Mother down for all of two seconds before he asked, "Where's Justice?" The man she'd said she'd married.

That shut her up. And there, staring him in the face, was the reason for his current lack of complete trust in the woman he'd known for years. Alex wanted the old, bossy, nosey Mother back. Not this snarly reminder of subterfuge and deceit.

Justice was one helluva fine man. He'd served Sasha and Dempsey, Sasha's handicapped daughter, faithfully, behind the scenes for years. After Dempsey's death, he'd whisked Mother off to some tropical Pacific island for an extended vacation. She'd needed the break. Alex thought they'd gotten married, although, in typical Mother-style, no one from The TEAM had been invited to her wedding. Until she'd returned and become increasingly harder to deal with, Alex hadn't thought to fact-check her story. Now he knew Justice had returned from their adventure alone. He'd taken a new job at a high-end hotel in Miami, Florida, and had severed all ties with multi-millionaire Sasha Kennedy.

"That's none of your business," she replied tartly. "My personal affairs are no one's—"

"Oh, come on, Mom," Jameson interrupted as his left hand circled her wrist. "We're all family here, TEAM family. Surely—"

"Stop calling me Mom!" She jerked out from under his touch. "You're *not* my family, Junior Agent Tenney. None of you are!"

"Excuse me?" Mark's head canted nearly to his shoulder at that vehemently stated demand. "You found Libby for me after those Russian's kidnapped her and buried her alive, didn't you? You tracked her to the roadside construction site where they'd left her trapped inside a stack of concrete planters. Those were nothing but coffins, *Mom*. It was fall in Wisconsin. It was cold. She would've died of hypothermia if you hadn't helped me find her. I wouldn't have found her by myself. You saved my Libby's life."

Alex kept his mouth sealed.

"And who picked up a weapon the day Interpol Director Peters came to kill me, David, Harley, and Mark during that Black Dragon Syndicate op?" Zack asked, his big hands splayed on the tabletop in front of him, across from her. "If you're not our overprotective Mom, who is?"

"But I—"

"But you helped me get to Izza and my unborn baby girl in time, Mom," Connor interrupted quietly. As usual, Izza was sitting beside him, her brown eyes big and shining with tears. His hand fell automatically over his diminutive wife's shoulder. "Without your help, those bastards would've beaten Izza to death, and you know it." Swallowing so hard Alex heard it, he pulled Izza under his arm. "We would've lost our sweet little Jamie that day, and I'd be a fuckin' mess."

"Yeah, but—"

"Yeah, but you and Ember spotted our SOS out in the Utah desert where the cartel dumped us," Izza added. "You stared at satellite feeds for days looking for us, Mom. I know you did."

Before Mother could growl again, Jameson told her, "You helped Eric, Hunter, and Adam locate Maddie and me after that shoot-out with Pops Delaney. He would've killed us, *Mom*."

She shot him a glare. The cords in her neck turned stiff and hard, but at last, she was fighting tears.

"And you helped Jameson, Harley, and Eric follow me to Boston when I went there to kill Delaney's daughter," Maddie piped up from across the table where she sat beside Mark. "I made a mistake that day, but you made sure I didn't get myself killed. Thank you, Mom."

"You helped me get China out of Wyoming," Maverick murmured darkly from the other side of Harley. "I thought she was dead when I finally extracted her and Kiri from that hellhole her sister had them in. I thought I'd lost her, but you sent Gabe and Taylor, that medical helo, and…" His voice ground to a full stop as he swiped a hand over his face. "Did you know she stopped breathing on that Wyoming hillside that night, *Mom*? Without you, I'd be dead now. Because it was you who helped save the woman who saved my gawddamned, worthless life!"

Alex opened his mouth to tell Maverick he was anything but worthless, but Adam spoke first. "You waltzed into Paul Reagan's mansion to find Shannon for me, to make sure she was doing okay, remember? He had her and Squeaks. He was blackmailing her, using her baby boy against her to keep her in line." Adam's eyes glittered with unshed emotion. "Squeaks was premature. He needed his mother. But Paul Reagan was killing her, Mom. Her own son of a bitchin' father kept that sweet little guy from his mother, wouldn't let Shannon see him, wouldn't even let her hold him unless she did what she was told. He wanted her to run his freakin' empire, when all she wanted was her son back. I'm with Maverick. Without you, I'd already be dead, because…" He lifted his eyes to the ceiling. "I can't live without my wife and son, *Mom*. Just. Can't."

Before Mother could reply, Taylor added quietly, "You helped Harley and Gabe find me after I'd been shot, before I knew who I really was. Before I met my people and the woman I married, the ones who truly love me."

Alex swallowed hard. That had been an excruciatingly difficult time in Taylor's life. It wasn't until he'd found his lost American Indian heritage that he'd finally become part of The TEAM.

"You helped Zack and Mark find me before that homeless nut job, Miriam, stabbed me again," Harley said quietly.

"Remember? She'd already stabbed me once. I was bleeding out. Her knife was still stuck in my ribs. I was out of my head and dying." Unabashedly, he ran a hand over his watery eyes. "You saved my life that night, *Mom*. Miriam stabbed Mark, too. You saved his life, too."

"You did," Mark said quietly.

"You found my finger," Beau added, his voice no more than a whisper. The little finger on his left hand was once again attached and functional. Psycho killer, Catalina Montego, had drugged Beau, then hacked his finger off with a gardener's branch clippers, in her effort to terrorize Alex and The TEAM.

"And I know you tracked down everything you could find about that failed mission overseas. You hacked the government's geo-satellites, I know you did. You broke the law to prove I didn't kill my men. You put yourself at risk to prove I was telling the truth, to keep me out of Leavenworth. Then you dug into the shitshow that was my childhood, and you found my real parents, damn it." Beau was wiping his face plenty by then. "You gave me my life back, Mom. There's a picture of my pretty baby sister hanging in my living room because of you." He pointed his finger at her. "You didn't have to do that, but you can't deny that you love me and McKenna. You've rescued all of us in one way or another. Why shouldn't we call you *Mom*, gawddamnit?"

"Because…" She sniffed back her tears, struggling not to cry. This was what she needed, her TEAM, the men and women she'd protected for years, standing up for her. Getting in her face and reminding her where she belonged. That she was part of them. That they needed her as much as she needed them. Alex couldn't have asked for more if he'd scripted this display of loyalty himself.

Jameson turned his dark glasses to Mother and gingerly cupped his left hand over her wrist again. "Beau's right. We call you Mom because we love you, *Mom*," he whispered, "and we know you love us. You're just having a hard time right now. We understand. All of us have lost people we love. It takes a long time to get straight."

"But you're… But I…" She was having a hard time swallowing. "I'm not your mom, damn it. I was Dempsey's, but now she's gone, and so's Justice, and… and…"

"So are Gorgeous and Crystal Love," Maverick breathed. Gorgeous and Crystal Love were the pure white Percheron horses, the mother and foal, that perished the night an arsonist torched China's barn in Wyoming. "So's my baby brother, Darrin, *Mom*," he said softly. "Think I don't miss them? I'll never get any of them back, but I've still got China and Kiri. I hope I've still got you."

Alex was the one swallowing hard then. He'd never known until much later how close Maverick had been to committing suicide after his baby brother was killed in Afghanistan. That was when Maverick quit The TEAM and walked from Alexandria, Virginia, to the center of Wyoming. There he'd finally found the peace he'd been looking for, at China Wolf's Wild Wolf Ranch.

It was Beau who'd finally cracked Maverick's hard shell during The TEAM's failed operation to stop Catalina Montego. Beau had been just as lost, just as broken and angry at the world, as Maverick then. They were brothers by different mothers, bound together by the twin demons of loss and heartache. In a convoluted way, during that op, Maverick became the big brother Beau never had during his miserable childhood. And Beau, the agent Alex had come damned close to firing, filled in for the younger brother Maverick desperately still needed in his life.

"Doesn't matter how or when it comes," Tripp muttered darkly. "Death is the greatest equalizer of mankind. It ruins us all."

Alex nodded his head at Tripp, thankful he now knew about Abdul Ikram. Tripp would always carry that guilt, but he'd found Ashley Cox now, and Alex knew damned well how quickly the right woman could change a hard man's heart.

"It's a cheating, lying bitch with no heart," Jameson murmured. He was still facing Sasha, his voice soft and low, his arm resting on the back of her chair now. "It doesn't ask permission, Mom, and it doesn't care who it takes from us, how or when. It just takes and takes until…" A tremendous sigh shuddered out of him. "…it feels like it sucks the life out of you. I know you miss Dempsey. We know you're hurting. We've all lost someone we'll never get back. But it sounds like you've been holding us together for a long, long time. That's why I've always called you Mom. How about you let us hold onto you for a while?"

Her lashes fell. She clenched her jaw, pursed her lips, and blinked down at the table. Those fingernails of hers were oddly quiet.

"You've been with me since I lost Sara and Abby," Alex reminded her gently.

Her chest heaved with another deep intake of air. Mother was suffering. How well Alex knew precisely what she was going through. After he'd lost his first wife and child, he'd been a royal pain in everyone's ass, pissed at anyone who got in his way, suicidal, too. But oftentimes, it was the biggest assholes who were hurting the most; who needed the most understanding and patience. The most love. Kelsey had given him all that, and more.

"It's different," Mother whispered to the table. "Helping you people is what I do. It's my job, not yours. Just like it was my job to take care of Dempsey, only I failed at that, didn't I?"

"No more than I failed Sara and Abby," Alex replied.

"But you were deployed. You weren't here when it happened, when they died. I was right there with her, and I… I…" Mother gulped so hard, Alex heard it across the table. "Me, of all people, I should've been able to save her… I'm a—"

"You're a millionaire," Beau said. "So what if you own a high-rise, a pharmaceutical research company, a hotel, and…?" He cocked his head at her. "What else?"

"ICan," Jameson replied, then added, "Her flagship gaming business. Clever name, Mom."

"And DoDCore," Mark said. "Her Department of Defense website, available only to government entities in need of a technological assist."

"It's called a bump," she said civilly, still studying the tabletop. Still drowning. Still so damned lost. But still one hundred percent the genius she'd always been.

Alex skirted the far end of the table, jerked one of the extra chairs away from the wall, planted his rear, pointed his elbows into his thighs, and leaned into the woman who'd once been a trusted friend. He held his hand out to her. Mother turned in her seat, looked at it, and finally took hold. Her fingers were ice. Alex cupped that cold hand in both of his and held on.

Interestingly, the nickname Mother began as a behind-her-back joke about her nosy, gossiping, interfering ways. Alex hadn't fully appreciated his genius techie back then. But the spinoff moniker, Mom, was kinder and gentler. It fit the woman she'd become. Alex could thank Jameson for that.

"Kelsey told me something a few years back," he told her quietly. "Like you and Justice, we had a helluva lot of crap to deal with when we first married. She'd just lost her two sons. I'd lost Sara and Abby a few years earlier. The pain was fresh. We were both ragged and raw, drowning in our own piles of grief. Not a day went by that one of us didn't feel like we were bleeding.

"But one morning at breakfast, she climbed onto my lap, took my big, fat head in her hands, and told me I could cry and curse God forever, but she wasn't leaving me." Alex swallowed hard at the tender woman he lived for now. "My sweet wife told me the only reason I was being such an A-hole—her word, not mine—was because grief lasts as long as true love. It has to; it's a measure of how deeply we love the ones we lost. And when the day comes that I lose her…"

He looked at the floor between his feet, his heart pounding like a son of a bitch. "I'll be just as big an A-hole as I was then." Alex lifted his chin and met Mother's teary gaze. "Like it or not, death leaves a son of a bitchin' crater inside of us, Sasha. We'll never stop missing the ones we lost, but only because we gave them our whole hearts."

The room was stone-cold silent when he finished. Alex had never shared so much emotion or personal information with his TEAM before. He might never again. But then again, he did trust everyone in this room with his life…

He'd learned a lot since Catalina Montego had crashed onto the scene two years ago. Exorcising her evil spirit from the District and Virginia had taught Alex how fast he could lose the very thing he'd always wanted, yet had ignored, whenever TEAM troubles came calling. Namely, his family. A guy didn't get many second chances. That was what Kelsey was, his second chance. He'd never deserved her, but God knew he needed her. And she'd blessed him with his third and fourth chances: his daughter Lexie Rose and his newborn son Bradley Patrick. And now, living with his elderly father's Alzheimer's, Alex was learning how to forgive, something he was still working on.

Everyone was listening, but he focused on the trembling woman at his knees. "I'd like you to manage all things technology related, Sasha. From concept to invention to patent, hell, to worldwide distribution, if DoD allows. You'll hire the people who'll do the best job for you. It's a big world out there and a new terrorist every day. Are you still part of my TEAM or not?"

"Thank you." She whispered so low he had to lean in to be sure he'd heard right. "I needed this." A tiny sad smile quirked one side of her lipstick-painted mouth. She squeezed his hand. "And I'm okay being called Mom. I'm staying. I'm in."

Jameson rapped his knuckles on the tabletop. "You heard her. Mom's staying! Let's celebrate, people!"

As a thunderous "Ooh-rah!" filled the room, Alex allowed a long, deep breath. His TEAM was back. All of them.

Chapter Forty-Five

Day forty-three and counting. Trish had been moved from the hospital in Alexandria to a nearby rehabilitation center. There Tripp met the indomitable Gracie Fox-Armstrong. She was one of the many physical therapists on staff, also Junior Agent Taylor Armstrong's wife. When Trish woke up—if she did— Gracie would be her personal trainer. She'd already assisted in treating Trish for her venereal diseases. Eventually, she'd teach Trish to stand again, how to walk, feed herself, and everything else active people did. Then she'd accompany Trish home to help her transition back into the real world.

But for now, Trish remained bedridden and unresponsive. One good side effect of her coma was that the drugs, booze, and smokes she'd used, were now out of her system. She'd detoxed under strict medical care, something she never would've done before her attack. Her cervical cancer hadn't required a complete hysterectomy, as Doctor Pitt had initially diagnosed. Instead, an oncology specialist removed it via what he'd called a simple trachelectomy. Didn't sound simple to Tripp, but the doctor assured Andy and Tripp that option gave Trish the best chance of being able to carry a pregnancy to term. Which was important to Andy. She'd started believing in miracles again. Tripp took the wait-and-see approach. This was Trish after all.

As unlikely as it seemed, she'd gained weight. The anemic, skeletal woman she'd been the night she'd nearly lost her life, was gone. Regular nourishment via a feeding tube did that. Her skin tone was more pink than gray these days. Chalk that up to Gracie, who tended to Trish's personal needs, daily cleanliness, and hair care.

If only Trish would open her eyes and tell him to fuck off. That was what Tripp lived for.

"Okay, steep hill up ahead, Pooh Bear. Time to dig in and give it your all," he told her as he manipulated her right leg into a smooth bend, followed by a gentle lift and a full extension. Gracie had taught him how to work his sister's limbs to prevent stiffness. "Pretend with me, you're the best downhill racer in the world. Uphill, downhill, doesn't matter. You can beat everyone else on this track. Here we go again."

Tripp talked throughout Trish's workout. It was his day with his sister. Ashley was working out at TEAM HQ with, of all people, Zack Lennox. He was teaching her self-defense; Jameson would eventually teach her parkour. Tripp and Ashley were meeting his mom at noon for lunch, before Andy took over sitting with Trish until 6pm. Ashley had the night shift, which meant Tripp would be back to sit with her and Trish until 10pm, when the facility closed its doors to visitors. They were the Three Musketeers, each keeping the others cheered up and filled with Doctor Smith's positive vibes.

But after hoping for a month and a half that Trish would finally wake up today—

Nope. Not going there. Tripp banished the very real, in-his-face fact that she might never recover. She was into the second month of her coma. She had no lingering complications from her surgeries. She wasn't on a ventilator and her incisions were healing. She just wouldn't open her eyes.

"Okay, Pooh Bear, you won that race easy," Tripp said after manipulating her leg for the twentieth rotation. "The crowd's on their feet. They love you, kiddo. And look at that cheater, Mitt. He thought he could slow you down by sidestepping into you, but you showed him. You go, girl!" Tripp whistled softly and made clucking, hissing noises, hoping it sounded like the clapping din of his imaginary crowd. "You're a star!"

After exercising her other leg through another imaginary twenty-lap race, he fastened the fluffy-lined booties Gracie had bought Trish around her calves and her always icy-cold feet. The slipper soles were covered with non-skid dots that had yet to meet the floor. But someday…

God, he hoped she'd open those snarky eyes soon.

Tucking her pajama pant legs into the booties, he pressed the Velcro straps in place. Her wardrobe now consisted of clothing designed to snap-on or wrap-around, anything to make dressing easy. This morning, Gracie had dressed Trish in loose-fitting, black silk pajamas with red piping on the edges. Trish's garish black hair-dye was growing out, as was the length. It actually shone from Gracie's careful attention now, and her natural curls were back in full force. Tripp couldn't remember the last time his sister had looked so much like herself.

Since he'd previously exercised her feet to keep them from curling, which was more like a massage than what he considered a workout, Tripp moved alongside the bed for her next sets. Taking hold of her right arm, he put one hand on her wrist, the other at her elbow, and stretched the limb slowly and gently into a wide quarter arc.

"Let's give all those fans of yours a great big parade wave." Tripp always put excitement into his voice. Somewhere inside that hard, banged-up head of Trish's, he hoped she was listening. "There you go. Not too high. Not too low. Jusssst riiiight."

Lowering her arm to her side, he repeated the rotation. "Good job, Pooh Bear. Ten more of these. Slow and easy. When we're through, I'll read something out of 'Winnie the Pooh.'" A very long time ago, in Idaho, Trish had adored the little, yellow, stuffed bear. Hence her nickname. Brothers loved to tease.

"Great! Now let's play ball." He raised her arm high enough to execute a full one hundred eighty degree stretch. "Volleyball, today. Remember when we used to set up the net across the backyard in Idaho? Man, I hated that Russian Olive tree hanging over our fence from Ruskin's pasture. The thing had ten-inch thorns, I swear. How many balls did we lose to that ball-eating monster. Ten? Twenty?"

She grunted. She'd made a noise!

Very carefully, Tripp relaxed her arm and leaned over her, their hands linked together under her chin. "I heard you. You're trying to talk to me, I know you are," he told her, his tears shimmering, making her a beautiful, blurry angel. The gold roots showing through the black, formed a halo at the crown of her head. "Do it again, Pooh Bear. Please. Say something to me, anything."

She didn't respond. Didn't open her eyes. Nothing. Which wasn't a surprise. Because of the damage to her throat, her thoracic specialist Doctor Pitt had performed a tracheostomy.

She now had a hole, aka a stoma, in an already damaged throat that allowed her to breathe. Once she regained full consciousness and strength, she'd have to learn how to eat through her mouth instead of the tube that ran through her nose into her stomach. Because of the way her throat had been cut, Doctor Pitt also planned a surgical procedure called a microlaryngoscopy, to repair the nerve damage to her vocal cords. If Trish put her mind to it, she'd be able to communicate vocally someday. Tripp still couldn't believe she'd survived.

"Aw, come on, Pooh Bear. Please. It's just me, your dumbass brother. Do it again. I don't care if you tell me to fuck off or go to hell. Honest."

She moaned. Out loud! At least she'd made something in her throat vibrate. She *had* heard him.

He loved it! "You're alive!"

Well, of course, she was alive. Tripp knew that. But now she was really alive!

Opening her eyes, she blinked. Three drowsy blinks, but by hell. She'd done that intentionally. He could've kissed her! So he did. Lifting her limp torso up from her pillow, just enough to ease his hands beneath her, he hugged the sister he'd been missing for a long, damned time. Gently, he kissed her cheek. While she lay there breathing in his ear, Tripp cried like a damned baby. "You're alive, and you're going to be okay, and—"

She managed a weak slap to his shoulder. Tripp eased her carefully back down. His heart had lodged up high in his throat. He was so damned happy. "I'm calling Mom." He had his cell phone to his ear by then. He couldn't wait to tell— "Mom! Trish is awake."

"She is!" Andy shrieked. "When?"

"Just now. Hurry. Get dressed. I'm coming to get you."

Ashley peeked into the room. "Oh, my gosh, is she awake? How wonderful!" She'd dressed in yoga pants and a plain white t-shirt this morning. She'd been excited, bouncing on her toes when Zack swung by her apartment and gave her a ride to TEAM HQ.

"Congrats," Zack said. Wearing a black hoodie and running pants, he took up the entire doorway behind her.

"It's a miracle," Tripp replied, so damned happy and relieved for his pain-in-the-ass sister. He couldn't get his eyeballs to man up and quit leaking, damn it!

Suddenly, Ashley had both arms around his neck and his forehead rested on her shoulder, while he quietly fell apart. Until then, Tripp hadn't realized how worried he'd been that he'd lose Trish. Or how much he loved her. Trish always had the knack of making him angry. But yeah. He loved his twin more than he'd ever tell the brat.

"How will Andy get over here?" Ashley asked.

"I'll go get her," Zack volunteered. "Sit tight, folks. I'll be right back."

Tripp glanced sideways at his twin. Trish was fingering the bandage on her neck. "I don't want to tell her what happened," he whispered after Zack left.

Ashley snuggled into him, her fingertips on his collarbone. "Why not? It's a miracle. She's lucky to be alive."

"But I don't want to scare her."

"Well, my goodness. Look at you!" Gracie exclaimed from the open doorway "Hi, Trish! My name's Gracie Armstrong. I'm your rehab therapist, nurse, and mentor. Basically, I'm here to help you get back on your feet. I brought you a get-well-quick present." She placed an electronic tablet on the nightstand near Trish's hand. "It'll help you communicate until you learn how to talk again. You can even play games on it or listen to music."

Gracie was one of those forever optimists, the kind of caregiver a patient wanted in their corner when they faced an uphill battle. She'd already proven to be a rock of positivity with Tripp, Andy, and Ashley. Watching her interact with Trish did Tripp's nervous heart good.

Trish patted her bandaged throat, her eyes wide and her lips moving, but no sound coming out.

"That's where your doctor performed a tracheotomy to help you breathe. You were assaulted, sweetheart," Gracie explained as she sat on the edge of the bed. "Some awful man tried to kill you. Do you remember anything?"

Trish shook her head.

"But Tripp and his guys shot that guy," Ashley explained quietly. "He's dead now, Trish. That jerk can't ever hurt you again. You're a survivor like me."

When Trish squeezed her eyes shut and her lips pinched, Tripp knew she was struggling with her new reality. He tugged Ashley into his side and let Gracie take over. She knew best how to help his twin understand what had happened to her. Trish had survived one hell of an attack, but this was her second chance—if she was smart enough to take it.

"Hey, listen. Why don't you and Gracie get better acquainted, while we grab a bite of lunch," Tripp told his twin. "Mom's on her way. We'll be right back."

But Trish wasn't having that. Shaking her head, she waved frantically for him to stay. Her eyes were bright and panicked.

Tripp never thought he'd see the day she would admit she needed him. He was at her side in a heartbeat. The moment he drew close, Trish latched onto his hand and pulled him down to her face. Like a drowning woman, she wrapped one arm around his neck, her chest heaving as she buried her face in his shirt.

Gracie moved out of his way and let Tripp settle beside his sister. He gathered her under his chin. "Hey, kiddo," he breathed. "You're alive, and you're going to be okay. Yeah, some idiot thought he could take you down, but you showed him. You're one helluva fighter. I'm proud of you."

She made a desperate sound deep in her throat, and her heart was pounding like a hummingbird was caught in her chest.

"Will she really be able to talk again?" he asked Gracie.

She crossed her arms over her chest, smiling, and her eyes on Trish. "It'll be hard, girlfriend, but I know a couple really good speech therapists, and with enough practice… Yeah. I've seen people overcome damaged vocal cords before. Plus, Doctor Pitt is one of the best thoracic specialists on the East Coast. If he says you'll recover, then trust me. It's a done deal."

Tripp patted his twin's back, something he hadn't done in years. "And I'll be here every day until you're back on your feet. Mom and Ashley, too. Oh, yeah." He motioned Ashley to join him on the edge of the bed. "Almost forgot. This is my girlfriend, Ashley Cox."

Blinking furiously up at her brother, Trish stabbed her finger at her stoma.

"I know. That rat bastard cut your throat, kiddo. He meant to kill you, and by all accounts, you should be dead. But instead, he's kicking up daisies, Pooh Bear. Not you. Look at you, still ready to kick the world's ass."

There was no sparkle of hope in her eyes. She didn't believe him.

"It's okay to be scared, Trish," Ashley offered extra-quietly. "That same guy tried to kill me two years ago. I was scared for a long time. So scared, I kinda forgot how to live. But if a scaredy-cat like me can learn to fight back, I know Tripp's badass sister can, too. One of his friends is teaching me how to box and about self-defense. Maybe we could spar together sometime."

Still cowering under Tripp's chin, Trish shook her head the slightest bit. This was a side of her he'd never seen.

"Oh, yes, you most definitely are badass, girlfriend," Ashley teased. "Tripp's been telling me stories about you guys growing up in Idaho. How you glued his coffee cup to the kitchen table one morning before school, and how he nearly jerked his throwing arm out of its socket trying to pick it up. How you put a plastic skull in the microwave one morning, so he'd find it when he fixed his oatmeal, and how he screamed like a girl."

The corners of Trish's lips curled.

"You've always been a pain in my ass. Don't stop now," Tripp added gently.

Another ragged cough escaped her.

He hugged his sister carefully. "We're just going down the block to a pub for lunch. Want me to bring you anything? Clam chowder? Waffle fries? Ice cream?" She'd adored strawberry ice cream when she was a kid.

Leaning back onto her pillow, she made a heart sign with her index fingers and thumbs.

"You want a Valentine?" Where the hell was he going to find something like that this time of year?

She shook her head and made the sign again.

"I think she's trying to tell you she loves you," Ashley said.

Trish nodded, those tired eyes washing over him. She pointed at her chest, then him, then made the sign one more time.

Tripp could have cried, but Gracie interrupted his meltdown by handing Trish a couple tissues. "She's tired, guys. Let's let her rest."

Tripp took a chance and told Trish, "I never stopped loving you, Pooh Bear."

She'd never liked his nickname for her. Predictably, she flipped him her middle finger. But for the first time in her life, Trish did it with a smile

Epilogue

There were good days. There were bad days. A good day was Trish impatiently wanting out of bed the minute Tripp arrived, then standing on her own two feet and walking a few steps to prove she could. A good day was Andy crying because her baby girl had just signed that she loved her mom and could Andy ever forgive her? Or the morning Trish shot Tripp two hands full of flying fingers, which Gracie translated into, "It's damned time you learn American Sign Language, so I can talk to you again, Trippster!"

Tripp had once hated her nickname for him almost as much as she'd hated being called Pooh Bear. Yeah. Good times.

A bad day was Tucker Chase calling to inform Tripp of everything he and his team had found in Doug Driscoll's basement apartment in nearby Arlington. Another body bag and another woman's lifeless, tortured body. A bloody stainless-steel table. Two damp drains in the concrete floor, both ripe with plenty of forensic evidence. Pulleys bolted to two-by-twelve-foot ceiling joists. A heavy chain attached to those pulleys. Meat hooks dangling at the end of that chain.

Tucker had already reported everything his team had found hidden in Driscoll's trench coat, the weapons he'd planned to use on Ashley. The sharp knives and rolls of fishing line. The wire, pliers, fishhooks, and duct tape. But the small ballpeen hammer and all those loose six-inch nails were the worst. The creepy bastard was one crazy motherfucker.

Jameson's profile had been accurate as hell. Not only did Driscoll reside close by and travel Interstate 395 on a daily basis, but he'd suffered a catastrophic injury as a small child, that resulted in him being medically castrated. Compound that glaring shortcoming—no pun intended—with his mother's bizarre compulsion to tell the world about his lack of manhood, and Driscoll hated women and pretty much all men. But he only vented his insane obsession on women because real men scared him. He was the ultimate voyeur, a photographer whose career field offered graphic stimulation, as well as vivid real-life scenarios to fuel his twisted need to prove he was still powerful…albeit in a pitiful, impotent way.

The altar where Driscoll commemorated his *work* yielded photos of eleven missing women. Tucker's team had already identified the four from Pennsylvania and the three from Massachusetts. Identification of the rest pended DNA results from the body bag found at the last crime scene. Counting the two that got away, Ashley and Trish, and the three murders from two years earlier, that made a grand total of sixteen women Driscoll had violated, intended to violate, or murdered. Not a day went by that Tripp didn't wish he could kill the son of a bitch again.

"Are you ready?" he called out from where he was sitting in Ashley's living room. Since his apartment had been an uglier crime scene than hers, he'd moved in with Ashley after Director Chase gave them the green light. Tripp had cleaned the mess in his place, then moved most of his stuff to storage. He'd only brought his clothes and his shaving kit with him to Ashley's.

October and November had been all about Trish's recovery. She was home now, and Andy was happier than Tripp had seen her in years. Christmas had come and gone. After an unseasonably warm December, January brought ice and snow flurries to the Eastern Seaboard. Despite the wintry weather, movers had packed TEAM HQ while all of the agents were on two-weeks holiday leave. Things were looking up.

And there she was, wearing a clingy sweater dress the same color as her eyes. Ashley no longer wore man-shirts or pants, but this was the prettiest he'd seen her. The dress hugged her curves and accentuated her plump cleavage in all the best ways. The fabric flowed like sapphire blue water over her figure, dipping at her waist, making his heart pump like crazy. The lace of a white camisole peeked above her breasts, framing them like two plump gifts he wanted to put his mouth and hands on.

She'd rigged part of her hair into a bun crisscrossed with golden wires and dotted with sapphire gems. The rest hung down her back in an ebony sheet of silky softness that rippled when she moved. But those matching blue, fuck-me heels… Not only did they make her legs longer, but the thought of them on his shoulders later today made Tripp hard as hell. He jumped to his feet, his throat dry, and reached for her hand.

"Let me look at you," he said, his voice full of gravel and grit.

"Are you ready?" she asked breathlessly.

"Baby, I am so ready. Oh, you mean to get going?"

She lifted her face to the ceiling and laughed. Seeing the tender expanse of sweet-smelling skin between her chin and chest was invitation enough. Tripp tugged her against his body and buried his face in the crook of her neck, breathing in the luscious scent of her hair. This shy, timid creature had become his reason for living. Ashley had changed his life and all of his toughest-dog-in-the-fight reference points. Tripp no longer lived for the hunt or worked nights for Lady Justice. He lived for Ashley, his mom, and his sister now. His TEAM and his life, not Ikram's. He'd done all he could while he'd served, and he'd come to realize it was time to let Abdul go. Now was Tripp's time to live.

"We're going to be late," she whispered, even as her hand curled around his neck and her fingers delved into his hair.

"Shall we?" he asked, going for gallant, but, no doubt, looking like the kid from Idaho that he'd always be.

"Yes. Let's." The excitement in Ashley's voice was a quivering livewire of need that jolted straight to his groin. If she even hinted at stepping out of that dress, he knew damned well they'd be late.

But now was not the time. They had some place to be, and they couldn't miss it. Not today. People expected them, especially them, to be on time.

Fighting a primal need to undress Ashley, Tripp held her winter coat while she slipped her arms into it. While she buttoned up, he shrugged into his leather jacket. His pistols stayed home today. He couldn't wear his two-pack holster under the get-up he'd soon change into. The small pocket pistol tucked in his inside jacket pocket would have to suffice. Tripp flipped his jacket collar up, because, today… baby, it was cold outside.

It took a half-hour to get to the chapel on Prince Street, Alexandria. After he parked his truck in the rear lot, Ashley went her way, carrying a garment bag with all her essentials.

The next time they met, they'd be different people. They'd be—

"Hey!" Jameson called from the open back door Ashley had just disappeared into. "Been waiting for you. Hurry your ass up, McClane!"

"Coming," he replied, on the run now.

Hurriedly, Jameson showed him where to change, then helped him dress. Adeptly, he straightened the front of Tripp's pin-tucked dress shirt while Tripp stuffed its long tails into his pleated, black, dress slacks. Jameson tied Tripp's bow tie as he slipped into the shiniest damned dress shoes in the world.

"What'd you do, spit polish these shitkickers?"

Jameson laughed, deep in his throat. "Leave it to you to call patent leather slip-ons shitkickers. Nope, just dusted them off while I was waiting for you. There. You look sophisticated enough."

Yeah, right. How would Jameson know what he looked like?

Tripp turned to the mirror, lifted his chin, and ran a quick hand over his clean-shaven chin. They said clothes made the man. Well, that was not him in the mirror. Looked more like a blond James Bond wannabe. But he'd paint himself and go naked if it pleased Ashley.

"How do I look?" Jameson asked.

The man was uncharacteristically nervous. He wasn't wearing his dark glasses. Tripp almost wished he were. Jameson's brown eyes were forever unfocused, his pupils small, never dilated. But friends didn't diminish friends, and Tripp wouldn't say or do anything to dampen his buddy's confidence. He cuffed Jameson's shoulder. "Who cares what you look like? You do know this day isn't about you, right?"

"Yes, but…" Jameson straightened his tie, then smoothed a hand down his sleeve. "A man can't afford not to make a good impression."

Tripp flicked a tiny string off his buddy's lapel. "Come on, Romeo. The music's playing."

"You first."

"Of course." Even best men knew when to step up and lead. They were in their place at the front of the chapel when the real music, the here-comes-the-bride tune, started. Tripp fastened his gaze on the back of the chapel. There she was. Ashley. The woman he adored and would spend the rest of his days worshipping. His heart scampered up his throat like some bonkers chipmunk at the sight of her.

"Well?" Jameson whisper-prompted. "How's she look?"

"Oh, yeah, sorry." Tripp cleared his throat. "Maddie's beautiful—"

"I already know that," Jameson hissed. "I need to know—"

"Settle down. Ten more steps, and she'll be right here. Three, two… Okay, reach for her."

Maddie stepped onto the raised dais and put her tiny hand in Jameson's outstretched fingers. "Hey there, handsome. Are you ready to do this?"

With a quiet groan, he tugged her into his side. "Been waiting my whole life for you," he whispered.

Man, the guy was smooth.

Tripp reached for his woman then, and Ashley folded under his arm like she'd always belonged there. At least, momentarily. The ceremony demanded a little more distance between groomsmen and bridesmaids, which Jameson had just realized as well. When Maddie separated herself from his side, Tripp escorted Ashley over to where the other maids-of-honor were standing and returned to his best buddy's side.

Tripp's hands were shaking, partially in support of his friend, but mostly because it should've been him standing with the minister, him announcing his marriage vows today. Him promising to love, honor, and obey the amazing woman who'd dropped into his life that dark Friday night. She thought he'd saved her? Not even close. It was Ashley Cox who'd turned everything she touched into gold, including him. He was just a hard, dumbass grunt who'd finally seen the light, and that light was the loveliest sapphire blue. God, he loved her.

Poor Jameson stuttered through his vows, until Maddie reached across the gap between them and took his hands in hers. His chin hit the front of his fancy ruffled shirt. He sucked in a deep breath. Something inside Jameson changed once he had a hold of his bride. His chest heaved with a full cleansing sigh. His broad shoulders squared, and he snapped to like the ninja warrior Tripp now knew he was. As usual, Jameson's head tilted down at the woman he'd never be able to see. The crazy-in-love guy poured out his heart in the longest romantic marriage vow Tripp had ever heard. When he finished, Maddie's eyes were bright and brimming.

She whispered her much shorter vows to him then. The minister declared, "By the power vested in me, I now pronounce you man and wife. You may kiss the bride."

Jameson wrapped one arm around Maddie's neck, and she melted into him. Her bridal bouquet dropped to her side. Ashley grabbed it before it hit the floor. Maddie slipped both arms around Jameson's waist. He slanted his head. She slanted hers. Jameson looked pretty damned satisfied when she moaned into his mouth as they kissed.

Tripp got it then. That minister hadn't married them; he was just another witness. This sacred promise was all on Jameson and Maddie. They'd married each other, bound themselves to love, trust, and honor each other. Man, the things a man finally understood once they were shoved in his face.

He looked past Jameson and Maddie to Ashley. Her teary blues were locked on him. Did she know? Could she possibly understand the depth of his love for her? He had to make sure.

When the newly married Mr. and Mrs. Tenney's steamy kiss finally ended, the minister turned Jameson and Maddie around to face their friends and family. They raised their hands, and a mighty, "Hoo-yah!" filled the chapel, as every damned, big-mouthed Marine roared congratulations Navy style, in deference to Jameson having been a SEAL.

By the time the procession followed the bride and groom into the vestibule, Tripp was climbing out of his skin. He had a good hold on Ashley's tiny hand, but he needed more. The minister stopped to speak with Alex and Kelsey. Jameson and Maddie were surrounded by friends and family. It was time. Before the doors closed, Tripp jerked Ashley back inside and out of sight. With all celebratory noises muted, there in the back of the church, he dropped to one knee. Once again, time stopped.

Ashley was looking down at him, her eyes shining.

He was looking up at her, his heart in his throat.

"What are you doing? We have a reception to be at in…" Ashley scanned the chapel for a clock, then shrugged. "…about thirty minutes."

"I love you with all my heart," he told her. Such pathetic words! They said nothing about the ache in his heart, nor the fire in his soul. Damn it, he was as bad at this, as Jameson had been with his vows.

Shoving his tux jacket out of his way, Tripp reached deep into his pants pocket and ran into his good luck charm, that pair of silk panties. Ashley didn't yet know it, but they went everywhere he went. Slipping past them, he pulled the ring out of his pocket. One big solitaire, it captured the light from the electric sconces lining the chapel's back wall and turned it into sparkling prisms, casting rainbows into Ashley's pretty eyes.

He lifted it up for her to take.

She didn't. She just looked at the ring, licked her lips, and stopped breathing. "Tripp, I—"

"I know you don't want to get married, and I know why. Your parents were a disaster, and I know you're scared, but…"

Her chest heaved with a larger than normal breath. She was visibly trembling. Man, he was messing this up so badly.

"But… Well… Damn it, I'm scared, too, Ashley, but I need the whole world to know you're mine, and I know that's not politically correct…" And now he was babbling! "You're a strong woman, and you can stand on your own, and you don't need some guy telling you what to do or give you permission, and I won't, but I—"

Ashley collapsed and landed on his knee. Just fell forward, took his hard head between her hands, and kissed the ever-loving shit out of him. Robbed his breath. Stole his heart. Vanquished every last nerve jitterbugging up his spine.

Tripp tucked the ring back into its silken nest in his pocket. He couldn't get another word out. Didn't need to. Not the way their tongues tangled. Not the way their hearts pounded in sync. Ashley breathed for him, and he breathed for her, the seal between their mouths and lips tight. Holding onto each other. Just holding on.

When at last they came up for air, she told him, "You're not just some guy, Tripp. You're my guy. Yes, of course I'll marry you."

"You will? Err, but I didn't ask you yet. Not really."

She nodded, her face flushed and her lips deliciously wet and shimmering. "Well, I'm asking you. I'm not my mom, Tripp, and you're nothing like my dad. We can make our own forever, but we'll do it our way. We'll do it right. Will you marry me?"

"Yes!" He scrambled to retrieve the ring. The world blurred into one shiny piece of rock once he slid in onto the delicate finger of the only woman in the world he adored. His ribs felt too tight for the warmth flooding his chest. But now, they had something to celebrate. He jumped to his feet and led her out of the chapel.

Jameson cocked his head when the doors opened and Tripp gestured Ashley out first. "Tripp! Where'd you go, man? Everyone's looking for you."

No way was Tripp making this day about Ashley and him. Instead, he slapped his good buddy's shoulder extra-hard and, with Ashley snuggled under his arm, he declared, "You old married man! Congrats, brother!"

That threw Jameson off track. Tripp knew his buddy was an only child. Which was why he used that word liberally. *Brother* meant something personal to Jameson. Damned if those dark brown eyes of his didn't water before he pulled his spectacles out and hid his emotions behind them.

Tripp didn't let Jameson turn maudlin. When Ashley slipped away to talk with Maddie, he grabbed Jameson by the back of his neck and muttered in his ear, "Damned time you did something smart with your life."

"Yeah, well…" Jameson's voice was too ragged.

Tripp could tell he was having a hard time. He slapped his friend again. "My turn next, and you'd better damned well be there, you son of a bitch."

"Always," Jameson growled. With one more hearty back slap, he regained his composure.

It was Maddie who spied the ring. "Ashley!" she squealed. "Did he…? Are you two…?"

So much for secrets. Before the wedding congrats turned into engagement congrats and stole Jameson and Maddie's thunder, Tripp captured Ashley's hand, lifted it high with his, and told the world, "Drinks are on Jameson!"

Later that night, Tripp lay on his back in Ashley's bed, exhausted and sated, with her tucked under his arm, and her left hand splayed over his bare chest. Every time the ring on her finger caught the tiniest ray of light from somewhere in the darkened room, it sparkled, and he smiled.

He was a changed man. The anger he hadn't realized he'd been carrying for so long was gone. He had Alex to thank for that. Because of Alex, Trish was also a different person. The darkness in her seemed to have disappeared, and Andy was happy as a lark.

Tripp had more responsibility, the kind that allowed him to continue his night job by doing it more efficiently. Hopefully, more effectively. Who would've thought someone like him would be responsible for The TEAM's new Civilian Anti-Terrorism Unit? That Alex had faith in him told Tripp plenty. But more than anything, he had Ashley. Funny how things changed the moment he'd cradled her in his arms that desperate Friday night. He hadn't been the same since.

And those fuck-me-blue heels? Best. Shoes. Ever!

The End

Thank you for reading Tripp and Ashley's story!

You are the key to this book's success.

Please tell other readers why you liked Tripp by leaving an honest review at the retail site where you purchased it.

Recommend him to your friends. Lend him. Most of all, enjoy him!

Other Irish Winters' best-selling series:

In the Company of Snipers

Alex

Mark

Zack

Harley

Connor

Rory

Taylor

Gabe

Maverick

Cassidy

Adam

Lee

Ky

Hunter

Eric

Jake

Seth

Beau

Renner

Beckam

Walker

Jameson

Deuces Wild
King of Hearts
Joker Joker
One-Eyed Jack
Ace

Hearts and Ashes
Smoke
Ash

SOBs Novels
Angel
Assassin
Vaquero
Coming soon:
Kruze Sinclair's story

To keep up with my new releases, giveaways, and actionable intel, sign up for my spam-free newsletter at IrishWinters.com.

Keep reading for another tasty tidbit!

An Unedited Preview of *Damned*

SOBs Novel, #3

Kruze Sinclair wasn't supposed to be there. The plan to leave Istanbul, Turkey, had been straight forward. All Senator Sullivan's black ops exfils were well-planned and scheduled ahead of time, vetted through whichever other spec ops teams were in the same country, and expedited accordingly. If the US Air Force couldn't accommodate getting an occasional unnamed hitchhiker out of Turkish airspace, the Navy always had resources available on the sly. Since civil unrest became the norm for this third world country, all US military departments operated more as distant, socially unwanted relatives instead of the besties they'd been during the decades of solid Turkey/American relations.

But like the shifting political landscape below, where Kruze found himself late this afternoon, things had changed between Turkey and America. Unfortunately, Istanbul, his way home, now lay on the exact opposite side of this godforsaken land. Early this morning, Sullivan had tasked Kruze, since he was *'in the neighborhood,'* to pick up some high and mighty journalist who'd gotten herself lost and captured by a rebel faction, in the edge of the Eastern Anatolia Region. Bordered by Georgia to the north, Iraq to the south,

Iran, Azerbaijan, and Armenia to the east, Eastern Anatolia was once again, the glow-in-the-dark hotspot of Eurasia.

The mountainous region was home to the often-disparaged Kurds. It was what some talking heads called their last holdout. Their Alamo. Kruze knew the history. After the first World War, thanks to then USA president Woodrow Wilson, Kurdish nationalists were guaranteed the eventual establishment of their own country, Kurdistan. But, like the treaties made with American Indians, it never happened. In 1920, the Treaty of Sevres between the Allies and the sultan of the Ottoman Empire recognized Kurdistan's autonomy. But the treaty was never ratified, due to a rising military star in Turkey, Mustafa Kemal Ataturk, the country's first president. Lack of that ratification left the ancient country of Kurdistan geographically spread across large portions of eastern Turkey, northern Iraq, and western Iran, as well as smaller portions within Syria and Armenia. Iran and Iraq were the only countries to officially recognize the autonomous portions of Kurdistan within their borders.

Which also explained the conflict between Turkey and Armenia. Back in the early 1900s, Eastern Anatolia Region had seen the demise, as in the outright genocide, of its Armenian population, by Turkey. The campaign against Armenians had been so ugly that, even today, it was forbidden to even speak the word 'Armenia' in Turkey. The powers that ruled Turkey were still changing the written history of that war to suit their whitewashed spin on the war crimes they'd committed against a population of well over a million innocent men, women, and children.

Which must be why Brianna What's-Her-Pain-in-the-Ass-Name, oh yeah, Banks, was here. She'd probably decided to write her own spin on the historical nightmare. Guess Mizz Banks hadn't received the royal treatment she'd expected, though. A rebel faction took her captive. The Turkish military now vigorously hunted for her with no intention of taking her, or her captors, alive. She'd had a death wish coming the moment she'd ventured into this mountainous warzone. Turkey intended to grant that wish, had even put a million US dollar bounty on her hard head. Kruze's job now was to find the prima donna and extract her pretentious ass without causing an international incident. Lucky him.

From the bottom of his former Navy SEAL heart, he detested journalists and reporters. Every. Last. One. Of. Them. That hatred stemmed from the fabricated untruths and fiction about his older brother's final foray into South America, the one that had nearly gotten Chance killed. Yes, those ugly stories. Because of them, Kruze carried one helluva grudge against the entire, star-studded, celebrity news reporting community. In his estimation, they were nothing but gold-digging liars, easily bought by whichever politically-driven megalomaniac offered the most pieces of silver. But that was another story and another grudge Kruze carried. Like he didn't have enough.

He lay perfectly still on a narrow granite outcropping, his binocs trained on the caravan of rusty jeeps, half-assed, ancient pickups, overburdened donkeys, and the scruffy militia, around four dozen strong, in the narrow valley below. His gear bag, filled with a weighty collection of survival items, lay beside him, his sniper rifle already on its bipod and aimed below.

Thank you, Jesus, his in-county sources had been spot on. They'd told him which band of rebels Banks had most likely tangled with. And bingo, there she was, her highness Brianna Banks, the latest know-it-all from one of many twenty-four-seven, capitalist, propaganda machines to hit America's big time. She was tripping along beside a dust-covered, rust-pitted older model Toyota pick-up, itself a DIY project, bristling with banners, armament, and enough rebels to void its shock absorbers warranty. If it still had one.

Most of these rebels were dressed in traditional baggy pants, ragged button-up shirts, vests, sashes, and leather boots. Nothing colorful. Everything dusty, dirty, and some shade of brown. Yet the entitled American woman among them wore a bright red scarf wrapped over her head and around her arrogant neck, making her a gawddamned target. Kee-rist! What did she think she was? Untouchable? Didn't journalists understand a gawddamned thing about this country? Guess not.

Kruze fingered the focus wheel on his compact binoculars to bring her in closer, watching her walk that dusty road with her head held high and her nose in the air. Despite the too-big-for-her-face Jacki-O sunglasses propped on her nose, she screamed Made in the USA and proud of it. Not the smartest declaration in this war-torn region.

She was definitely under close guard. Two armed men followed behind her. When she slowed, bent over and rubbed her bare foot, one shoved the butt of his rifle into her back. Which, oddly, raised the hackles between Kruze's shoulder blades into dinosaur stegosaurus plates.

When she fell to her knees, those plates stiffened more. Even high on the hillside like he was, he could hear the ugliness in their voices. He didn't know their language, but he knew by the tone that they were mocking her. Calling her vile names behind her back.

His harsh opinion of the American woman changed—a little. She was still an arrogant piece of entitled ass, and for sure, she had no business being in this war-torn part of the country. Her ignorance had put her life—and now his—at risk. Damn the mentality that made foolish, entitled American princesses like her.

A single glint created a tiny prism inside the outer ring of his binocs' lens. Kruze shifted his view to the opposite side of the canyon. Well, what do you know. A robed man stood across from Kruze's position, the long rifle in his hands also aimed at the caravan below. The guy was probably after the reward on Banks' head, a lucrative offer in any part of the world, but especially here. Whoever he was, he'd be everyone's best friend by nightfall—if he made the shot, and if he could prove he and he alone had killed the American journalist. Which meant he'd be after some kind of trophy. That red scarf would do. Or her head…

"Shit," Kruze hissed. He flattened to his ledge, needing to stay the course, save the girl, do his hero thing, then get the hell out of there.

He had two choices. Plan A: Shoot the assassin before he got a shot off and killed Princess Banks, or fire into the caravan to create a distraction. But even if those worked, there was no guarantee Banks would take advantage of it and run for her life, or that she'd get away if she did. These mountain people weren't stupid. The lived on what they hunted, for hell's sake. They'd run her down in no time, might even beat her for causing trouble.

Steadying his rifle scope across the canyon, Kruze opted for the direct approach: Shoot the motherfucker. One round ought to create enough distraction to separate Banks from her marching buddies. Getting down this side of the canyon in time to rescue her would take a couple minutes, though. She might not have that kind of time.

Plan B it was. Instead of taking out the assassin first, he called out to the men below, pointed to where the assassin now hunkered down, and yelled, "Turkish Army! Hadi! Hadi!" Which he hoped meant hurry, hurry.

That put a wrinkle in things. The brave assholes below scattered and took up defensive positions. The assassin ducked down and recalculated. Kruze grabbed the opportunity is distraction provided, clutched his rifle over his head, and slid down the nearly vertical face of his side of the canyon. A loud cry went up below, but no one fired at him. That was nice.

He landed boots first, then pointed up at the precise lookout of the assassin, and yelled, "Shooter!" His Turkish wasn't good; his Kurdish and Farsi weren't much better. But most Kurds knew enough English to understand what he was trying to help them. They reacted as any targeted gang would. The assassin got one more shot off, but it went wild, as every rebel soldier in that convoy peppered his location with enough lead that they knocked a small landslide loose.

Kruze took advantage of the fog of war. In three quick steps, he grabbed the flustered American woman by her hand, ripped that stupid red scarf off her head, tossed it to the dirt, threw her over his shoulder in a fireman's hold, and ran in the opposite direction.

"What? Wait. No, stop! I can't leave." She wanted to argue? Now?

"Shut the hell up. I'm here to save your stupid ass. Stop kicking!"

He didn't plan to go far, just needed to get to the last vehicle in this roughneck convoy before that rockslide buried them all alive. While the rebels were busy being heroes, Kruze hurried to get Banks out of sight. Once they noticed she was missing, they'd come unglued. But they'd also expect her to run in the opposite direction. Kruze didn't plan on being that kind of stupid. He tossed Banks to the ground beside the last vehicle, a square-fender jeep that looked like it'd been in WWII.

"Get under here and shut-up," he ordered.

She stood there blinking at him like a… a woman.

Kruze stepped into her personal space, towering over her, and still breathing hard from that slide down the mountain. He was damned if he was going to take any lip.

That did the trick. Mizz Banks tugged her skirt up and dropped to the ground, then flattened her body, and scurried on her hands and knees beneath the undercarriage. While she rolled over and shifted her backside into one of the ruts, Kruze tugged his blanket, which was plenty ratty and dirty, from inside his camouflaged jacket and climbed down with her. Before Banks could pitch another hissy-fit, he rolled onto her much smaller, narrower body. A less than ladylike grunt ground out of her. He shook the blanket out as far as he could, given the restricted space under, then tossed one end of it over his legs and pulled the other end up until it covered his shoulders and head. And her.

By the time he'd finished, Kruze was on his belly and face to face with Mizz Brianna Banks, breathing the same air. She whimpered when his full weight mashed her into the dirt. Well, too damned bad.

"Shut it, Princess. I'm only here to get you out of the country alive, not marry you."

"Th-thanks for helping me," she whispered. Banks almost sounded sincere. That should've altered his opinion, but it didn't. Journalists just like her had made his brother Chance's life a living hell for too damned long and in too many ways. They'd known nothing about the details of his covert op into South America, less about Kruze and Chance's mother's death, which had happened during the same time. So what'd they do? They'd invented, hypothesized, and outright lied, created sensational, twisted tales full of so much crap, that Chance had come damned close to committing suicide. He'd lost most of his SEAL team on that op, and had nearly lost his life. America's press corps thought they could say whatever they wanted under their first amendment rights? Well, Kruze had news for them, this woman in particular, and it started with a vehement effing F-off!

By the time he was through remembering why he detested journalists, Kruze was flaming pissed all over again. Gawddamnit, yes, he was the emotional middle brother of Scarlett Sinclair's three boys, and he'd struggled with the shortcoming all his life.

But like his friend Julio had taught him to do, Kruze forced his mind and soul back to zero. Breathed in. Breathed out. Tried like hell to let the past go, to forgive and forget and—yeah, not happening. Not only no, but hell no. He'd never forgive the press for their lies or his mom for not telling him she was dying of cancer. Or Chance for wanting to kill himself after he came to in the hospital and found out he'd lost everything. What a fucked up month that had been! How was a man ever supposed to get over all that?

Didn't matter how much Kruze had tried, he plain didn't know how to let those sorrows and grudges go. He'd adored his mom, still did, and he would always idolize his older brother. Losing his mom had been gut-wrenching, but losing Chance at the same time? That would've been the cruelest blow. Kruze didn't know how to get back to the man he'd been before Chance had almost pissed his life away. Didn't know if he wanted to. Pagan, the youngest Sinclair, seemed to have found a way to deal with those betrayals, but Kruze didn't know where to begin.

In the still of his mighty struggle to zero his anger, Kruze's mind settled on the sensation of the much smaller heart pounding against his belly. The journalist's heart. Odd, that the steady thump of this foolish, selfish woman's blood flowing through those chambers grounded him in the middle of a nightmare situation that could still get them killed. Yet it did. There was something familiar to this moment, something tugging at the back of his memories. He almost felt—better.

No, gawddamnit. Kruze shrugged that notion aside. Miss Brianna Banks was nothing to him. She wasn't brave, surely wasn't any kind of patriot. She was a user, a prima donna of the highest magnitude, some rich man's privileged daughter. All she'd wanted when she'd sneaked into Turkey was a sensational story that would sell. She wanted to be famous.

He might block his thoughts and opinions, but Kruze could still smell the sweet, musky scent of her body, the perfumed oil in her straggly hair, and her fear. Red scarf or not, arrogant or just plain stupid, Banks was awash with panic. She was breathing hard, scared for her life. She damned well should be. She'd brought this shitstorm down on herself. His job was just to get her dumb ass safely back to America. He didn't have to like her to do that.

The Earth quaked. Then roared. *What now?* Kruze ducked his face into Banks and lifted his arms over her head, shielding her from the furious cloud of rocks and dirt suddenly pummeling the convoy. The landslide had arrived. Thick dust and all sizes of rocks battered everything in its way, like a dry ocean wave, make that a tsunami. Kruze could barely breathe. The landslide's throaty roar turned into bouncing thunder that grew closer and closer until—

BANG! BOOM!

You have got to be kidding me! A boulder as big as a gawddamned house—an American house, not the hovels these poor mountain people lived in—landed square behind the convoy. It nearly kissed the rear gate of the jeep he and Banks were hiding under. Holy shit! Talk about one helluva close call. A yard nearer and it would've crushed the jeep and them with it.

Shock waves from the impact shook the ground. Kruze worked his jaw to keep his eardrums from blowing out, even as he stiffened his body and enclosed Banks in as much safety as he had to give.

When the thunder ceased, so did the shooting. Smaller rocks continued to rain down on the convoy. Kruze guessed the rag-tag army was hiding under the rest of the vehicles if they were smart. At last, the rockslide slowed to a trickle of bangs, thuds, and hisses, then stopped.

With his entire body still wrapped protectively around Banks, Kruze cocked his head to better hear what was going on beyond what had proven to be the perfect hiding place.

More yelling. More bellowing. But the noises sounded crazy-happy instead of pissed, angry, or hurt. A roar went up and shooting recommenced—until some guy with voice, as deep as that growling landslide, started singing a somber, respectful song. The yelling and shooting ceased as quickly as it had begin. Given the diversity of dialects, Kruze didn't understand everything word being sung, just *'Pesnê,'* their word for praise.

Well, I'll be damned. They'd killed the assassin, and now, these simple mountain people, as rude and cruel as they could be, were praising Allah. The reverent song lasted for all of five minutes. Once it ended, the rebels circled the massive rock that could've crushed Kruze and Banks to death.

"I'm scared," Mizz Brianna Banks whispered, her breath a soft warm feather that didn't feel half bad when she huffed into the hollow of his sweaty neck.

Kruze retracted his arms from around her head and his hands from her face. "Deal with it," he growled quietly, his elbows now tucked to his side and his hands flat to the dirt. He was ready to push up and away. Any minute now…

"They stopped shooting. Why don't we make a break for it?"

"Because here is safe; out there is certain death. Keep quiet." These guys would expect them to run. Kruze didn't intend to be that kind of stupid. He wasn't moving until he was sure he and Banks could get away without being seen or shot in the back.

Kruze was all male. A former Navy SEAL, he'd seen combat in some of the world's worst places. He was bigger boned, thicker muscled, and a helluva lot heavier than the dainty, entitled celebrity mashed beneath him. He was one of

America's baddest badassed warriors, by hell, and he could be a mean son of a bitch when the situation demanded. He'd faced death too many times to count, and he'd ended every HVT he'd ever been ordered to hunt. He'd survived the harshest weather, in the worst places, and the worst kinds of disasters known to man. He wasn't made to fail.

But he wasn't immune to the soft, feminine curves against his belly and thighs, or the tender brush of this woman's breasts against his much harder chest muscles, with every breath she took. Or the quivering tones of pure terror in her voice, and that heart, its beat so loud he was fairly certain it was climbing up her throat. He'd seen terror before, in the eyes of men, women, and little kids without hope. Brianna Banks was each of them all over again, her pride and ego stripped away, willing to do anything to survive.

If she were alone, she'd probably think she stood a chance running from those men out there. She'd bolt. Which proved yet again, she had no business being this deep inside Turkey's Eastern Anatolia Region. Do-gooders like her should've stayed home where they belonged. Because, when they didn't, once they'd overstayed their welcomes—if they'd ever been welcomed in the first place—some unfortunate SEAL team received orders to retrieve the idiots. And sometimes those men died. For what? The life of a journalist who'd turn on them as soon as there was money to be made in the press? Kee-rist! When would people learn?

Growling, Kruze forced his focus back on the endgame of getting Banks out of his life and himself back to the States. He'd been down this road before, and because this woman was who she was and did what she did for a living, he didn't care if she was scared or not. She should be.

Inhaling a deep, quiet breath, he wondered how long their reprieve would last. Not long. He'd no more than exhaled, when one of the rebels yelled, "Americans!" Every fighter around that rock scrambled in all direction to find him and Banks. More bellowing. More gunfire. Ouch. Damn it. A ricochet caught Kruze's left biceps. High. Just skimmed the meaty muscle near his shoulder joint; nothing to worry about. He'd treat it later.

It was all the boots pounding past their location that concerned him now. He and Banks were literally hiding in plain sight. It'd only take one sharp-eyed man or woman to spot them and raise an alarm, maybe kill them both where they laid. Yet Kruze knew the jittery nerves of an army under attack, especially after a boulder the size of Rhode Island landed where it had. These guys were hyped-up on adrenaline and fueled by religious zeal. They fanned out in all directions and up both sides of the canyon. Again, not a good time to make a break for it.

Fortunately, enough rocks and dirt had blocked one side of the Jeep, enough to provide a quantum of cover. Kruze shifted his hips, aware that his thigh holster might be digging into the trembling body beneath him, but not caring one bit if it was. He knew he was being an ass, but he refused to baby Banks. She'd asked for this, well, hello Karma. She was going to get precisely what she'd had coming to her.

Turkey was off limits to United States civilians due to its high level of terrorism, arbitrary detentions, and, oh, guess what? Increased risk to Americans! Wanna bet Banks hadn't checked with the US State Department before she'd trotted her privileged ass across whatever border she'd breached to get here? Journalists! The bane of every active duty soldier, airman, sailor, and Marine. Probably Coasties, too.

Planning how to get her out of this country alive, Kruze watched out both sides of the jeep's undercarriage as far as he could see. By the time the ragged rebel army returned from their futile search, they were still agitated but also hungry and tired. The few women in the convoy had set up camp, and delicious aromas wafted from the landslide-free side of the road.

Most of the dust from the landslide had settled, the sun was gone, and night had fallen. In developing countries like Turkey, electricity was not readily available everywhere or to everyone. The farther a man got from the cities, the fewer amenities. In mountainous altitudes and narrow canyons like this one, the sun went down extra early, night was a helluva lot darker, and it would only get colder.

Not that Princess Banks was cold yet. She couldn't be, not wedged under him and into the rut like she was, not with his massive body providing enough body heat to melt ice and keep her warm. But they couldn't stay where they were much longer. Hiding in plain sight was only good in small doses. Plus, the miracle of the boulder still attracted plenty of attention. Too soon, these wild men would start drinking and dancing around that big rock, praising Allah with gunfire and song. Therein lay the real problem—how to get the hell out of Dodge before this op turned into a bigger clusterfuck than it already was.

He doesn't remember me. After all these years, he's forgotten that night in Paris. The revelation shouldn't hurt, but it did. Of all the men in the entire United States who could've, should've been sent to rescue her, why on earth did it have to be Kruze Sinclair? Not that Bree cared. He'd certainly had no trouble leaving her before, and she'd bet her bottom dollar, he'd do it again.

About the Author

Irish Winters…

…is a best-selling author who, when she isn't writing, dabbles in poetry, grandchildren, and rarely (as in extremely rarely) the kitchen. More prone to be outdoors than in, she grew up the quintessential tomboy on a dairy farm in rural Wisconsin, spent her teen years in the Pacific Northwest, but calls the Wasatch Mountains of Northern Utah, home. For now.

She believes in making every day count for something, and follows the wise admonition of her mother to, *"Look out the window and see something!"*

Connect with Irish online:

On Facebook: https:/www.facebook.com/author.irishwinters

On Twitter: https://twitter.com/irishwinters1

Or at http://www. IrishWinters.com

www.ingramcontent.com/pod-product-compliance
Lightning Source LLC
Chambersburg PA
CBHW030955190726
48285CB00004BB/1324